Sarah Pernell is a
in Rugby. She is m
microbiologist, she
particularly the early medieval period. *The Gift & The Promise*
is her first novel.

The Gift &
The Promise

Sarah Pernell

PIATKUS

For more information on other books published
by Piatkus visit our website at
www.piatkus.co.uk

First published in Great Britain in 1999 by
Judy Piatkus (Publishers) Ltd of
5 Windmill Street, London W1P 1HF

This edition published 1999
email: info@piatkus.co.uk

The moral right of the author has been asserted

A catalogue record for this book is available from the British Library

ISBN 0 7499 3082 9

Set in Times by Action Typesetting Ltd, Gloucester

Printed and bound in Great Britain by
Mackays of Chatham plc, Chatham, Kent

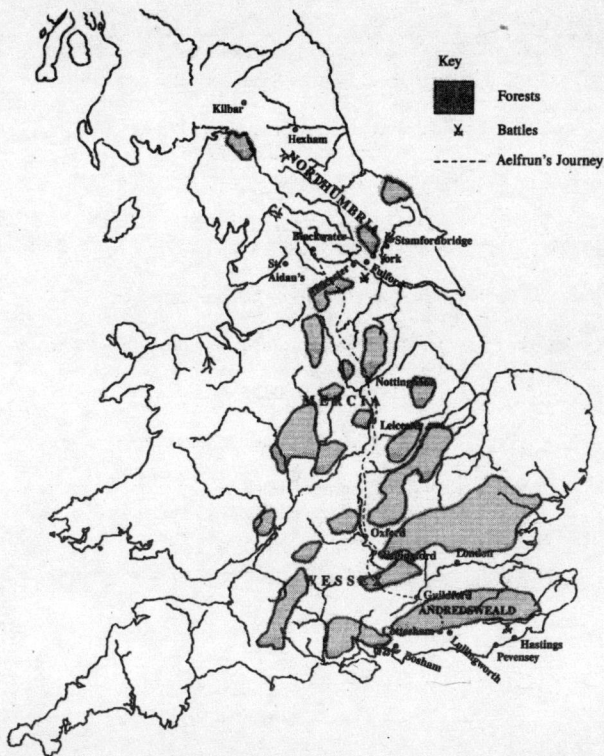

Key

Forests

Battles

Aelfrun's Journey

Kilbar

Hexham

NORTHUMBRIA

Blackwater

Stamfordbridge

St
Aidan's

York

Fulford

Nottingham

M E R C I A

Leicester

Oxford

Wallingford

London

W E S S E X

Guildford

ANDREDSWEALD

Chichester

Hastings

Bosham

Itchingworth

Pevensey

I

April 1056

Aelfrun tried to concentrate on what her father was saying, but felt a strange nervous fluttering deep in her belly.

'You do understand what an honour this is for our house?' Wilfred said with irritation.

Aelfrun nodded meekly, staring at her shoes. She wondered if she were dreaming; it hardly seemed possible that a man such as Godmund Edgarson had actually asked for her hand. Her father was neither rich nor influential, and until this morning Lord Godmund, who was both, had not visited her home for at least seven years.

She'd been twelve years old, and Godmund had been a grown man even then. She couldn't remember his face: he'd seemed kind, and he'd come to invite her parents to his wedding. 'What became of his wife?' she found herself asking.

'Cengifu?' Wilfred said surprised. 'Haven't you heard? She died in childbirth last year. The baby died too, so there's only one child for you to worry about – a daughter.'

Aelfrun wondered anxiously what it would be like to be a stepmother. No one had asked for her consent to this marriage, but as the eldest of six poorly dowered sisters she knew she should be grateful for any offer at all.

'The wedding will be soon,' Wilfred said, remembering contentedly Godmund's generosity over the settlements. 'But don't think I'll be wasting a fortune on it,' he hastened to add. 'Lord Godmund does not to wish there to be any great to-do made of it.'

'No, of course not, Father,' Aelfrun said.

Wilfred lived well enough himself – his plump cheeks and

straining paunch were evidence of that – but his own children would have gone in rags if his wife had not been such an efficient manager of the little he allowed her. Lazy, greedy and selfish, Wilfred worried over his pennies while his cunning, dishonest steward, Folca, steadily robbed him of pounds.

Wilfred, of course, knew nothing of this, and nor did he know, as he dismissed his daughter, just how angry and frustrated his steward would be when word of her betrothal reached his ears.

Thegn Godmund was in a foul mood, riding in gloomy silence, ignoring the four heavily armed ceorls of his escort. He was an attractive man, tall and well-built, and usually with a smile that made him seem almost handsome. He looked older than his thirty years, the bright copper-brown of his beard showing traces of grey, as did his hair which he wore quite short, in the fashion of a court much influenced by the king's Norman friends. It was his eyes, however, that aged him most. Dark grey and full of sadness, they reflected all the grief and pain that had soured and embittered him since the death of his wife barely a year ago.

Godmund felt a pang of remorse for his surliness. How could he expect any of his ceorls to understand what he suffered? Wulfhere, just fifteen, could know nothing of love; Alfgar, grizzled and scarred from a hundred fights, took his love where he found it; while Orric and Alfred, well, no one could describe either of them as passionate men. He almost smiled at the thought.

There were times on this journey when he'd been tempted just to turn his horse and go home. How could he even think of marrying with Cengifu hardly cold in her grave? But there was no real choice but to go on. For eight long months he'd stayed away from home, drowning his grief in strong drink in the company of Earl Leofwine, his friend and lord. It was Leofwine who had finally ordered him home to mind his affairs, and Godmund, angry at first, had soon discovered that his friend was right – he had responsibilities he couldn't just ignore. His steward, Dunn, had managed his estate well enough, but his hall was in disarray and his five year old daughter, Ceolwynn, was running wild like any peasant child, undisciplined and untaught. Ceolwynn meant all the world to him – but she had needed a mother, and quickly!

Godmund had not chosen his new wife ill-advisedly. He knew Wilfred and his stern, austere wife well enough to know that any

2

one of their daughters was sure to be hard-working and frugal. He didn't need her to bring a large dower, he just wanted a woman to manage his household, raise his daughter and give him unquestioning obedience and loyalty. But with his wedding now only hours away, he suddenly found himself wishing he could remember what the girl was actually like.

Aelfrun had hoped for a new dress for her wedding, but Wilfred had no intention of wasting money.

Now her mother was pulling out Aelfrun's clothes from her coffer and throwing them haphazardly across the huge bed that all six girls shared, picking up one garment after another to hold up against her daughter.

'The blue,' cried Estrith, producing a tunic of fine, deep blue wool. 'She looks lovely in this, and it has no darns.'

Her mother lifted the hem to examine the embroidery edging it. 'This was your own work, was it not Aelfrun?' she asked. Aelfrun nodded. 'Good, it will do no harm to let your husband see that you do not lack accomplishment.'

Her sister Wilburg came in with a bowl of warm, herb-scented water and Aelfrun began to wash, her thoughts in turmoil. There were questions she longed to ask, but her mother just tutted impatiently and handed her a clean shift. Aelfrun obediently slipped it over her head and sat down on a stool while her mother combed and replaited her hair, winding it through with some gold-threaded braid – a lucky find at the bottom of Estrith's box.

Her sisters, meanwhile, were still running through their coffers to find the prettiest of their jewels and ornaments for her approval. She chose a brooch of silver set with lapis lazuli, and a girdle of fine grey leather fastened with an intricately worked silver buckle, all the time submitting with outward calm and patience to these ministrations yet delighting in the warm-hearted envy of her sisters and the grudging and unexpected praise from her mother. Finally she was dressed to everybody's satisfaction, and suddenly, there was no escape from the fact that she was about to exchange irrevocable, indissoluble vows with the man who from this day onwards was to share her life, and her bed.

Now she was walking towards the church with her sisters giggling and whispering behind her. 'How do I look?' she asked anxiously, clinging to Estrith's arm.

'Terrified,' her sister answered bluntly.

Godmund, standing at the front of the church with her father, turned to watch her come in. Ah! that one, he thought with relief. He saw a young woman, slender but not tall, with light brown hair and pretty, dark eyes edged with long curling lashes. These eyes were her most attractive feature, her slightly sallow skin being lightly marked by some childhood illness, and her mouth being just a shade too small and too straight for beauty. Above all, what he saw was a women who bore no resemblance at all to Cengifu, and this pleased him well.

No Mass, it seemed to Aelfrun, had ever ended so quickly. Now they were all out on the church porch with the whole village looking on and the priest standing ready to say the words over them. She glanced shyly up at Godmund and he gave her a quick reassuring smile before turning back to listen to the priest, who had begun the ceremony. Aelfrun made her responses with growing confidence, suddenly happy that from now on she would be mistress of her own hall, free forever from her mother's sharp tongue and her father's petty meanness.

In just minutes it was done; they were married. Aelfrun took her husband's arm and allowed herself to be led back to the hall where the usual three days of feasting and celebration were about to begin.

'Does this marriage please you?' Godmund asked unexpectedly.

'To you, my lord, how could it not?' she replied, already beginning to feel more at ease in his company. He laughed and indicated that she should seat herself on one of the large oak chests that stood against the wall. She sat, eager to please.

'I hardly gave you time to prepare yourself, did I?' Godmund said ruefully. 'I hope this small gift will make amends.'

She took the small leather bag he offered her, smiling up at him shyly. Excited as a child, she tipped the contents of the bag onto the palm of her hand and gasped with pleasure at the string of fine amber that was revealed. 'It's lovely,' she cried, 'beautiful! You are most kind.' He was smiling at her, but his smile was strangely distant. Aelfrun felt a small shiver of misgiving. 'I have longed to ask,' she said, breaking at last the uneasy silence that had suddenly fallen between them, 'why did you choose *me* to be your wife?'

Godmund was a little startled by the question. He thought hard for the right thing to say. 'I remembered you from past visits to your father's hall,' he lied. 'I thought you a pleasant child, now grown into a very attractive and charming young woman. In all other respects, also, I heard nothing but good of you. You seemed to me the perfect choice.'

'Estrith is prettier,' she commented, glancing at him sideways to see his reaction.

'Estrith?' he asked, puzzled.

'My nearest sister,' she explained. 'She is quite lovely; or there's Wilburg, who would have been a good choice too.' She really did want to know why he had chosen her.

'Are you saying I've made the wrong choice?' Godmund replied with mock alarm. 'Or do you want me to marry *all* your sisters?' he added, laughing, but he very much wanted to change the subject. If she wanted him to speak words of love, well, that he could not do. 'Shall I tell you about your new home?' he asked quickly. 'What would you like to know?'

'Yes,' she answered, nodding. 'Tell me about Cottesham, about your people. Do you think they will like me?'

'They will like you very well, Aelfrun,' he replied seriously, 'but it is more important that they respect you. I expect order and efficiency in my hall, so you must be ready to deal hardly with any of my servants who try to thwart your will.'

'Are they so difficult to govern then?' she asked, alarmed.

'Not at all,' he reassured her, 'lazy and ill-disciplined of late, but nothing that a firm hand cannot control. When I'm away, you may rely on Dunn, my steward, who will do all he can to help you.'

'What of your daughter? Will she welcome me?'

'She still grieves for her mother, but I'm sure that, in time, she will give you her love. Ceolwynn is an affectionate child, very pretty and full of life. You will need a firm but gentle hand there — she can be headstrong.'

Aelfrun was touched by the warmth he showed in speaking of his daughter. Her own father had never shown such affection towards any of his offspring, not even his two sons.

'My wife's father,' he continued, and then faltered, 'I mean...'

'I understand what you mean,' she said, reaching out to touch his sleeve, a gentle, intimate gesture that surprised him. 'I know how hard it must be for you not to think of her still as your wife, even now.' Godmund looked at her, his expression unreadable. Her dark eyes met his and she gave him a smile of sympathy and understanding, but he looked away again, saying nothing.

'Cengifu's father,' he began again, 'shares my hall. You will like him, I'm sure. He's a lively old man and a wonderful story-teller; but his health is not always good and he does need some care.' He decided not to elaborate on this, she would learn soon enough about Rurik who was now prone to strange, violent moods when only his growing feebleness prevented him from being an actual danger to others, but Aelfrun, Godmund decided, would find this out for herself soon enough.

For the next few days he put himself out to be charming and attentive, not because he wanted Aelfrun to learn to care for him, but simply because it was in his nature to be gentle and courteous. The effect on Aelfrun, however, was overwhelming. By the time they were ready to leave for Cottesham she was deeply and utterly in love with her husband and only a little sad to be leaving her home and family. It was her sisters, she knew, whom she would miss most of all, especially Estrith; but Estrith had her own plans and found an excuse to take her sister aside just before she left.

'Aelfrun, when you are settled will you send for me?' she pleaded. 'Please, Aelfrun, ask Godmund if I can join your house-hold. I'm sure he would be willing to please you in this.' Estrith clutched her sister's arm so tightly that Aelfrun was amazed at her vehemence.

'Of course I will ask,' she answered, guessing at once that her sister's eagerness was not caused solely by sisterly affection. 'It's Wulfhere, isn't it?' she teased. 'I hadn't realized it was you that had caused him to sing and whistle all the day.'

'Oh I know nothing can come of it, but I do so long to be near him.'

Aelfrun understood, none better, how her sister felt and promised to see that Estrith was at Cottesham before the summer was out. They hugged one another to seal the promise, then Aelfrun found herself bidding farewell to all her family, and ensuring that all her bride goods had been safely loaded onto the pack mules, ready for the journey.

They rode out of Wilfred's village on a fine morning, past freshly ploughed fields where ragged, barefoot peasants broadcast beans from seed bags slung around their necks. Some looked up as the riders passed by and Godmund was mildly surprised by their sullen expressions. Folca the steward, who was overseeing the sowing, watched the couple pass, and Aelfrun turned her head away so that she need not return his greeting. The man made her shiver; the thought of his eyes on her body filling her with a kind of loathsome dread.

Folca glared after them venomously. For years Aelfrun had been at the very heart of his ambitions and this unexpected turn of events had filled him with fury. It had given Folca particular pleasure to imagine buying Wilfred's daughter with money stolen from his master's own purse, but now all hope of marriage to any one of his lord's daughters was gone. With Aelfrun married to such a powerful thegn as Godmund, no silver in the world would buy a mere steward into Wilfred's family.

Aelfrun, still uneasy, spurred her horse into a fast trot. By the time Godmund caught up with her she had managed to collect herself sufficiently to laugh and exchange pleasantries with him. She was foolish to be so frightened of a man who had never by word or deed offered her any harm or insult. Yet she was afraid of Folca.

As the road carried her closer and closer to her new life, Aelfrun put any unpleasant thoughts behind her and began to enjoy the day and dream of what the future might hold.

Wulfhere, riding behind them, was also thinking of the future, but rather less cheerfully. Godmund was wrong to think that Wulfhere knew nothing of love. Three days he had just spent in the company of the loveliest girl he had ever met. It was clear that she liked him; she could easily have avoided him, but she hadn't. He grinned happily to himself and formed the sound of her name in his head, revelling in its sound: Estrith, Estrith. His thoughts were filled with her fair, delicate beauty, her sweet voice and gentle manner. But she was a thegn's daughter – small chance for a poor, unlanded ceorl to aspire so high. Still, there could be no harm in dreaming, surely?

Their two-hour journey was over and now Godmund came to help Aelfrun out of the saddle. Willingly she slipped down into his arms, but he released her quickly, turning with delight towards the small child running towards them, followed by a man who was, Aelfrun guessed, the steward, a priest and a

7

small group of household servants, all of whom were eyeing her with curiosity.

The child threw herself into her father's arms and Godmund, after a quick hug, wasted no time in introducing her proudly to his new wife. The child was lovely, Aelfrun saw as she knelt to give her a kiss and a warm smile. Aelfrun was, above all, a very practical and sensible young woman and had decided early on that to win the affection of the man she must first win the affection of the child, and this she intended to do.

Ceolwynn returned the kiss promptly enough, knowing that this was expected of her, but then stepped back uncertainly. When her father had promised her a new mother, she had envisaged another Cengifu, tall, fair and beautiful. This woman was not what she had expected and she viewed her with suspicion.

Aelfrun returned her solemn stare with another smile. 'Shall we be friends?' she asked, taking one of Ceolwynn's hands into her own. Ceolwynn put the fingers of her free hand in her mouth and nodded reluctantly. Saying nothing, she allowed Aelfrun to keep hold of her hand.

Aelfrun stood up again and looked to Godmund for his approval. He was certainly pleased, but his smile, she saw, was for Ceolwynn alone. Quickly suppressing the sharp pang of jealousy that stabbed her, Aelfrun turned to meet Dunn Oswaldson, her husband's steward, and the short, round priest, Father Eadric, whose dark eyes beamed a welcome.

Godmund suggested they make a brief tour of the village so that she could see and be seen by his people, and this she agreed to quite readily, eager to learn as much as possible. Ceolwynn, aware that Aelfrun was now absorbed in adult conversation, managed at last to slip free of her stepmother's hand and made her way back to the hall.

There was little to surprise Aelfrun in her new home. The peasants, barefoot and dressed in the uniform hodden-grey of their class, went about their work in the same way here as anywhere, although she did notice that they looked more cheerful and went about their duties with more willingness than she was accustomed to seeing under Folca's rule. Their cottages looked much the same, wattle and daub with thatched roofs and sunken dirt floors and, in winter, a low wood or wattle partition to separate the family from their beasts. Furthest from the hall were the flimsy hovels belonging to the poorest of Godmund's people, but, on the whole, the cottages were in good repair, and some even had walls of coloured daub to make them look brighter and more welcoming.

Finding herself walking with Dunn, Aelfrun tried to make conversation. 'You are young to hold a steward's post,' she said, then added hastily, in case he should think this a criticism, 'but I know that my husband thinks very highly of you.'

'Thank you,' he replied with a grateful half smile. 'I do my best, although sometimes I fear that my best is hardly good enough.' There was a heaviness in his tone that intrigued her.

'You sound as though you find your duties burdensome,' she said curiously.

'No,' he protested. 'It's just that it saddens me to stand by helpless when God chooses to bow down with sorrow people that I know so well.'

Aelfrun stared at him, not quite understanding his meaning but finding herself warming to one who obviously took his responsibilities very seriously.

Dunn noticed her puzzled expression. 'Earlier this week,' he explained, 'I saw hanged a man who was kind to me when I was a boy. He deserved his fate, I know. He was caught stealing a flitch of bacon from another man's house, and though his punishment was just, I am sad for the man who once taught me to make a whistle from a reed, and for his wife who now has no man to help her.'

'What will happen to her?' Aelfrun asked with concern.

'Well,' he said, 'she is a slave, but as the offence was not hers, my lord is not likely to treat her, or her young daughter, harshly.'

Aelfrun was silent for a few moments, and Dunn glanced shyly at her. He liked what he saw; a firm, thoughtful profile and, apparently, a concern as deep as his own for the welfare of the poor folk. Unexpectedly, she turned to him and their eyes met. They both laughed, a little embarrassed, and looked away again.

'My husband,' Aelfrun told him, 'has said that I may choose a slave to be my personal maid. Do you think this woman would serve?'

Dunn's face lit up briefly. 'Why yes, she might. Eadburg is clean, presentable and hard-working. You could do worse.'

'Then let her present herself to me tomorrow and we will see.'

Dunn was impressed with the way she had taken so swift a

decision. In fact, as she entered the hall on the arm that Godmund turned to offer her, Dunn found that he liked his new mistress a great deal more than he had anticipated.

Godmund's hall was far larger than Wilfred's: a good hundred feet in length. It had taken several days to clear out all the old rushes and replace them with new, and it had been Dunn who had thoughtfully had sweet herbs mixed in with them to cast out the old smells; and even the dogs had been chained up safely at the far end of the hall so that the bride could enter her new home with dignity.

Rurik was, as usual, on his stool by the fire. Godmund brought his wife to him and waited, a little apprehensively, for the old man's reaction. Rurik had approved his decision to remarry and had agreed that one of Wilfred's daughters would do well enough, but Godmund was still a little uneasy.

'Well,' Rurik said brusquely, looking her up and down in an appraising, hawklike manner, 'won't you give an old man the pleasure of a kiss?' Aelfrun quickly did so and Godmund relaxed. The old man would be all right. Aelfrun seemed to have surmounted the twin hurdles of acceptance by both Ceolwynn and Rurik. Neither had been too fulsome in their welcome, to be sure, but he was confident now that all would be well.

In his casual way Godmund did all he could to make Aelfrun feel comfortable in her new home: he introduced her to the ceorls and servants; he agreed immediately to her choice of personal maid and formally, in front of all, he handed her the household keys to hang at her girdle, firmly establishing her in her position of mistress of his hall.

He also made sure that the small feast they enjoyed at supper did not degenerate into a riotous, drunken revel; warning his ceorls beforehand that, until Aelfrun had left the hall, they were to refrain from the bawdy talk and jests that commonly accompanied a bedding.

When the time came for them to leave the hall, he touched his wife's hand lightly. Startled, she almost dropped the cup that had stayed almost untasted throughout the proceedings. The hall was packed with strangers, everyone from the village was there, even the skin-blackened charcoal burner from his hut deep in the woods. Aelfrun was suffering from an agonizing shyness,

10

compounded by her only-just-realized fears of what was about to come.

'Would you like your woman to go with you, to help you make ready?' he asked, leaning his head close to hers.

Aelfrun nodded, her tongue suddenly too dry to shape any words. She rose, red with embarrassment as she felt all eyes upon her. The maid, Eadburg, guided her from the hall and to Godmund's private chamber. Aelfrun didn't need to be reminded that this was the room he had once shared with Cengifu, or that this was where his daughter had been born, and where his wife and baby son had died.

Aelfrun allowed the maid to help her out of her gown and to unbind her hair, but then she dismissed her, suddenly anxious for a few moments alone. She was not, of course, totally ignorant of what was to about to happen to her – no one could be who lived in a world where servants and guests alike slept and coupled without shame in the darkened recesses of a communal hall. However, it took some time before she felt calm enough to finish preparing for bed.

The bed was covered with soft furs of bear and wolfskin. An oil-lamp burned on a small, low table, casting a soft, yellow light over the room, and there was already a bowl of water there. She washed herself, then knelt to say her prayers. When Godmund finally arrived, closing the door firmly on those who had the temerity to follow, he found her already in bed, combing her hair with the handsomely carved ivory comb that had been a wedding gift from her sisters.

He stood watching her without speaking for several moments; for so long, in fact, that she blushed furiously and her arm faltered in its long, sweeping strokes. Was he anticipating the moment when he would make her his wife in truth? The thought sent a small frisson of pleasurable excitement through her that even her nervousness could not suppress.

'Cengifu had the most beautiful hair I have ever seen,' he blurted out suddenly. 'Danish fair it was, and so long that you could have drowned in it.'

Nothing he could have said would more effectively have destroyed what little confidence Aelfrun possessed. Hurriedly, she put down the comb and hid herself beneath the concealing covers. Godmund, however, was no longer looking at her, but at

11

some distant point over her left shoulder where the past beckoned him. She had never before felt so plain and undesirable.

She waited for him to give some indication of what he expected her to do, but Godmund turned away from her wordlessly. He began to undress, slowly and without eagerness. Aelfrun felt a small surge of indignation and pulled the skins up to her chin with rather more force than she had intended.

A soft knock at the door broke the uneasy silence, and at Godmund's gruff command to enter, a serving maid sidled in carrying a jug of wine on a wooden tray. She placed it on the table, carefully removing the bowl of water with her free hand as she did so, and at Godmund's nod of thanks she hurried out, her eyes averted from the bed and her cheeks pink.

'I thought you might need this,' Godmund said kindly, indicating the wine. 'It will help calm you; I noticed you drank little earlier.'

'Thank you,' Aelfrun replied woodenly, still smarting from the hurt of his earlier, unthinking words.

He poured the wine and handed her the cup, standing over her dressed only in his hose. Her attention was caught by the small reddish hairs that curled over his chest and she had to stifle the panicky giggles that threatened to erupt for no reason at all. She buried her face in her cup and thought frantically of sobering things.

'You're not afraid, are you?' he asked. She shook her head, untruthfully, but wouldn't look at him. She sat stiffly, sipping her wine, the covers pulled up defensively as Godmund watched her, contemplating without any great pleasure what he was now obliged to do. He had bedded other women since Cengifu's death, but only whores and bored court ladies looking for excitement. This, he knew, was very different. Here in his own bed, not just for an hour or a night but for a lifetime, it felt like a betrayal. He almost wondered if he could go through with it, but the thought of the ribald speculation that would follow his unexpected return to the hall gave him pause. He downed his own wine in one purposeful gulp. 'Are you ready?' he asked abruptly, reaching for her cup without waiting for a reply.

Aelfrun finished the wine hurriedly and handed the cup back, sliding further under the covers as if to make herself as inconspicuous as possible. Godmund doused the lamp, plunging the room into utter blackness, and she felt the weight of him settle on the other side of the bed as he removed his hose and slipped under the furs himself.

They lay in silence, their bodies barely touching, with Aelfrun holding her breath as she waited; but she had to release that breath, and several others, before Godmund eventually turned towards her and reached across to place a hand on her thigh, sending through her an unexpected but pleasurable shiver of anticipation.

She half turned towards him, seeking his lips with her own, reaching out clumsily to hold him, shocked at her own response to the feel of his naked body under her hands. He returned her kiss briefly before starting to caress her clumsily with rough, ungentle hands. She tensed slightly, aware, even in her inexperience, that this was no tender, gentle lover. His hand groped firmly, demandingly, between her thighs, forcing them apart until he had room to enter her, giving her no chance to respond to the insistent demands of his searching fingers.

She gasped, shocked and frightened by his lack of tenderness. Tears welled in her eyes as he mounted her without a word, taking her quickly and perfunctorily, hardly noticing her sharp cry of pain as the virginity she'd been so glad to offer him as a treasured gift, was taken from her as casually as something insignificant and worthless.

Rhythmically, bruisingly, he moved above her till his breaths became shorter, harder, his thrusts more rapid and imperative and then, with a moan that carried in it a name that was not hers, he spent himself in her.

She knew then, with dread, that she was bound for ever to a man who was still married in his heart to a woman long dead, and that he would never let her forget it.

II

Summer 1060

The baker, hearing the blast of a distant horn, left his ovens and walked to the door. And Ceolwynn slipped out from behind him, clutching a large chunk of bread still warm from the oven. She glanced guiltily about her, but was already too late. The sound of the horn had drawn Aelfrun out of the still room just in time to prevent her escape.

Caught in the act, Ceolwynn waited patiently for the torrent of complaint which was sure to follow her desertion of the hot, stuffy hall and the endless round of spinning and sewing which made up her days.

'You cannot be trusted, can you Ceolwynn?' Aelfrun snapped. She snatched the bread from Ceolwynn's unresisting hand. 'Do I starve you?' she asked. 'Do you really need to beg food from servants?'

Ceolwynn hung her head. The smell from the bake-house had been irresistible, and Ceolwynn, blessed with her father's charm and her mother's beauty, found it easy to persuade her father's servants to do anything at all that she wanted.

'I am most truly sorry,' she now offered meekly, but Aelfrun, impervious as always to her coaxing ways, just glared at her.

'You make no effort to mend your ways,' she chided. 'Only the good Lord knows what will become of you if you cannot learn some self control. Who will want to wed a maid as headstrong and unskilled as you seem likely to become? We'll probably never find any man fool enough to take you.'

It was absurd of course, even Aelfrun could see that. With those sparkling deep blue eyes and hair the colour of pale copper bathed in sunlight, Ceolwynn's beauty alone would be enough to draw men like flies to honey. She felt a sharp surge of envy, quickly suppressed, at the thought of the child's many advantages – including an indulgent father.

Ceolwynn shuffled restlessly under her stepmother's fierce scowl, and Aelfrun sighed. 'And what about Estrith?' she asked reproachfully. 'Has she been left to manage all that mending alone? I'm surprised at her for letting you slip away so easily.'

'Oh, it's not Estrith's fault,' Ceolwynn put in hastily. 'I told her I needed the privy.'

'Lies too!' Aelfrun cried, quite shocked.

'I didn't lie, truly,' Ceolwynn protested. 'I did need to use the privy; it's just that I forgot to go back.' She put on her most penitent expression, but was unable to resist the temptation to add: 'That was Wulfhere's horn, wasn't it? You can always tell. My father will soon be here.'

Aelfrun stifled the impulse to slap the child's smug smile, knowing that any punishment was more than likely to be over-ruled as soon as her husband arrived. In Godmund's eyes, Ceolwynn could do no wrong.

A familiar bitterness almost overwhelmed her. If only Ceolwynn had come to love her, she thought unhappily, perhaps Godmund might have valued her more. His indifference was a cruel and constant pain. She really had tried so very hard to please him and to be a good mother to his beloved daughter. She'd tried everything to win the child's confidence and trust, but Ceolwynn remained wayward and stubborn, thoughtless and disobedient.

Godmund spoilt the girl quite shamelessly whenever he was at home, pampering the child with small gifts and allowing her to leave her lessons to hawk and to hunt with him all the day. Aelfrun's attempts to make Ceolwynn respect and obey her just made her sound sharp-tongued and shrewish.

Ceolwynn was by now casting eager impatient glances towards the road, and Aelfrun decided not to pursue the matter any further. Godmund had been away for several weeks and she longed to see him again. 'Go and find Dunn,' she ordered briskly. 'Ask him to come to me at once.'

Ceolwynn sped off, her sandalled feet sending up small bursts of dust from the sunbaked earth. Aelfrun went back to the hall to find Estrith waiting, as eager and excited as a child. Aelfrun felt sad for her.

'You know that Godmund is looking for a husband for you, don't you?' she warned kindly, slipping an arm about her sister's waist. 'He'd be very angry if he found out about you and Wulfhere. I was wrong not to do more to discourage you.'

Estrith sighed. 'We've done no wrong, we love one another. Would a marriage between us really be so terrible?'

'Do you really imagine our father would allow a match between his daughter and a landless ceorl?'

'One day Wulfhere will prove himself in battle and the king will make him a thegn and reward him with rich estates,' Estrith replied, not quite joking. They both laughed.

Dunn had just hurried in, closely followed by the servants he had summoned on the way. Ceolwynn, skipping with excitement, was not far behind.

'Is it my lord?' Aelfrun asked with undisguised eagerness.

Dunn nodded. 'Yes,' he said, 'but not alone. Two strangers ride with him.'

'Hurry then,' she said, 'and see to it that there is enough wine and ale in the hall.' She turned quickly towards Ceolwynn and Estrith. 'Make sure that fresh straw is laid in the hall,' she said, 'sufficient for at least a dozen men to sleep on, while I see to it that there is bread and meat for all.' Then added to herself, It was thoughtless of my lord not to have sent some warning so that all might have been prepared.

The girls left at once, but Dunn hung back for a moment to speak to her. 'It is good that lord Godmund should have returned to us at last,' he said with a smile. In these past few years he had shed his youthful uncertainty and now had the confident, assured look of a man who knows his place in the world and is content with it.

'Indeed,' Aelfrun replied gladly, her stern features softening in response to his smile. 'I expect he will stay now until after the harvest, perhaps even until Christmas.' Her usual harassed frown had been swept away by hopeful expectation. She looked almost pretty.

'Let us hope so,' Dunn answered. He seemed reluctant to leave and she looked at him questioningly. 'Please don't think it impudent of me,' he blurted suddenly, 'if I say that it gives me much pleasure to see you so happy. Forgive me.'

Aelfrun smiled at him warmly. Often lonely and unhappy, she

16

found his friendship as much a comfort to her as Estrith's affection. 'I forgive you,' she laughed, the fleeting touch of her hand on his arm making him blush.

They said no more, but as he left she stood for a few moments, thoughtfully watching his departing back.

Godmund's guests caused Aelfrun some surprise, for one was no stranger at all but her own young cousin, Cenred. She hadn't seen him for several years and was fascinated by the changes she saw in him – the chubby, sometimes irritating small boy was now transformed into this tall, blond youth smiling down at her.

'I am most glad to see you, cousin,' he said warmly, his voice deeper than she had expected. 'It has been too long.'

'Indeed it has,' she agreed with equal warmth, holding both his hands in hers and looking at him appraisingly from arms' length.

Aelfrun hadn't realized how much she had missed all her own family, though Cenred had never been an especial favourite.

Estrith was fidgeting restlessly at her side and she stood back to let her greet her cousin. She was relieved that, in the excitement, Estrith had managed to conceal her interest in Wulfhere, which had started to become worryingly obvious.

Godmund was waiting to introduce their other guest and Aelfrun turned to him now with a welcoming smile. This young man was not only a stranger, but also a Norman – common enough at court where the king surrounded himself with his French and Norman friends, but very much a novelty here where foreigners were unknown.

He was about sixteen, she guessed, perhaps a little younger. His dark hair was so short that she might almost have thought him a clerk, were it not for his aristocratic manner. His brown eyes twinkled in a face so bright and friendly that it was impossible not to smile back at him. He carried himself with great assurance. She thought him handsome, in a boyish way.

'Aelfrun, this is Renaud de Lassay,' Godmund said, placing a friendly hand on the young man's shoulder. 'Renaud is in the service of William fitzOsbern, the Duke of Normandy's own right hand, his greatest friend.'

'Oh!' Aelfrun replied, trying to look suitably impressed. 'It is indeed an honour to have the representative of such a great man as our guest. Welcome to our hall.' She kissed the young man heartily on the lips, as was the custom.

The familiarity of the greeting never failed to startle Renaud but he returned it with enthusiasm. 'The honour is all mine,' he replied in quite reasonable but heavily accented West Saxon, 'since I can claim no share at all in my lord's fame.'

Everyone laughed delightedly, pleased that he had made the effort to learn their tongue.

'Come,' Aelfrun said, 'meet the rest of my family. This is my sister, Estrith.' Renaud cheerfully accepted a kiss from the pretty girl with corn-gold hair. 'And this is my daughter, Ceolwynn.' He bent to receive the child's greeting and was immediately struck by her merry eyes.

'Ah! This is the mischievous one, yes?' he asked, whispering so that only she could hear. She grinned at him. 'I think I too am the mischievous one, so we shall be the allies, no?'

Ceolwynn nodded agreeably, taking to him at once.

'Are you here on your lord's business?' Aelfrun asked.

'Yes, I am. My lord holds land in England, given to him by your king. I am here to learn the ways of an English manor so that one day I might look after his interests. Though I have to confess,' he added guiltily, 'I have spent more time at court than in my lord's fields and byres.'

Aelfrun laughed. She found it quite impossible to imagine this boy as a steward. 'And are you enjoying your stay here in England?' she asked with genuine interest.

'Very much,' he answered, surprised to find that he really meant it. He'd hated England at first, despising all Saxons and making little effort to understand their barbaric language and customs. Cenred's friendship had changed all that, and he'd soon come to appreciate his English hosts. He was ashamed now of the way he'd behaved, but he'd been filled with fury and resentment at being sent away while his lord and Duke William fought to hold the duchy of Normandy against its many enemies. 'Everyone has been most kind to me,' he continued, embracing them all with his charming smile, 'and I am most grateful that Lord Godmund should have invited me to his home. Osbern fitzOsbern, my lord's brother, holds lands of the church at Bosham, and I was to have gone there; but the company of such beautiful and delightful ladies is far preferable to me than that of monks and priests.' He chose not to add that it was Osbern who had reported his lack of diligence to his brother – a complaint which had led to Cenred appealing to Godmund on his behalf.

The unaccustomed compliment startled Aelfrun and Estrith. Ceolwynn giggled at their confusion, and Wulfhere, hovering nearby in the hope of stealing a moment with his beloved, glowered sullenly.

'Enough,' Godmund roared good-naturedly. 'Lead us to food and a cask of good ale. My wife,' he said turning to Renaud, 'provides us with meals that would put the king's own cooks to shame.'

Aelfrun glowed in his praise and gladly led the way into the hall where all was now ready. Godmund smiled at her, pleased as always to find everything so well ordered. He had no regrets about his marriage, and it never occurred to him to wonder if Aelfrun might be less than satisfied with her side of the arrangement.

They went first to Rurik, who hardly ever moved now from his stool in front of the fire, except to sleep wrapped in his cloak beside it. It was one of his better days and his head was clear and unconfused. He saw Ceolwynn and smiled. It was Ceolwynn, who loved him dearly, who would always bring his food, finding for him the tastiest morsels and cutting his meat into tiny pieces for him. He raised his hand as she came near and she hurried to take it, eager to tell him about their visitors. Rurik listened, a wary eye glancing over her shoulder. Strangers always worried him and he studied the two young men with suspicion.

'Ah,' he growled at Cenred, once he was convinced that the visitors offered no kind of threat, 'so you're kin to that oaf, Wilfred, are you?' He ignored Renaud.

'Rurik, please,' Aelfrun hissed at him in an agony of embarrassment, 'these are our guests, and Wilfred *is* my father.'

Rurik pretended not to hear her protest. 'So,' he asked, taking in Cenred's long hair and newly sprouting beard, 'it pleases you to ape the Dane now, does it?'

'It is the fashion,' the lad replied testily. 'Many young men at court have begun to grow their hair long again.'

'I suppose you're all sick of looking like a pack of Normans, eh? No offence, young fellow,' he added, addressing Renaud for the first time. 'I suppose you're one of them – a Norman, I mean?'

'I am,' Renaud answered, quite unruffled. 'But I too like this fashion. If I did not have to go home soon, I would perhaps grow my hair.'

19

Rurik looked at him approvingly. The boy knew how to make himself agreeable, and how to keep his temper when provoked. Ceolwynn, he noticed, was hanging on his every word. The boy had charm, too, like Godmund. For some reason, he suddenly found himself annoyed by Ceolwynn's liking for the Norman; it seemed almost like a defection. His budding approval of Renaud evaporated completely and he glared at him.

'I think we are ready to eat now,' Aelfrun put in hastily. 'I'll send your food over to you soon, Rurik,' she promised.

'Whenever it pleases you,' he replied sulkily.

Aelfrun sighed in exasperation, but Rurik had turned his back on them all to warm himself at the fire.

Ceolwynn slipped inside the stable door and looked curiously at Renaud, who was sitting hunched over a large pile of horse harness, a polishing cloth in his hand and a deep frown of concentration on his face.

'Why are *you* doing that?' she asked. 'The grooms do all that work here.'

'Ah yes, but if I learn to do it well, myself, then I will know when my own servants have not done it well. I will know all their tricks, eh!'

'That sounds like something my father might say,' she commented.

Renaud laughed. Godmund had indeed said those very words. He'd taken very seriously his offer to train his charge and, during this last two months, Godmund and Dunn between them had made sure that Renaud had every opportunity to learn exactly how an English manor was run. 'Did you come to have a horse saddled?' he asked. 'Are you going riding?'

'No, there's a new litter of kittens in the hayloft. I came to see if I could find them. I like kittens, don't you?'

'I do not dislike them; they will grow into cats, and cats are useful.' He returned to his work, rubbing vigorously.

'Do you like Cenred?' she asked after a few minutes of companionable silence.

'Yes, he has been a good friend to me. He helped me to learn your language and made sure that I knew the correct way to behave at your king's court. He also warned me whom I should be careful not to offend, which is very important when you mix with powerful men. Why do you ask?'

'I think my father is planning that I should marry him. I overheard them talking.' She twisted some straw between her fingers, staring down at her handiwork as though it were the most important thing in the world. Renaud knew that she was waiting for him to comment, but he wasn't sure what he should say.

'Don't you like him?' he asked eventually.

At home, he would have scorned the company of a mere girlchild, and would have been ridiculed had he sought it, so the closeness of the friendship which had sprung up between them was a constant surprise to him – even more that he should enjoy her company as much as he did.

'I don't know,' she replied thoughtfully. 'He hates to lose when we play dice. And he told me off for putting a mouse in Aelfrun's sewing chest.' She giggled, and hugged her knees gleefully, enjoying the memory of Aelfrun's scream.

Renaud didn't answer for a few moments. He liked Aelfrun and didn't care to see her teased. On the other hand, if he rebuked Ceolwynn, she wouldn't talk to him about her fears. He had grown very fond of the child and was unwilling to lose her trust.

'Well,' he said at last, deciding to make no comment at all about the mouse incident, 'it will be many years before you have to marry anybody, and these early arrangements often come to nothing. I shouldn't let it worry you yet. Even if you did have to marry him, I'm sure you will like him better when you are older. He can be quite good company.'

He hoped his words would reassure her, but inwardly he doubted if she would ever find Cenred to be an agreeable companion. Cenred's pleasures, usually involving taverns and brothels, were unlikely to appeal either to the child that Ceolwynn was now or to the young woman she would eventually become.

However, Ceolwynn had lost interest in the conversation and was now climbing the ladder into the hayloft to find the kittens. 'Don't touch them if their mother is near,' he called after her warningly. 'She will scratch you if you do.'

'I'll be careful,' she called back, hauling herself over the edge of the loft and disappearing into its shadows.

The child was going to be beautiful, Renaud mused, and she would be wealthy too, if Godmund had no sons. Cenred was wise to establish an early claim. But he didn't much like the idea of a match between Ceolwynn and Cenred, who was too selfish and demanding for a girl of her temperament. Nor did he have her bright, inquisitive mind – he would surely stifle her. He shook his head sadly and suddenly found himself thinking about Aelfrun, who had always been very kind to him. Her obvious unhappiness saddened him, and he was puzzled by Godmund's behaviour towards her: always polite and courteous, but treating her more like a valued servant than a wife.

'Is Aelfrun truly afraid of mice?' he called out, quite intrigued by the thought that anyone could fear such a commonplace creature.

'Of course not, she was just startled,' came the muffled reply from the back of the loft. 'Oh good, here they are, I've found them. Do you want to see the kittens, Renaud?'

'No, not really. I've seen kittens before.' He examined his finished work carefully and gave a grunt of satisfaction. 'I'm going now,' he shouted, heaving the harness up onto the wooden pegs in the wall.

There was a thump as Ceolwynn threw herself down at the edge of the loft, sending a shower of hay and dust over Renaud standing below. Her face appeared, grinning down at him. 'Where are you going to?' she asked.

Renaud made a point of brushing himself down and coughing reproachfully before replying. 'To find Dunn,' he said. 'I believe,' he continued, screwing up his nose with distaste, 'that I am to learn how a sheep's feet should be trimmed.'

'That's all right then,' she said with satisfaction. 'One of our tenants is sick and Dunn has gone with Aelfrun to see what help the man's wife will need with their farm. You'll be able to keep me company.'

'Oh, will I really?' Renaud answered mildly. 'I'm glad that I shan't be put to the trouble of having to make the decision for myself.'

Ceolwynn deliberately ignored his sarcasm. 'You can help me down now,' she ordered imperiously, swinging her legs over the top of the ladder and starting to climb down with one hand decorously holding her skirt in place. Renaud laughed and obligingly reached up to guide her down.

'I have to take some gifts to Father Eadric's house: bread and honey, cheese and wine. You can help me carry them,' she said as they left the stables.

'I'm at your service, my lady,' he replied with an exaggerated, sweeping bow.

She led the way through the village to the dairy, where they found four withy baskets piled high with food and drink. Renaud selected the two heaviest for himself.

'Tell me, why are we taking food to the good Father?' he asked with interest as they neared Father Eadric's large, neat cottage just beyond the church. 'Is he ill?'

'No, he's well enough. It's not for him, it's for Betta.' She ducked her head, stepped down into the cottage and called out: 'Betta, it's me, Ceolwynn.'

'Come in, come in,' a voice called from a corner on the other side of the fire. A huge iron pot simmered over the flames, filling the cottage with the appetizing smell of stew.

As his eyes became accustomed to the gloom, Renaud was able to make out the largest woman he had ever seen, giving suck to a tiny baby almost lost to view in the folds of one enormous, exposed breast. On the floor at her feet played two more infants, each tied securely on to a peg in the wall to keep it from the fire.

'This is Betta, Father Eadric's wife,' Ceolwynn explained. 'She's just had a new baby. Renaud helped me carry these baskets over to you, Betta.'

'Thank you,' the woman called out over the noise of crying infants. 'You are most kind.'

Renaud nodded and retreated quickly, waiting outside until Ceolwynn finished her visit. 'That's Father Eadric's *wife*? Your priest is married?' he cried out in astonishment as soon as they were clear of the cottage door.

Ceolwynn was surprised at how shocked he sounded. 'Yes, why not?' she asked, puzzled. 'Do priests not marry in Normandy?'

'Well, yes,' he conceded reluctantly, 'but it is very wrong and Duke William, I know, is determined to stop it. I'm just surprised that a woman as devout as your stepmother would have permitted such a thing. How many children do they have?'

'Eight, I think, but three died very young, and one drowned in the mill-stream last summer. The eldest, Bedric, is just a simpleton, poor boy.'

'It may be God's judgement upon them,' Renaud said severely.

'You don't really think that, do you?' she asked, obviously upset.

Renaud immediately regretted his words. 'We will forget it,' he said placatingly. 'This is your home and these are your customs. If the Church here permits such marriages, then who am I to disagree?' He looked up at the sound of a cart rattling over the bridge and saw Aelfrun seated up beside the carter with Dunn riding at her side. 'I think our little holiday is over,' he said ruefully. 'We must find out what our next tasks are to be.'

Ceolwynn nodded without enthusiasm. 'When I have daughters,' she grumbled, 'I will not be so cruel as to make them work without rest from daybreak to sunset.'

Renaud roared with laughter and soon she was forced to give up her scowl and laugh with him.

Summer slid into autumn and everyone rejoiced at an abundant harvest. The barns were full, the tithes all paid, and it was time to make merry at Godmund's harvest feast. Everyone was welcome, even the beggars who waited patiently for the scraps that were sure to come their way.

Godmund himself was seated with Cenred, Dunn and Renaud at the head of the board, their conversation loud and boisterous. The women, as usual, sat separately at tables arranged at right angles to the main one, and Ceolwynn sat with Aelfrun, but she was not too disappointed as, by carefully making sure that she placed herself at the end of her own bench, she found herself quite close to Renaud at the top of his.

Unexpectedly, he caught her glance in his direction and winked at her across the table. She grinned back, but as he turned away, his head cocked to catch what Cenred was saying, a sudden panic made her palms sweat and her heart beat very fast. One day, perhaps quite soon, Renaud would have to leave. She might never see him again.

Ceolwynn usually liked to listen to the adults' talk – she sometimes heard interesting things she wasn't supposed to know – but today she found their conversations dull. She amused herself by watching the antics at the lower end of the table, where serving maids weaved in and out, skilfully evading the grasp of men determined to grab a handful of buttock or steal a kiss. Sometimes a girl would not be quick enough and there would be a shriek, a slap and the sound of laughter.

Tiring of this, she turned her attention once again to her

24

father's end of the table, where they were discussing the sons of the late Earl Godwine, who were the queen's brothers and the most powerful men in the kingdom, save for the king himself.

'What sort of man is Harold Godwineson?' Aelfrun asked. 'What little word we have here speaks well of him,' she said, 'but you, my lord, spending as much time as you do at court, must know if what we hear is truth.'

Godmund, who hadn't missed the note of discontent in her voice, smiled good-humouredly and finished his ale while he mulled over his answer.

'He's a strong man with many noble qualities,' he replied at last, addressing the company at large and barely glancing at his wife. 'He's forthright, honest and capable, but,' he added, 'he has his faults – profanity being one of them, and one that greatly offends the king.' He paused to call for his cup to be refilled before continuing. A moderate man, he preferred not to use the drinking horn which, since it was impossible to put down until drained, quickly led to drunkenness. 'Harold's popular enough,' he said, 'both at court and with his own people of Wessex; far more so than his father, Earl Godwine. And Harold is careful not to offend. Some might say he's cunning rather than clever, and they may be right.

'Apart from my good friend, Earl Leofwine, I know Tostig best of all the Godwinesons – I have always admired him more than I do Harold; but Tostig is stubborn and will never change direction nor listen to advice once he has set his mind on a particular course of action.'

'Ah! Northumbria,' Cenred muttered knowingly.

'Northumbria, indeed,' Godmund agreed. 'I have never known Tostig quite so unreasonable as he is over the government of his earldom, replacing Danish laws with Saxon, crippling his people with taxes ... there's something almost *driven* about him. He's very jealous of Harold.' For the first time he looked directly at his wife. 'I expect Cenred could tell you more about Harold than I can,' he said. 'He is, after all, a Wessex man and his father's lands lie near Bosham, Harold's own home.'

Aelfrun, unwilling to have her conversation diverted to her cousin, had another question. 'Have you met the lady Edith?' she asked, referring to the woman known as the Swan-neck, Harold's long-time mistress. 'They say she is very lovely.'

25

'Once or twice and, yes, she really is quite beautiful, very quiet and dignified. Her children, I am told, are quite remarkable for their handsomeness, ability and good manners, but I'm sure my own daughter,' he added, eyes twinkling at her, 'will outshine them all when she goes to court.'

Ceolwynn grinned back at him and only Renaud noticed Aelfrun's distress as her husband diverted his conversation away from her once more. He watched her struggle to hold back the tears.

Not for the first time, Renaud failed to understand Godmund's heartless treatment of a charming and intelligent wife who so obviously adored him.

He glanced at her again. She was still struggling, so he hastily entered the conversation in order to give her time to compose herself. 'Your king,' he said, catching Godmund's eye, 'is a most admirable man. It is remarkable that one who holds such power should be capable of such,' he paused, 'self-restraint. His goodness and piety are an example to us all.'

'He is pious, yes,' agreed Godmund, calmly holding Renaud's stare and silently acknowledging his slight hint of cynicism. 'But what of the future? He is ailing and leaves no heir. We'll need strength, not goodness, when Edward dies.'

'But for nearly twenty years he has brought peace and contentment to England,' Cenred argued. 'Our roads are safe to travel and our merchants prosper. Only the squabblings of certain noble earls has disturbed our peace; is this not so?'

'That's true enough, Cenred. He has done well enough in all but one respect: he leaves no strong, healthy son to follow him.'

'My own lord, Duke William, is not without claim to the throne, I have heard,' Renaud remarked innocently. 'King Edward's mother was, after all, sister to Duke William's grandfather.'

There was a sudden hush. Godmund laughed lightly to break the tension. Gradually the chatter resumed.

'There are claimants,' he said, 'nearer to home than the Duke of Normandy, and I daresay the king will name one of them his heir before too long. There's his nephew, Edgar, and Sven of Denmark, of course: not a popular choice, but more acceptable than William.'

'It is rumoured,' Renaud persisted, 'that he's already promised the throne to Duke William. Normandy was the king's home when he was young and friendless – perhaps he wishes to repay a debt. Besides, he may not live until Edgar reaches manhood; the child is only eight years old. Who would support a child king?'

Godmund suspected that he was being baited. 'I'm sure these fair ladies must find such talk tedious,' he said, firmly closing the discussion. 'Aelfrun, will you play for us?' he asked.

Aelfrun, still smarting from his slights, shook her head. 'I play indifferently, my lord. Let Estrith play. I believe you will find that more pleasing and her voice is sweet.'

Godmund made no argument but waved a hand casually in agreement and Estrith, blushing, hurried to take down the small, round lyre from its peg on the wall. She set it on her knee and ran her hands lovingly over the smooth, polished maple wood.

She played well, holding her audience captive as her pure, true voice led them through her sweet, sad song of lost love and tragic but heroic death. As the last note died away, the whole hall seemed to heave a collective sigh, and it was some moments before normal conversation resumed. Godmund smiled approvingly and beckoned Estrith to his side.

'Well done,' he praised her warmly, offering her ale from his own cup. Thirsty from singing she drank deeply and gratefully, but all the time she waited with apprehension for his next words, convinced that these attentions were leading to something disagreeable.

She was right. 'I have good news for you, Estrith,' he said. 'I have found you a husband.' Seeing her stricken look, and mistaking its cause, he hastened to reassure her. 'Have no fear. I promise you are not to be sent far away. It's a local thegn I have in mind for you, and he is both young and handsome enough. He's asked to meet you soon, if this is agreeable to you.'

Estrith cast him an anguished look. 'Oh no!' she cried, making the first excuse that came into her head. 'I have been considering whether my future might lie in the convent rather than in marriage.' Suddenly fearful that she had gone too far to withdraw, she added: 'At least, I would like more time to make up my mind.'

'Indeed,' Godmund answered, more than a little displeased. 'If this is truly what you wish then I would hesitate to stand in your way. I will see if the young man will wait.'

'Thank you, Godmund,' she replied, grateful to have won for herself a breathing space.

27

Godmund's manner towards her cooled a little. Glad to escape, she quietly left his side and returned to her place beside Aelfrun, who was both surprised and annoyed that Godmund had made no mention to her of a prospective suitor.

'You don't really mean it, do you?' Ceolwynn whispered to Estrith. 'You don't really want to be a nun, do you?' she asked, envisaging Estrith with her lovely hair shorn and her knees raw from constant prayer on a cold, hard chapel floor. She loved Estrith, who often calmed the troubled waters between herself and Aelfrun, and was horrified by the prospect of losing her as well as Renaud.

'I don't want to talk about it now,' Estrith hissed, and Ceolwynn subsided into a hurt silence.

After a while she began to feel even more aggrieved. No one was paying her any attention at all. Her father was talking to Dunn about pigs and pannage; Cenred and Renaud looked as though they were competing to see who could down the most horns of ale; Estrith and Aelfrun had begun a game of chess. Ceolwynn sighed heavily and looked around for something interesting to do.

All at once she noticed her grandfather seated on his usual stool before the fire, his bowl untouched in front of him. It was awful to have forgotten about him, especially at a feast. She slid off the end of her bench and made her way over to the fire, stepping carefully over the men who had already succumbed to drink and fallen to the floor. Rurik did not look up at her approach, so she slipped her arms around his neck from behind and pressed her cheek to his, enjoying the silky feel of his long, white beard on her skin.

'I'm sorry I didn't come sooner,' she whispered apologetically in his ear. He patted her hand and recited mournfully:

> *Girls do not love me, no one visits me, I*
> *cannot move about; ah, Death, why does it*
> *not come for me?*

'You know that's not true,' Ceolwynn rebuked him fondly. 'You just want to make me feel guilty, and you forget that I know that poem too. What about:

> *I am bent in three and old, I am peevish and*
> *giddy, I am silly, I am cantankerous.*

Is that not you?'

Rurik laughed and picking up his bowl began to eat. Ceolwynn leant against him, humming softly. Suddenly, without warning, Rurik leapt to his feet, hurling his bowl into the fire and almost knocking her to the floor.

'Blood and fire,' he thundered, drawing every eye in the hall. 'They bring nothing but blood and fire.' He turned to point a finger waveringly, accusingly, at Renaud, who lowered his drinking horn in amazement and confusion. 'A curse on all Normans,' Rurik raged on, 'they will bring death and destruction upon this house.'

Frantically, Ceolwynn tugged at his arm to try to get him to sit down again. 'Calm yourself, Grandfather,' she urged soothingly, 'there are no enemies here.'

Rurik turned to her, suddenly calm and frail again as the borrowed strength drained out of him. 'Oh sweet lass,' he breathed in anguish, 'beware the Norman, I beg you.'

He reached out, plaintively, a look of infinite suffering in his eyes. She stepped forward as if she could stop him falling with her own small body, but Godmund was there before her, wrapping his powerful arms around the old man to carry him to his place.

Before he got there, he knew that Rurik was dead.

The last flickering flames of Rurik's funeral pyre spluttered fitfully and died away.

Ceolwynn shivered and wrapped her cloak more closely about her shoulders. 'If my father should die, I shall have lost everyone I love,' she observed to Renaud. 'Once you and Estrith have gone, that is.'

Renaud smiled to himself. 'What about Aelfrun? Surely you must love her?'

'Well, sometimes,' she admitted grudgingly, 'but she could be kinder.'

'And so could you,' he answered.

'What do you mean?' she asked.

Renaud wondered whether this pampered child could ever understand what it felt like to be lonely and unloved. He sighed, thinking both of Aelfrun's sadness and of a childhood he preferred to forget.

His father, Robert de Lassay, had held rich and fertile lands in southern Normandy, very close to the French border. Renaud should have been able to look forward to a happy and secure future, but before he was three years old, plague had carried off both his parents, changing everything.

He had been his father's heir, but was too young to inherit. Guy, his cousin, had been given control of his estates and care of Renaud himself. Guy, however, eager to exchange temporary for permanent control of Renaud's lands, subjected the boy to a regime which was as brutal and hazardous as he could make it – stopping only at outright murder in his attempts to ensure that Renaud would never reach his majority. In time, even the servants learned to treat the boy with such cruelty and contempt that vicious beatings, neglect and semi-starvation were all Renaud could ever recall of his early childhood.

Chance alone had saved him from an early grave. When he was seven, his late father's overlord, William fitzOsbern, hunting in a nearby forest, had been forced by a sudden storm to seek shelter at Lassay. It was fitzOsbern who had appointed Guy as Renaud's guardian, though he himself held the actual wardship. This unannounced visit gave Guy no time to conceal the state of his young cousin and fitzOsbern, to his horror, found his ward half-naked, lice-ridden and emaciated.

Renaud's life had changed overnight. Scrubbed raw and dressed in the spare clothes of one of fitzOsbern's pages, he had been taken into fitzOsbern's household as a page himself, and had grown to manhood on fitzOsbern's estates at Breteuil.

It had not been an easy life – he had had much to learn and the other pages had, at first, laughed at his ignorance and rough behaviour – but soon he had learned how to carve and wait at table, to serve wine and dress his lord. He had learned not to scratch, spit, fidget or wipe his nose with his sleeve, and how to speak gently in the presence of a lady. Eventually he had found acceptance among his peers, and had formed a lasting friendship with one Hugo of Caen, a fellow page who had taken him under his wing.

He was no longer a page, of course. In fitzOsbern's household he had received the military training and education appropriate to his rank and future knighthood. He had learned to ride and to wrestle, to hawk, hunt and to swim. In fact, in William fitzOsbern's house Renaud had learned what it was to be truly happy and content – but he had never forgotten the pain and isolation of those early years.

What could Ceolwynn possibly understand of all this? What could he possibly say which would make her see that it was not Aelfrun who was cruel and unkind?

'Aelfrun is, I think, very lonely here,' he began tentatively. 'She is always a stranger, because no one really cares what she thinks or feels. She is very unhappy, and this makes her a little sharp in the tongue, I think you say.'

Ceolwynn was taken aback. She had never given any particular thought to Aelfrun's feelings. 'She doesn't like me,' she retaliated, a little sulkily.

'On the contrary, I think she tries very hard to like you, it is you that makes this difficult for her – remember the mouse, eh! You are not quite the dutiful daughter that she would wish for, but she loves you just the same.' He smiled at her kindly. 'Tell me,' he said, changing the subject and leaving her to ponder his words in her own time, 'why is your grandfather not buried here with these others?' He indicated with a wave the graves in the churchyard behind them.

'The people are afraid of his ghost. They believe that he would haunt them if he was buried here.'

Renaud nodded with understanding. He had already discovered for himself that these Saxons were a very superstitious people. 'And do you not fear this?' he asked.

'Oh no! His ghost would never harm anyone here,' she answered confidently, 'but I think he would have liked it better this way. He used to tell me about the way his people built huge funeral pyres on board their longships and sent them blazing out to sea. I wish we could have built a ship for him.'

They were both quiet for a few moments, then Renaud said, 'Just before he died, your grandfather said some strange things. He seemed to fear that I could bring you some harm. Yet no one here has treated me with any fear or suspicion, even though the last words of a dying man might be taken as some kind of omen.'

'Oh, there's no great mystery,' Ceolwynn replied almost cheerfully. 'Grandfather was often like that, nobody would have paid much heed to his words.' Her tone was so light and dismissive that Renaud was at once reassured. 'In fact,' she went on, 'they were probably more worried that he might find an axe and deal with you himself.' She grinned at him ghoulishly. 'That would have been shame indeed, a guest slaughtered at our very board.'

She laughed at his slightly shocked expression, and Renaud smiled. 'Shall we go into the church for a moment?' he said. 'I didn't know your grandfather well, but I would like to say a prayer for him.'

She nodded and they walked in silence to the church, Ceolwynn thinking once more of his remarks about Aelfrun. Perhaps he was right: she hadn't been kind to her stepmother. Rurik's death had reminded her forcefully just how fragile her little world really was. Her father was seldom at home and Estrith might soon be married, or in a convent. Perhaps it was time to make a friend of Aelfrun. She resolved at once to make more effort, and told Renaud so. He was pleased, but might have been rather less so had he appreciated that her motives were not entirely selfless.

Father Eadric was just leaving the church as they arrived at the door. He nodded briskly to them in passing and warned them to take care lighting their candles, the church's aged timbers were very dry after a long, hot summer.

Inside the church, Renaud finished his prayers and waited for Ceolwynn to finish hers. He had, of course, often attended Mass during his stay, but he was usually bleary-eyed and sleepy, hiding his yawns beneath a bowed head. He never troubled to look around him, his thoughts more often on breakfast than on his devotions.

Now he observed the simple thatched wooden nave built without transepts, and, in the pale light of the candles, he noticed for the first time the beauty of its decoration. The walls and pillars were handsomely carved. The altar-cloth was a masterpiece of the embroiderer's art, and the tall cross that rested upon it was of gold, ornately fashioned and studded with several small precious stones. He wondered if it was of Eastern origin, carried here, perhaps, by some marauding Viking long ago.

In wall niches on either side of the church stood tall statues of the saints in finely carved ivory, their faces eerily lifelike in the flickering candlelight.

The floor was bare, packed earth where most of the congregation stood to worship, although there was a bench to one side for the very old and the infirm. The altar, however, stood on a part of the floor which, as he knelt to pray, caught Renaud's eye. It was a small area of brightly coloured mosaic, quite out of keeping with its surroundings. He stepped back a pace to view this unusual flooring better.

'Do you like it?' Ceolwynn asked, observing his interest. Prayers finished, she had risen to her feet, dusting down her tunic in unconscious imitation of her stepmother. Renaud found the gesture quaintly adult and endearing.

'Yes, it's quite beautiful,' he replied. 'Where did it come from?' He had seen such mosaics before and knew quite well that they were not of Saxon workmanship.

'It was already here, part of some old ruins, when the church was built by my father's great-, great-grandfather, Cotta. He settled here and gave his name to Cottesham.'

'Is there more like it in the village?' he asked, kneeling to run a hand over the tiny bits of tile.

She hesitated and he looked at her questioningly. 'Can you keep a secret?' she half whispered although there was no one else to hear.

'Of course,' he replied, and wondered what sort of a secret she could keep hidden in a community as small as this.

'There is another place, a ruin, but no one else knows of it. I could take you there, but you must swear, here in this church, never to tell a soul. It is my secret place and I am the only one ever to have been there. Will you swear?'

He tried not to smile at the earnest, trusting little face staring up at him with such intensity. He was young enough not to have forgotten about childhood secrets and understood how important such a private place must be.

'Of course I swear,' he said, 'and I am honoured by your trust in me.'

'Put your hand on the altar and swear it,' she insisted.

Obediently, he reached across and laid his right hand on the altar-cloth. 'I swear by all the Holy Saints, and on my own life, never to reveal the secret place of my friend Ceolwynn, to a living soul.' He turned his head to look at her. 'Will that do?'

She nodded and made to leave, beckoning him to follow. The

sun was beginning to set, but it was still lighter outside than it had been in the church.

'Do you want to see it now?' she asked. 'There may be just enough light, if we hurry.'

'Why not?' he agreed, and waved for her to lead on.

She took him out beyond the palisade, then down a rough path used to drive the pigs to and from the tall woods ahead. They had barely entered the edge of these woods when Ceolwynn left the path and slipped down a steep bank thick with generations of dead beech and oak leaves. Under the dense canopy of the trees daylight faded rapidly and Ceolwynn drifted ghost-like in and out of a grey mist.

'Wait, Ceolwynn,' Renaud called. 'I hadn't realized it would be so far, or so dark. We should go back, we won't be able to see anything at all.'

'It won't matter, you'll see,' she called back. 'Look, we're here.'

At the bottom of the bank she began to clear away the leaves from between the partially exposed roots of an ancient oak tree. He caught up with her and saw a gap, a cavity even blacker than the surrounding gloom.

'Come on,' she urged, and disappeared into the darkness.

Renaud had to get down on his hands and knees to slither through the hole between the roots. Inside, it was even blacker than he had imagined, and as quiet as the grave until he heard the scrape of Ceolwynn's attempts to strike a light with flint and tinder. Then he caught sight of her face bent low over a small oil-lamp as it flickered uncertainly into life, and soon the whole chamber was illuminated by its warm glow. What he saw then was so totally unexpected that he gave a gasp of surprise and pleasure.

The space was some six feet square, though anyone taller than Ceolwynn would be unable to stand upright, and even she had to stoop a little. The floor was decorated with a mosaic which proved beyond doubt that this was just part of what had once been a room of great size, now covered and obscured by centuries of soil and forest growth. All that remained of the mosaic was a vine-patterned border, which clearly formed a corner of that long-vanished room, and the legs of a dancer poised gracefully in mid step, captured in time.

The unshod feet were slim and feminine, the nails painted a

34

bright and garish red. Brushing aside the loose leaves, Renaud revealed the diaphanous folds of her gown, the pattern on its hem and a bunch of bright ribbons trailing gaily from an invisible hand lost for ever in the forest floor.

'Well,' Ceolwynn asked in a throaty whisper, 'what do you think of it?'

'It's wonderful,' he replied in an awed voice. 'I could not have dreamt of its like. What artistry, to have captured in cold stone the very essence of life. I can almost see her dancing in my mind, just from that which remains.'

She smiled at him warmly, pleased that he felt just as she did.

'Look at this,' she said, crawling past him to clear yet more dirt and leaves away from the floor. 'It's almost overgrown. No, here it is!' She moved aside, still on her knees, so that he could see what she had uncovered.

There in the mosaic was a small, brown, curly-haired dog leaping playfully under the feet of the dancer, twisting in the air, red tongue flapping and tail wagging joyfully.

'He's almost alive,' Renaud exclaimed, reaching out to run his fingers over the vivid, vigorous shape as if in disbelief.

'What people do you think made things like this?' Ceolwynn asked him.

'I cannot answer you,' Renaud admitted ruefully, 'but I have heard tales in my own land about such ruins.'

'You have them there too?' Ceolwynn was surprised.

'Oh yes, and I believe they are to be found even in far-off lands. It is said that they were made by a people who came from the south hundreds of years ago, but I don't know if that be true.'

'What do you think they were like, these people?'

'Who knows? It is said that they must have been giants, so large were the buildings they made.'

'Giants!' Ceolwynn breathed, impressed. 'What do you think happened to them? Where did they go? Do you think they will ever come back?'

Renaud paused. He didn't really have any belief in giants himself, but he could see that she longed to believe in them.

'It is said,' he invented on the spur of the moment, 'that they remain the guardians of the lands they lived in, and that they but sleep, hidden from the eyes of man, until they are called forth in time of grave danger.'

Her eyes, bright and shining in the lamplight, opened wide. 'What sort of danger?' she whispered, as if the giants themselves might hear. 'Who may call them forth?'

'I don't know,' he replied, finding himself in difficulties as his invention began to show signs of growing beyond his control. 'All I can say is that the giants sleep and wait. That's all I know.'

'Do you think they are here now, in this place?' she whispered almost fearfully, believing every word. Renaud groaned inwardly as everything he said spawned yet another question. 'Do you think that this is where they wait for their return?' she went on slowly, this time not waiting for his answer. 'Is their sleep deep and untroubled, do you think, or is this the place where giants dream?' Her rapt expression told him that she was lost in the fantasy of his creation.

'If it is anywhere, then yes, I could believe it is here that your giants lie. Does it comfort you to know that your father's lands may be guarded by warriors mightier than, say, Wulfhere?' he teased. She laughed and was distracted from her imaginings.

'Look at this,' she said suddenly, drawing his attention to where the roots of the tree had forced their way down through the walls of the building, breaking them down but at the same time preserving small areas upright between them. In places he could make out faded patches of paint on plaster and Ceolwynn, pleased by his obvious interest, held up the lamp so that he could see better. False panels decorated with make-believe vases, flowers and fruit had been painted on the walls, and the effect was magically life-like. Renaud shook his head in wonderment.

'The lamp was here already,' Ceolwynn told him, 'and so was the oil-jar, but it was empty. Aelfrun measures out the oil very carefully to stop the servants wasting it. So it wasn't easy to get some, but I managed.' She proceeded to shine the lamp around the room and he noticed that she had made a tidy heap of her treasures in one corner.

There was some pottery, most of it broken, but the oil-jar and several glazed dishes were intact. He was careful not to draw her attention to the normal, human size of these things. There were some small items of jewellery and some coins; all very tarnished, but undoubtedly silver. Above all, he saw a bowl of the whitest chalcedony; translucent, polished to a waxy lustre and faintly encircled with bands of a bluish-grey tint. Its shape was exquisite;

deep, rounded and gracefully symmetrical. Renaud thought he had never seen anything so beautiful, so perfect, in all his life.

Cradling the bowl lovingly in his hands, he wondered aloud: 'How could anything so delicate and lovely have survived all this? You are very lucky, Ceolwynn, to have found this place, these things. Why don't you take them home and use them?'

'Then it wouldn't be my secret place any more and they'd dig it all up to see what else might lie here.' She thought for a moment. 'You have the bowl,' she said suddenly, delighted at her own inspiration. 'Take it to remember me by, because you are my true friend.'

Renaud felt he ought to refuse the gift, but knew in his heart that he couldn't bear to do so. 'I accept your gift,' he said with a formality that surprised her, 'but I have nothing of equal worth to give you in return. So, I will make you this pledge. I vow that if ever you have need of me, then you have but to summon me and, if it is within my power, I will repay you with any favour you have to ask.'

'Like the giants?' she asked.

'If you like,' he agreed, 'just like the giants.'

They crouched facing one another, each a little shaken by the intensity of the moment and hesitating to end the silence between them. At last, the lamp began to splutter and fade and the moment passed.

'We must go,' Renaud said, carefully tucking the bowl inside his tunic. 'People will begin to wonder if we have been spirited away by elves.' He wriggled out first, leaving Ceolwynn to snuff out the lamp and follow, scuffing up the leaves behind her to hide the entry once more.

It was full dark now, but a clear night and a bright moon made it possible for them to find their way home without difficulty. They walked in silence, each of them aware that this evening had forged between them a bond that neither time nor distance could ever break.

They were not to know that time and distance are not the only destroyers of friendship.

III

October 1060

'Renaud,' Aelfrun remarked as they shouldered their way through the market-day crowds, 'we know so very little about you, or about your home and family. Are you, perhaps, betrothed, or married even, to some fair lady who languishes, pining, for your return?' She spoke playfully, in case he should be offended by her curiosity.

'There's little enough to tell,' Renaud replied, pausing to shield her as the crowd surged apart at the sound of a cheerful warning cry. A baker skilfully manoeuvred his way through with a stack of trays balanced on his head, waving his thanks. 'I am my father's heir,' Renaud continued as soon as it was possible for them to walk side by side once more, 'but since I've not yet come of age, his estates are not mine to control. So, until then, I've no real fortune except the patronage of a good man, for which I am grateful; and no, I am neither married nor betrothed, for who,' he added, smiling, 'would have one such as I?'

'I'm sure there's many a pretty maid at our English court eagerly awaiting your return, even if the ladies of Normandy are blind to your charms,' Aelfrun laughed.

'Perhaps,' he grinned, but then, unexpectedly serious, he went on, 'but there is a lady in Normandy who has my heart.'

'Oh!' Aelfrun exclaimed, intrigued. 'Who is she? Is she very beautiful?'

'All women are beautiful,' Renaud answered with no hint of mockery. 'Little Ceolwynn has the beauty of the rising sun, colourful and bright but as yet lacking the full heat and brilliance to come; Estrith makes me think of birdsong and cornfields and long, hot summer days; and you have a beauty that is of the calm of twilight when the day's work is done, sweet and restful.'

Aelfrun blushed, unaccustomed to compliments. 'And what of your love?' she asked quickly, to cover her embarrassment.

'Ah,' he sighed, 'my lady has the beauty of a moonlit night, cool and dark and still. Her hair is as black as the raven's wing, her skin the colour of new milk. She walks in grace like the roe in the forest glade, and her voice would make the very angels hang their heads for shame.'

Aelfrun stared at him, amazed to hear any man speak so. 'For shame,' she said, tapping his arm reproachfully, 'you are teasing me.'

'No, indeed, I speak the truth, for Emma is everything I say, and more. She's the sister of my good friend, Hugo; his twin,' he added. 'Once I believed she cared for me as I care for her, but she is to wed another, a man as loathsome in both manner and appearance as he is in reputation.'

'Poor child,' Aelfrun murmured with sympathy, 'no doubt she was forced to it.'

'I wish that it were so,' he replied bitterly, 'but the truth is that he is rich and I am not.'

They walked in silence for a while, stopping occasionally to examine the goods on offer at each stall. Then Aelfrun caught sight of Estrith and Ceolwynn watching a group of tumblers.

Ceolwynn was having the most exciting day she had ever known, unaware that it was Renaud who had suggested the outing to Godmund to ease the sadness of Rurik's passing. Godmund had agreed and they were making a festive day of it.

It had been a merry, uneventful ride to Lullingworth. Once there, Godmund had wandered over to the horse lines. He had almost made up his mind to buy Ceolwynn a horse for her birthday, but so far had found nothing he liked.

Wulfhere, who had followed him, was wondering how he could get Estrith alone, and what he could buy her as a love gift that would not invite question. Eventually, he made some excuse and slipped off to find her, succeeding at almost the same moment as Aelfrun and Renaud.

'I never knew there could be so many people in one place,' enthused Ceolwynn. 'And there are houses with rooms upstairs for people to live in, not just for haylofts and storerooms. Is London like this?' she went on breathlessly, eyes filled with wonder. 'I never knew cloth could be dyed so many colours, did you?' To please Renaud she had made a genuine effort to be nicer to Aelfrun, and had been rewarded with such real warmth and affection that she felt quite ashamed of her past behaviour.

Aelfrun smiled tolerantly at the torrent of exclamation and question.

'Look!' Ceolwynn cried suddenly, 'a bear. Can I go to see the bear?'

'I'll take her, if you like,' offered Renaud.

Ceolwynn seized his hand to drag him away, and Aelfrun turned to Estrith and Wulfhere who were standing, close together, next to her. 'I must find Godmund,' she said in her usual brisk way. 'Will you come with me?' Estrith looked at her pleadingly and glanced towards Wulfhere. Aelfrun sighed. 'Ten minutes then, no more,' she agreed. 'But stay where you may easily be found,' she cautioned, and wondered if she should speak to Godmund about these two. He would find out one day, and would be sure to blame her for her silence.

Ceolwynn walked across the market-place with Renaud, revelling in the sights, sounds and smells from all sides, familiar yet exotic in their sheer intensity. The scent of spices would waft from one direction, to be replaced by the smell of fresh-tanned leather or roasting meat or new bread, all depending on which path you chose to walk. There was a jostling and a familiarity that was at once both welcoming and a little intimidating. A burly butcher's apprentice winked at her as though they were old friends, and a blind beggar clutched at her skirt with a vice-like grip that frightened her.

Renaud sent him off angrily; the man was a fraud, he told her. He'd seen him earlier, drinking and roistering with no sign of blindness about him then.

They finally reached the bear which, close to, Ceolwynn found something of a disappointment. Its muzzle was grey with age, its expression tired and dejected as it pawed half-heartedly at the iron collar and chain that secured it to a stout post.

Ceolwynn began to push her way through the gathering crowd in order to get a better view. Renaud, too, had noticed the sorry state of the old bear, its teeth and claws drawn, eyes watery as though with unshed tears. It was then he saw two men bringing out their dogs; large, ugly mastiffs, whining and straining at the leash in their eagerness.

Renaud had expected a dancing bear show, but it was now clear that what had attracted such a large crowd was a bear-baiting. Wagers were being laid and money changing hands, the excitement growing in proportion to the anger and fear of the bear and the maddened yelping and snarling of the dogs.

Catching sight of Ceolwynn's bright hair, Renaud dived after her. 'Come away,' he ordered peremptorily, 'you do not want to see this.'

'Why not?' she grumbled. 'I wanted to see the bear. Why do we have to go?'

'It is a baiting,' he replied with disgust, 'but that poor old bear stands no chance at all. It's not a fair fight and I do not care for it.'

Ceolwynn cast a last backward glance at the bear and felt moved to pity. 'Can't we do anything?' she asked, taking Renaud's hand in hers.

'No, and it would be foolish to try. Let's just find something more pleasant. Are you hungry?' he asked, and at her eager nod said, 'Come on then, we'll find something at the food stalls by the church. A drink would be welcome, too.'

They wandered off, chattering and laughing, unaware of Wulfhere and Estrith closeted together in a nearby doorway.

'Our situation is hopeless,' Wulfhere was saying miserably. 'If you don't accept Lord Godmund's choice of husband for you, he'll expect you to take the veil.'

'There is another choice, Wulfhere,' she insisted, 'if only we have the courage.'

He looked at her quizzically.

'We run away,' she said. His shocked expression made her hurry on. 'We could go to Flanders or Normandy where you could take service with another lord.' Wulfhere frowned unhappily. 'It's worth the attempt, isn't it?' she asked desperately. 'If you truly love me, that is.'

He turned his head away from her to stare out across the market-place. What she asked was impossible, yet the alternative was almost beyond bearing.

'Wulfhere?' she pleaded, frightened by his silence.

Fastening her with his eyes, he gripped both her hands in his, desperate to make her understand how hard it was for him to deny her. 'Estrith, listen to me please,' he began painfully. 'You know I love you with all my heart. You are all that I have thought about or dreamt of for nearly five long years, hoping and praying for some miracle that would make you mine. But this,' he concluded sadly, 'this you cannot ask of me. I cannot in honour desert my lord, save that he willingly release me.'

'But you are a free man, Wulfhere,' she argued fiercely. 'There can be no shame in seeking service with a new lord.'

'You know it's not so simple. Flanders and Normandy are the refuge of traitors and exiles. I know I am free to leave my lord, but not to steal away what I, at least, regard as the chiefest treasure of his house.'

'Then I must marry as Godmund bids,' she answered coldly, withdrawing her hands. He felt the hurt in every movement of her body and longed to pull her close to him, promise that he would do whatever she wished, anything, to keep her love; but he knew he could not do it.

She left him then, rushing away through the crowds so he shouldn't see her tears. He chased after her, calling her name, but if she heard him she made no sign of it.

He caught up with her at the horse lines, where Aelfrun was admiring the pretty roan mare that Godmund had finally chosen for his daughter. Seeing her sister's distress, Aelfrun quickly drew her away from the crowd. Estrith, confiding everything, smiled wanly at her sister and allowed herself to be hugged.

'I wish I could help, truly I do,' Aelfrun said unhappily. 'Do you want me to speak to Godmund? He might listen to me.'

'No,' Estrith sighed, shaking her head. She was well aware that Aelfrun had no power to sway her husband. 'He would probably just send Wulfhere away, and that would make things even worse for him. Godmund has all his loyalty, you know – more than he realizes.'

They had moved back into the main market square where Renaud and Ceolwynn joined them.

'We are having a most wonderful time,' Renaud informed them cheerfully, 'are we not, my little friend?' Ceolwynn stuffed the last of a sticky oatcake into her mouth and licked her fingers, nodding enthusiastically.

At that moment, Wulfhere's concerned face appeared briefly out of the crowd. It vanished again, but it was obvious that he was headed in their direction. Impulsively, Estrith grabbed Ceolwynn's arm and pulled her briskly away.

42

'Come, show me where you bought your honey cakes, Ceolwynn,' she said, and Ceolwynn found herself dragged off. Before Wulfhere could reach them, both Ceolwynn and Estrith had disappeared.

Wulfhere stood looking at Renaud and Aelfrun with an expression of stupid surprise on his face. 'Oh!' he said, 'I was sure I saw the lady Estrith here with you. I have something for her.' Clutched in his fist was a small silver ring, but he wondered if she would accept it from him now.

'I expect you'll run into her sooner or later,' Aelfrun said matter-of-factly. 'Would you mind going back to tell my lord Godmund that we will wait for him here, if he has finished his day's business?'

'I'll go at once,' the young man replied, having no real choice.

Renaud, watching all this with veiled amusement, was, however, far from unsympathetic. The loss of his own love didn't stop him hoping for the happiness of his friends. 'You look hot,' he remarked to Aelfrun. 'There's a stall over there which sells quite a drinkable ale. Would you like some?'

'Thank you, yes. The day is hotter than one might expect so late in October.' She took off her cloak and held it over her arm. 'I'm sorry that we are to lose you so soon,' she said, 'we shall all miss you, especially Ceolwynn.'

'I shall be sorry too, but the time, sadly, has come. I go back to the court with Cenred in a day or two, although he tells me that first we are to visit his father's house.'

Aelfrun frowned. 'Yes,' she said, 'he has important matters to discuss with his father, it seems.' She sounded so very disapproving that Renaud glanced inquiringly at her.

On an impulse, Aelfrun decided to confide in him. 'Cenred wants Ceolwynn to be his wife, and my husband has indicated that a betrothal between them would not be displeasing to him. Cenred goes to secure his father's approval and consent.'

'I already knew something of this. Ceolwynn herself told me; you know the child has ears everywhere. She seems no happier than you at the prospect.' He took her cloak and folded it over a barrel to make a seat for her. 'Might I ask what your objection is?' he asked, returning to their discussion.

'I'm not sure. I can't honestly say that I have any reasonable objection,' she admitted. 'I just feel that for Ceolwynn to marry

43

Cenred would be a mistake. It's hard to explain, but I don't believe she could ever be content with him.'

'Is contentment the best she can hope for from marriage?' he asked.

'How many of us can marry for love?' she returned. 'If we cannot have love, then surely contentment is the very least we can hope for?'

'And if we do marry for love, does contentment necessarily follow?' He paid for their drinks and handed her mug to her.

'Not always, but I imagine that marriage between two people who truly love one another must be an enviable state. My husband's first marriage was one such.' She sighed, lost in her own thoughts.

'What if the love is one-sided?' he probed, watching her face. She looked at him sharply, jolted by the closeness of his question to her own reflections.

'Then probably neither party can ever be truly content. One will be striving constantly to achieve the unattainable, while the other will always long for the one that he, or she,' she added hastily, 'has not.'

'So what then is your receipt for a perfect marriage? What would you wish for Ceolwynn?'

Aelfrun peered into her mug reflectively. 'Friendship, I think,' she answered. 'Friendship lasts when passion and beauty are spent; it supports you in time of need and shares with you your joys and sorrows.'

She had become very solemn and Renaud, who had just at that moment noticed Godmund walking towards them, quickly made up his mind to make her laugh. She never looked her best, he thought, when she was looking serious or thoughtful.

'I will agree with you, in part, but does passion really have no part to play in this ideal marriage of yours?' he asked mischievously. 'I think I would prefer a lover. Friendship is all very well, but there's not very much you can do with a friend on a dark winter's night, is there?'

Aelfrun almost choked on her ale. 'Enough,' she cried, laughter replacing her momentary shock.

Godmund, coming to meet them, saw Aelfrun just at that very moment, her face alive with laughter, her eyes sparkling and animated. Unaware of his approach, she continued talking and joking with the young Norman and Godmund found himself pausing to watch her curiously, almost as though he was seeing her for the first time, through the eyes of a stranger. Gone was the self-conscious humility she always displayed in his presence; she was not trying to please, she was simply enjoying herself.

She half turned to put down her mug and saw him standing only a few feet away. He watched the sudden change come over her; the smile was no less welcoming, but it had become meek, not joyful. Her eyes lost their sparkle and became anxious and fearful. He felt a strange and powerful sense of loss. It is me that diminishes her so, he thought, and the knowledge was unexpectedly painful.

He held out his arm to her. 'I am grateful for the care you have taken of my wife,' he said pleasantly to Renaud, 'but now I intend to steal her back, if she is agreeable?'

'Of course, my lord,' she answered, slipping gracefully off the barrel and shaking out her cloak. 'Did you wish to speak to me about something?'

'No. I thought you might like to walk with me by the river. It's cooler down there and would refresh you before the journey home.' Turning to Renaud he said, 'Dunn has gone on ahead, but you could try to find Wulfhere and the girls and tell them to be at the tavern where the horses are stabled in about an hour.'

Renaud nodded and moved off, whistling gaily to himself and well pleased with the results of his efforts to reveal to Godmund's blinkered eyes a more lively and joyful Aelfrun. The look of astonishment on his face had been most gratifying.

'You seemed very merry when I arrived,' Godmund remarked as he led his wife towards the river. 'What were you talking about?' He hadn't meant to ask, for fear he might sound jealous, but curiosity got the better of him.

'Oh, we were just talking nonsense,' she replied quickly. 'Did you know,' she said, 'that in Normandy they find a good, honest kiss of greeting quite shocking.'

'Yes, I did,' he laughed, 'in fact, I must admit to a guilty pleasure in watching their discomfiture.'

Now they were moving away from the square and down tiny streets and passages where small, ragged children played in the dirt and women with tired faces and work-worn hands shrieked

45

messages to one another across the narrow divide.

The air was so still, Aelfrun thought, that it seemed to fasten stifling fingers around the throat and raise beads of sweat from every pore. Gratefully they reached the end of the last evil-smelling alley and found themselves out on the grassy slope that led down to the river and the cool shade of the willows.

Godmund spread their cloaks on the ground under the lacy curtain of branches. They sat bathed in dappled shadows as a restless breeze stirred the leaves and made the sunlight dance skittishly around them. Aelfrun slipped off her shoes and allowed her feet to dangle in the cool water, giving a soft sigh of pleasure as it lapped around her ankles.

Godmund watched her thoughtfully, studying with new interest the curve of the long lashes on her cheeks as she leant back with eyes closed, supporting herself on arms braced slightly behind her, her pose artlessly drawing his attention to the soft rise and fall of her breasts.

As the river water began to dampen the hem of her tunic she moved to pull her skirt up higher, unaware of his steady gaze. After checking no one else was near, she bared her legs to the knee, giving Godmund a shamefaced grin. 'It's so hot,' she excused herself. 'I wish I had not worn wool today.' Godmund smiled but said nothing. His strange mood puzzled and worried her. She couldn't remember another time since their marriage when he had deliberately sought out her company without some clear purpose in mind. 'Have you had a successful day?' she asked conversationally, hoping that she had done nothing to anger him.

'Fair enough,' he answered. 'Have you always had that?' She followed his gaze to the small, brown mole below her knee. 'I don't recall seeing it before.'

Without thinking, she blurted bitterly, 'Well, that's hardly surprising, is it?'

He was startled by the sudden anger in her voice. 'What do you mean?' he asked. Appalled at herself, Aelfrun shook her head in an agony of shame and confusion, but Godmund, stirred by her sudden flash of spirit and annoyed that she seemed to be retreating from him again, grabbed her by the arms and gave her a small shake. 'Tell me,' he insisted, but frightened she turned her face away from him. 'Do you know, Aelfrun,' he said, more gently, 'today, for the first time, I realized that I hardly know you, my own wife. I brought you here so that we could talk, alone, away from too many listening ears, but now I have made you angry. Won't you tell me why?'

Aelfrun swallowed hard. Still frightened, she knew that if she kept silent now, she might never again find the courage to speak her mind. 'I long for a child, Godmund,' she began hesitantly, her voice trembling. 'I will never feel that I am your wife in truth until I have borne you a child, a son.'

It was not the answer he had expected and he stared at her uncomprehendingly. 'Is that all?' he asked, kneeling in front of her so that she was forced to look at him.

'All?' she repeated, shocked out of her meekness. All at once, the pent-up frustrations of years burst forth in a torrent of furious words punctuated with sobs. 'Is that all?' she cried with tears streaming down her face and her small fists pummelling ineffectually at his chest. 'You spend your nights in the hall in the company of servants while I lie awake, wondering if you will come to me, praying that, just for once, you will. You stay away and pine for what you have lost while I burn with shame; and you ask me, is that all?' She stopped to gasp for breath. 'She is gone, Godmund,' she almost shouted at him, 'but I am here, warm and alive, and I love you. Why is it so hard for you to love and want me too?'

She sat weeping uncontrollably, her hands before her face to conceal her tears. Her head-dress had fallen to the ground; her hair, hanging in plaits now half unbound, gave her an innocent, child-like look that touched Godmund to the heart. Feelings that he'd denied himself for so long began to sweep over him, almost frightening in their intensity.

'I do love you, Aelfrun,' he whispered, pulling her towards him until her head rested against his chest. Gently stroking her tangled hair he murmured soft, unintelligible words of comfort. He raised her chin and kissed her, holding her close and feeling the soft curves of her body beneath the coarse cloth of her tunic. Her lips parted willingly under his, returning kiss for kiss, and suddenly he found himself holding her closer, surprised by her response and at the passion which began to stir impatiently and demandingly within him.

Unprotestingly, she allowed him to raise her tunic and caress the soft skin of her thighs, covering her sun-dappled nakedness with gentle kisses. The touch of his lips on her breasts made her flush with desire, but suddenly she realized that he intended to take her there on the ground, under the sky and with the crowded market only a short walk away.

'Not here, not now,' she protested weakly. He looked around.

'We're well hidden by the trees,' he reassured her. 'Do you really want to stop now, my love?' he whispered teasingly. For answer she pulled his mouth back to hers and kissed him hard, leaving him breathless. He made love to her then as if for the first time, whispering words of tenderness and endearment that etched themselves joyfully onto her heart, so honestly were they meant.

Later, as they lay quietly together, each lost in their own thoughts and feeling no need for words, he took her hand tenderly in his, brushing his lips against the tips of her fingers in a silent gesture of homage. In that moment Aelfrun knew with sweet certainty that whatever memories lingered in his heart, the ghost of his dead wife would never come between them again.

If Renaud, predictably, was the first to guess at the change in their relationship, then Dunn was undoubtedly the second. He saw it in the way their eyes met as Godmund reached up to help her from the saddle, and in the way in which he held her longer and closer than was strictly necessary. The pain was sharp, but he was truly and unselfishly glad for both of them.

'What shall I do with these, mistress?' asked Eadburg, Aelfrun's maid, indicating the bales of cloth that Aelfrun had only just remembered to buy before they left.

'Put them in my sewing chest, for now,' Aelfrun answered, reluctantly pulling herself away from Godmund's possessively encircling arms to give the maid the key from her girdle.

'You're to have a new gown, I hear,' Godmund remarked affably to Ceolwynn. She nodded, yawning. Godmund smiled. 'I think this child will be asleep on her feet before much longer,' he said, and with Ceolwynn on one side and Aelfrun on the other he made his way to the hall, his arms around them both.

Dunn watched them go, pondering on the changes a day could bring.

He shook his head wonderingly and decided not to eat in the hall that night. His presence, he thought sadly, would hardly be missed.

Four days later, the day after Ceolwynn's tenth birthday, Cenred and Renaud left together. She'd found it a puzzling few days; on the surface nothing had changed, yet in some indefinable way, everything was different. Her father and Aelfrun, she noticed, had been especially light-hearted.

Estrith, on the other hand, had seemed strange and distant, reluctant to talk and unusually snappy. As if to compensate, Ceolwynn discovered she had a new and persistent companion in Cenred, who had taken to dogging her footsteps and making himself agreeable to her in his ponderous way. It seemed to confirm her suspicions that he had marriage in mind, and she gave some serious thought to the matter. She supposed she liked him well enough, but he was certainly not so interesting or amusing as Renaud.

On her birthday, Cenred gave her a pretty gilt workbox to hang at her girdle, a gift both charming and well chosen, not at all what she would have expected from him. Cylindrical in shape, it contained needles, scissors and threads of many colours.

'It is a very beautiful gift, Cenred,' she said, turning the box over in her hands to admire the workmanship. 'I will treasure it.'

'It is a gift for a maid on the threshold of womanhood,' he replied in stilted tones, 'when it is time to put aside childish toys and take up the tools of life.'

Aelfrun, seated beside them sewing, lifted her eyebrows at this speech and wondered how long he had rehearsed it.

'I am most grateful, thank you,' Ceolwynn said, reaching up to kiss him. She was taken aback by the enthusiasm with which the kiss was returned, and surreptitiously wiped her lips on her sleeve.

'I hope that you will think of me kindly each time you use it,' Cenred struggled on.

'I'm sure I shall,' she responded politely, and made to hang the chain of the box at her girdle.

Just at that moment, Cenred made a clumsy attempt to take her hand in his. The box was knocked to the floor, Cenred stooped hastily to retrieve it, banging his head painfully against Ceolwynn's as she bent to do the same. He leapt back, burbling an apology, only to step on the tail of a sleeping dog which squealed loudly and promptly sank its teeth into his calf. Frantically, he tried to shake off the dog, but only succeeded in kicking over the stool on which Aelfrun had carefully laid out her skeins of thread, now thrown all over the floor.

At last the dog let go, and Cenred, red-faced, attempted to regain his dignity and blundered on with his speech. 'I look forward to our next meeting, when I hope ...,' he caught Aelfrun's warning look and remembered that he was, as yet, to make no mention of his hopes to Ceolwynn, 'you will too,' he finished lamely and foolishly.

'Yes, of course,' Ceolwynn replied, out of her depth now in this odd conversation. She looked around desperately for some help, but suddenly everyone seemed to be very busy doing something else. Her father was helping Aelfrun pick up her threads, and Renaud, his shoulders heaving most strangely, was not looking her way at all. Cenred abruptly abandoned his attempts at courtship and limped from the hall without another word. Ceolwynn heaved a sigh of relief.

The rest of the day was easier, she found. She fell in love with her new palfrey at first sight, naming her Rowan. Aelfrun gave her a bridle decorated with bells and bright ribbons, and Estrith had a pretty silver brooch for her. Renaud, too, had managed to find her a gift, a small carved wooden bear bought from a legless cripple outside the church in Lullingworth.

'It's to remind you of our day at the market,' he told her. 'The bear was hardly the best of the day's memories, it's true, but I thought you would like it.'

'Yes I do,' she replied warmly, 'very much.'

'And you'll keep it to remind you of me?'

'Oh, you're not going to fall over or anything now, are you?' she giggled.

'I don't think so. No, quite steady,' he answered. 'No dogs attached, see?' They both collapsed, convulsed with mirth. Renaud sobered first. 'He really can be quite likeable, though; Cenred, I mean. We shouldn't really make fun of him. If you were to marry him, I'm sure he would be kind.' When she didn't answer, Renaud changed the subject. 'The man who carved this bear is a craftsman of great skill, but his legs were crushed by falling masonry while he was working on the king's new abbey at West Minster. I'd intended to ask your father if he could find the man some employment here, but perhaps he might be more willing if you were to ask. Would you?'

'Yes, of course, but you could have asked him yourself; he likes you, and he has been very good-humoured lately.'

To her surprise, he kissed her lightly on the top of her head. 'Yes, he has, hasn't he?' he agreed, and smiled.

They were walking back to the hall when Ceolwynn saw her father with Dunn outside the blacksmith's shop. She shot off to show him the bear and make her plea for the woodcarver. Renaud forlornly made his way to the stables to check that all was in readiness for the departure at daybreak.

Village life could be dull and the departure of lively and interesting visitors was always much regretted. Aelfrun, however, was especially sad, aware that in some subtle and inexplicable way, Renaud had been responsible for the many happy changes in her life. 'Good fortune go with you, Renaud,' she wished him sincerely. In a low voice, she added, 'I hope that when you return to Normandy, you will find that your Emma has had a change of heart.'

'Small chance of that,' he answered, leaning forward in the saddle to catch her softly spoken words, 'but my thanks for your good wishes. I shall miss you all.' He took a last drink from the parting cup she held out to him, then turned his horse to follow Cenred.

Ceolwynn, waving even though their backs were turned, suddenly remembered something and raced after him, grabbing hold of Renaud's stirrup to get his attention. Breathless, she gasped, 'Did you remember the giant's bowl?'

'Of course,' he replied affectionately. 'How could I have forgotten it? It's safe here in my pack, and will always make me think of you and my happy days here.'

Satisfied, she released his leg. 'Farewell, then. May God go with you.'

'And with you, little one,' he responded, moving on as Cenred threw them an impatient glance.

'My father said he would see what he could do,' she called after him, reluctant to let him go. He waved an acknowledgement, understanding what she meant, and looking back just once, he saw her standing in the road where they had parted, watching sadly as her friend left Cottesham, perhaps for ever.

IV

January 1063–September 1065

'Have you seen your father?' Aelfrun asked, raising her voice above the din. In winter anyone whose work did not have to be done elsewhere, crowded round the fire in the hall. The air was filled with noisy chatter and the shouts and laughter of children.

Ceolwynn shook her head and wondered at the hint of excitement in her stepmother's voice. 'Try the stables,' she suggested. 'He probably went there to find some peace.'

Godmund looked up from his gear as Aelfrun came through the door, his frown at having been discovered changing to a smile as soon as he saw her. The wolfhound at his feet thumped his tail heavily in greeting, making no effort to rise. Old and arthritic, his useful life was long over, but Godmund spared him out of affection. Aelfrun stroked the old dog's head, raising a small cloud of dust and hair, then hovered uncertainly in front of Godmund until he laid down his sword and looked up at her expectantly.

'We are going to have a child, at last,' she said in a rush, her eyes full of happiness, 'in May, or early June, perhaps.'

For a moment, Godmund looked as though he hadn't heard, but then he stood up, all the colour draining from his face. This was not what she had expected and she began to think that he did not share her joy; but then she remembered how his beloved Cengifu had died and understood the fear he felt for her.

She reached up to cup his face between her hands. 'You have no need to fear for me, my dear lord,' she said. 'I'm strong and healthy, with a body made for childbearing. Come,' she urged, 'tell me you are glad.'

He held her hands and stood back as if to examine this strange new person she had become. 'You're right, I am afraid for you,' he answered seriously, 'but of course I'm glad, more than glad.' He hugged her tightly, then hastily released her for fear of doing her some injury.

She laughed at him, lovingly, and placed his arms around her again so that for a few quiet moments they were locked together with his cheek resting gently on the top of the head which lay so trustingly on his chest.

'May or June,' he mused. 'A good time. The baby will have time to grow strong before winter comes. ... Come, sit with me a moment,' he said at last. 'There's something I should tell you. No, don't look so anxious, it's nothing that you should let upset you.'

Godmund had been stealing himself for this moment for some days, and was uncomfortably aware that this was a particularly bad time to tell Aelfrun what was on his mind, but he also knew there would never be a good time.

Earl Harold, seeking revenge against an old enemy, Gruffydd, King of Wales, had burned the town of Rhuddlan where the king had been holding his Christmas court, and had destroyed most of Gruffydd's ships. Gruffydd had managed to escape, but Harold, out for blood, had called upon his brothers, Tostig and Leofwine, for help – and Godmund, as Leofwine's man, would soon have to join him.

Aelfrun listened in silence while he explained all this, but exploded in uncharacteristic fury as soon as he'd finished. 'How can you tell me that I should not upset myself? You say that you fear for me, and then calmly tell me you are going off to fight a war. Am I supposed to have no fear for you, who goes into even more certain danger than I?' With a brisk movement she wiped a tear from her eye and tried to pretend that she wasn't crying.

'Not a war,' he argued, 'merely a campaign.'

'Oh!' she snorted derisively, 'I suppose, then, that in a campaign no sword will be drawn in anger and the Welsh will invite you all peacefully into their land. Take it, they will say, since this is only a campaign there is no cause for us to resist you.' This time she couldn't stop the tears flowing.

'Aelfrun, please don't,' he pleaded. 'You know that I cannot choose to go or not to go. If I could, do you think I would leave you alone at a time like this?'

Aelfrun knew he was right; her tears would change nothing and would only distress him further. Stifling a sob and wiping her face with her sleeve, she attempted a wan smile. Tentatively, he put his arms around her again, and this time she made no resistance, succumbing gratefully to the warmth of his embrace, accepting what little comfort he could offer.

Over the coming months, Godmund was away from home for weeks at a time, as Harold, reluctant to ease the pressure on his old enemy, pursued the campaign even through the winter. By May, the push for final victory was well under way, with Harold gathering a fleet in Bristol and his brother, Earl Tostig, advancing on North Wales with a mounted force. In the second week of May, Godmund arrived home at Cottesham for a brief visit.

Aelfrun was overjoyed to see him and rushed about with great energy, organizing everything for his comfort and ignoring her maid Eadburg's warnings.

'I cannot stay long,' Godmund told her regretfully as they sat at meat. 'Another day, no more.'

Aelfrun smiled, content just to have him there. It had been a long time, she thought, since they had all sat together at this table. Dunn was there, which pleased her. Since he'd married Wulfrun a year ago, he seldom joined them in the hall.

Estrith had finally agreed to wed the young man Godmund had found for her, but had delayed so long that the suitor had grown impatient and found another wife. To her relief, Godmund had lost interest after that and had let the whole matter drop. Unfortunately, her feelings for the now forgiven Wulfhere were unchanged, which worried Aelfrun, since loyalty to her sister meant deceiving her husband.

'How much longer is this fighting going to last?' she asked Godmund despairingly. 'I live in fear for you, my lord.'

'I'm certain it will all be over soon,' he assured her. 'We'll soon be closing the trap which will catch our Welsh mouse once and for all, have no fear. These Welsh scurry off into their mountains as soon as they see us coming and avoid hand-to-hand combat. That's what makes it so hard to crush them completely.' He smiled at Aelfrun, who said nothing. She was suddenly very pale and looked frightened. 'What is it?' he asked at once, full of concern. 'Whatever's the matter?'

Eadburg, never far from her mistress, guessed at once what

was amiss. 'You leave her to me, my lord,' she ordered Godmund, and helped Aelfrun to her feet. Ceolwynn, as white-faced as her father, came to take her other arm. Estrith, as practical and organized as her sister, had already left the hall to make sure that everything from linen to birthing stool would be ready.

Aelfrun gave her husband an anguished look. 'It's too soon,' she said, more bewildered than frightened now.

'Don't you fret about it, my love,' Eadburg comforted her. 'I'll look after you and see that all comes right. Come away now. No, my lord, you stay here. It isn't fitting that you should see what's to be seen now.'

Obediently, the thegn made way for the slave and sat down, full of anxiety, to wait out the next few hours.

'My son,' Godmund breathed in awe. He looked at the tiny bundle in his arms and shook his head wonderingly. 'I had forgotten,' he said, 'just what such a moment as this felt like, to hold your newborn child for the first time.'

'He's small, but healthy,' Aelfrun murmured, smiling weakly at him from her bed. Godmund laid the sleeping child gently in his wooden cradle and took his wife's hand in his, holding it to his cheek for just a moment.

'And you, my dear one?' he asked tenderly.

'I am very happy,' she answered contentedly, then yawned, unable to help herself. He smiled and released her hand, tucking it carefully beneath the covers.

'I must leave you to sleep,' he said.

'No,' she protested, pulling herself painfully into a sitting position, 'don't go, please. You have to leave so very soon. If I sleep now you may be gone before I wake and you have not yet told me what you want to call your son.'

'What would you like to name him?' he asked.

'I had thought, perhaps, to name him for your father.'

A shadow crossed Godmund's face. 'My first son lived for a few minutes only,' he explained sadly, 'but there was time enough to baptize him. Edgar was the name he was given. I do not care to use it again.'

'Forgive me, I didn't know. How about Siggi?' Aelfrun offered. 'Siggi Godmundson,' she said slowly. The baby stirred and opened his eyes for a moment. 'There, you see,' she cried, delighted, 'he answered to his name. He must be called Siggi.'

'It shall be as my lady wishes,' Godmund agreed gallantly. 'After all, how can I refuse you anything on this day.' He sat down on the edge of the bed and fed her honeyed sweetmeats from a bowl. 'Which reminds me,' he went on, 'I must give you a gift in exchange for your gift to me, though there is nothing I could give you which would be even half so precious. What would you like?'

As it happened, Aelfrun had already half-planned her answer to this question. Never again would her husband be as anxious to please and to reward her as he was at this moment. Even so, she hesitated, drawing a deep breath before she spoke.

'The most precious gift you have in your power to grant me,' she began, 'is my sister's happiness.' Godmund stared at her, a look of confusion on his face.

'I don't understand,' he said.

'Estrith wishes to marry, but only your consent and assistance can smooth the obstacles that lie between her and the man she loves.'

'Who is the man?' Godmund asked.

'Wulfhere,' she blurted, as if saying it fast would make it more palatable.

'That puppy has dared to court my own wife's sister?' he said incredulously.

'I knew you would be angry,' Aelfrun said unhappily. 'I should not have asked you, forgive me.'

'No,' he answered stiffly, 'I made you a promise and must at least consider the matter now that you have asked it of me. I owe it to you.'

'It's not a debt that you are obliged to honour, my lord.'

'Now you are angry with me,' he sighed again. 'Let's not quarrel on such a happy day.'

'I don't want to quarrel, my lord,' Aelfrun answered him pleadingly, 'I only want you to listen, and to be just.'

'I swear if that boy has done anything to shame your sister, he will pay for it.'

'He has not,' Aelfrun hastened to assure him, 'and Wulfhere is a grown man and a man of honour, as my sister is an honourable woman. They have loved one another since first they met, over seven years ago. Think of it, my lord; they have remained constant for all that time, even knowing how hopeless was their love.'

'How long have you known?' Godmund asked. She didn't answer. 'I see,' he said. 'I am disappointed that you have deceived me, Aelfrun.'

'I didn't mean to,' she said miserably. 'I wanted to tell you, but dared not. I love them both.'

'It saddens me that you feared me too much to tell me what was going on under my own roof. I should have been told,' he reproached her.

Aelfrun hung her head, too exhausted to argue further; and Godmund, seeing her weakness, was ashamed of his anger. He kissed her and stroked the hair away from her face.

'I made a promise,' he said, 'and I will seek a way to keep it without disgracing your father's house. Trust me to do my best, but I cannot promise more than to make an honest effort on his behalf.'

'Oh, Godmund, thank you,' Aelfrun cried joyfully. 'I do love you so.'

'But why,' Leofwine asked, puzzled, 'should I want to send one of your men to my brother Tostig?'

Godmund stirred up the fire and turned the spit. Fowl fat sizzled and hissed in the flames and a gust of wind, acrid and smoke-filled, blew through the open doorway making both men cough. Godmund moved to pull across the hides that served as a door, shutting out the sight of smouldering fields where sudden bursts of spark and flame glowed redly against the evening sky and the bodies of captured Welshmen dangled from the trees, a grisly warning to their countrymen. It was hardly a glorious campaign, Godmund thought, this burning of villages and taking of hostages, but if Harold was right it would force the Welsh to abandon the king who had brought such suffering upon them, and make peace on English terms.

'It's not just that I want Wulfhere to be your messenger,' Godmund explained. 'I'd like you to send, with your letter, your personal recommendation of him to your brother.'

'Wulfhere,' Leofwine said thoughtfully. 'Isn't he the tall, brawny fellow; very fair; built like a brace of oxen?'

Godmund grinned at the description: 'That's him. The fact is, I want him to have the opportunity to distinguish himself, to prove his courage and ability. He's not likely to do that with us here, is he? Our part of this campaign is entirely punitive, and we're not likely to come up against anything more threatening than a pitch-fork.'

'Why is it so important that this particular ceorl of yours sees a bit of real action?' Leofwine asked. 'You don't, by any chance, want him out of the way, do you?' he suggested.

'No I do not,' Godmund denied vehemently. 'I shall explain,' he continued. 'I would like you to help young Wulfhere to attain the status of thegn so that he can marry my wife's sister. If you can persuade Tostig to look upon him with favour, then perhaps Wulfhere's own efforts may be all that will be required for your brother to present such a recommendation to the king.'

'Ah!' Leofwine exclaimed with an exaggerated air of revelation. 'Now I see,' he went on, 'either your man gets his promotion, or he dies in the attempt. What will your womenfolk say if the lad comes home in a cart?'

'That is a risk we all take. But, believe me, I would prefer that he lives and prospers. Help him, Leofwine, as a favour to me.' Leofwine nodded and Godmund smiled with pleasure.

'One more thing,' he added. 'I have not told the lad that I know where his hopes lie. He must believe that all he achieves is by his own efforts.'

'So it shall be,' Leofwine answered. 'I see no reason why your man shouldn't leave tonight, under cover of darkness.'

Later on, Wulfhere, called to attend his lord, was surprised to find Godmund with the earl's chaplain and clerk as well as the earl himself. He hovered uncertainly in the doorway until Godmund, looking rather pleased with himself, beckoned him forward. Earl Leofwine smiled agreeably, while the chaplain and the clerk, like a pair of solemn crows, stared at him with frank curiosity. The clerk handed him a sealed letter which Wulfhere took uneasily, glancing at Godmund for explanation. It was the earl who answered his look, explaining where he was to take it.

'Once there, you will stay with my brother Tostig and obey his orders in all things. Is that clear?'

'Very clear, my lord,' Wulfhere answered, a thrill of excitement coursing through him. 'When shall I leave?'

'At once,' Leofwine replied, handing over a sketchy route that the clerk had managed to produce from among his papers. 'Take a good horse and remember that you are in enemy territory. Keep out of sight and destroy the letter if you cannot avoid capture. You may go now.'

Wulfhere, still confused by this rapid, unexpected turn of events, threw one last look at Godmund.

'Take care, lad,' the thegn said kindly. 'May God go with you.'

By August, it was all over. The Welsh had finally rebelled against Gruffydd and had sent his head to Harold as a peace-offering. There had been no pitched battles in which a young man might prove his valour, but Tostig, amused by his younger brother's curious request, had shown his letter to Harold and given him an idea.

Wulfhere had accepted without hesitation Harold's challenge to go alone into Wales with secret letters for the most important local chieftains, offering generous terms in return for the over-throw of Gruffydd, their king. It was dangerous work, and although it was arguable whether his secret mission into Wales precipitated or merely accelerated Gruffydd's downfall, still he had played his part, and bravely.

His reward had been all that he could have hoped for, and only two weeks after the Welsh capitulation, the king had confirmed his new status as thegn and granted him a small estate in Northumbria, making Tostig his new overlord. Unaware that he had had some of the most important men in the kingdom acting on his behalf, Wulfhere had been overcome by the speed of the events which had changed his life.

Now, for the last time, he was going back to Cottesham, riding at Godmund's side as an equal. 'I just can't believe it,' he told Godmund wonderingly. 'I shall wake up and it will all have been a dream.'

Godmund listened for what seemed like the hundredth time to the story of Wulfhere's brief audience with the king at Gloucester. He heard again how all the details had been noted in the great book and how he had been told the rights, privileges and duties that went with his new rank and property.

'You will have to marry, of course,' Godmund mentioned nonchalantly.

Wulfhere immediately blushed and Godmund had to pretend a need to adjust a stirrup to hide his laughter. After a moment, he went on: 'I know you no longer have any duty of obedience towards me, but I hope that your old loyalty and respect will incline you favourably towards a suggestion of mine, since, to my knowledge, you have demonstrated no particular preference of your own in this matter.' Wulfhere looked devastated and Godmund continued straightfaced: 'You will need a wife of good family, but ...' he shook his head doubtfully, 'a bit of land in Northumbria and no real lineage of your own to offer is not going to attract too many proud fathers with daughters to marry off, is it?'

'I suppose not,' Wulfhere conceded in a small voice.

'No, it will not,' Godmund went on, enjoying himself immensely. 'However, I have the answer. I have a cousin. She is, to be sure, a little long in the tooth, but I'm certain she's still capable of breeding – if you waste no time. She's no beauty, I have to admit, but she would bring you a handsome dower.'

'It is good of you to take such an interest, my lord,' Wulfhere began desperately.

'My dear Wulfhere, your welfare is of the deepest concern to me and, knowing that, I am sure that you will be only too happy to accede to my suggestion.'

'I am most grateful, but—' Wulfhere tried again.

'There is no need for thanks,' Godmund interrupted cheerfully, holding up a hand as if to stave off a flood of gratitude. 'I am happy to be able to do this service for you. There is no more to be said.'

Wulfhere was lost for words. His thegnship was too new for him to feel confident about defying the man whose word, only days before, had been law to him. His look of misery was eventually too much for the older man.

'On the other hand,' he said casually, 'you could, I suppose, have my wife's sister, Estrith.'

Stunned, Wulfhere reined to a halt and Godmund had to half turn his horse to enjoy the look on his victim's face. The laughter in his eyes betrayed him, and Wulfhere finally realized that Godmund not only knew his secret but was prepared to give him without argument the one thing that would make his life complete.

'You knew,' he said incredulously, 'and you were not angry?'

'I was at first,' Godmund admitted, 'but things have changed. Remember though,' he cautioned, 'mine is not the final say; there are still Wilfred's wishes to consider.'

'How long have you known?' Wulfhere asked, still dazed with relief and happiness.

'Since May. My wife told me on the day our son was born.'

Wulfhere nodded thoughtfully. It was all becoming clear to him now. Godmund had given him his chance and in doing so had given him everything. He would never forget it.

The floor of the weaving shed where Aelfrun and Ceolwynn worked alongside their serving women, was just bare earth flattened and made smooth by the feet of generations of women.

'I wonder what Estrith is doing now?' Aelfrun mused. 'Life must be very different for her up there in Northumbria. They say the people are quite wild and their language scarcely comprehensible.'

This was a softer, more contented Aelfrun than the sad young woman Renaud had known. She was a little plumper now, and the old severity had disappeared from a face that laughed and smiled far more often and more readily. Her only sadness was also her joy, since Estrith was now far away from them.

'I'm sure she will be very happy as long as she has her Wulfhere beside her, don't you?' Ceolwynn answered with a smile. 'Those rough Northumbrians will soon come to love her; she is so good and kind.'

'Yes, you're quite right. Oh, Siggi no! Don't do that.'

Her small son, busy rolling loom weights across the floor and chortling happily to himself, had failed to lift two weights at once and one of the heavy clay rings had tipped over, catching the end of his finger. The shed rang with the sound of his frightened howls.

Ceolwynn rushed to her brother's rescue, lifting him up into her arms, kissing his sore finger and whispering soothing words until he hushed.

'There's no need to pet him so, Ceolwynn,' Aelfrun complained. 'He was hardly hurt at all. The child is spoilt enough without you forever running after him.'

'He's adorable. Aren't you, my lamb?' Ceolwynn protested, hoisting him high and swinging him around until he screamed with laughter, his pain quite forgotten.

Siggi was everyone's favourite, there was no denying it. He was two years old, a happy, cheerful child secure in the knowledge that he ruled his entire world.

61

In looks, Siggi favoured his mother, with hair of a rather uninteresting brown and a face with more character than beauty. His eyes, too, were like hers; large and dark with long, curling lashes. They gave him a look of angelic innocence which was surprisingly deceptive, since he was full of mischief. To see him so strong and healthy, a worthy son for Godmund's house, filled Aelfrun with great pride.

She was proud, too, of her stepdaughter. At fourteen, Ceolwynn was now a lovely young woman, fulfilling all the promise of her childhood. Her hair was lighter than it had been, but its copper sheen raised it far beyond the commonplace. She was tall and slender, already half a head taller than Aelfrun, and her deep blue eyes sparkled with ready laughter.

For the past two years she had been formally betrothed to Cenred and they were to marry soon after she reached her sixteenth birthday. Her early fears about this marriage had lessened with the years, and as her new home would be less than half a day's ride from Cottesham, she knew that she would not lose touch with those she loved. This knowledge had brought her great comfort. How dreadful it must be, she had thought, to leave your home and travel far away, perhaps never to see your family again. She guessed that Estrith, in her northern home, must miss them all very much.

A shaft of sunlight shining through the half-open door made Ceolwynn sigh heavily as she resumed her seat at the loom.

Aelfrun could see how bored she was and suggested she take Siggi out into the sunshine.

Ceolwynn leapt up and gave her stepmother a quick kiss of gratitude. 'I won't take my eyes off him,' she said as she scooped him up in a wriggling armful.

Godmund's fishponds, towards which they walked, provided fresh fish both for the village and for market, but for Siggi they were just another source of amusement. He loved to watch the big fish swim round and round, then leap to snap at the bread he threw on the water.

Ceolwynn was on her way to the kitchens to get some bread for them to take when she saw Hild, Eadburg's daughter, helping to spread some clean laundry out on the bushes to dry. She waved.

'We are going to sit by the ponds,' Ceolwynn said. 'You can

come if you like.' Hild was as much a companion as a servant and Ceolwynn enjoyed her company.

Hild grinned. If her mistress ordered it, she could not be refused permission to go. Ceolwynn waited while the girl hooked a shift onto a convenient twig and spread out the last of the clothes, then together they strolled off with Siggi swinging happily between them.

They had just crossed over the palisade when Dunn drew up on his small, shaggy pony. 'Hello,' he said in surprise. 'I thought you'd be heading for the woods.'

'Why?' Ceolwynn asked, puzzled.

'Had you forgotten? They're driving the pigs to mast today. Siggi would love it ... Pass him up,' he offered, 'and I'll meet you by the pens; you'll run faster without him.'

Gratefully, Ceolwynn handed over her brother and with Hild close behind raced back through the village to the pens, where all the pigs were being gathered together from the fields and cottage gardens, ready for the drive up into the beech woods. Once there, the pigs would be left to fatten over the winter, and in the spring her father would be paid a pannage fee based on how many inches of fat they had put on.

The drive was always great fun and very, very noisy. The swineherds would collect their sixpences from those whose pigs were to be driven, and then with spears and the trumpeting of horns would goad the beasts along and try to keep them to the path. The other villagers would follow, just to join in the fun.

Dunn arrived just as the drive began and handed back his charge, then with the little boy carried alternately on their shoulders, Ceolwynn and Hild followed the drive until they were exhausted.

At the edge of the woods they stopped to rest, not far from the place where Ceolwynn's ancient ruin lay hidden. They slumped down on a log and shared with Siggi the bread that had been intended for the fish.

It had been such a long time, Ceolwynn realized, since she'd last felt the need to visit her secret place that she'd almost forgotten it: but she remembered it now and smiled to herself, thinking of the day she had taken Renaud there. 'Hild,' she said suddenly, 'you'd better go back now. I'll come on later with my brother.'

Hild frowned, disappointed at having to go back, but having no argument to offer, left.

After she had gone, Ceolwynn stared pensively down at her brother grubbing in the dirt at her feet. 'You're filthy,' she told him absently.

At the sound of her voice he looked back at her over his shoulder and chuckled for no reason she could see. She stroked his silky baby hair and wondered whether she was ready to share with him her secret. He wouldn't understand, of course, but if she started taking him there often enough, he would soon learn that it was their secret place and not to speak of it as he grew older. The words of a song she had heard a minstrel sing came into her mind and she sang it softly to herself as she pondered:

> ... *I have a hut in the wood, none knows it but my Lord; an ash tree this side, a hazel on the other, a great tree on a mound encloses it ...*

Abruptly, she made up her mind. She wanted her brother to grow to manhood knowing that she was his friend as well as his sister. He would not even be four years old before marriage took her away from him, but a shared secret would help to bind them through the years no matter what else separated them. They would sit in the lamplight, she thought, and she would watch his eyes grow round with wonder as she told him the tales that Rurik and Renaud had told, so many years ago, and in the telling she would keep her memories alive.

'Come on, little fellow,' she said, hoisting him into her arms. 'I'm going to take you to meet some giants.'

V

September 1065–January 1066

'What is it you want, Hugo?' Emma asked irritably.

He uncoiled himself languidly from his place in the window seat and wandered over to where Emma sat, her lap full of discarded sewing. 'Can a man not visit his dearest sister without being accused of wanting something from her?' he asked.

'No,' she replied acidly, 'I do not believe you have come for the sole pleasure of my company. It's not your way.'

Hugo laughed. 'Actually, I have news that might interest you.'

He drifted back to the window. Emma refused to be drawn and picked up her sewing once more.

'Renaud de Lassay is here in Caen,' he told her casually. Emma stabbed her finger with her needle and watched the blood make a small red stain on her work. 'He said he'd very much like to see you again.'

'Renaud de Lassay?' she mused. 'The name is familiar.'

Hugo laughed, not in the least fooled. 'Come now, how could you forget such an ardent lover.'

'He was never my lover,' she returned sharply. 'He was just a boy when I last saw him.'

'Well, he's a boy no longer,' Hugo remarked with a wicked smile.

'You seem to forget that I am a married woman.'

'Rumour has it, my dear, that you yourself forgot that little detail a long time ago.'

Emma paled. 'What rumours?' she asked, obviously alarmed. 'Things would not go well with me if my husband was to hear such talk.'

'Don't fret,' he said, serious for once, 'I was only guessing.

Shall I tell Renaud, then, that you do not wish to see him?'

'Yes. No, perhaps it might be entertaining. Bring him tomorrow. My husband goes hunting with the duke in the morning so we may be quite private.'

Emma's husband, Roger de Virar, was a cold and humourless man to whom a wife was a possession valued only in terms of the advantage it brought to himself. It had come as a great shock to Emma to discover that she herself meant far less to him than the property she had brought with her. Pampered and admired all her life, she had confidently expected her husband to be yet another devoted admirer. Learning that he was not had dealt a severe blow to her pride.

'That may be difficult,' Hugo was saying, interrupting her thoughts. 'Our Renaud has become something of a favourite with the duke, and may himself be expected to accompany the hunt.'

'Really?' she said.

'Yes, indeed. Duke William himself conferred arms on the boy during the Breton campaign last year. So, as I say, it may not be so easy for him to get away.'

Emma was not now to be put off. 'If he wants to see me enough, he'll think of something.'

Hugo smiled, then became unexpectedly serious. 'You must be careful, you know. I fear for you if Roger should ever come to learn of your, shall we say, diversions.'

Emma shrugged, pretending a nonchalance she didn't really feel. 'Roger pays little enough attention to me when he's here.'

'Oh, he would care, Emma, believe me, he would care.'

Emma nodded, accepting his warning – Roger de Virar truly was a man to be feared. 'Thank you for your warning, Hugo, but you need have no fear for me. I will be careful, in all I do.'

'That would be wise,' he said, stooping to kiss her cheek in farewell. 'Until tomorrow then, my dear Emma.'

'Until tomorrow,' she agreed, wondering if Renaud would make an agreeable husband if Roger should die.

But why was Hugo so anxious to bring her together with Renaud? Her brother was, she knew, a mischief-maker. What mischief was he up to here?

Emma was quite right to suspect her brother's motives. Hugo had recently had a falling out with his sister's husband over the matter of a loan asked for and refused. It amused him to think of the pompous Roger being cuckolded. He'd been delighted to run into Renaud in the duke's household and it hadn't taken long for him to realize that the means for his revenge was at hand.

A close friendship had sprung up between Hugo and Renaud during their boyhood in fitzOsbern's household. Hugo had been his young companion's defender and protector and Renaud, never forgetting this, gladly forgave him all his many faults. It was as a visitor to Hugo's own home in Caen that he had first met and been captivated by the fair Emma.

Meeting again, here in Caen, it wasn't difficult for the two young men to recapture their cheerful camaraderie nor for Hugo to persuade Renaud to renew his friendship with his sister. Even so, it was with some misgivings that Renaud found himself, the following morning, walking at Hugo's side towards Roger de Virar's large town house.

Caen was Duke William's favourite city and he was transforming it. Many new stone houses, of which de Virar's was but one, had been newly built, and two new abbeys, St Stephen's and Holy Trinity, had been founded by the duke in return for the Pope's recognition of his previously forbidden marriage to Matilda of Flanders. The effect was impressive.

Renaud gazed at the changes in admiration.

Emma would be twenty-one, a year older than himself, he thought, and if Hugo was anything to go by, then maturity could only have enhanced and refined her already startling beauty. His mouth felt dry as they climbed the stairs that led to her private rooms. What would he say to her? What would he feel? Was he still in love?

A young page showed them to a small room where food and wine had been laid out. There was no sign of Emma, but the page carefully filled their cups, bowed politely and left. Hugo watched with veiled amusement as Renaud paced nervously to and fro. He guessed his sister planned some dramatic entrance, in which assumption he was soon proved correct. Emma swept into the room dressed in a dark red gown that managed to emphasize both the whiteness of her skin and the silken darkness of the hair which hung unbound far below her waist.

'Oh!' she cried, as if their appearance had been totally unexpected. 'That stupid boy, he was told to let me know when you arrived. Please forgive me. If I had known you were here, I would, of course, have been ready to greet you.' She waved a hand towards her hair in a prettily apologetic gesture to show that they had caught her totally unprepared.

'Think nothing of it,' Hugo offered with a grin that informed her that he at least was not taken in by her play-acting.

She ignored him and turned all the warmth of her soft, dark eyes on Renaud. 'My dear, dear friend,' she said. 'It's been so long.' She took his hands and gave him her most adoring look. 'I cannot tell you what it means to me to see you again. How handsome you have become.'

Renaud was completely overcome. She was perfect. The love he'd tried to forget flooded back tenfold, and he found himself just holding her hands, utterly lost for words, while Hugo, seeing that any extra effort on his part would be quite superfluous, made an excuse and left.

'I thought you would have quite forgotten me,' Renaud got out at last.

'Forget you! How could I? I think of you all the time. How cruel to accuse me of such inconstancy.'

'But you married another?' he said, a note of puzzlement in his voice.

She sighed heavily and allowed a single tear to decorate her cheek. 'I was a child; I did what I was told was best for me and for my family; but it was always you I loved, dearest Renaud.' To his surprise she put her arms around his neck and kissed him with unexpected passion. 'Do you love me still?' she breathed, holding him so close that he could feel her heart beating.

'Oh yes, yes,' he answered fervently, forgetting the scornful words of rejection she had poured on him in the past, 'even more than ever.'

'Come,' she said suddenly. 'Sit down and tell me all that has happened to you these past five years. Hugo tells me you have been in England.'

'I did spend nearly two years there, yes,' Renaud replied, taking the offered seat, 'but my lord fitzOsbern called me back unexpectedly.' He laughed. 'It was quite a relief to return. I thought I would never have the chance to gain my knighthood, but my lord saw to it that I did.'

'He must think well of you; as, I believe, does another William,' Emma probed.

'The duke, you mean?' Renaud said. Emma nodded and passed him a cup of wine. 'Yes, I have been lucky enough to catch his eye, if only because my own lord is constantly in his company.' Emma nodded again. 'Well,' he went on, 'when I was last here in Caen, one or two comments I made about the new buildings apparently found their way to his ears, and his approval. Since then the duke seems to like having me about and does occasionally ask my opinion on his projects. He doesn't actually care about my opinion,' he laughed ruefully, 'but I think he enjoys talking to someone who shares his interest.'

'So you have no real position yet in his household?'

'Not really, although I have been told that I may hope for something soon. My lord fitzOsbern insists that I would be foolish to refuse an offer from the duke; should he make one, of course.'

Emma was very annoyed with Hugo for having misled her. Still, it was, after all, only a little dalliance she intended at present. Time alone would tell whether the pursuit of Renaud de Lassay would prove worthwhile.

'What are your plans now?' she asked. 'Will you stay in Caen for some time?'

'Certainly, as long as my lord chooses to stay. Longer possibly, if the duke offers me some employment.'

'Then there will be opportunities for us to meet again?'

'Yes, of course; but I doubt if we will be able to meet as privately as this in the future. Your husband would, I'm sure, be unhappy about such visits, even in the company of your brother, and I would have no doubts cast upon your honour.'

Emma turned away to hide her smile. 'Most assuredly we shall meet again, and privately,' she said, turning back and laying her hand meaningfully over his. A look of total confusion flooded his face. 'I think,' Emma continued, running her fingers almost imperceptibly the length of his hand, 'that you can trust me to take whatever steps I think necessary to protect my own honour.'

Renaud met her eyes and saw that he hadn't mistaken her meaning.

'I will send a message by one I can trust: Richard, the page who brought you here. You should go now,' she said.

He rose and would have kissed her, but since Hugo chose that moment to return they parted with just a clasping of hands.

On the way back to the duke's new stone fortress Renaud was

unusually quiet, but Hugo made no attempt to interrupt his thoughts. Whistling softly and cheerfully to himself, he began to savour the pleasure of his revenge on Roger de Virar.

Emma stretched luxuriously, shamelessly revealing her naked body to her lover's eyes and making no effort to cover herself with the furs scattered all over the bed and on the floor. Renaud paused in his dressing to pull some of them back onto the bed. Emma laughed.

'Come here,' she ordered, holding out her arms to him imperiously.

'I have to go. We take too many risks.' Emma pouted and he gave in, going to sit beside her on the bed and taking her in his arms. 'I still have to go,' he said.

'Go then,' she replied pushing him away in annoyance. 'It's nothing to me whether you go or stay.'

Renaud sighed; he still found her quite as captivating and exciting as ever, but she was volatile and he did sometimes find her sudden mood changes a little tiresome. Now, realizing that the hour was getting very late, he rose to leave.

'I am going to have a baby,' Emma said abruptly. Renaud sat down again.

'Is this true?' he asked. He knew her well enough by now to appreciate that she was not above using a dramatic statement like this just to get his attention.

'Yes, it's true.' He could see from her face that she meant it.

'Is it possible that Roger could be the father?'

'Yes,' she said doubtfully, 'but whether he will believe it or not is another matter. His first two marriages were both childless.'

'What do you think he'll do if he doesn't believe you?' He pulled the furs up over her as he spoke and this time she didn't argue.

'I don't know.' For the first time she looked frightened, as if in telling him she had forced herself to face up to the reality of her predicament. 'He will have to be told soon,' she said forlornly.

'It is *my* child, isn't it Emma?' She looked at him in surprise and prepared herself to display anger and indignation, but he met her look firmly and she realized that even though he loved her, Renaud had no illusions about her; not any more. He had come to know her too well.

Gently and a little sadly she ran her fingers down his cheek. She had never wanted a child and it had come as a shock to learn that her tried and tested methods of avoiding pregnancy had finally failed her. Despite all her efforts she must have conceived, she calculated, almost the very first time they had lain together.

'Yes, that at least I can promise you,' she answered him. 'There has been no one else since that day when Hugo first brought you to me.'

'Except Roger.'

'Except Roger,' she conceded.

'If he casts you off, you must come to me. I will protect you and acknowledge my child.'

'He won't do that. He would do nothing that would expose him to ridicule. He will find other ways to punish me.'

'He's a brutal man, Emma,' Renaud said worriedly. 'I fear for you, and our child, in his hands.'

Emma shook her head. 'Whatever his suspicions, he will have no proof,' she said resolutely. 'Nor will my family let him harm me. Don't worry, I think Roger would rather be reasonable than lose face.'

Renaud put his arm around her protectively and let his hand rest on the place where his child was growing. The thought filled him with awe.

He held her hand tightly in his. 'You must never doubt that you are all I have ever wanted, and if you had only been free there would have been no need for any of this, I would have made you my wife.'

Emma smiled a little. After Roger's indifference, Renaud's adoration was like balm to her wounded pride. 'Well, I am not free,' she sighed, swinging her long, white legs out of the bed. She stood in front of him draped in wolfskin and pulled his head to her breast in a gesture unusually tender. 'I think you know,' she said, 'that this must be the last time we meet like this.'

Renaud looked up at her quickly, opening his mouth as though about to argue, but then he simply nodded agreement and they hugged briefly. She leant forward and kissed him once on the lips and again on the forehead.

Renaud rose to go, then hesitated, unable to believe that everything between them could end like this, so suddenly and so finally. 'You will send for me if you need me, won't you?' he insisted.

'Go,' she urged, 'it is late.' He picked up his cloak and walked to the door. 'Renaud,' she called. He turned. 'You may be sure that I will never tell him who the father is, but be careful all the same.'

Roger de Virar stared stonily at his wife as she told him the news. She stood boldly in front of him with her head held high and a totally false air of assurance.

'So, and may I know who is the father?' he asked, his voice controlled but full of contempt, his eyes as cold as grey marble.

'You are my husband,' she replied with an expression of surprised innocence.

Without another word Roger stood up and struck her so hard that she spun half across the room before she fell weeping to the floor. He walked over to where she lay, blood pouring from her nose and mouth, one eye already swelling. 'Who is the father?' he repeated, kicking her sharply in the ribs. She curled up in a ball, frantic to protect her unborn child. He laughed, a vicious, ugly sound. 'Can I at least assume that you do know who the father is?'

She glared up at him, sudden defiance sparking in her dark eyes. 'You are,' she whispered painfully through swollen lips.

He smiled at her sourly. 'I suppose it is possible,' he agreed, staring down at her thoughtfully. After a few minutes he bent and pulled her to her feet, bruising her arms with the force of his grip.

'What are you going to do?' she asked.

Without answering he dragged her out of the room and up to her own apartments. Alys, her maid, startled by her mistress's bloodied face, rushed to help her, but Roger pushed her roughly out of the way.

'Get out of here and stay away until you're sent for,' he ordered. 'Your mistress will not need you.'

The frightened maid needed no second bidding but fled to the kitchens.

Roger, meanwhile, had thrown his wife face down upon her bed and ripped the gown from her back, leaving her naked and defenceless. Her eyes opened wide with shock and disbelief as he pulled off his wide leather belt, wrapping the end of it around his hand, a grim smile playing about his lips. Terrified, she tried to hurl herself across the bed, but he grabbed her hair and held her, raising the belt high.

'No!' she shrieked as the belt descended, but the blows continued without mercy while she screamed and writhed and wept in agony and terror.

At last he seemed to tire and she could hear him panting heavily beside her. Trembling with pain and fear, she prayed for him to go, but Roger hadn't finished with her yet.

She screamed again as she felt him mount her, her bleeding, tortured back forced to take the almost unendurable pain of his weight and the abrasive drag of his tunic with each brutal thrust. Finally, he pulled her down onto her knees and raped her again, cruelly and unnaturally, completing her humiliation and leaving her crumpled and weeping on the floor until he chose, hours later, to send Alys to tend her.

Renaud had heard nothing from Emma for several weeks and she had not appeared in public since their last meeting. He was fairly sure that she must by now have told Roger of her pregnancy, but what had happened? Had she been sent away, into a convent perhaps? He was so engrossed in his worries that he didn't hear the duke speak to him.

'Renaud,' William said loudly and sharply, 'would you do me the honour of answering my question?' Renaud started and stared at him in confusion. The duke had spoken with impatience but with a glint of sympathetic humour in his dark, intelligent eyes.

He was a remarkable man, this Duke of Normandy, bastard offspring of a warrior prince and a tanner's daughter. He'd been only eight years old when his father, Duke Robert, had died on a pilgrimage to the Holy Land, so it was something of a miracle that he'd kept a hold on his dukedom. He had, of course, been fortunate in his protectors, but this would have availed him nothing had he proved weak and unfit to rule. However, William had grown strong and powerful, proving himself ruthless and relentless towards his foes.

'I beg your pardon, my lord,' Renaud replied, flushed. 'I didn't hear the question.'

'Perhaps I should apologize for disturbing your thoughts,' William remarked drily. 'Might I know what matter it is that you find so absorbing?' There were a few sycophantic titters from the

73

courtiers which William silenced with a look. 'Never mind,' he continued dismissively. 'I was asking whether, in your opinion, the feeling in England is favourable towards me as a successor to King Edward. You have lived among the people as well as at court; what is the popular view? In the light of Earl Harold's oath, will the Witan, the earls and their thegns support and uphold my claim when the time comes?'

Renaud hesitated. He knew the answer, but also knew that it could hardly be agreeable to the duke.

Earlier in the year, Earl Harold had been taken prisoner by Count Guy of Ponthieu after his ship had been driven onto the French coast by a storm. William, seizing his opportunity, had offered a generous ransom in return for custody of the Saxon.

Renaud had not been at court during this time, but later he had met Earl Harold at the Norman court in Caen. Harold had cut a handsome and prepossessing figure with his long Saxon-fair hair and luxuriant moustache, and Renaud was surprised to find him both approachable and easy-going, courteously professing to remember him and quite willing to talk about Renaud's friends in England. From him, Renaud had learned of the death of Cenred's father and Ceolwynn's betrothal.

It had been impossible for Renaud not to find himself admiring Harold all the more for his ability to behave with such quiet dignity under humiliating circumstances. At all times he had appeared even-tempered and seemingly relaxed, despite his ambiguous position: half guest, half political prize.

Renaud could never be certain in his own mind just which of these two very clever and subtle men, Harold or William, was actually telling the truth about the disputed oath-swearing that had occurred at Bonville-sur-Touques; an event upon which William now based his claim to the English throne.

Renaud would have liked to know the truth, but it made no difference to his ultimate loyalty, which lay always, of course, with Duke William, who was still, he realized, waiting for his answer.

'I would say that they might accept you, my lord, if Earl Harold stands by his oath to support your claim and the king makes no other designation: but in all honesty, I believe that a Norman claimant would have to be almost their very last choice for king. As for Harold standing by the oath, it is already

74

rumoured, as you must know, that he claims it was made under duress and he refuses to be bound by it.'

'Well, that is a frank if not a pleasing answer,' William commented, 'but it's always wise to know one's true position. You are not the only one to have told me this unpalatable truth; although others have, perhaps, put it a little less bluntly.'

With that, the indefatigable Duke of Normandy strode from the room followed by his courtiers and servants.

At the door he turned back. 'Arrange a time to speak with me privately,' he said. Then he was gone.

Renaud sighed. He was free at last to try to find Hugo and see if he had any news of Emma. Before he could leave, however, he was approached by a tall, thin clerk with an anxious frown and an armful of papers.

'You wanted an appointment?' the man said in a voice as thin and reedy as himself. 'Straight after Mass, tomorrow morning.' Renaud nodded his acquiescence. 'Don't be late. The duke will not be kept waiting.' He was gone in a swirl of black robes before Renaud had a chance to respond.

He found Hugo in the mews. The falconer standing beside him gave Renaud a polite nod and then, with a gloved hand, carefully replaced in its cage the small hawk he had been holding.

'Hugo, I have to talk to you.'

'What's the matter?' he asked.

'Have you seen Emma recently? Or heard from her?'

'Well, no, not for some weeks, but that's not unusual. Why?'

Renaud hesitated. He was fairly certain that Hugo knew of his relationship with Emma, but it had never been mentioned between them. Hugo obviously knew nothing about the baby and Renaud felt very uncomfortable about telling him. Drawing him away to a quiet part of the courtyard, he said, 'Emma is with child, Hugo.'

An expression almost of glee passed over Hugo's face, but it was quickly replaced by one of concern. 'You fear for her?' he asked.

'Like you, I have heard nothing from her. Roger must know by now.' He saw that Hugo was well aware of the implications. 'As her brother, you are the only one here who has any right to demand to see her. If he refuses you, you could send for your father. Roger dare not refuse him access to his own daughter.'

Hugo nodded. 'I will go to the house and see if it appears that the servants have had orders to keep people from her,' he said decisively. 'We may be fearing for her needlessly.'

'I hope that may be so. Will you go now?'

Hugo heard the urgency in his voice and agreed to go at once.

Now that he had placed the problem of Emma in Hugo's hands, Renaud was free to worry about why the duke should want to meet him alone. The following morning he presented himself with some trepidation outside the chamber where William usually began his day's business. Not everyone was as punctilious as the duke about attending early Mass and this was a relatively quiet time of the day for him; a time to discuss details with his clerks, or to talk privately without the usual crowds to speculate on his conversations.

Eventually, Renaud was ushered in.

'Ah, Renaud,' William began, smiling affably. Renaud relaxed a little. 'I knew your father quite well, you know,' the duke continued conversationally. 'A stubborn man, as I recall, but honest and loyal for all that – qualities which I am led to believe you share.' He paused as if waiting for some response.

'I am grateful for your good opinion of me,' Renaud said.

William continued to study him thoughtfully. 'You are soon to come of age, are you not?' he said, and Renaud began to suspect that this must surely be leading up to talk of his long-delayed inheritance.

'Yes, my lord, within the month,' he replied with some eagerness.

William, however, seemed in no hurry to tell him what was on his mind. He waved Renaud to a seat and sat opposite him drumming his fingers thoughtfully on the edge of the table. 'Your cousin, Guy de Lassay, has ruled in your stead since your father's death?' he said at last.

'Yes,' Renaud agreed sourly.

William leant forward and held Renaud's eyes with his own. 'Your cousin has proved himself to be a very useful man, Renaud. He has done much in these past years to keep my border safe from the French.'

'I will do as much for you, my lord, when I come into my own,' Renaud insisted.

'I have decided, Renaud, that Guy shall keep your father's lands in his own right. It is a fitting reward for the good service he has given me all these years.'

Shocked beyond words, Renaud felt faint. He clenched his fists in helpless rage and struggled to keep his temper.

'I know that you have relied upon an income from Lassay to maintain yourself,' the duke continued, ignoring Renaud's obvious distress, 'but I will see to it that you will not be left without the means appropriate to your rank.'

'But it's not fair,' Renaud burst out, unable to contain himself any longer. 'Guy has no right to what is mine.'

'Lassay would only be yours, Renaud,' William rebuked him sharply, 'if I chose to make it so, and for some very good reasons, I do not so choose.'

Aware that the duke would only be provoked by further displays of anger, Renaud took a deep breath and tried another approach. 'I just don't understand what I have done to deserve this, my lord,' he said unhappily. 'I've always believed that I have served you and my lord fitzOsbern well.'

'So you have,' William agreed. 'My decision,' he said, 'has nothing to do with you. It is not intended as a punishment.'

'It feels like a punishment,' Renaud returned bitterly.

William smiled a little. 'Lassay is a small, insignificant manor that you haven't seen since you were a child,' he said almost impatiently. 'There are greater prizes to be won in this world, believe me, and in my service you will be in a very good position to win them.'

'In your service, my lord?' Renaud asked cautiously.

William studied his young liegeman thoughtfully. 'Yes. I have a task for you,' he said. 'I want you to return to England,' he went on, much to Renaud's surprise. 'It is already known that you have been trained to oversee one of fitzOsbern's estates, so your return should arouse no suspicion. However, you will, in fact, be in my service.'

'What is it that I am to do?' asked Renaud, more than a little puzzled.

'You speak the Saxon tongue, do you not?'

'Yes, well enough,' he answered, then added, smiling at the memory of Ceolwynn's teasing, 'but my accent gives me away.'

'It is enough that you merely understand it. In fact, it would be better if it were not generally known that you speak it at all. I want you to go among these Saxons, listen to their words, then send to me all those snippets of news and gossip which are unheard by men too lofty to heed those beneath them.'

'You want me to be a spy?' Renaud asked with a small frown.

'Shall we say that I would like you to be my eyes and ears in England, so that I may know for certain who is my friend and who my enemy. There are of course many others in my pay about the Saxon court, but few of them have the advantage of speaking the language. You, I'm sure, will find it easier to discover the secret thoughts and intentions in men's hearts. What say you?'

Renaud hesitated, but knew it would be unwise to show the duke that he was reluctant to undertake any service asked of him. 'Very well,' he agreed, still a little doubtful. 'It shall be as you wish.'

William gave a grunt of satisfaction. 'It may not seem an especially noble position, I'll grant you,' he said, 'but you will not find me ungrateful, Renaud. Remember, one day *I will* be king in England.'

Emma had been confined to her apartments and had seen no one but Alys since the day of her fearful encounter with her husband. Her back was healing but she was listless and apathetic, still shocked and terrified by her experience.

Alys had a warm heart and had been horrified at the injuries Roger had inflicted on her mistress, bathing her wounds tenderly and murmuring incoherent words of comfort as though to a child.

Emma now sat passively as Alys, crooning softly to herself, combed out her long, black hair. Sometimes the comb caught in a tangle, but Emma hardly seemed to notice when once she would have slapped her maid for her carelessness. Her hands were folded protectively over the faintly visible curve of her belly, reassuring her that the baby still lived despite all that Roger had done. Alys was now aware of her mistress's pregnancy, and it hadn't taken her long to guess the cause of Roger's fury.

'How long does he expect to keep me prisoner here?' Emma said angrily, showing for the first time a spark of spirit.

Surprised, Alys stopped combing and leant forward so that her mouth was close to Emma's ear. Having seen what Roger was capable of, she wasn't going to take any chances. 'Your brother has been asking after you,' she whispered.

'When?' Emma asked frantically, turning and grasping Alys's hands in her own. 'Tell me. What did my husband say? Will Hugo come back?'

'I can only tell you what I have heard, mistress, and I beg you keep your voice down, do.' The fear in her manner made Emma cast a nervous glance towards the door. 'Your brother was here yesterday,' Alys continued, still in a whisper. 'I don't know what he was told and the master was not in the house, but the steward has orders to admit no one when he is from home.'

'Did Hugo say he would come back?' Emma asked again.

'I would think it likely,' Alys conjectured. 'Surely he would think it strange not to be allowed to see his own sister?'

Emma nodded thoughtfully. She wondered if Renaud confided in Hugo. 'Would my husband allow young Richard to come to me here, do you think?' she asked, considering the possibilities open to her.

'Richard has gone, my lady.'

'Gone!' Emma exclaimed, suddenly alarmed. 'Where has he gone?' Richard was the only other person who could name the father of the coming child. Had Roger guessed as much?

'I don't know.' Alys replied with a shrug. 'He was just gone, the day after ...' She didn't finish, but Emma knew exactly what she meant.

'Alys,' she said turning to look over her shoulder, 'would you be prepared to do something for me, something very brave?'

The steady brush strokes faltered and Alys's voice trembled as she asked: 'What do you want me to do?'

'Take a message to my brother.'

Terrified, Alys nearly dropped her brush. 'Oh, I dare not, mistress, truly I dare not. I beg you not to ask it of me.'

She was near to tears, and Emma was disturbed to see just how much fear the thought of her husband's displeasure could inspire.

'Then will you at least try to watch out for him when he comes again?' she urged. 'You might be able to get some word to him then without arousing suspicion.'

'I will try, mistress,' Alys replied hesitantly. 'I promise I will if I can. Forgive me, I'm too afraid to do more.'

Renaud knew that his fears were justified as soon as Hugo told him that he had been refused entry to Roger's home. 'What do we do now?' he asked.

'*We* do nothing,' Hugo answered. 'You must remember to show no interest whatever in the matter. I shall speak to Roger and demand to see Emma.'

This had proved more difficult than expected. Roger had smoothly put him off with one semi-plausible excuse after another, until Hugo had decided to go again to the house in Roger's absence, but the steward had again turned him away.

Just as he had been about to leave, however, a maid, rushing out with an armload of linen, had collided with him in the doorway. She had been knocked to the ground, blocking his way and obliging him to stretch out his hand to help her to her feet. The steward had watched the encounter with irritation as the girl had gabbled a torrent of apology and thanks, and Hugo had almost missed the hurried message contained in the flood of words.

'The only words I caught were that she's well, but needs my help,' Hugo explained to Renaud soon after. 'It was really difficult to make out any message at all.'

'Well, at least we know she's alive. I'd believe anything of that man. What happens now?'

'I'll send for my father, as you suggested. He'll be more of a match for Roger.'

Renaud heard the self-reproach in his voice and shared his feelings of helplessness. 'You did your best, Hugo. There's no need to feel ashamed that you could do no more,' he comforted him.

'None of this would have happened at all but for me.'

'What do you mean?'

'It doesn't matter,' Hugo answered after a moment's hesitation. He couldn't bring himself to confess that it was his scheming that had caused all this. 'If I send a man now, my father could be here tomorrow. He'll not waste any time if he believes that Emma is in any danger.'

Hugo was right; his father, Humfrey, rushed into Caen from his outlying estates as soon as he received word. Humfrey adored his twins, born unexpectedly late in life to a wife who had, up until then, presented him with a succession of sickly infants, all but two of whom had died at an early age.

Although ordinary in appearance, Humfrey was a man of great energy and determination and it was not long before he had confronted his son-in-law, demanding to see his daughter without delay. Seemingly unperturbed but inwardly furious, Roger invited him to visit, with Hugo, the very next day.

Roger de Virar now realized that it would be impossible to keep his wife shut away without some explanation. He considered the options. He could expose her shame and shut her away in some convent, or he could acknowledge her bastard as his own and keep Emma under his roof and control.

This last course had its attractions. Their last encounter had been surprisingly enjoyable, for him at least. Coming to a decision he climbed the stairs to Emma's room. As he entered, she jumped to her feet and stood facing him with all the courage she could muster. Her husband's presence seemed to fill her small robing room and Emma had to fight the urge to tremble as he stared unpleasantly at the slight but increasingly obvious swell under her robes. He waved a dismissive hand towards Alys, who fled only too willingly.

'I have decided,' he said without preamble, 'to forgive your past indiscretion and allow you to resume your position as my wife.' Emma felt an overwhelming sense of relief flood over her, and realized how certain she had been that he was fully capable of killing her. 'You may sit,' he said. 'As for the bastard you carry,' he continued, pausing to enjoy the sudden alarm in her eyes, 'since I have no child of my own body, at least in yours I may have an heir of my own upbringing. It is to be hoped that you bear a son.'

'There will, no doubt, be conditions?' she asked, watching him cautiously. She was convinced that he would not allow the matter to be closed here.

Roger laughed. 'I am glad to see that confinement has not dulled your wits. Yes, there are indeed certain conditions if some terrible accident is not to befall our poor child in the future.'

'Tell me then,' she said with resignation.

'First, I want to know the name of the child's father, and whether he is aware that this child is his. Secondly, I will require you to swear an oath that you will never again sully the name of my house with your shameless liaisons. Finally, you will swear never to divulge to any other person what has passed between us here today, or at any other time.'

Emma knew that Roger would never believe the child was his. 'I will comply with all but your first condition,' she replied with a courage she was far from feeling. 'I will never tell you who the man is, but you can rest assured that he knows nothing of the child.' The lie came easily to her lips.

Roger wondered briefly whether it was worth further 'persuasion', but decided against it, not now with her damned father making such a fuss. He would have liked to hear the truth from her, but there was no real need; the page had told him everything – eventually. 'Very well,' he conceded. 'Dress yourself suitably and join me for supper in the hall.'

'As you wish,' she said meekly. He walked over and held her chin roughly in his hand, forcing her head upwards.

'There will be no second chance for you,' he said.

'I understand,' she answered, frightened again by the menace in his voice.

'And you are grateful for my forgiveness?'

'I am grateful,' she agreed.

'Good,' he said, slowly releasing her at last and walking over to the door. 'Then I shall be pleased to give you many opportunities to show your gratitude.'

'You are my husband,' she said dutifully, struggling to keep the loathing from her voice. 'I shall do all that is expected of a wife.'

'Yes,' he said with a hateful smile, 'you will indeed.'

'It was very strange, Renaud,' Hugo told him the following day. 'Roger entertained us as if there had never been any difficulty, and Emma quite calmly told us she had not been receiving visitors as her condition had made her feel unwell, but that she was delighted to see us both now. My father was furious with me for dragging him here on a wild goose chase, causing him to make a fool of himself by demanding to see his daughter when there was no obstacle at all.'

'But *we know* that Emma was in trouble, Hugo. She was forced to speak and act as she did, fearing to do otherwise with Roger there.'

'No, you're wrong; that was what was so strange,' Hugo replied insistently. 'Roger did leave us alone; he almost made a point of doing so, and I'd swear there was no one else to overhear our conversation, yet still Emma said nothing.'

'Did you question her?'

'Of course; she just laughed and said I was foolish to worry about her.'

'Did Roger say anything about the baby?'

'Oh yes, he made a great show of paternal pride. He obviously intends to accept it and that would appear to be the end of the matter.'

'You are convinced then that he and Emma have come to some understanding?'

'So it would seem. I must go now.' Hugo squeezed his shoulder reassuringly, 'I'm sure we need not concern ourselves any further about it. Emma is a grown woman who makes her own decisions and takes her own risks. You will soon be in England, out of harm's way. This matter is closed and it will be better for everyone if it is never spoken of again. Are we agreed?'

Renaud nodded slowly. 'If that is what you believe is for the best,' he said reluctantly.

Hugo left him then, content that the events he had mischievously set in motion had at last come to a satisfactory conclusion. Renaud, however, was less certain.

VI

January 1066–October 1066

'Come dance with me, little brother, dance,' Ceolwynn shouted over the almost deafening racket of trumpet, horn and drum. Full of energy and just a little tipsy from the free-flowing mead, Ceolwynn grabbed the small boy's eager hands and swept him into the middle of a hall fragrant with the scent of spices and the earthy greenwood smell of holly boughs and ivy. Tonight was the very last night of those cold but carefree days between Christmas and Epiphany when no work was done that didn't have to be done and the hours were filled with gift giving, feasts and revelry. Gleemen played and mummers mimed, tumblers and jugglers entertained in every corner and young men, flushed with drink and eager to impress their sweethearts, tested their strength with noisy bouts of wrestling.

Father Eadric, flushed and puffing, joined in the celebrations with wholehearted enthusiasm while Betta, his wife, sat near the fire with her newest babe in her ample lap and a generous jug of ale at her side. Heaving with merriment, she shared a joke with Aldhere, the legless carpenter, who rocked merrily back and forth on his little wheeled cart and blessed the day he had come to Cottesham, where Godmund's generosity had created a secure and valued place for him. The village, too, had benefited from Aldhere's presence for he had a keen and unerring ear for news and gossip.

Aldhere had, in fact, heard some quite interesting rumours very recently, but since it wasn't wise to talk too loudly about an ailing king and a dubious succession, he held his tongue and just enjoyed the festivities. 'The good Father will have to set himself a penance for his excesses,' he said jovially, giving his companion a broad wink.

Betta chuckled heartily. 'He'll have to fast for a week,' she cried gaily.

Dunn, coming up to them at that moment, was compelled to smile by the sheer force of their laughter, even though he had no idea of its cause. 'May Wulfrun sit with you, Betta?' he asked. 'She's near her time and much afraid. I thought you might comfort and reassure her.'

'Of course, my dear. Sit down here by me, love,' she urged. The girl sat down obediently, glancing timidly at her husband for his approval.

Avoiding her eyes, Dunn gazed around the hall in a restless, searching way until Aelfrun, standing near the door with her feet tapping busily in time to the music, caught his glance and smiled. Discomfited, he smiled back and hastily returned his attention to the little group beside him.

'There's nothing for you to fear, lovey,' Betta was saying, squeezing his wife's knee, and Dunn left them to make his way to Aelfrun.

'There you are!' she chided gently. 'We hardly see you in the hall any more. You must be very happy now that you are to have a child.'

'I'm content enough, my lady,' Dunn said.

He lapsed into silence, standing uneasily by her side as if afraid that to move away might seem ill mannered. Aelfrun sighed inwardly in frustration and found herself having to suppress the urge to kick him. It was almost impossible to find in this aloof, cold man the dear friend she had once known, and greatly missed.

Dunn stared at the floor, hating the way he must sound to her now. The banter, the easy companionship that had seemed so natural during the years when Aelfrun had been alone and friendless, could now all too easily lead him to expose his deeper feelings, bringing nothing but shame and disgrace. To keep his distance from her was painful to him; to be close to her like this was agony.

Aelfrun, irritated by his silence, was about to move away herself when Godmund arrived with Siggi slung playfully under one arm and Ceolwynn, quite breathless, on the other. They surrounded her, all talking at once – even Godmund, made young again by the joy he had found in his family.

Ceolwynn was enjoying herself, firmly dismissing from her

mind the thought that this would be the last Christmas season she would spend in her father's hall. This time next year she would be Cenred's wife. 'Come dance with me,' she cried, seizing Dunn's hand and dragging him away.

Aelfrun stared after them both with a baffled frown creasing her brow. 'I wish I knew what was the matter with that man,' she grumbled.

'I don't think marriage agrees with him,' Godmund remarked, 'but I can't fault his stewardship. No man could work harder or serve my interests better.'

Aelfrun was pensive. 'It's since his marriage that he's changed most. Wulfrun was a poor choice for a man like Dunn.'

'That is a harsh judgement, and one unworthy of you,' Godmund reproached her teasingly. 'Wulfrun is not strong, it's true, but there is no harm in her.'

'You are quite right,' Aelfrun agreed with a sigh, 'it was unchristian of me to be so lacking in charity.' Then, with a mischievous grin, she added: 'But I still think I could have found better for him had he asked me.'

Godmund opened his mouth as if to speak, but whatever he had been about to say was lost for ever as, with a loud crash, the door was flung open.

All eyes were drawn towards the stranger standing in the doorway, the reins of his horse still in his hands. A groom hurried forward to relieve the man of his horse, glancing back regretfully as the door was closed behind him. Godmund, recognizing the newcomer as one of Leofwine's men, strode forward to welcome him.

'Leofwine, Earl of Kent and Essex, sends you greetings,' the messenger declared entering the hall. 'Let it be known that on the fifth day of January, in this year of our Lord, 1066, our beloved King Edward departed this life, in peace and in the presence of his queen and council. God rest his soul.'

The gasp from the assembled company that greeted this pronouncement was quickly silenced by Godmund's raised hand. He could see that the messenger had more to say, and so it proved.

'King Edward, in his dying hour,' the young man continued, 'named Harold, Earl of Wessex, as his successor and heir to his throne. This being undisputed by the Witan, on this very day, the

Feast of the Epiphany, Earl Harold was crowned King of England.'

William of Normandy, hearing of Harold's accession while hunting in the forest of Quévilly, immediately abandoned the hunt and stormed back to Rouen with a face quite black with rage. Harold's insult, as he saw it, left him no choice now but to fight for England's crown.

Renaud, trailing at the rear of the hunt, heard the news third hand from Hugo, who had heard it from a page who had been at the duke's side when the messenger arrived. 'Is it true, do you think?' he asked.

'The man who brought the news was himself at West Minster when the king died,' Hugo said.

'So,' Renaud murmured, drawing the word out slowly as he dwelt on the implications. 'Then my services will not be needed after all,' he said, a huge wave of relief flooding over him. He'd never wanted to be one of William's spies and being chosen had done little to soothe the resentment he still felt at William's refusal to grant him his birthright.

Hugo was staring at him in astonishment. 'Not needed!' he exclaimed. 'Good God, man, this is the greatest opportunity you've ever had. I'll wager the duke is even now planning to raise an army to invade England. Don't you see, victory would mean a whole country as the spoils of war? The duke's loyal followers will be rewarded with land, Renaud, land! Our work has only just begun.' With a loud shout of excitement he spurred away.

'It was my brother Tostig, you know, who killed him, in the end,' Leofwine confided, scratching his ear and looking bored. He hated being here in London almost as much as Godmund hated being kept away from Cottesham, but neither of them had much choice. Harold wanted his brothers, Gyrth and Leofwine, at his side during these troubled and uncertain times; Leofwine, in turn, had demanded the companionship of Godmund, his friend.

A mood of tension had prevailed since Harold's crowning: everyone waited to see what William of Normandy would do. Now, as the summer dragged on, William still made no move. The Saxon militia, known as the Fyrd and made up of contingents from every village in the country, had been on standby since early spring; but there had been no invasion and at the beginning of September the men had finally been sent home.

'How so?' Godmund asked.

'King Edward was very fond of Tostig,' Leofwine answered. 'It broke his heart to take Northumbria from him and send him into exile, but it was Harold who encouraged him to do it. Do you think he should have done that?'

'Tostig left him no choice,' Godmund answered frankly. 'I liked your brother Tostig. I always believed him to be an honest and honourable man, but you know as well as I do that his rule in Northumbria was far too harsh. If he had been prepared to listen to the complaints of his thegns, to understand that the ways of the north are not necessarily worse than our ways, they would never have turned against him and forced King Edward's hand.'

'Edward would have done nothing without Harold's advice,' Leofwine argued. 'But is it right for brother to turn against brother?'

'It's not for me to comment, is it? However, I will venture to say that I believe that Harold has always acted in the best interests of the country, and that he regarded Tostig as a worthwhile sacrifice to peace. A massive armed rebellion in Northumbria would have done immense harm and King Edward acted, quite rightly, to prevent that. Does that content you?'

'I hate all this feuding, Godmund,' Leofwine said with unexpected passion. 'The house of Godwine will destroy itself, I know it. While we wait to see what William will do, Tostig nips at our heels with his constant raids on the southern coast. Sooner or later he will have to be destroyed, that much is certain, but to Harold that is simply a military necessity. How can he forget so easily that Tostig is his own flesh and blood?'

'He doesn't forget,' Godmund assured him slowly, 'but now he is king, he stands apart. We have always to remember that Harold *is* England and the house of Godwine no longer has first call on his loyalty.'

Leofwine knew all this but still found it hard to accept. For several minutes he did not speak.

But then he walked to the window. 'Why doesn't he come?' he cried out impatiently, staring towards the south.

The day was hot and sultry, the air in the London streets stinking and oppressive, increasing Leofwine's mood of tension and frustration. 'Let us ride out with a hawk on the wrist and try to forget William and Tostig and all other plagues on our peace of mind,' Godmund suggested. 'What say you?'

'An excellent idea,' Leofwine replied, perking up at once. It was then that a sudden noise from the streets caught their attention and Leofwine peered curiously out of the window, beckoning Godmund to join him. 'Something's afoot,' he breathed. They exchanged a glance of growing excitement and unconsciously their hands moved towards the swords hanging at their belts.

Outside, crowds were forming, breaking up and reforming as news and speculation passed rapidly from mouth to mouth. It was impossible to hear what was being said and the two men hurried down the narrow staircase, to find a messenger from the king already at the door.

'What news, man?' Leofwine asked eagerly, grabbing him by the shoulder.

The man, breathless from fighting his way through the crowds, gasped, 'King Harald of Norway has landed a great army in the north. Lord Tostig is with him, proclaiming himself Earl of Northumbria once more.'

'Tostig again!' Leofwine cried bitterly.

Godmund sighed and addressed himself to the messenger. 'Is that all your message?' he asked.

The messenger shook his head and quickly told them that the king was already on his way northwards, intending to gather an army to him as he rode. Leofwine and Gyrth, his loyal brothers, were to send their own housecarls to join him, but they themselves were to stay in the south and keep watch for any signs of activity on the part of William of Normandy.

Leofwine nodded grimly, then, dismissing the messenger with a handful of coins, he gave orders for his men to leave at once. That done, he stood in brooding silence for several moments. Godmund gave him a questioning look.

'We're going hawking, I believe,' Leofwine responded calmly, and walked out of the door.

Duke William had found it no easy matter to win the support he needed for an invasion of England. He had too few ships and, as his council took pains to remind him, his vassals were under no obligation to supply him with the military assistance needed for an overseas expedition, and showed little inclination to do so.

It had taken patience, persuasion and promises of rich rewards of English land to convince these same vassals to double their prescribed quotas of men and arms, yet still this had not been enough. Further help from outside Normandy, however, would not have been forthcoming without a more righteous cause than the mere avenging of an insult. So William had sent emissaries to Pope Alexander II who, persuaded more by the political situation than by the justice of the cause, had eventually given full Papal approval and sent William a consecrated banner to draw men to his side. The proposed expedition had now become a crusade and pledges of support for William had at last flooded in.

William set about the formidable task of building his fleet, and while the Saxon Fyrd waited in vain throughout the summer of 1066, William's shipwrights and craftsmen were hard at work, grumbling at the speed forced upon them and shaking their heads over ships hastily thrown together from such rough and unseasoned timbers.

Not so the ship that had been a gift from William's wife, Matilda. Long and slender, high of prow and stern, the *Mora* was truly the longship of William's Viking ancestors, but her brightly coloured sails and gilded decorations declared also that this was a ship worthy of a king. On the sternpost she carried a wooden effigy of William's father, Duke Robert, which Matilda knew would please her lord, and, in the prow, the brazen figure of a child holding a bow.

By August, over 500 ships were assembled at the mouth of the Dives. But now it seemed that God frowned on their enterprise. For a whole month, foul weather and unfavourable winds made the crossing impossible.

William, with unusual patience and calm, struggled to maintain morale and keep his men fit for action as conditions worsened and tempers grew short. Old rivalries flared, quarrels broke out and the desertions began.

Deciding that any action was better than none at all, on 12 September, four days after the English Fyrd had been stood down, William moved the fleet to St Valery, from which point the crossing would be shorter and there would, he hoped, be less likelihood of being sighted by the enemy before the dawn landing on the English coast. This move cost William several

a mistake about you. I'm going to look closely at this idea of yours; I think it has merit.'

As it turned out, three such timber castles had eventually been prepared, though William had made no further comment on Renaud's part in the matter. Now, thanks to the duke's kind words, Renaud was confident that as long as he survived the forthcoming battle, and William triumphed, his future in England was assured.

That night, restless with excitement, he paced the decks waiting for the trumpet call from the *Mora* which was to be the signal for the fleet to sail. At last, just after midnight, it came, but they had been at sea for less than an hour before he found himself clinging to the ship's rail, trying desperately hard not to be sick. He couldn't remember the voyage being as bad as this when he had first sailed to England nearly eight years before, but then, he thought miserably, he hadn't sailed on a clumsy, overloaded transport ship with the smell of vomit and horse piss all around him. The sound of a man retching close by made his own stomach heave in sympathy. He moved away, wondering to himself just who in all William's proud army would be fit to fight a battle on the morrow.

The night was dark under a new moon, the air filled with curious, almost disembodied sounds which made the close-bounded world of the ship seem wonderful and strange. As he regained control of his stomach, Renaud stared out into the darkness, listening to the hiss and splash of the sea and the muffled snores of men sleeping cloak-wrapped on deck. Flapping sails and creaking timbers struck an eerie counterpoint to the whinny of a nervous horse and the rattle of harness. Far ahead, a mere gleam on the horizon, he could see a light shining ghostlike at the masthead of the *Mora*, guiding them all to their destiny – be it fortune or death. It rose and fell with each swelling movement of the sea, like a fallen star caught on the crest of a wave.

Slowly but inexorably the world Ceolwynn knew was becoming a little less sure, a little less safe.

When had she realized that things were never going to be quite the same again? Had it been when her father had ridden away that first time with a strange, grim look on his face and no word of when he might return? Had it been when the Fyrd had been called out, making the threat of invasion seem suddenly very real? Or had it been in April when the tailed star had flamed through the night sky and prophecies of doom and ill omen had been on every tongue?

She sighed. The year had been full of tragedy and portents. In early February Betta had collapsed and died as she hastened to Dunn's cottage where Wulfrun, already several hours into her labour, had drifted into unconsciousness. Father Eadric had rushed from his wife's body only just in time to administer the last rites to the dying girl and to the poor, malformed babe that God in his mercy had not allowed to live.

Godmund had come home briefly in the spring, bringing a gift in time for Siggi's third birthday. His talk had been all of war, and Aelfrun had listened quietly to his news: of Tostig's attacks on the coasts and the Isle of Wight; of the watchfires and beacons that had been set up to give warning of William's approach; of the difficulties of keeping so many men under arms; of feeding them, training them and keeping them fit and ready for action.

As the time for him to leave had drawn near, Ceolwynn saw that her father would be grateful for a little time alone with his wife, and so she had made her farewells and taken her brother away to their secret place where, for an hour, they had crouched in the mysterious lamplight while she had told him stories and listened to his happy prattle.

They'd seen little of Godmund since and missed him greatly, but it was late September now and, as winter closed in, the likelihood of war receded. Soon the weather would make a Norman invasion impossible and, in the north, King Harold had once again proved himself a worthy warrior king.

'Do you think Father will be home soon,' Ceolwynn asked hopefully, 'now that the king has won such a great victory?'

'I pray so, daily,' Aelfrun answered softly, glancing up from her sewing. 'At least we know he was not at Stamford Bridge, so we need not fear for him on that account.'

The Saxons had suffered a crushing defeat at Fulford a week ago, so the news of King Harold's victory at Stamford Bridge had come as a great relief. Both Tostig and Harald of Norway had been killed, removing the threat from the north.

'Do you think Wulfhere might have been there?' Ceolwynn

asked, then regretted the question. Aelfrun would be sure to start worrying if she thought her sister might be widowed with no one close to comfort her.

Aelfrun's reply, however, was calm and realistic. 'I think it more than likely,' she said, 'perhaps at Fulford also. Each day that passes without word from Estrith leads me to hope that all is well.'

Ceolwynn nodded agreement and raised her work to her lips to bite the thread with her teeth, but, seeing Aelfrun's frown of disapproval, hastily put it down again and reached for the scissors in her workbox.

They were busy sewing for Siggi the first set of clothes that marked the end of babyhood, and the task gave them both great pleasure. Tiny shirts and tunics, doll-like leggings and caps appeared under their flashing needles. In the warm hall with its comforting fire and familiar faces, it was possible to forget for a while the worries of these past months.

It was a cold, dull morning with no real sight of the sun. Aelfrun, still sleepy, gave a yawn and put aside her sewing. At her feet lay the pair of handsome young greyhounds that had been her gift to Godmund after his old wolfhound died. For warmth she tucked her toes cosily under the haunches of one of them and the dog raised its head to lay it heavily across her knee, gazing up at her with placid brown eyes. Absently, she began to stroke the smooth, sleek head. 'He will surely be here for your birthday, and there is still the wedding to be arranged,' she said suddenly.

It took Ceolwynn a moment to realize that Aelfrun's thoughts had drifted back to Godmund. Mention of the wedding was an unpleasant reminder that, war or no war, her own life was about to take a new and alarming turn. She had grown up with the fact of her betrothal to Cenred, but all at once the talk was all of marriage and it seemed that now there was to be no escape from it. A feeling close to panic washed over her. 'Perhaps the wedding should be postponed,' she suggested tentatively. 'With all the uncertainty over what William of Normandy plans to do, I expect Cenred, and my father, would prefer to delay matters a little.'

'Nonsense,' Aelfrun laughed, 'William of Normandy is not about to spoil *my* daughter's wedding. Nothing will do that.'

But Fate plays cruel tricks and should not be tempted. Nothing, like never, is a word to be used with caution, for even as she spoke, William of Normandy's fleet was already casting anchor in Pevensey haven.

Duke William scanned the coastline, searching in vain for some sign of the Saxon defenders he was sure had to be here somewhere.

He knew, of course, that the Fyrd had been stood down – his spies had told him that even before he sailed – but even so, he thought, surely someone must have sighted the fleet by now and given warning. Some local resistance, at least, was to be expected: but, as his scouts reported, there was nothing. So where were the Saxons? Where was Harold?

Line abreast, the mighty fleet anchored along the shore and as the disembarkation began, William waited aboard the *Mora*, well aware that his forces were now at their most vulnerable and that an attack before all the horses and armour had been unloaded would be disastrous.

Nothing happened; there was no surprise attack, no sudden ambush, and the landing continued without mishap until at last the duke prepared to step down from his ship to lay claim to his inheritance. It was a long-awaited moment and one that William had hoped would be both dignified and memorable, but in his eagerness he stumbled and fell, throwing out his hands before his face to save himself.

There was a muffled gasp from those around him and, as he straightened with his fists full of sand and shingle, he could sense the dismay in his followers and, for just one moment, he wondered fearfully whether this might not be some dreadful omen.

Suddenly, from the crowd, a voice rang out loud and clear:

'Comrade, you hold England, O future King.'

There was a roar of appreciative laughter and William nodded gratefully to the quick-thinking soldier who had cried out in such a timely manner. 'Quite so,' he agreed, 'but now we must set about the business of securing more than a handful, I think.' There was more laughter which soon dispelled any last remaining fears. 'Have we any news yet as to Earl Harold's whereabouts?' William asked.

One of the scouts stepped forward. 'We have a prisoner, my lord,' he offered.

'Then bring him here at once,' William cried out in exasperation. 'I must know where Harold is.'

Hurriedly the captive peasant was brought before the duke and, as a torrent of questions was hurled at him, stood trembling in dumb silence for several minutes before anyone realized that they had forgotten to bring an interpreter.

Just at that moment, fitzOsbern spotted Renaud walking his unsteady horse up and down the beach and sent one of his men to fetch him.

'Ask this man where is Harold,' the duke ordered, brusque and impatient, as Renaud came up to them. 'Get as much from him as you can, by whatever means.'

Renaud turned to the Saxon and began his interrogation, hesitantly at first but with increasing confidence as his tongue remembered the words. Their prisoner, however, could tell them little beyond the fact that the Fyrd had been recalled and that Harold had gone north to fight back an invasion by his brother Tostig and the Norwegian king.

'North?' William wondered softly. 'Truly, God is with us. I wonder, my lords, who it is that soon we will have to fight for this land, the King of Norway or the Earl of Wessex.'

'How best can we use this advantage?' asked fitzOsbern.

William stared silently out across the English countryside. 'We must find a better defensive position, away from these coastal marshes,' he said at last. 'Renaud, you will stay to see to the building of one of your castles here at Pevensey, but we must send out reconnaissance parties to find a better site for our camp and test the strength of any local resistance. Are we in agreement?' There was a general murmur of acquiescence.

Renaud, livid at once again being left out of any real action, threw a despairing glance at fitzOsbern, who shrugged and shook his head.

By the following day the army had been moved to Hastings, and Renaud, who was now responsible for the erection of the remaining two timber strongholds at this new camp on the heights overlooking the town, fretted at such mundane duties.

'Never mind,' Hugo consoled him cheerfully, 'you're better off than I am.'

The two friends were sharing a fire with a small group of Breton mercenaries who were more than half way through a cask of looted ale and had by now forgotten how much they disliked it. Renaud raised his voice to be heard above the noise of their tuneless singing. 'How so?' he asked, unconvinced.

'I have to ride with Roger de Virar,' Hugo complained, helping himself to a generous hunk of the pork roasting over the flames. 'I know as well as any man that an army has to forage to survive,' he went on, 'and of course it is always the peasants that suffer, poor devils; but by God that de Virar really enjoys it all, the looting and burning, rape and murder. It sickens me to see that hideous smile on his face when all around him helpless women and children suffer and die.' An involuntary shudder emphasized his words.

'I wish Harold's forces would get here,' Renaud muttered irritably. 'We came to fight, not to terrorize peasants.' News of Harold's victory at Stamford Bridge had just reached them.

'I've heard Harold's army is resting in York,' Hugo remarked. 'He may not even have heard of our landing yet.'

Renaud gave a low whistle of surprise. 'So we have plenty of time to prepare for him,' he commented. 'Will we be moving on to take Winchester, or London?'

'Not necessarily. Our duke has a different strategy in mind; his old favourite "wait and see".'

'But surely we should advance at once?'

'No, the aim now is to wreak as much havoc as possible in these, Harold's own lands, drawing him to the defence of his people before he has time to regain his strength and assemble any greater force. If the plan works, he could be here at any time – I hear it took him only four days to get his army from London to York.'

'Harold is certainly a force to be reckoned with,' Renaud commented, throwing what was left of his dinner into the fire. He sighed heavily. 'It would seem, then, that de Virar will not lack sport over these next few days.'

'My God! I hope Harold comes soon,' Hugo said. 'A good fight, man to man, is one thing, but I don't think I have the stomach for such work as this. Perhaps you're the fortunate one after all.'

Renaud nodded thoughtfully and wiped his greasy fingers on the tunic of one of the now snoring Bretons. Hugo, laughing softly, followed suit.

'Talking of de Virar,' Renaud said casually, 'has he made any mention of his son, by any chance?'

'To me?' Hugo answered, as if surprised.

'Why not? You are the child's uncle.'

'I thought we had decided that the whole matter was closed and not to be discussed between us,' Hugo hissed, casting a nervous glance over his shoulder.

'I merely ask, as a friend, whether your sister and nephew are in good health; that is all.'

'They are both well,' Hugo muttered grudgingly. 'They have named the boy Geoffrey and, as far as I can tell, Roger is quite as besotted with him as any other father is with his first-born.'

'Geoffrey,' Renaud murmured under his breath. 'Thank you, Hugo,' he said. 'I have longed to ask.'

'Take my advice,' Hugo replied, getting to his feet, 'if you value your life, don't ever ask again. Who knows,' he said with a warning glance directed at the sleeping mercenaries, 'where a man like de Virar has his ears.'

Aelfrun's father, Wilfred, was undoubtedly possessed of more than his fair share of weaknesses and vices, but cowardice was not one of them. Faced with a Norman army virtually at his door, he made the bravest yet the most foolish decision of his life: he resolved to stand and fight.

'This is madness, my lord,' Folca protested, so appalled at Wilfred's intent that he quite forgot to maintain his usual veneer of servile humility. 'These Normans are bent on destroying all in their path – no one is safe who stands against them. To attempt to fight such fiends would be sheer folly.'

'By God! I *will* fight,' Wilfred exclaimed, too excited even to notice the contempt in his steward's voice. 'See to it that the women and children are safe in the hall with the doors securely barred from the inside; then see that every able-bodied man we have is properly armed.' Proudly, the old thegn lifted and waved aloft his massive, double-edged sword.

'I beg you, my lord, reconsider,' Folca persisted, stepping back a pace, out of harm's way. 'Order everyone into the forest until all danger is past.'

'Never!' Wilfred cried. 'No man will take from me what is rightfully mine.'

At another time this declaration might have amused the larcenous steward, but in the present circumstances Folca was in no mood for humour.

Wilfred gave the sword a last swing and started to rub the rust of disuse from the blade, dismissing his man with an impatient wave of the hand. Folca had no choice but to accept that his master was beyond all reason. So, with his head full of plans to save his own skin, he left to carry out his orders, herding all the women and children of the village into the hall and leaving it to Wilfred's wife to take charge and set them to barricading the doors. Next, he saw that every man and boy over ten years of age was armed with whatever weapons were available: axes and shields for the lucky ones, sharp farm tools and heavy, wooden clubs for the rest.

When all was ready and there was nothing left to do but wait, Folca slipped away to his cottage and, hastily dousing the fire, dug up his stolen treasure from its hiding place beneath the hearth stones.

He waited until he could hear the tramp of marching feet and the rattle of harness before making his escape through a gap in the badly maintained palisade, scrambling out of the ditch on the other side. Head down, he ran through the fields and into the woods, panting under the weight of the bag he carried.

In the distance he could hear Wilfred shouting orders and calling his name, and even before he was fully out of earshot he could hear the clash of arms and the cries of pain that followed. He felt no sense of guilt or shame. For a moment he rested, leaning against a tree to catch his breath.

He would have to plan his next move carefully, but he wasn't too concerned about discovery. Wilfred had refused to listen to the rumours of the Norman atrocities, but Folca *had* listened and was sure they were true. He was also quite certain that there would soon be no one left alive to denounce his perfidy or question his new-found wealth.

He was just about to make a final decision as to his direction when he was overcome by an unexpected and irresistible compulsion to make for Cottesham. He saw himself suddenly as the bearer of tragic news to the lady Aelfrun, and the thought of her shocked, grief-stricken face brought a vicious grin to his mean features.

With a mirthless chuckle he set about tearing his clothes and soiling them liberally with handfuls of mud. As a finishing touch he drew his knife and, with no hesitation at all, dealt himself several superficial cuts and scratches, smearing the blood generously over his face and clothes.

So engrossed was he in his work that he failed to hear the rustle of dead leaves and the sound of small twigs cracking beneath an unshod foot. Had he looked up at that moment he might have glimpsed a small, dark figure darting for cover, might have seen a pair of sloe-black eyes widen in surprise at the chink of silver as he picked up his heavy bag.

As Folca disappeared once more into the trees, Nest, the Welsh slave girl who served Wilfred's wife, watched him go. It wasn't difficult for her to work out just what the steward was up to, but, much as she loathed the man, she didn't blame him for his defection. Like him, she saw no cause to die for Wilfred's folly. She felt no love, no loyalty, for Wilfred's house.

Nest had been only eight years old when Saxon soldiers had raided her own village. She had seen her father and infant brothers slaughtered and had watched terrified as her mother had been dragged away, screaming for her children. There was no telling what had become of her. Nest had been quite fortunate, she had been sold as a slave.

Wilfred's wife had been a harsh mistress, heavy-handed and impatient with a frightened child who for many months had been unable to understand the commands given to her. Her daughters had been less cruel, and Nest still remembered Aelfrun's kindness to her in those early days, but it had been Wilfred himself who had made her life most miserable.

Wilfred had been attracted by the child's exotic beauty and had liked to touch her in ways that she had found both alarming and confusing, but which she had been helpless to prevent. She had tried to avoid being alone with him as much as possible, but one cold winter's evening, just before her twelfth birthday, Wilfred had raped her for the first time, ignoring her struggles and frightened tears.

In the years since then, Nest had twice had to procure the means of ridding herself of the results of Wilfred's unwanted attentions. This time, however, all her potions and charms had failed her and when at last her belly had swollen beyond all concealment, her mistress had discovered the truth.

Her rage had been terrible to see, but for once she had stayed her hand. Nest was, however, to be sold into a brothel; a fitting place for such a slut, her mistress had insisted venomously. Wilfred, quailing before his wife's fury, had agreed without argument and had not the invasion driven the matter from everyone's mind, Nest would have been sold days since. As it was, in the resulting confusion Nest, like Folca, had seized the opportunity to make good her escape.

Now, as she stared after the absconding steward, she wondered whether she would be able to kill him and steal his silver. She had both a knife and the advantage of surprise, it was true; but, on the other hand, her pregnancy made her slow and clumsy. If she should miss her first strike, she realized, he would be sure to overpower and disarm her. A shudder of fear and disgust passed through her at the thought of being helpless in Folca's hands. Regretfully, Nest abandoned any idea of following the steward and, hitching up her skirts, hurried away in the opposite direction.

To a man, Wilfred's household fought bravely for their lives and their homes, all resentment of their master forgotten in the common peril. There was never, of course, any hope at all of an effective resistance against William's mounted, armoured knights. Wilfred maintained only two trained men-at-arms, and his sons had never yet been tried in battle. Within the space of an hour, not one of the defenders was left alive. Before he could strike a blow, Wilfred himself had been ridden down, crushed beneath the hooves of a dozen horses. His eldest son had been felled by a sword-thrust only moments later, and the youngest, just fourteen, had died defending his mother and sisters, pinned by a spear to the door of his father's hall.

In the hall itself Wilfred's wife and daughters listened to the battle sounds with fright-whitened faces, their hands pressed over their ears to blot out the screams of dying men.

Surrounded by their servants, they stood pressed against the wall furthest from where the battle raged, and waited for the inevitable. Small children hid their faces in the folds of their mothers' skirts and their frightened sobs mingled with the murmur of prayer all around them.

As the sound of fighting died away, the barred and barricaded doors began to shudder beneath the blows of the victors. The shouts outside had changed their tone, becoming charged with coarse jests and ribald laughter. Even though the Norman tongue was unknown to them, no woman there could mistake what was intended once the soldiers broke through.

'Each of you knows what you must do,' Wilfred's wife said sternly to her daughters as she removed her knife from her girdle. Wilburg burst into tears and her mother glared at her fiercely until the girl regained control. 'If any one of you lacks the courage,' she went on, 'you may ask another to do it for you.' The sound of splintering wood made her hesitate briefly before she continued. 'We have no time left,' she said heavily, 'we must begin.'

Dry-eyed, she kissed each of the four girls in turn, starting with the youngest, whose freckled face wore an expression of blank incomprehension, and ending with Wilburg who had never expected her life to end at twenty, before she had even begun to live it.

Finally, she turned to her servants. 'Do not think that submission to these devils will save your lives,' she warned them bitterly. 'They will use your bodies, but know for certain that they will not spare any one of you. To submit to them will be to suffer twice over, I promise you. The only thing you can hope to save is your honour.' She turned to face her daughters, watching them briefly as with tearful hugs and kisses they bade each other farewell; then, without another word, she plunged the knife into her own heart.

When the Normans broke through they stood momentarily aghast at the blood-soaked scene before them. Nearly thirty women and half as many children lay dead on the red-stained rushes.

Deprived of their sport, the Normans searched furiously but in vain for even one woman left alive, kicking and stabbing at the bodies in savage, frustrated anger. With nothing else left to do, they looted the hall, then fired it, before moving on to the next village.

VII

October 1066

'Listen to your brothers, Harold,' Gytha insisted. Earl Godwine's widow found it hard to accept that her sons had long since grown beyond her control.

King Harold shook her hand away impatiently and she staggered, clutching at the edge of the table to stop her fall. In the moment of shocked silence that followed, Gyrth rushed to his mother's aid while Gytha, with the consummate skill of an experienced manipulator, clutched dramatically at her heart and glared reproachfully at her eldest surviving son.

Harold was tired, sore and, above all, infuriated by the number of hours wasted in argument when one swift, decisive action could well bring them victory. He was sure that surprise, his favourite tactic, used so successfully against Norwegian Harald, could also defeat the Bastard. The Witan, giving up the struggle to persuade him against any precipitate action, had finally departed the council chamber, leaving Harold's brothers to try what further persuasion they could.

Now, Harold scowled at his mother across the table. 'I will lead my own army to defend what is mine,' he shouted. 'I need have no fear of God's anger; I have broken no honestly given oath and there is no good reason for me not to face this spawn of the tanneries who would be king.'

'All know that the Pope has declared himself on William's side in this,' Gyrth argued, 'and that you, as a result, are excommunicate. This may weaken the resolve of some of your followers. Let one of us take command and then there can be no doubts in any man's mind.'

Harold slumped against a pillar. Unutterably weary, he tried to

104

close his ears to the barrage of argument so that he could concentrate on his new plan of campaign. He knew that his brothers meant well, but they failed to understand that a true king could not fight for his throne by proxy. This was his fight, and by God he would fight it; but what had he done, he asked himself bitterly, that God must challenge him again so soon? Wasn't the sacrifice of a brother, once dearly loved, enough to ask of a man? Just when would he be allowed at last to rest, and to grieve for Tostig, his foolish, misguided brother?

Only days after his victory at Stamford Bridge, the news of William's invasion had forced Harold to rush back south and recall the Fyrd, but while his army slowly reassembled and he kicked his heels in London, William was growing ever more firmly entrenched on the coast, looting and pillaging unopposed. With each passing day the sufferings of his people grew, and Harold knew he could wait no longer.

Gyrth was still talking, his voice low and urgent. 'Stay here in London and wait for reinforcements, Harold,' he pleaded earnestly. Reluctantly, Harold forced himself to concentrate on his brother's words. 'Let *us*,' Gyrth went on, waving a hand towards Leofwine, 'attack William; then, should we fail, you can still lay waste every inch of land between here and the sea. Even the Bastard's army cannot survive a winter without food and shelter.'

'Do you agree with Gyrth, Leofwine?' Harold asked wearily, without turning round. There was some sense in what they had to say and he was prepared to listen, but the thought of destroying his lands and thereby condemning his own people to death by cold and starvation, was repugnant to him.

'Yes, I do,' Leofwine answered forcefully. 'It would be folly for you to risk your life now. We can afford to lose an army, but we cannot survive the loss of our king.' He waited a moment to see if Harold would speak, but when the king said nothing, he continued in a softer, more persuasive tone. 'You need time to rest and strengthen your hand. We can give you that time. For the love of God, brother, be advised by us.'

'Listen to your brothers,' Gytha cried again and Harold, angered beyond all reason by her shrill voice and her constant refusal to accept his decisions, immediately forgot his resolve to consider his brothers' proposal.

By the Rood! he thought furiously, she might have ruled his

father, but she would never rule him. 'I will do what I know to be right,' he roared, slamming the table with his fist and sending the cups flying. 'I will not wait. The Bastard cannot be left to pillage and destroy my lands for one day longer, nor will I allow him to escape back to Normandy unpunished.' Shocked into silence his family stared at him. 'This very day I will send ships to block his retreat, then we'll move swiftly and attempt to take him all unawares. He'll expect us to wait for men from the north and west, but our own housecarls and our south-eastern fyrds should be sufficient either to surprise and defeat him, or, at the very least, to hold him until our reinforcements arrive.'

He didn't add what they all knew; that the housecarls – although a substantial army in themselves of at least 2,000 well-armed, professional fighting men – were only just recovering from the battle at Stamford Bridge. They were wounded, bruised and exhausted. William's troops, on the other hand, were fresh, well rested and well aware that their retreat had been cut off. Should the Normans fail, there would be no place to hide and no mercy for them in a hostile English countryside. Such knowledge, as all men knew, put courage in a man's heart and strength in his arm. But no matter!

Shaking off his weariness, Harold now set about calling for his scribes and couriers, rapidly issuing orders, detailing his plans and quickly infecting his brothers with his own enthusiasm.

Gytha, defeated, left with an angry swirl of skirts.

'Leofwine,' Harold instructed, 'I'll leave it to you to see that our south-eastern fyrds are met together at some suitable point on the Hastings road, no later than two days hence.'

'What place do you suggest?' Leofwine asked. He knew that further argument would be of no avail and would serve only to delay matters. Accepting that fact, he was now fully committed to following his brother's commands.

Harold thought for only a moment. 'At the hoar apple-tree where the road from Hastings forks at Caldbec Hill. The place is well known and cannot be mistaken.'

Leofwine nodded in agreement and then, with nothing more to be said, left to carry out his orders.

Outside in the courtyard, Godmund waited to hear the news. Leofwine's grim expression told all. 'He means to fight again, so soon?' he asked, but it was not really a question. 'I had hoped to visit my family first,' he added wistfully.

'We leave almost at once,' Leofwine replied, dashing all hope. 'We are the lucky ones, Godmund,' he consoled him. 'Think what it must be like for those poor devils who have spent these last weeks in the saddle or fighting. They're brave fellows, God knows, but this is asking much of them.'

'Their king asks as much of himself,' Godmund reminded him.

'Have you *seen* Harold lately?' Leofwine asked rhetorically. 'I tell you, the man is black and blue. For days he was so stiff and sore he needed help even to dress himself, and half his army is in no better case.'

They started to move away together towards the stables. It was the afternoon of 11 October, and each one of them had less than three days to live.

Godmund, travelling in the vanguard of the advancing English army, reached Maidstone late the following day. Already the town teemed with soldiery and Godmund's search for a night's shelter for himself and his band produced only a filthy, bug-infested inn that offered food every bit as unappealing as its accommodation.

There were several new men in Godmund's war band now, including Brand, just a spit boy in the Cottesham kitchens until Godmund's last visit home. The boy was barely ten years old, but he had mounted an amazingly persistent campaign to persuade his lord to let him join his company, and Godmund, half amused, half irritated, had finally given in. He found no cause to regret his decision: the boy worked tirelessly and with unfailing cheerfulness.

Their night in Maidstone was no more comfortable than they had expected, but at least it was no worse. They left at dawn, abandoning the main road just a few miles out of the town to travel the ancient trackways through Andredsweald, a tortuous, wearisome route which left both men and horses exhausted. They travelled slowly all through the day, their path frequently blocked by large bands of foot-soldiers also making their way through the forest, reaching the meeting place late in the evening of 13 October. The remainder of the army continued to pour into the camp throughout the night.

Godmund sought out Leofwine just before dawn. He'd spent most of the night trying to find food for his men, who had fasted all that day, but food was in short supply. They'd found enough to go round eventually, but, like almost everyone else in this turbulent camp, they were all now heavy-eyed from lack of sleep. The earl, too, looked weary, but he greeted his friend with obvious pleasure and offered him breakfast, which Godmund declined having eaten already with his men.

'How goes it, my lord?' he asked, casting an approving eye over the highly organized bustle of Leofwine's camp.

'Well enough,' Leofwine answered through mouthfuls of bread. 'Our scouts report that William seems to have feared a night attack and has had his army stood to arms all night, so at least they'll be no more wakeful than we are.' He waved a hand towards the space next to him on a fallen tree.

'Numbers?' Godmund queried, sitting himself down.

'Fairly even, I should say. William has perhaps 8,000 men in the field. He's still busy calling in his foraging parties so there's no doubt we caught him on the hop, Harold was right about that!

'We have the select men of the southern, eastern and western shires, and Harold brought south with him some of the men of the north who fought at Stamford Bridge, so they are here. Then, of course, there are the housecarls – mine, Gyrth's and Harold's. It's a formidable force, nearly every man of them trained in arms to some degree. Harold decided not to call out the Great Fyrd and he's probably right: frightened peasants armed with nothing but hoes and sickles would be more hindrance than help against William's mercenaries.'

'Can we expect any more support?'

Leofwine shook his head. He leaned forward to tighten his shoe fastenings, then looked up quickly as a young man, breathless with excitement, galloped up and wheeled his horse to a dramatic halt. 'They are on the move, my lord,' he cried. 'The king has sent me to tell you that it is time to take up our positions.'

Leofwine, leaping to his feet, grabbed his helmet and hauberk and then, having thrust them under one arm, placed his free hand on Godmund's shoulder. 'This is it,' he said, grinning humourlessly, 'we are in God's hands now.'

Godmund pulled himself up with a good deal less energy than his lord. 'I'm beginning to feel my years,' he remarked ruefully. 'Still stiff from yesterday's ride.'

Leofwine laughed, then became serious. 'We will meet them on the ridge at Santlache,' he said. 'It is the king's choice, and a good one, I do believe. William has many archers and a strong cavalry, but by forcing them to attack uphill and over such rough and marshy ground, my brother hopes to give our stout infantrymen the advantage. The steep slopes of Caldbec Hill behind us will prevent William from attacking from the rear, while at the same time blocking our own retreat.'

Godmund nodded thoughtfully, seeing the sense in this. 'It's a fight to the death then,' he said heavily, 'every man will see that there can be no retreat.'

'Exactly,' Leofwine agreed. 'Listen, Godmund,' he said unexpectedly, 'I want you to join my housecarls, old friend. I probably won't get the chance to speak with you again before this day is won or lost, but I would be content to know that you were fighting at my side, as you did in Wales, remember?'

'I would be proud to do so, my lord,' Godmund replied, deeply honoured by the invitation to join Leofwine's hand-picked, highly trained professional warriors, only the best of whom would be chosen to form their lord's shield wall. 'I must find my own men now and give them their orders,' he said, 'then I'll meet with you later on Caldbec Hill.'

The two men embraced clumsily before hurrying about their business.

From his vantage point at the top of Blackhorse Hill, William of Normandy surveyed for the first time the Saxon forces ranged against him, inwardly admitting to a grudging admiration for his adversary which he would never have confessed aloud. Harold had moved with remarkable swiftness and purpose; he had chosen a defensive position which almost negated William's own advantages; and he had managed to assemble at very short notice a considerable army of singularly well-accoutred soldiery.

It was impossible at this distance to distinguish between Saxon and Norwegian workmanship, but William suspected that much of the Saxon armour and weaponry must have been stripped from the dead at Stamford Bridge. Certainly, Harold was not the man to let such an opportunity go to waste.

'This won't be the easiest battle I've ever fought,' William fitzOsbern reflected morosely, staring out across the steep slopes facing them. Riven by countless small gullies and strangled by almost impenetrable undergrowth, the terrain over which they must attack presented a considerable obstacle in itself. There had thankfully been no rain: mud would have made it impossible to get across.

William remarked with some satisfaction, 'I knew that if I made his lands bleed, Harold would be sure to rush to their defence. If he'd waited for reinforcements ...' He shook his head slowly, leaving his doubts unspoken.

Up on the Santlache Ridge opposite, each division of Harold's army hurried to take up its position. Clearly, Harold could not have expected the Normans to have moved up so speedily from Hastings; it was still less than two hours since sunrise.

'It's still a larger army than I, for one, anticipated, in the circumstances,' fitzOsbern commented, observing Harold's deployments with interest.

The Saxons, with no cavalry and very few archers, were establishing a front line of perhaps 1,000 men, presenting an unbroken wall of shields against which the attackers must hurl themselves. Behind this, the rest of the Saxon army formed a solid phalanx some twelve ranks deep.

'There is the king,' cried out Robert de Mortain, 'I see him now.'

William scowled. 'You mean the Earl of Wessex,' he rebuked his half-brother sharply, but his eyes followed with curiosity Robert's pointing finger.

Harold had positioned himself at the very crest of the hill – his standards, the Dragon of Wessex and the Fighting Man, were plain to see. William guessed Harold's brothers would be close by their king, surrounded by housecarls and slightly behind the massed front ranks. He stared out across the narrow divide and silently made his plans while Robert and fitzOsbern waited patiently. At last he seemed satisfied and the three men rode swiftly back to the waiting army.

Renaud, busy preparing his gear and listening with half an ear to the complaints of Hubert, fitzOsbern's disgruntled squire, watched excitedly for the return of the duke. The squire grumbled on, oblivious that Renaud's attention was fully engaged elsewhere. He was a Gascon and could talk for half an hour without drawing breath – or so it seemed to Renaud.

'Look!' Renaud interrupted eagerly, cutting across the seemingly endless tale of woe the Gascon was recounting. 'Lord fitzOsbern comes this way, he must have his orders. It cannot be long now.'

Hubert stalked away to fetch his lord's armour, muttering angrily about the arrogance and ill-manners of all Normans; but Renaud hardly noticed his departure. After all the long months of waiting, all the frustrations of inactivity, he was at last about to have the opportunity to grasp his future with his own hands. Trained for war since childhood he had yet to fight in earnest, and the thought of battle excited him beyond measure.

The squire returned just as fitzOsbern arrived, his horse barely skidding to a halt before its rider threw himself from the saddle. 'Help me into my hauberk, Hubert,' he shouted, his face alight with the lust for battle. 'It begins,' he said.

Renaud waved away the squire and set about arming fitzOsbern himself, pulling the heavy mail hauberk over his head and carefully positioning the slit in the waist over the hilt of the sword worn underneath. FitzOsbern had spared no expense on his armour. His hauberk, with its short, wide sleeves and skirt split front and rear for ease of riding, extended upwards at the back to form a protective hood. The inside was padded to help prevent chafing, and to protect his lower legs he wore mail chausses tied at the back of the calf with thongs of leather. His cone-shaped helmet with its long nasal to shield the face, was forged from the finest steel, as was the straight broad blade of his sword, the wooden hilt of which was inlaid richly with silver and decorated with niello.

'It's a long time since you did me a squire's service,' fitzOsbern remarked once he was fully accoutred.

'I wanted to speak to you,' Renaud replied. There had been little opportunity to do so lately and there were unanswered questions. 'Why did you let the duke keep Lassay from me, my lord? You could have persuaded him otherwise.'

A look of annoyance flashed over fitzOsbern's face. 'This is hardly the time to talk of these things,' he answered with some impatience, turning his back and preparing to mount.

'There might never be another time, for either of us,' Renaud reminded him soberly.

FitzOsbern turned to face him. 'You hold me to blame then?'

'I have loved you as a son would his father, my lord, yet I feel

111

you have betrayed my trust.'

'Renaud, Renaud,' fitzOsbern sighed, placing a gauntleted hand heavily on the young man's shoulder, 'believe me when I say there was really never any chance of you inheriting Lassay. You were just a child and Guy had far too long to establish himself as the duke's loyal vassal. I became your protector for your father's sake, but I could see what would happen. I couldn't have prevented it, I swear: but what I did do,' he added, 'was to encourage those talents in you that would one day persuade the duke to regard you with favour.'

'Talents?' Renaud queried, curious despite himself.

'People like you, Renaud,' fitzOsbern said. 'Even as a child you had a way of getting people to talk to you, tell you things. It's not easy to mistrust those we like.'

Renaud was shocked. 'Then you always intended me to be the duke's spy?' He shook his head in disbelief. 'What honour could there be for me in such a part?'

'I believed you might be useful that way, yes,' fitzOsbern admitted uncomfortably. For the first time he saw the situation from Renaud's point of view and had the grace to feel a little ashamed. 'As for dishonour, there is no shame in serving your duke in this way; many noble lords do so without hesitation. 'Come,' he said, suddenly brisk and anxious to drive away the misery he saw in his young companion's eyes, 'grant me your pardon for what was no more than an error of judgement. Let us put the whole matter behind us; we have more urgent matters to hand and no more time to waste.'

Renaud knew there was no more to be said. 'Your chausses have yet to be tied,' he pointed out.

William looked relieved. 'Make haste then, lad,' he said, smiling. 'We must be gone from here.'

He mounted as soon as the last thong had been tied, reaching down to receive his mace and the long, kite-shaped shield which, more than anything else, distinguished the Norman from the Saxon in battle.

Putting aside all resentment to concentrate on the coming battle, Renaud had much to ask the battle-hardened fitzOsbern.

'It will be our archers and infantrymen who will first try to create gaps in the shield wall,' fitzOsbern answered in reply to Renaud's eager questions. 'Then it will be our turn. Once we break through, they will be hard pressed to withstand the weight of our cavalry.'

'You make it sound easy, my lord,' Renaud said with cheerful confidence as he mounted his own horse.

He needed no help with his arming since his hauberk was made of leather, not mail, and weighed far less than fitzOsbern's. His helmet, too, was lighter, lacking the nasal and made of a far inferior steel. None of his armour fitted particularly well as, unable to afford the cost of having it made for him, Renaud had bought all of it from a widow whose husband had died on one of William's many earlier campaigns. It was not a good fit, but it had been cheap and had allowed Renaud to spend more on a decent horse, a heavily muscled black stallion with an evil temper but a great deal of courage and spirit.

'Never think it, my boy,' fitzOsbern replied grimly. 'This will be a long and bitter fight. Those men over there will be fighting for their homes and families. Don't underestimate them.'

Renaud nodded soberly, realizing suddenly that this day might be his last on God's earth. He crossed himself.

Hubert the squire handed him his lance. Then Renaud, dismissing his grim and morbid thoughts, rode after fitzOsbern, catching up with him close to where Duke William, from his safe vantage point, watched and waited as, to the sound of trumpets blaring, his archers began their advance.

There had been a time, perhaps even more than one, during that long-drawn-out day, when Renaud had been convinced that defeat was inevitable. The Saxon line had seemed unbreakable, throwing back wave after wave of attack. The archers had made no dent at all in its ranks; the infantry had not only been forced to struggle uphill through the mire, but also through the massed ranks of their own retreating archers. All this under an unrelenting hail of missiles from the English: javelins, axes, spears, even stones. Duke William, despite his loud cries of encouragement, had been unable to disguise his concern during those early stages of the battle.

The inexperienced Breton cavalry, and even the Norman and Franco-Flemish divisions, had been forced to retreat from the unbroken shield wall, and if some of Harold's less disciplined fyrdmen, in the mistaken belief that the whole Norman army was in retreat, had not given chase, then that first disastrous attack would have left the Saxons virtually unscathed. As it was, these unarmoured fyrdmen in their leather tunics and caps, had left themselves exposed to a fierce cavalry attack in which Renaud, for the first time, had killed his man: one quick, clean thrust of his lance through an enemy neck and it was done. There had been no fear, no hesitation, no regret. The Saxon, hardly more than a boy, had stared up at him with a startled, slightly baffled look, before collapsing in a fountain of blood. Renaud had withdrawn his lance and rejoined the fighting.

During the short lull that followed the collapse of William's first attack, Renaud managed to wrestle the hauberk and helmet from a dead Fleming. The quality was good and he was grateful that he would be better protected once they engaged the more formidable housecarls.

The second attack fared little better. Duke William had joined the fighting, sometimes on foot, and at one point had been thought killed; a belief which might have been catastrophic had not the duke scotched the rumour by throwing back his helmet and showing himself to his men.

The day wore on and by mid-afternoon William knew that if his third attack failed then he, and his near exhausted army, would undoubtedly be doomed; so he combined all three of his divisions and prepared to mount a final attack. He planned to use a volley of arrows, directed over the heads of his own men, to distract the Saxon lines as each wave of his army moved forward; but first, he ordered his men to rest and eat.

Renaud found Hugo during this brief respite and was heartily glad to see him.

'None of this is as easy as it sounded, back in Caen,' Hugo said wryly.

'Come now, Hugo,' Renaud urged him. 'This is no time for doubts. Do you really think our duke could lose? Surely not?'

'Of course not, forgive my foolishness. I'm just a little tired. Tell me,' he said, changing the subject, 'didn't you live here once? There may well be men you know up there on that ridge. Does that thought trouble you?'

Renaud frowned. Until this very moment the thought had not occurred to him at all. 'It was a long time ago,' he said uneasily. 'I was just a boy. I hardly remember anyone I knew in those days.'

This was not at all true. Hugo's innocent question had conjured up memories better left forgotten on such a bitter day as this.

Unbidden, visions of those pleasant times flooded into his mind: carefree days spent with Cenred in the London stews; the kindness of his welcome in thegn Godmund's home, the thegn's patient and good-natured tutelage and the sweet and gentle smile of his wife. Above all, he remembered the wholehearted friendship of Godmund's beautiful, impetuous daughter and the precious gift she had given him. 'Ceolwynn,' he whispered softly to himself, and suddenly all his dreams of wealth and conquest turned to ashes.

Brand shivered in the cold, pre-dawn air and tried to convince himself that it was just cold and not fear that made him tremble so. He was dreadfully afraid and had no idea what he should do. No one he knew had come back into the woods, but other men, panic-stricken and wild-eyed, had seized the horses he had been set to guard, and he had been helpless to stop them. The only one he had managed to hold on to had been his lord's grey stallion.

As dawn began to creep across the sky, Brand summoned up all his courage and left the shelter of the woods to search for his master's body, dragging the reluctant, struggling horse along with him. Already, in the treetops, the crows were assembling with bright predatory eyes.

Brand knew there was no point in hoping that Godmund might have survived the carnage. The upper slope of the Santlache ridge was thick with the bodies of men, thousands of them, and horses in their hundreds. And the sight of severed limbs and smashed skulls made the boy want to vomit. The enemy had carried the day.

He could have made for home, away from this horror, but Brand had one last duty to perform for his lord and this he would do. For over an hour he searched among the bodies, constantly alert for signs of the enemy, unaware that Duke William, now King of England, had already given permission for the removal and burial of the Saxon dead. At last he found the place where Godmund had fallen, surrounded by the men who had defended him to the last, just as he had defended Earl Leofwine and his king.

Fighting back his tears, Brand was able to thank God that at least his lord was in one piece. If he could get the body across the horse, then he could get it home. He bent down and rolled the body of another man off Godmund's legs, wiping his hands on his leggings as they came away all bloody. Suddenly realizing that the blood of a man several hours dead on a battlefield should not still be warm and sticky, he returned to the man he had just rolled over in the hope that he would not only be alive, but might also be someone he recognized.

The man was heavy and Brand had to struggle to turn him over onto his back, hampered by the press of dead men all around him. A small groan soon convinced him that he was right, the man was still alive, and he redoubled his efforts until eventually he found himself staring into the bruised and bloodied features of the one he knew to be his mistress's cousin, Lord Cenred.

Already, looters were at work on the field, stripping the dead of their valuables. Having no choice, Brand sought one out, a tall, savage-looking woman, and begged her help in exchange for all but Godmund's sword.

With Cenred and the dead Godmund straddled across the back of the horse, eventually Brand and the woman left the battlefield behind them and started to make their way northwards in the wake of those Saxons who, on Harold's death, had fled the field with bands of Norman cavalry in hot pursuit.

They made their way towards the village of Crowhurst where, as Brand's companion assured him, they would find shelter and aid for the wounded man, but was not an easy road to travel, littered as it was with the bodies of yet more Saxon dead. The Normans had chased the Saxons even into the forests to stop them regrouping, slaughtering any man who found no place to hide. These bodies provided fresh pickings for Mab, as the woman called herself, and Brand, stiff-backed with disgust, walked on without a glance as she pounced on each new corpse, crowing delightedly at every worthwhile find.

About a mile from Santlache they came upon a sight which cheered Brand just a little. A large party of Norman knights had been lured into a deep and hidden gully where they had been ambushed and slain. Here, it was Norman bodies that lay piled deep, and although Brand realized that the incident could have made little different to the outcome of the battle, it was good to see that Saxons were still capable of striking a blow in their own defence.

116

When they reached Crowhurst, Mab led them to the cottage of a man called Penda who made his living as a brewer. Brand, noting the man's restless, fidgety hands and sly, rat-like face, disliked him on sight and tugged nervously at Mab's sleeve. 'Can we trust him?' he whispered anxiously as she helped him get Cenred into the cottage while Penda led the horse with its remaining burden into the stable.

Mab shrugged. 'If you can pay him, Penda is your man. He will help you as long as he can turn a profit by it.'

'But I can't pay him,' Brand cried in alarm. 'I gave you everything.'

'There's the horse,' she replied, grunting a little as she lowered the dead weight of Cenred's unconscious body onto a bed of straw and stinking hides.

'But I need the horse,' Brand protested, 'and you said you would help me get home. You lied to me.' He put his hand to Godmund's sword and glared at her defiantly.

Mab quailed in mock fear, then laughed at him. 'Put away your weapon, my little fighting cock,' she said shaking her head in amusement. 'God knows you are hardly big enough to lift it, let alone use it. Have no fear; I said I would help you and Black Mab always keeps her word.'

Slightly reassured, Brand turned to look at Cenred, who was still breathing.

He started to pull off the young man's hauberk, wincing at the way in which repeated heavy blows had pounded the mail through his tunic and into the flesh of his back and chest.

Mab brought water and clean rags and pushed Brand out of the way. With unexpected gentleness she began to bathe and bind Cenred's wounds, talking to him all the while as though he might hear and be comforted. 'Find me some cobwebs,' she ordered once, and Brand, eager to help, obeyed willingly. He handed them carefully to Mab, who laid them gently over each freshly washed wound to help stem the flow of bright blood.

'Will he live?' Brand asked.

'He may,' she replied, probing carefully at the blood-matted hair over Cenred's left ear. 'The wounds in his chest would probably have killed him by now had they been going to,' she went on, half to herself. 'The blow to the head may be serious, I cannot tell. If he recovers at all, he may be left half-witted by it; who

117

knows? He's weak, but he's stopped bleeding. That's good. As soon as he begins to come round, we'll get some food into him to build up his strength. The rest is in God's hands.'

Satisfied that Mab knew what she was doing, Brand sat down quietly at the table to watch her work.

Penda came back before she'd finished and scowled at the wet, bloody mess she'd made of his bed. 'What trouble have you brought me now, Black Mab?' he asked sourly.

'You owe me a favour, you evil old bugger,' Mab replied.

'All right, all right,' he interrupted hastily. 'Just tell me what you want of me, that's all. Then you and your friends can be gone from here just as soon as you like.'

'You've heard that the king is dead?' she asked.

'I've heard,' he replied indifferently. 'So, we'll have a new king. The battle is over and done; I don't know what you need me for.'

'Word is that the Bastard will not rest until he's destroyed all who fought for Harold,' she said. 'They're slaughtering our wounded, on and off the field, and I've heard they've even mutilated the poor king's dead body.'

Penda nodded. 'And I've heard,' he offered, 'that they're killing any man bearing marks or wounds on his body that he cannot prove were not earned on the ridge at Santlache.'

Brand, who had not known this, widened his eyes in shock. The danger on the road had been far greater than he had known.

'Exactly, and we have a wounded man in our care.'

'So you bring me fugitives now,' Penda growled. 'Do you want to see me dead, woman?'

'It wouldn't break my heart, since you ask,' she answered drily, 'but if you help us we can be gone by daybreak and your dirty little skin will be safe.'

'Spare me your insults and just tell me what you want.'

'Food, a night's shelter and the hire of your horse and cart, with the boy's horse as surety for payment.'

'But what if I don't get them back,' Penda argued unhappily. 'I'll have lost my cart, won't I?'

'You'll get them back, I swear it,' Brand cried out.

'You have my word on it, Penda. I will go with them and bring the cart back myself.'

Penda scratched pensively at his crotch and cast shifty eyes around his unwelcome guests. 'What payment did you say?' he asked.

Mab smiled. 'Three shillings,' she said.

'Five,' he countered.

'Four,' she replied with finality.

Penda nodded agreement and they slapped hands on the deal.

'You'll be able to give me the money, won't you?' Mab asked Brand when they were alone again.

'My mistress will,' he mumbled miserably. 'She will be very grateful to you.'

'But will you tell her about our bargain, my fine lad? Will she be so grateful when she knows what I have here in my bag?' Mab dangled in front of his eyes the bag containing, amongst other things, the armbands and brooches taken from Godmund and Cenred. She raised Brand's chin with the point of her knife, forcing him to look at her and frightening him with the glittering menace in her eyes.

'I won't speak of them,' he hastened to assure her. 'They are yours; it was agreed between us.'

Mab jerked the knife and then, as Brand jumped back in alarm, used it to cut two huge wedges of bread from a fresh loaf, grinning at him wickedly as she did so. Brand laughed weakly and they sat down together to a meal of bread and new cheese, raw onions and mugs of the brewer's second best ale. It was the first food Brand had eaten since dawn the previous day and he ate ravenously, but as the last crumbs disappeared, exhaustion overcame him and he fell asleep where he sat, his head cradled in his arms.

Ceolwynn knew that her father was dead as soon as she heard the wailing that accompanied the cart rumbling over the bridge. She put down her sewing and got to her feet, glancing towards Aelfrun whose face was ashen and whose hands gripped her needlework with white-knuckled intensity.

Ceolwynn gently prised the clutching fingers loose from the cloth and took Aelfrun's hand in her own. 'Courage, dearest Aelfrun,' she murmured gently. 'I may need your strength to lean upon, as you may need mine.'

Aelfrun allowed herself to be led towards the door. Servants followed, whispering and sighing, filled with the same terrible foreboding.

Hild, who had been playing a game with Siggi, now swept the boy up into her arms to stop him running after them all. She had once had a fancy for one of the young lads who had recently joined Godmund's small troop, but at this moment she felt both sad and grateful that nothing had come of it. She, at least, had no one to cry for, she told herself firmly.

The cart had stopped outside the hall and Ceolwynn, seeing the strange woman holding the reins, felt a surge of hope. Surely no stranger would be the one to bring her father's body home? A moment later, recognizing Brand, she felt her heart thud painfully.

The boy was cradling a man's head in his lap, a blond head that she knew could not be her father's. Father Eadric was staring into the back of the cart and when Brand spoke to him she saw the priest's face crumple in grief as he made the sign of the cross. All hope fled.

The band of women who had followed the cart into the village, wailing and keening for their own, now parted to allow their lord's wife and daughter to take possession of his body.

'I brought him back to you, my lady,' Brand said hesitantly as Aelfrun stared unspeaking at the jute-wrapped bundle that might have been anything, a roll of cloth or a bale of fleeces perhaps, but which was, in fact, all that remained of the man she had loved with all her heart and soul.

Ceolwynn sobbed once then stood silent with the tips of her fingers pressed to her lips, the grim reality of the moment stripping away all her courage.

'Lord Cenred lives,' Brand told them, just to fill the agonizing silence.

Cenred opened his eyes and struggled weakly and unsuccessfully to sit up. 'Aelfrun,' he croaked hoarsely, reaching out a hand towards her. 'All is lost, cousin. Godmund, the king, his brothers, all dead, dead ...' he tailed off hopelessly as if unable to believe his own words.

Aelfrun dragged her eyes away from her husband's body and took Cenred's hand in both of hers. 'Don't try to speak now,' she said gently. 'You must rest and regain your strength.'

Dunn had brought hurdles and had been waiting quietly for Aelfrun to decide what she wanted done. At first he couldn't look at her, her pain was too much for him to bear, but since it was soon clear to him that she was far too dazed and confused to think

120

of practical matters, he suggested that if Ceolwynn were to share a bed with her stepmother, the wounded man might be made comfortable in Ceolwynn's bedchamber. Aelfrun gave him a pale, grateful smile and signalled for Cenred to be lifted down.

Once Cenred had been carried away, Dunn climbed up into the cart to help pull Godmund's body within reach. As they lowered him onto the makeshift stretcher, Aelfrun reached out to try to draw back the sacking from his face.

'Wait!' a gruff voice commanded, and startled, Aelfrun obeyed as the tall, ugly woman who had been driving the cart, heaved herself down and strode towards her. 'Before you see him, lady, let Mab wash him for you and leave him tidy like. It's my trade, mistress, laying out the dead, and you'll be pleased with my work, I promise you. It will only grieve you more to see him as he is right now.'

'There is nothing that could give me more grief than I feel at this moment,' Aelfrun sighed wearily, 'but I thank you for your concern. Do, then, what must be done.' She let her fingers brush lightly over the sacking that covered her lord's face before turning to Brand. 'I owe you a great debt, Brand. You have been brave and loyal and shall be rewarded.'

'I could have done nothing without Mab,' the boy replied truthfully.

'Mab shall have her reward, too,' Aelfrun promised absently. She had already forgotten who Mab was. 'Go now,' she ordered, her voice trembling, 'eat and rest. We will talk later.' Her self-control was beginning to crumble and she hurried away before the tears could flow.

The small, sad crowd dispersed, the horse with its empty cart was led away, and Ceolwynn, forgotten by everyone, was left all alone. Blindly and without purpose or direction she began to walk, finding herself suddenly, but without any real surprise, close by the secret place which for so long had been her refuge in time of sorrow.

She crawled into the comforting, womblike cavern, spurning the lamp and deaf to the agitated rustlings of small creatures disturbed by her intrusion. She sat crouched in the enveloping darkness, feeling nothing, thinking nothing, hugging her knees and hearing nothing but the beating of her heart.

Sadly, the numbness couldn't last. Her thoughts refused to be shut out; they crowded relentlessly into her tired head, jumbled and confused but demanding to be recognized.

'Where were you?' she railed senselessly at the guardian giants that had peopled her dreams. 'I believed in you,' she protested with weary hopelessness, rocking to and fro in an agony of rage and pain. 'Why did you fail me?' she cried, but only silence answered her.

The sun was sinking fast as she made her way home again, pale with anguish, but strengthened in resolve. I am my father's daughter, she told herself with a proud lift of the head. His blood flows in my veins, his courage and strength will sustain me. There was no time to waste in futile weeping. Her father was dead, a sea of tears would not change that, but Cenred, her betrothed, was wounded and needed her. Siggi, and Aelfrun too, would need all her love and care in the days to come – but even that, she knew, would not be enough to ease her pain.

'I will avenge you, Godmund Edgarson,' she screamed soundlessly at an indifferent sky. 'Before God, I swear I will avenge you.'

VIII

October–December 1066

Cenred opened his eyes. Beside him Ceolwynn sat with a pile of mending in her lap, so absorbed in her work that she hadn't noticed him wake. He wondered with drowsy curiosity what she was doing here at his bedside, but the question seemed of no great importance; his mind demanded no answer. He lay still, content to study the shadow of the dark lashes on her alabaster cheeks and the sweet curve of soft lips pursed in concentration.

She sighed just once, a sound of such heartwrenching sadness that he reached out to touch her, but before he could speak, a wave of memory flooded over him, dark and bloody. He cried out, forcing himself upright with a suddenness that caused him to fall back with a gasp of pain.

At once she was at his side, her face full of concern, but he could read relief there as well. 'At last,' she breathed, more to herself than to him; then, more briskly, she added: 'We had begun to despair of you ever coming back to us.'

Cenred frowned. 'Have I been sick so very long then?' he asked, becoming agitated and struggling to rise.

Ceolwynn stroked the damp hair back from his face with soothing fingers. 'Hush now, lie still,' she said. 'You've had a fever, but your wounds mend and you'll soon be well again.'

'There was a boy,' he said, trying hard to remember.

'Brand,' she confirmed, nodding. 'He brought you back, and he brought my father's body.' A tear rolled down her cheek. 'Do you think you could eat something?' she asked.

He ignored her question. 'Fetch Aelfrun,' he said, suddenly urgent. Startled, Ceolwynn jumped to her feet. 'Go,' he insisted as she hesitated still, 'fetch her now.' His voice was suddenly

123

sharp and commanding, all trace of confusion gone. 'I must speak to her at once.'

She hurried to find her stepmother, who had spent the past two days and nights in ceaseless vigil beside her husband's body, fasting, unsleeping, praying until he had finally been laid to rest in the churchyard. Now she lay in the deep sleep brought about by a draught that Eadburg had persuaded her to drink.

By the time Ceolwynn had managed to rouse her and bring her to Cenred, he was already out of bed. Both women at once berated him for his stupidity, and Cenred, holding up a hand to still their clamour, conceded enough to sit back down on the bed, acknowledging his weakness.

He had to breathe deeply for several moments before he was able to speak. 'Cousin,' he said at last, addressing Aelfrun. 'You must listen well for what I have to say is very important.' Aelfrun nodded and sat down as Cenred started to tell his tale. 'When Godmund fell,' he began, 'Earl Leofwine had already been killed, as had his brother Gyrth.

'I had managed to work my way up to a position beside Godmund, who, like myself, had fallen back to join the royal housecarls in defence of the king. When I saw him there, I moved closer so that I could fight and die at his side, for it was clear by then that there was small chance of victory.

'The king refused to leave the field, although to have done so would have given us the chance to fight another day with the support of our northern lords. Harold was a brave man,' he mused, half to himself, 'but in this I believe he was wrong. Anyway,' he hurried on, 'we were defending ourselves against an elderly knight and two younger men, his sons as I was later to discover. We killed them all.' He paused to sip some water from the cup that Ceolwynn handed him; then he continued. 'The fighting went on, hour after hour; the more we killed, the more they came at us, but we stood our ground. Believe me, we gave them no easy victory.'

For just a moment his eyes flashed with furious pride and Ceolwynn, meeting that fierce glance, felt a oneness with him that made her for the first time genuinely glad that her father had chosen this man for her husband.

The moment passed and Cenred resumed his grim account of Godmund's last hours. 'Suddenly,' he said, 'even above all the noise of battle, we heard this dreadful scream of rage. It chilled the blood, I can tell you, but before we had time to think any more about it, a troop of Norman cavalry, fresh and well-armed, attacked us with such terrible ferocity that it was impossible to withstand such a charge. Our shield wall was finally broken, Godmund fell and almost in the same moment I was struck down and knew no more.'

By this time there were tears on Aelfrun's cheeks and Ceolwynn squeezed her shoulder comfortingly. 'Is this necessary, Cenred?' she asked plaintively. 'Isn't it enough that my father is dead without us having to listen to all of this?'

'No, let him speak,' Aelfrun interrupted her. 'I need to know exactly how he died. I want to be able to see him in my mind, to remember him, so brave and strong, right up until the end.'

Cenred shook his head, almost impatiently. 'That's not why I'm telling you this,' he said. 'Listen. After the battle, the Normans were swarming everywhere over the field, slaughtering the wounded and seeking to name all those thegns who had taken up arms against William. We are all to be declared "traitor" to our new king and our lands made forfeit in consequence – as I learned later when, for a time, I regained consciousness and could hear the sound of Norman voices above and around me. I soon realized, dazed as I was, that the battle was indeed lost and so I lay still, feigning death, and thus it was that I overheard that which concerns you, cousin.'

'What was it you heard?' Aelfrun asked with shock and surprise.

'The man who had attacked us so fiercely, he was son to the elderly knight who had died earlier by Godmund's hand. He was with another knight, one who addressed him as Hugo; any other name for him I do not know, but he was full of rage and hate, screaming vengeance on Godmund's house for his dead father and brothers. The second knight tried to calm him, but apparently, from what I could hear, without much success.'

'I don't understand,' Ceolwynn said, her brow creasing in perplexity. 'How did he know the name of the man who had slain his kin? And, since my father was already dead, what further vengeance could there be left to take?'

'I, too, was puzzled by this,' Cenred answered, his voice growing weaker as the effort of talking took its toll. 'That they knew Godmund by name did seem passing strange, though there were many Normans at King Edward's court who could have put a name to him, it's true; but I will come to the point.

'This Hugo swore an oath that he would seek out and destroy any male of Godmund's house, whether father, son or brother. I heard the other Norman protest at that, but then I must have passed out again. After that I remember only the boy, Brand you called him, and a painful jolting in the back of a cart.'

'You are telling me then,' Aelfrun said in a small frightened voice, 'that there is some hate-crazed Norman, determined to take my son's life, who could arrive here at any moment.' Cenred nodded wearily. 'What shall I do?' Aelfrun cried out, but if Cenred had any advice to offer he was now past giving it. Exhausted, he had collapsed back on the bed and was soundly, deeply asleep.

The threat to her son roused Aelfrun as nothing else could and forced her to make plans for the future.

She called together all those whose advice she trusted: Dunn, Father Eadric and Aldhere the crippled carpenter, whose practical good sense and keen awareness of events she had long since learned to appreciate, and explained to them everything that Cenred had told her earlier.

It was hardly a private or quiet conference. They formed a group about the fire, and all around them the air hummed with half-heard chatter, shouted orders and all the workaday sounds of a busy hall. Aelfrun wondered at such curious normality when nothing in their lives could ever really be normal again. The greyhounds lay down at her feet, but they were restless, rising every few minutes to pace up and down. It had been too long since they had hunted, she mused, stroking one velvety ear, but this brought fresh pain as she remembered that never again would Godmund ride out, hawk on wrist, nor chase the hart with these fine hounds at his side.

Angrily she dismissed these sad thoughts from her mind. She turned to her steward. 'What say you, Dunn?' she asked.

Ceolwynn and Father Eadric were now also looking towards him expectantly and Dunn shifted uncomfortably under their intent scrutiny. 'Well,' he began with a nervous cough. 'Firstly,' he asked, 'can we be sure that Lord Cenred was not mistaken in what he heard?'

'We cannot be sure, of course we cannot,' Aelfrun answered him. 'But nor can we sit idly by and wait for proof. My son's life could be the price we pay for certainty.'

Dunn nodded. 'True enough,' he agreed. 'We have to accept that the danger is real. What else do we know? We know that this Norman, whoever he may be, knew my lord Godmund by name and will have little difficulty discovering where his home, and therefore his kin, are to be found.

'On the other hand, it's doubtful that he would be given leave to pursue a personal vendetta while his duke strives to secure his hold on his new kingdom.'

'You believe we still have some time then?' asked Ceolwynn hopefully.

'Probably. Time enough to make plans and avoid overhasty action.'

Aelfrun looked relieved; she had half feared that Dunn would advise her to flee at once. 'I don't want to be driven from my own home,' she said, 'but my cousin's words have filled me with dread. If only we knew who this Hugo might be, I would throw myself upon his mercy for my child's sake.'

'If you were to appeal to our new king for his protection,' Father Eadric offered, 'it is possible that this threat could be removed altogether. I have heard that he is a just man.'

'That is an idea which holds promise,' Dunn agreed, 'but such an appeal would take time and we have to decide whether it is safe for the lady Aelfrun to stay here while we wait.'

Aldhere interrupted them with a loud clearing of the throat. 'The decision, it seems to me,' he said when he had their full attention, 'cannot be whether or not the lady should go, but whither? There can be no place for her here now, nor for her childer. Aye, I mean you too, mistress,' he said in answer to Ceolwynn's stricken expression. 'We shall have a new master here as soon as our new king turns his attention to rewarding his supporters.'

A grim silence greeted his words as each one of them was forced to recognize the truth of what he said. Aldhere leaned forward from his little cart to throw another log on the fire, jerking back sharply as it crackled and sparked. Still no one spoke and Ceolwynn found herself wondering if this long nightmare would ever end.

127

'We will go to my father's house,' Aelfrun said at last. 'We are his kin and he will not turn us away.' Her voice was bleak and Ceolwynn, who had heard something of the miserable life led by the occupants of Wilfred's hall, felt a sinking of her own heart at the prospect of that thegn's cold charity.

'A wise choice,' Dunn said, nodding his agreement, 'but your father's lands lie much closer to the southern coast and the Norman army may not be far distant. There is so much we cannot be sure of at this time. Was your father at the battle? Will he keep his own lands? Are the roads safe between here and there? Before you can think of leaving we must send a messenger to be sure that all is well.'

'That sounds like good sense to me,' Aldhere said.

'And you, Father?' Aelfrun asked the priest, who jumped as though stabbed with a bodkin.

'Oh! Oh yes, quite the best thing, yes. Your father's house, certainly,' he gabbled, clearly unaware that the discussion had moved on.

'Are you all right, Father?' Aelfrun asked, worried by his strangely distracted manner.

'I think I know what troubles him,' Aldhere said. 'Those of us who keep our ears to the ground,' he said, 'and some of us are better equipped than others so to do,' he added with a wry glance at his stumps, 'have heard things both good and bad about the man who has made himself our king. One thing we have heard is that he has no love for our English priests and what he calls their lax and ungodly ways. I think Father Eadric has just realized that he, too, may well be in danger of losing his home and his living once a Norman becomes lord here.'

'Father Eadric is not lax and ungodly,' Ceolwynn cried indignantly. 'How can you say such a thing, Aldhere, you who have received nothing but kindness at his hands?'

'Hold fast, mistress,' Aldhere protested. ''Tis not me that says it, but the Norman's words as I have heard reported.'

'Oh, I see,' she mumbled, embarrassed by her own outburst.

'Aldhere is right,' the priest agreed sadly. 'But forgive me, it is the safety of my young lord which must come first. Will you send a man to the lady Aelfrun's father today, Dunn?'

'I may as well see to it at once since there can be little more to discuss until we have his report. Have I your leave to go, my lady?'

'No, wait,' she said. 'There is one other matter which we must discuss at this time.'

Dunn looked back expectantly. Aelfrun's wretchedly unhappy expression tore at his heart and if his death at that very moment could have changed the past, he knew he would gladly have made the sacrifice.

'I cannot go empty-handed to my father's house,' she said slowly. 'What money does ... did ... my husband keep by him?'

Dunn, who had been dreading this question, coughed uncomfortably before answering. 'My lady,' he said, 'be sure that you will take with you every penny I can lay hands upon, but I fear that what silver there is, is little enough.'

'How much?' she asked.

'About twenty shillings, perhaps a little less,' he answered unhappily. 'My lord spent a great deal this past summer on armour and weapons for his men,' he hurried to explain as her eyes widened in shock. 'He bought horses, too, and much expense was incurred by my lord having to spend so much time at court.'

'I understand,' Aelfrun replied heavily. It was a great blow, knowing that Wilfred would be far from happy about supporting three almost penniless dependants. 'What about the rents?' she asked hopefully. 'It's barely three weeks since Michaelmas; surely those paid in silver cannot all have been spent – not yet?'

Dunn looked glum. 'I'm afraid they have, my lady. Lord Godmund instructed me to send all monies to him in London so that he might pay his debts. I have been able to keep back only enough to see us through to the next quarter-day.'

'Well then,' Aelfrun sighed, rising from her seat, 'it seems that we will just have to sell our few trinkets and make the best of things, won't we Ceolwynn?' She attempted a brave smile but it was not a success.

'But I don't understand,' Ceolwynn argued, looking from one to the other of them in bafflement. 'We're not poor. My father was a rich man, surely? How can we suddenly be poor?'

'Your father's wealth lay in his land, child,' Aelfrun replied gently. 'Now that the land is to be handed over to our enemies, we have nothing save what we can carry away with us.'

'Dunn,' the girl protested, seizing his arm and giving it a small, insistent shake, 'you always seem to know what to do when things go wrong; you must be able to think of something.'

Ceolwynn's faith in him did nothing to alleviate Dunn's already overwhelming sense of helplessness; but for her sake he allowed himself to consider, for what seemed like the hundredth time, their limited possibilities.

But Dunn was forced to admit himself defeated. 'You could stay until the Christmas rents are collected,' he said reluctantly, 'but I had hoped to see you safely away before then. The longer we wait, the greater the danger. Who knows when this Hugo will come?'

Aelfrun agreed. 'We will wait only as long as it takes for our messenger to return and for my cousin to regain his strength, then we will leave. It is decided.'

For Ceolwynn the enormity of it all began to sink in. They would be outcasts, homeless, little more than beggars. She looked over to where Siggi played catch-the-ball with his nurse, laughing his infectious, innocent laugh, all unaware of what had befallen them. Tears sprang to her eyes. 'Tell me we won't have to go,' she sobbed, but no one answered her.

For the first time she began to understand that she must leave Cottesham for ever, and, as the emptiness she felt at last gave way to the agony of loss, she collapsed onto the rushes and wept as though her heart would break.

In the days that followed, Aelfrun kept herself busy sorting out the clothes and linen, dishes and kitchen utensils they would be forced to carry with them to help lessen the impression of beggary. Dunn rode into Lullingworth to sell some pieces of jewellery: silver belt-buckles and brooches; a golden armband; a silver cloak pin set with garnets and a necklace of gold and rubies. The only item Aelfrun refused to allow herself to part with was the amber necklace that Godmund had given her on their marriage.

Ceolwynn helped with the preparations, but all the while part of her waited for some happening, some unexpected event that would change everything. Aelfrun understood and gently tried to convince her that it was useless to hope, that nothing would alter the way things were, but stubbornly Ceolwynn clung to her conviction that a miracle would happen.

Something did happen, and although it was not the miracle

Ceolwynn had hoped for – far from it – it did change Aelfrun's plans quite considerably.

It happened on the day when Black Mab finally announced her intention to depart, forcing Brand to tell his mistress of his promise. Aelfrun, who felt that she owed the woman a debt no money could repay, gladly gave up the four shillings owed and saw her on her way with good will and kind words.

Brand stood staring down the road for some minutes to make sure the robber woman had truly gone, and so was the first to see the dirty, dishevelled figure of a man approaching, with a pronounced limp, from the opposite direction.

Folca, for it was none other, was well pleased by Aelfrun's devastated reaction to his terrible news. With malicious, secret pleasure he poured out his dreadful tale; he shed tears and bared his wounds for all to see; he described in graphic detail all that he imagined must have happened to Wilfred and his family, and dwelt at length on his own valiant efforts to fight off the invaders.

Aelfrun, who had thought herself too numb to feel more pain, heard now her poor, defenceless mother and sisters had been tortured, defiled and eventually slaughtered by a merciless soldiery and discovered that her capacity to suffer grief was, in fact, quite without limit.

In the days that followed, Folca managed to insinuate himself into the household and into the confidence of Aelfrun's advisers. If Aelfrun herself had any doubts about her father's erstwhile steward, she kept them silent. The passage of years had diluted the loathing she had once felt towards him, and in his presence she now felt no more than a mild dislike and a vague disquiet.

So, when Folca was admitted into their councils, she treated him with courtesy. Only Godmund's greyhounds, growling low whenever Folca drew near, showed any distrust of the man.

With the change in circumstances, a new destination for the fugitives had to be decided upon. Cenred was now well enough to join in the discussions, but Aelfrun was disappointed and worried by the slowness of his recovery. He remained weak and easily exhausted, able to rise from his bed only for short periods, and only if no real demands were made upon his strength. Aelfrun began to doubt if he would be fit to travel in the near future, but it was Cenred himself who broached the subject, making it clear that when they left he would not be one of their number.

'I would only slow you down,' he told them.

No one argued; he had only said what they were all thinking.

'If Cenred is to stay, I will stay too,' Ceolwynn announced unexpectedly, folding her arms and glowering defiantly.

'But you can't do that,' Aelfrun gasped, horrified.

'Why not? We are betrothed; it is my duty to stay by him. And what harm can there be in my waiting to see what happens? When Cenred is well again I shall go with him and we will be married. Until then, I will stay.'

Cenred glanced at her with startled gratitude at this sudden display of loyalty. As she stood there with her eyes full of fire and such a fierce, determined expression on her face, Cenred felt a stirring in his loins that made the prospect of marriage unexpectedly agreeable.

Aelfrun, less pleased by her stepdaughter's pronouncement, turned on her with almost equal fierceness. 'It's impossible,' she protested vehemently. She turned to Dunn for support, then the priest, but they agreed that Ceolwynn would not be in immediate danger.

'Right then,' put in Aldhere, 'if that's agreed then we should get back to the original purpose of this meeting, which was to decide where our young lordling should seek refuge.' He paused reflectively. 'Perhaps, my lady, you could disappear into some town and set yourself up in some way of business.'

'There is not enough money for that,' Dunn said, worried by the rapid depletion of Aelfrun's meagre funds.

Folca, who had hidden his own treasure high in the hollow trunk of an oak in the nearby woods, gloated inwardly at this. All was as he had long desired it; this proud thegn's daughter now had neither husband nor wealth, and in his twisted mind he believed himself at last avenged for the imagined spurning of his non-existent suit so many years before.

'Have you any other family – uncles, cousins – who might take you in?' Dunn asked, his brow creased with worry.

'Estrith and Wulfhere!' Ceolwynn cried out excitedly, interrupting whatever answer Aelfrun might have made. 'Wulfhere can't have been at Hastings; Cenred has already told us that the northern armies were not at the battle. Don't you see what that means? They have no reason to take his lands away from him; you would be safe there.'

'You're quite right,' Dunn agreed, brightening a little, 'but Northumbria is so very far to travel and many dangers may now lie on that road.'

'But it is the only place left for us to go,' Aelfrun said with decision. 'We will go to Northumbria, and soon. There seems to be no reason now for delay.'

'Then, since Lord Cenred cannot be your escort,' Dunn said, 'I beg leave to accompany you, my lady.'

'Gladly would I have your company,' his mistress replied, 'but who will manage the estates if you are not here?'

'Does that really matter now?' he asked drily. 'I wouldn't be looking after *your* interests any more, my lady, and, even if the choice were mine to make, I'm not sure I'd stay here under a Norman master.' As if to prove his sincerity, he began to unbuckle the steward's keys that hung at his belt. 'Let Folca run things here,' he said. 'He can take a chance on holding the post when the Normans come, if he wills.'

Folca, who had great faith in his own destiny, saw another profitable opportunity beckon and turned to Aelfrun with an ingratiating smile.

'I'm not sure,' she began hesitantly. The sight of Folca's wolfish grin had awakened memories she found disturbing. Her father's people had been miserable under his rule. But he had done her no harm; her fears had probably just been those of a silly, impressionable girl. She pushed aside her nagging doubts and nodded her agreement. 'I am happy to accept your offer, Dunn, and you, Folca, may stay here as steward until ... well, time will tell.'

For Folca, it all made sense to him now; he had only to convince the new lord of Cottesham of his loyalty and his future was assured. A Norman usurper, faced with a bitter and hostile peasantry, must surely see the value of a loyal, well-disposed Saxon in his service.

Aelfrun, already half regretting her decision, reluctantly handed him Dunn's keys. He took them almost greedily, closing his broad, damp hands about hers and holding them prisoner in his clammy grasp. She withdrew them quickly, suppressing the urge to wipe them on her skirts; then, with the dogs padding in her wake, she left to order supper and the lighting of the torches.

Then Dunn and the priest and Aldhere drifted away.

133

Only Folca remained, with Ceolwynn and Cenred. Ceolwynn began to find something sinister in the looks he gave her, the meant-to-be reassuring pat of his hand on her arm. Since Aelfrun trusted the man, or so it seemed, this made Ceolwynn feel guilty, and thrusting aside such unworthy thoughts, she bestowed on him one of her most engaging smiles and tried not to notice the way his strange yellow eyes seemed to glitter almost balefully in the firelight.

'It is strange, is it not,' the new, though as yet uncrowned, King of England asked of his clerk, 'that two men, each of whom has been promised a reward of land, should both ask for the same insignificant estate.' He leaned forward on his elbows and studying the two men over the tips of his steepled fingers, he asked: 'Is there something special about this manor of Cottesham of which I am unaware?'

The clerk began an intense scrutiny of the documents in front of him, running one finger rapidly up and down the pages and frowning in concentration. Renaud, waiting beside Hugo, who kept darting venomous looks at him, wondered at the speed at which the king had managed to obtain so much information. He supposed, quite correctly, that the spy network, of which he had once so nearly been a part, must be far larger than he had ever imagined.

'No, my lord,' the clerk said at last. 'I can find nothing out of the ordinary. Godmund Edgarson held this and several other manors scattered throughout Sussex, Surrey and Mercia. Cottesham was his chief, though not his largest holding, and appears to be reasonably prosperous. The manor consists of some twenty hides of good arable land and pasture, plus an area of forest, mainly beech, oak and elm, encompassing a further—'

The papers were snatched rudely from his hands and tossed onto the table. 'I don't need an inventory,' the king growled, as a pain passed quickly but disturbingly through his belly. William returned his attention to the two young men anxiously awaiting his decision. 'I could,' he said, fixing first Hugo, then Renaud, with his hawklike stare, 'ask each of you to state your reasons for wanting this particular piece of property, but I have a feeling that to do so might only confuse matters. However, I can see from the stubborn looks on your faces that this is a matter over which two good friends could fall out.'

'I hope not, my lord,' Renaud protested, 'such is certainly not my intention, and I trust that Hugo is of the same mind.'

Hugo, who was scowling with unaccustomed ill-humour, grunted an unconvincing agreement.

'Be that as it may,' the king replied, 'I think this is a decision to which I must give more thought. It's something of a judgement of Solomon, is it not?' he remarked jestingly. Only the clerk laughed, a shrill titter that caused William to wince and send the man away with an irritable wave of the hand. 'I shall let you know my mind in a day or two.

'It would make things easier, though, if you were to come to some mutual agreement over this, or perhaps neither of you should have Cottesham if that would ensure peace between you.'

'No!' Hugo protested loudly, but William quelled him with a look.

'Enough!' the king growled, as the pain tore savagely at his bowels. 'This land has yet to be won,' he reminded them sharply. 'Only a fool thinks to slice his loaf before he has baked it,' he said. 'London is not yet ours, and men still rally to that untried cub they call the Aetheling. Even the earls of Northumbria and Mercia have promised him their support. Rumour has it that their sister, Harold's widow, is to bear a child, though an infant would be small threat, even if the rumour be true. But still,' he said, 'we should never underestimate our opposition. Harald of Norway made that mistake, remember?'

The pain came again, but this time it was not so quick to retreat. He cradled his stomach and closed his eyes.

'My lord?' Renaud queried anxiously.

William sighed. He quite liked the company of these eager young men, but at this moment he wanted nothing so much as to be rid of them. 'I will inform you of my decision later,' he said, trying not to gasp and cursing inwardly at his growing certainty that his pain was caused by the onset of dysentery.

'You have my leave to go,' he said curtly.

Renaud and Hugo backed gratefully out of the royal presence.

'What game are you playing, Renaud?' Hugo hissed as soon as they stepped outside the door. 'You know why I want Cottesham; I've sworn an oath. Why do you seek to thwart me in this? What possible interest can you have in the matter? Withdraw your request if you value my friendship.'

135

'I do value your friendship, Hugo,' Renaud answered him, 'and I understand your grief and anger. You have lost almost all of those you held most dear; but still I say to you, you are wrong, very wrong, to want to vent that anger on the innocent.' Hugo was still scowling, but he seemed to be listening, and Renaud began to feel hopeful that at last he might be getting through to him. 'You would not thank me,' Renaud persisted, 'if, when your anger had cooled, you found you had committed some unworthy act and I had done nothing to prevent it. Just listen and let me try to explain. Remember when you asked me if I had friends on the ridge at Santlache, friends against whom I had taken up arms?'

Hugo nodded and, as Renaud continued, the two of them fell quite naturally into step, their heads close together in the unconscious, companionable way of old friends. 'Godmund Edgarson,' he went on, 'the man whose kin you have sworn to destroy, was both my friend and mentor during my stay in England, years ago. He welcomed me into his home, his family became mine and I grew to love them all. He was a good man and my heart grieved at his death, but I know that in war men die, friend and foe alike. You, too, must come to accept that, Hugo. Godmund was no murderer; he couldn't choose, in battle, whom to kill or not to kill. Besides, even if I didn't believe that you would eventually see that for yourself, your oath means nothing; Godmund had no male kin that I ever heard of.'

'If that be so,' said Hugo triumphantly, seizing on this last comment as though Renaud had just fallen into some carefully laid trap, 'why, then, are you so anxious to "protect" me from myself? If that was your only reason for wanting Cottesham, then with your own lips you have admitted that it is no reason at all.'

'I didn't say it was the only reason,' Renaud countered. 'My interest in Cottesham is not to thwart you, my friend, but to find for myself a place in this hostile land where I may be less hated than elsewhere. I want to make my home here, but I don't want always to be feared and despised as a conqueror and despoiler. There may be some small chance of that for me at Cottesham, where once I was known and made welcome.'

Hugo's tense, angry expression slowly evaporated. There was no doubt in his mind that Renaud was speaking the truth and he allowed himself a sympathetic, if rather superior, smile at the younger man's naivety. Did the poor fool really believe that a

Norman master they already knew would be any more acceptable to these defeated Saxons than one they didn't know?

'So Godmund had no father, brothers, sons?' he asked. Renaud shook his head. 'You swear it?' Hugo insisted.

'I can swear only to that which I know, but, to the best of my knowledge and belief, what I have said is true. There are no surviving males of Godmund's line.'

Hugo walked in silence for several more minutes, pretending to come to a decision he had already made. Together they passed through a gate in the city wall, then waded and squelched their way through the rain-soaked Norman encampment.

'I do believe,' Hugo reflected conversationally as he tugged one foot free of the mud and kicked away the heavy clod of earth that clung to it, 'that this is the wettest place on God's good earth.'

'Yes,' agreed Renaud, 'but rain is better than frost.'

'Ah yes,' Hugo replied sagely, grasping the allusion, 'and we've had plenty of that lately, have we not?'

'Indeed we have,' Renaud agreed once more.

Hugo draped an arm about Renaud's shoulders in a brotherly fashion, and Renaud, hiding his relief, knew that he had won.

Aelfrun, unaware that there was no longer any threat to her son's life, left with him and Dunn for Northumbria in the middle of December, fearing to delay any longer. The news that Archbishop Stigand and the young aetheling had at last submitted to William and that London was on the point of surrender had reached them on the seventeenth of the month, and there was now a grave risk, they believed, that the vengeful Hugo might, before long, be ready to seek them out.

Hugo, however, even if he had not already abandoned any thoughts of vengeance, was in no position to threaten anyone. He, in common with both his duke and the mighty fitzOsbern, had succumbed to the scourge of dysentery and had been forced to retire to his waterlogged and stinking tent.

He was still confined to his pallet long after the duke and fitzOsbern had recovered, and when victory finally came he was still bedridden and subject to the untender mercies of his squire, Ralf. So he had been unable to make the journey to London where Renaud, sent ahead to help with preparations for the coronation, had already found himself a comfortable billet on the north bank of the Thames, close by the place where William would soon start to build his White Tower.

Events moved very fast as December drew to a close, and by Christmas all the preparations for William's crowning in Edward's abbey of West Minster had been completed.

Christmas morning dawned cold but clear, and Renaud was up and about his master's business before the sun had fully risen. He was excited and full of high spirits, glad that the fighting was at last over and that after the duke's coronation, which was to take place this very day, there could be no more doubt about who was king of England.

He strode briskly through the streets of London town, answering the stares of the few citizens already abroad with a confident, good-natured smile. The stares of these Londoners, he had found, were more of curiosity than hostility, and some of them, especially the women, responded to him with smiles of their own; some tentative, others quite brazen and inviting.

It was strange, he thought to himself, how quickly they seemed to have forgotten the rape and burning of Southwark, just across the river, barely three weeks ago.

It had been an unpleasant episode, but it had proved once again that Duke William was not a man to flinch from bloody deeds in order to gain his own ends or avenge an injury.

Suddenly hungry, Renaud stopped to break his fast with the purchase of a hot meat pie, dallying a little – since the pie-seller was both young and pretty – to sharpen his Saxon with flirtatious banter.

He had always been much impressed by the sheer size and obvious wealth of the city, but on this particular morning, if only for the briefest of moments, London seemed almost beautiful to him. A fresh snowfall in the night had cloaked and carpeted every street and alleyway, hiding the dirt and disguising the stink and squalor of the poorer streets. Trees and rooftops, handsomely bedecked with sun-spangled icicles, glittered in the sunlight, and the great river Thames, gleaming like polished silver, flowed purposefully between banks edged with virgin white. It was with real regret that he watched the town wake up and the crisp new snow turn first yellow with the contents of emptied chamber pots, then black with the tread of countless feet.

The silence of the early morning quickly gave way to the

raucous calls of tradesmen, and then, as the city gates opened to let in the countryfolk, to the rumble and clatter of cartwheels and the thudding tread and mournful lowing of oxen.

Renaud stood back to let pass the heavy wagons full of eggs and fresh vegetables, sacks of grain, dairy produce and live fowl ready for the butcher's knife; the larder on London's doorstep spilling out onto its streets.

Suddenly realizing that the hour was growing late, he hurried on his way. He would have to make haste if he was to have time enough to return to his lodgings, have his horse saddled and make his way to the abbey in time to take his place with the guard assigned to hold back the expected crowds.

He reached the river where he trotted up and down the water's edge, growing more and more anxious as the minutes passed, until at last he spied what he was looking for, the small Flemish trader called the *Dove* which had dropped anchor late yesterday. Her captain carried letters for both the duke and fitzOsbern, and, although there was no real urgency about them, fitzOsbern was hoping for word from his much-missed wife and would not wait for the captain to make his own arrangements for delivery.

The mutual and abiding love between fitzOsbern and his wife of nearly thirteen years was well known, and Renaud felt great respect and affection for fitzOsbern's lady and understood his lord's fears for her health.

He rushed aboard the ship, the gangplank fortunately already being in place, breathlessly offered his credentials to the captain, obtained the letters, then tore off at an undignified pace back to his lodgings.

If Renaud had hoped that William's crowning was to be an end to England's sufferings, he was doomed to disappointment. The Londoners, presumably resigned to their fate, had gathered in large numbers outside the abbey, watching quietly but without apparent hostility as the regal procession made its way with all ceremony from Westminster Palace. They cheered a little as William, most splendidly dressed and mounted on a handsome white palfrey, rode past with his head held high and his eyes fixed majestically on the road ahead. Close behind him rode his brothers, Robert and Odo, and his friend fitzOsbern.

Renaud tried to signal his lord that all was well, that his wife had written, but the Seneschal, like his duke, looked neither right nor left and didn't notice him. The remainder of the Norman barons followed behind this august group and then, last of all, came the English lords, led by Archbishop Stigand and the brother earls of the north, Edwin and Morcar.

When they all dismounted and disappeared through the great west door of the abbey, Renaud, waiting outside in the cold, would have given almost anything to have been inside watching the anointing of a king. As it happened, few men saw the historic moment, for as the barons' roars of acclamation for their new king resounded from inside the abbey, the nervous soldiery outside, convinced that the English barons had turned on their duke, attacked the passive, waiting crowd and began to fire the surrounding houses.

Alarmed by the screams from outside and the smell of burning, almost everyone in the abbey rushed out, leaving a pale and shaken king and a mere handful of Norman barons inside.

Aldred, the Archbishop of York, recovered quickly and continued the ceremony. Anointing William with holy oil, he signed for him to make his solemn vows of kingship. William struggled with the unfamiliar English, but his words echoed hollowly throughout an empty church and his heart was heavy with the dread of premonition. Was this another omen? he wondered fearfully. Had God been angered by his ambition, his cruel determination to seize what he believed to be his?

Outside, Renaud had managed to restrain the men under his own command, but watched with mounting horror as, with the situation quite out of control, other officers joined with their men in an orgy of pillage and rape.

Suddenly, out of the seething mass of people, a small child, losing her grasp on her mother's hand, ran screaming and panic-stricken across his path. He reined back in time to prevent himself riding her down, but the child stumbled and almost fell beneath the hooves of an oncoming destrier. In one swift movement, Renaud swooped down and scooped her up, but when he handed her back to her mother the woman gave him a look of such loathing and contempt that he turned away, shamed despite himself for the actions of his fellows.

What did he expect, he asked himself bitterly? Gratitude?

After the ceremony, Renaud managed to approach fitzOsbern and hand him the letters, taking care to place the one in Adeliza's handwriting at the top of the pile.

Later, in the quiet of the evening when fitzOsbern had read his wife's letter and smoothed away the lines of worry from his brow, he described to Renaud all that had gone on in the abbey that day, and shared the young man's distress at the unhappy aftermath.

'Anyway,' he concluded, 'William is now, without question, king, and I am to lose a loyal servant.' Renaud raised his brows quizzically at this and fitzOsbern smiled, hoping that his news would help lift the young man's spirits. 'He won't be in any mood to tell you about it just at the moment,' he said, 'but the king has decided to allow you your will over that land you wanted. You are to be the new lord of Cottesham.'

IX

January 1067

It wasn't long before Dunn began to have serious doubts about the wisdom of their journey. Everywhere, bands of dispossessed, frightened peasants crowded the roads, carrying all their possessions on their backs or pushing in front of them small hand-carts piled high with household goods, tools and baskets of squawking fowl. They all had horrifying tales of destruction, rape and slaughter to tell, and they were all too afraid to return to their homes.

There were other, less pitiful, refugees on their road, however. Wealthy merchants, fearful for the safety of their costly goods, had packed up their businesses, lock, stock and barrel to make for the relative safety of more northerly towns. They travelled with well-armed retainers and Dunn often sought out their company for safety and companionship.

'It won't be for long,' a dealer in furs and amber had confidently assured them as they left Oxford behind and headed towards Buckingham where their roads would part. 'Once all the excitement dies down and the soldiers get their fill of looting, I dare say our new king will soon make it safe for me, and others like me, to set up shop here in the south once more,' he predicted with irritating complacency. 'It makes sense to get out of the way until order is restored, though. No thieving mercenary is going to line his purse with profit from my merchandise, not if I can help it.' He settled his fine, squirrel-lined cloak more comfortably over his shoulders and summoned one of his servants to bring him a flask of wine.

'Doesn't it anger you that this bastard Norman has killed our own rightful lord and seized our land by force?' Dunn asked

142

indignantly. 'Are you content to name such a one, king?'

'English, Norman, Dane, what does it matter?' the man replied with an airy shrug. 'All kings need trade and thus will always need tradesmen and merchants. They despise us, but they will protect us. Do you really think it matters to most people who is king? Look at them,' he said, pointing first to a ploughman at work in a distant field, and then to a group of peasants resting dejectedly at the side of the road, 'do you think it matters to them who is their lord? Of course not,' he answered himself. 'Each one of them is content as long as he has a roof over his head, a bit of land to till and food in his belly. That is all they have any right to in this world and they care not who gives it to them.'

Dunn was furious but wisely held his tongue. It would serve no purpose to argue that better men than this overfed, self-satisfied oaf had died rather than accept a Norman usurper, and Aelfrun, whose son lay in her arms unaware that he had lost a father and been dispossessed of his inheritance all in one fateful day, bowed her head and wept secret tears beneath the concealing hood of her cloak.

At Nottingham they met with their first disaster. Dunn's cob and their packhorse were stolen while the weary travellers slept at a small inn just outside the town. Aelfrun's palfrey, by far the better horse, was untouched; but Aelfrun opined, quite correctly, that the mare, unused to strangers, had proved too difficult to handle.

'We must get the town reeve,' Aelfrun insisted. 'The thief must be caught and brought to justice.'

Dunn thought carefully. 'It would take too long, my lady, and it's unlikely that we'll see those horses again, even if the reeve is willing to devote time and effort to the task of tracking down a thief in such troubled times. I'm afraid the law may be of little use to us in these days.'

'Has it come to this already?' she said, shocked to find yet another of life's certainties disappearing.

'Only for a time,' Dunn comforted. 'Despicable he might have been, but that merchant was right about one thing; Duke William will be sure to restore order as soon as he is able. It is in his own interests to do so.'

'Have we enough money to buy another mount?'

Dunn, who held all their silver, emptied his purse onto an

upturned bucket and counted the pennies. 'Enough for a mule, perhaps, but it would leave us with almost nothing for food and lodging. There is no help for it, I must walk.'

'But how far have we still to go?'

'Not more than a hundred miles, I would say; only five days if God is with us.'

'We could share the riding,' Aelfrun said.

'My lady, you are not accustomed to walking long distances. Forgive me, but I think it would slow us too much if you were to attempt it. Please be guided by me in this.'

To his relief, Aelfrun accepted that he was right without further argument. They took to the road again, Aelfrun sharing her saddle with Siggi and Dunn walking briskly at her stirrup. The boy clutched the reins proudly in his chubby fingers and grinned at them both.

They had had to abandon many of the goods the packhorse had carried, selling them in Nottingham for a fraction of their worth, and now lacked even a change of clothing.

Hampered by the inevitable loss of speed and their increasingly shabby and travel-stained appearance, they seldom travelled now with larger companies and found themselves more and more often alone in country that was strange and sometimes, to Aelfrun at least, a little frightening. The mountains through which they passed, although scarcely more than high hills, were far beyond the experience of even Dunn, the more accustomed traveller, while Aelfrun, who had never before travelled more than a few miles from home, found them at once both beautiful and menacing.

As they climbed higher the weather became colder, the wind fiercer and more penetrating. The high, windswept moorlands and bleak, rocky outcrops seemed forbidding and unwelcoming. It wasn't long before they found their woollen cloaks woefully inadequate for keeping out the chill, and Dunn's shoes had almost worn through, causing him more discomfort than he let her know.

They saw fewer people on the roads as they moved further north and villages became few and far between. Hunger and cold soon began to take a toll and their previously rapid progress slowed considerably, although Dunn did manage to get his shoes cobbled at last, in a village where an elderly thegn, well past his fighting years, had, in his eagerness for news, received them graciously and seen them on their way with enough food for two whole days.

144

This was to be almost their last piece of good fortune. Not long afterwards they crossed the Northumbrian border and found themselves in what seemed to be a deserted land. It was as though the inhabitants of every village had fled at their approach, leaving fields and byres standing empty and every crib and storehouse picked clean.

Still the journey dragged on. December slipped relentlessly into January, the new year bringing with it still colder winds and the threat of snow. They were reduced to eating anything they could find, even a vile, sour porridge made from the oats scraped out of the bottom of a bucket found in an empty stable.

With his feet blistered and raw, Dunn now tired easily; and when heavy mists shrouded the hills they huddled miserably in the shelter of rocks or trees, waiting for the weather to clear rather than risk losing their way. With each new delay it seemed more and more likely that they might never reach their destination.

Then, just when their spirits were at their lowest ebb, help came at last in the form of a grey-bearded shepherd clad from head to foot in sheepskins so thick and heavy that he looked more sheep than man.

He had been watching their stumbling approach up the steep, rock-strewn track for some time, eyeing them suspiciously from his rough wooden shelter and half minded to set his dogs on them if they came too close. When they came near enough for him to be sure that they posed no threat, he tied up the dogs and stood in the doorway until they came up to him.

'You'll be strangers here?' he said in a reasonably understandable West Saxon and with cold, unwelcoming eyes.

'Good friend, have you food to spare for hungry travellers?' Aelfrun asked desperately. 'We can pay you; we're not beggars.'

'I can see that, lady,' the shepherd replied without warmth or interest, 'but I have nothing to sell.'

'Please,' she pleaded, disguising her fury at his indifference, 'you must have something. Look,' she said, parting her cloak, 'my child is sick with hunger and cold. Help him, I pray, even if you won't help us.'

Exposed to the cold air Siggi began to cough, the dry, rasping sound filling the silence that followed his mother's plea. He looked pale and ill, his stomach cramped with hunger.

The shepherd thawed immediately, reaching up to take the boy from her arms and carrying him into the hut, where he set about feeding him bread soaked in a bowl of fresh ewe's milk.

Dunn helped Aelfrun down and hobbled the pony before following his mistress into the shelter.

How strange it was, Aelfrun reflected a little later as she devoured a dish of boiled cabbage, that only weeks ago she would have been appalled at the thought of spending a night in a shepherd's hut with no more to eat than bread and cabbage – cattle fodder which even peasants scorned.

Siggi had already fallen asleep and, while the shepherd showed him how to stuff their shoes with straw for warmth and comfort, Dunn was busy bathing his sore feet. She watched his head bobbing up and down as he nodded and talked quietly with their host, and her heart filled with gratitude for his unswerving loyalty and devotion. She thanked God for him.

The morning dawned fine and clear, with the sun copper bright in a cloudless sky and little or no wind to chill the warmth of its rays. They made an early start, setting out again in far better spirits and carrying in their bags a half loaf of bread, some ewe's milk cheese, a small chunk of raw goat's meat and a few wizened apples. The shepherd had carefully pointed out their route into the Blackwater valley, assuring them that it was really not very far now and that their journey's end was almost in sight.

Then at midday, the weather changed again. Cold winds blew and squally showers soaked their clothes and turned the track to mud. It was a great relief when, some hours later, by the fast-fading afternoon light, they saw at last a huge, dark lake at the end of the valley, the village of Blackwater clinging tenaciously to the slopes above it.

They left the woods and hurried down the last few miles of road, but Dunn knew almost at once that his worst fears had been realized. The village was deserted. A hide door flapped drearily in the wind as they passed, and he thought he heard a hen scratching in the dirt, but it was just a bundle of dried skins rasping against a wall as it swung to and fro.

He stopped walking and the pony came to a halt beside him, cropping the grass at the roadside as Aelfrun allowed the reins to drop from her fingers. She didn't have to ask him why he had stopped; the defeated slump of his shoulders told all.

146

'We may as well go on,' she said at last.

Wordlessly, Dunn began to walk again.

'Where would Wulfhere's hall be?' she asked, looking about her anxiously. She knew it would make no real difference, but part of her believed that things would be better if only they could take shelter in Estrith's home, but there seemed to be no sign of a hall here, just abandoned huts and cottages.

Dunn, who had only just remembered that a Northumbrian thegn seldom had his hall in one village, but usually somewhere between the several villages of his holding, broke this news as gently as he could. Aelfrun's face fell still further.

Suddenly, a movement caught Dunn's eye and he turned sharply, just in time to see an old woman darting for cover. 'Wait,' he called after her. 'Wait, we mean you no harm.'

She hesitated and glanced back at them. Aelfrun raised a hand in greeting and this seemed to reassure the old woman sufficiently for her to allow Dunn to approach.

Ragged and filthy, her grey hair hanging unbound and unkempt in knotted strings, the old woman waved and pointed in an agitated manner and it seemed to Aelfrun that she answered all Dunn's questions with a shake of the head, which was not encouraging. Eventually, he returned with his news.

'The woman says that everyone here has fled into the hills.'

'But why?' Aelfrun asked with a puzzled shake of the head. 'These villages can be in no danger from the Normans.'

'It's not easy to understand her, her Saxon is very different from ours, but it would seem that it's the Scots that are the danger. Earl Tostig's invasion and King Harold's death have left this part of the country wide open to attack. She says they are savages, the Scots,' he continued bleakly, 'enslaving captured women and children, but slaughtering the old and infirm, burning them alive.'

'Heaven shield us!' Aelfrun gasped, terrified.

'They've not entered this valley yet, but she says it will only be a matter of time. After all the fighting this summer, there are too few men left here now to defend their villages.'

'What shall we do?' Aelfrun asked despairingly. 'We must hide, too, I know, but is there any food here?'

'She says she has had none herself for two days, and I suppose we must believe her.'

147

'So, we must follow the rest of the village into the hills and hope we find them before it's too late,' Aelfrun sighed wearily, passing Siggi into Dunn's arms before dismounting. Dunn nodded, too dispirited to speak. 'Well then,' she said, suddenly more positive, 'we must see if this woman has a fire so we can cook what little we have left.'

Dunn untied their bundle from the saddle and gave it to her before leading the pony away to stable it. Aelfrun, with Siggi trailing listlessly in her wake, followed the old woman into her cottage, almost gasping with pleasure at the sudden blast of warmth from the fire. By the time Dunn came in, she already had the meat simmering in a big pot over the fire, and the old woman, once she realized that they intended to share their food with her, went off to rummage in a corner, returning with a few shrivelled turnips, a small block of salt, some onions and a few handfuls of barley.

Aelfrun noticed the look of anger on Dunn's face, but shook her head at him silently. She couldn't bring herself to blame the old woman for wanting to hold on to what little she had.

'I don't think we should waste too much time here,' Dunn said, running his fingers thoughtfully through his stubbly, new-grown beard. It made him look much older, Aelfrun thought, and was startled to find herself thinking that it also made him more attractive, a thought which made her flush with shame. 'If every village for miles around is either deserted or destroyed,' Dunn continued, 'then until the Scots have had their sport and head back across the border, we must stay out of sight. I suspect it might have been safer for us to have braved the Normans.'

'Do you think we should go home again then?'

'Eventually, yes; when the roads are safe to travel once more; but you do realize, don't you, that Cottesham will no longer be your home?'

She nodded. 'I have to go back, if only to make sure that no harm has come to Ceolwynn. We should never have left her.'

'You must not reproach yourself. It was your son who was in real danger and we cannot return until we know that he will be safe. Until then we must go up into the mountains.'

Aelfrun felt intimidated by the high, misted peaks all around, but she nodded to show that she accepted his decision. 'Why didn't the old woman go with them?' she asked curiously. 'Did you ask?'

Dunn nodded: 'She says she's too old to go scrambling about in the mountains and that on her own she will be quick enough to hide when danger comes.'

'She wasn't quick enough to hide from us, was she?' Aelfrun commented tartly.

Dunn watched her as she moved about doing the simple womanly things that came as naturally to her here in this hovel as in her own hall. She hung up their damp cloaks to dry, moved Siggi so that he was at a safer distance from the fire, tasted the stew and finally set about making up beds for them all using fresh straw from an empty cattle shelter.

Seeing his eyes on her, Aelfrun stopped and smiled at him quizzically, making him look away quickly in embarrassment.

After their meal, Aelfrun settled down to sleep on the bed of straw she had made, with Siggi lying between her and the old woman.

Dunn banked down the fire and put more water and barley in the pot to cook slowly for the morning, stumbling a little for lack of a rushlight or candle to light his way. When he'd finished he lay down just inside the door, wondering if he should mount a watch through the night; but before he could decide, exhaustion overcame him and he slept.

The next morning he rose early and went to feed the pony. As she made for the bucket he carried, he saw with a sinking heart that she was quite lame. A quick examination of her legs confirmed his fears that she would be unrideable for many days. They would have to finish this terrible journey on foot.

He fetched the saddlebags from the hut and began to redistribute the contents, putting as much as possible into his own bag so that Aelfrun would have less to carry. In the bottom of one of her bags he found a small cloth bundle of personal possessions, each one a gift from those who loved her most dearly: an ivory comb, an amber necklace, a velvet pincushion crudely embroidered by a child's hand. Impulsively, and with a quick glance to make sure that she hadn't yet woken, he stripped off one of his own armbands and slipped it inside, smiling ruefully to himself at the folly of the gesture. Even if she found it, he thought sadly, she would never see the significance of the addition.

'Do we have to leave now?' Aelfrun asked sleepily, waking and seeing him ready packed.

'As soon as you've eaten,' he told her.

He broke the news about the pony. Aelfrun listened with weary resignation, but made no comment. 'It will be even colder up in the hills,' he hurried on, hating to see the tired, almost defeated look in her eye. 'So Ulla has gone to see if she can find some warmer clothes for us.'

'Is that her name?' Aelfrun asked with a brave show of interest. She splashed her face with water from a pail and wiped Siggi's with a wet cloth before spooning out the stew.

The door slammed open suddenly and Ulla staggered in with an armful of clothing which she dropped in front of them without a word before disappearing again.

They finished eating, then quickly sorted out some suitable things to add to their gear. Aelfrun pulled on an extra woollen tunic, but had to cut one down raggedly with a knife to fit Siggi. There were sheepskins as well, which they managed to pin inside their cloaks to make warm linings, and a child's woollen hood which covered Siggi's head and shoulders.

The addition of a small axe to Dunn's limited armoury completed their preparations and they were finally ready to begin their search, leaving with no thanks or farewells since Ulla had disappeared and didn't even watch to see them go.

Siggi, obviously stronger and more boisterous with a few good meals inside him, skipped ahead of them down the road chasing a leaf caught by the wind. Aelfrun smiled briefly, watching him, but the smile soon turned to a worried frown.

'Do you know where we are going?' she asked Dunn.

'Ulla told me the way and which landmarks to look for. We must follow the lake until we reach an old stone cairn. Here, we must leave sight of the road and start to climb up into the hills, following an old deer track, which should be clear to us, until we are through the forest.'

'What then?' she asked, following his gaze up to where the bleak, high moor met the concealing, sheltering woodland.

'Well,' he said thoughtfully, 'that may be the difficult part – trying to recognize the different markers and signs that will lead us across the moors. We should be safe from the Scots up there, but we must take no chances. If we haven't found your sister by nightfall we'll have to be watchful; there may be wolves.'

'It's not so very cold yet,' Aelfrun remarked with surprising calm, 'I doubt if wolves will be hungry enough to trouble us, but what shall we eat,' she asked practically, 'if our journey takes longer than we think?'

Dunn, who hadn't wanted to think about this possibility, cursed inwardly at the uselessness of an education which had left him so ill equipped to serve her in this time of need. 'I should never have been the one to come with you,' he reproached himself bitterly. 'You should have had an escort who could hunt for you and defend you. What use is a *steward* in these times?' he cried out in anger and self-contempt. 'What use is Latin, when just knowing how to set a snare could be enough to save our lives?' Turning to face her as she stood watching him with astonishment, uncertain how to deal with such an unaccustomed outburst, he carried on heatedly: 'I am deeply sorry, my lady, that I have proved so poor a protector.'

'How can you say so?' she argued with a fierceness that matched his own. 'We are alive and well, and almost at our journey's end. No man could have done more.' To his amazement she closed the gap between them and putting her arms around his neck, kissed him soundly on the lips. 'Thank you,' she said, and kissed him again, more gently.

He protested, resisting the temptation to wrap his arms around her and hold her close. 'A better man would have saved you much hardship and hunger.'

'There can be no better man than you, Dunn,' she answered gravely. 'Do you think I could have come so far without you, my dear friend and comforter? Whenever I need a strong arm to lean upon, you are always there. You alone have made it possible for me to bear my great sorrow and loss.'

'You know why, don't you?' he blurted out, unable to stop himself. She released him and put a finger to his lips. Their eyes met and he knew he must say no more. Aelfrun turned to hurry after her son, now several yards down the road, and he watched her go with joy in his heart.

At last, he thought gladly, she knows that I love her; and for now that was enough.

'A dust of dried dung will see him right, mistress,' the serving woman insisted.

Estrith looked at her husband shivering feverishly on a bed of bracken and shook her head. Once again the deep axe wound in his shoulder had reopened and, as his life's blood seeped slowly but relentlessly through the bandages, he grew steadily weaker.

'I have seen men die of such treatment,' she argued wearily.

'He will die within hours, lady, if we do nothing to stop the bleeding.'

Estrith went to the entrance of the cave which sheltered them and stared out across the mountains. She blinked back tears and prayed that she would make the right decision. Wulfhere's life was in her hands.

Wulfhere had been wounded at Fulford, fighting beside Earl Morcar against Tostig, his erstwhile lord.

In the last hour of the battle he had received a blow from an axe which had, at first, presented few problems, and he had returned home with all that remained of the small force he had led into battle. Then, a few days later, news had reached them of William's invasion and Wulfhere, whose wound had not even begun to heal, had sent his men to join King Harold in York.

By the time the Scots invaded the north, Wulfhere had been too weak to do more than order a retreat into the hills. Now, less than six weeks after Harold's victory at Stamford Bridge, he was obviously close to death.

'Fetch the blacksmith, Edgiva,' Estrith said at last, turning and facing down the older woman who glared back furiously.

'On your head be it,' Edgiva said coldly as she moved to obey. 'If you choose to ignore my advice, then I hope you have the strength to bear the consequences.'

'Don't be angry, please,' Estrith pleaded.

It had taken them a long time to win acceptance here in the north, where, as foreigners, they had been regarded with suspicion. Wulfhere's stand against Earl Tostig's heavy-handed rule had earned him the respect of the local thegns, but Estrith suspected that the loyalty of the people was a fragile thing, not to be tested beyond endurance.

'I know you have done your best, but now we must try something else,' Estrith said, this time more firmly. 'It will soon be too late. Once when we were hunting, my horse tore itself on a broken branch, and the blacksmith sewed the wound with horsehair and dressed it with moss. It healed well and quickly.'

'A horse is not a man,' the maid countered, unconvinced.

'They are both flesh and blood,' Estrith replied. 'Waste no more time, I beg you, but do as I bid.'

Edgiva left, muttering crossly, and Estrith busied herself preparing an infusion of soothing herbs: thyme, fennel and feverfew. Blowing on the bowl to cool the potion she sang a charm on each of the herbs, then knelt beside her husband and, raising his head, coaxed him tenderly to take a few sips. She was holding him still, with his head pressed to her breast, when Edgiva returned with the blacksmith and his boy.

The man had the bone needle and strands of hair ready in his hands. 'I've not done this to a man before,' he cautioned her gruffly. 'You'll not hold me to blame if it goes amiss?'

Estrith shook her head. 'I will pray for God to guide your hand,' she said, unwrapping the bandages carefully from around the wound. 'Do you want me to hold him still for you?'

'It would be easier for us if you were not here, mistress.'

He peered at the wound and gave a small grunt of dismay at the signs of infection.

Estrith seemed reluctant to leave, but Edgiva took her arm and led her outside.

A fierce wind buffeted them cruelly as they left the cave, whipping at their cloaks.

The cave they had just left was the smallest of a group of three, the others providing shelter for the villagers, their dogs and their fowl. The rest of the livestock had been penned securely in a small gully blocked by a rockfall at one end and a wattle fence at the other. This refuge was well known to the villagers, since border raids were far from uncommon, but limited grazing and heavy snowfalls made a lengthy stay impossible at this time of year. Leaden skies and chill winds now gave warning that soon they must return into the valley.

There were about twenty people here, most of them women and children. The men, for the most part, were either long in years or, like the blacksmith, essential to the village. Very few of the younger, able-bodied men had returned from the battles of Fulford and Stamford Bridge.

The two women made their way to the second cave and a space was made for them at the fire. Someone handed Estrith a bowl of hot broth which she accepted gratefully, suddenly aware that she had not eaten all day. Wearily she sat listening to the conversation around her, with one eye on the entrance to see the smith return. It was not the smith, however, who came in next, but a young boy called Ulf whose grandmother had stayed behind in the village. He made his way over to Estrith and tugged on her sleeve.

'I have been to take food to my grandmother, Ulla,' he told her, wiping his dripping nose on his sleeve.

'That was kind of you,' Estrith replied, puzzled, wondering why she had been singled out to receive this particular piece of information. 'She was safe and well, I hope. Has there been any sign of the raiders?'

Ulf shook his head solemnly. 'Your sister has been there,' he said.

Estrith's weariness disappeared. 'Which sister?' she cried eagerly. 'It was Aelfrun wasn't it? Was that her name? Where is she now? Was she alone?' She had gripped the boy by the shoulders and each question was punctuated by a small shake.

'She didn't say what the lady's name was,' answered Ulf, slipping out of her grasp, 'but she was with a man, probably a servant, and she had a small boy. Grandmother told them to come here by the long road because she was sure they would lose themselves if she sent them the short way.'

Estrith nodded, knowing that only those born and bred in these hills could find their way on the pathless moors. 'It's Aelfrun and her son, I know it. How long ago did they leave?'

'Soon after yesterday sunrise.'

'They should have been here by now,' she fretted. 'We must look for them. You, Ulf, take some of the other boys and follow the long road back to the village, spreading out to look for tracks. There will be a reward for the one who brings them safely here to me.'

Full of enthusiasm, Ulf left on his mission.

The sound of crying drew Estrith to her other duties. In a large wicker basket her infant sons had woken from sleep and demanded to be fed. She carried them away from the crowd around the fire and, sitting cross-legged on the floor, she put them to the breast, turn and turn about, under the enveloping folds of her cloak.

She looked up unabashed as the smith entered the cave and approached her. 'My husband?' she asked.

'The bleeding has stopped and if you can keep him still for a few days, all may be well, though he'll not have good use of that left arm ever again. The fever is the danger now: it weakens him and makes him restless.'

'Thank you, Thorkil, I am grateful.'

'I have heard, lady, that there may be kin of yours lost on the hills. If you wish, I will join the search for them.'

'That would be another debt of gratitude I owe you, Thorkil,' Estrith replied gratefully. 'You are a kind man.'

The smith looked a little uncomfortable at this praise and hurried away. Edgiva came over to help wash the babies and change their linen.

'Well,' she offered grudgingly, having been to see the sleeping Wulfhere, 'he does seem a bit better.'

Estrith smiled. 'Look after the children,' she said contentedly. 'I must go to him now.'

She was still with Wulfhere when Thorkil came back. He stood in front of her with a sombre expression on his craggy features and she felt her heart sink as he continued to stand without speaking for what seemed an eternity.

'Have you found them?' she asked, her voice trembling and her face drained of colour.

Thorkil stretched out his hand and opened his huge, calloused fist to reveal to her grief-stricken eyes a broken ivory comb and the tattered remains of an embroidered pin-cushion.

There was blood on them both.

Another two minutes, three at most, would have seen them safely back under cover of the trees. A stream, not wide but too deep and fast-flowing for them to cross, had blocked their path and forced them back onto the road where it was spanned by a small timber bridge.

Dunn was already on this bridge when the attack came, so sudden and unexpected that he hardly had time to unhook the axe from his belt and shout a warning before the riders were upon him.

Aelfrun, trailing several yards behind with Siggi, heard his cry and looked up, but it was too late. She watched in horror as a small band of ragged Scots, mounted on ponies every bit as shaggy and unkempt as their riders, bore down upon Dunn who, in a half crouch, waited for them with his axe held defiantly in both hands.

155

'Run,' he screamed again. Aelfrun hesitated barely one second before snatching up her son in one arm and hoisting up her skirts with the other.

She ran for the cover of the trees with a speed only possible through sheer terror. Her heart pounded as though it would burst, her lips moved in soundless, desperate prayer, but all was in vain. Dunn fought valiantly, but hard as he tried, he managed to win for them only a few brief seconds before a blow from a club smashed his right arm and a series of blows brought him first to his knees, then felled him altogether. It was the woman now who interested the raiders, and they left Dunn bleeding on the ground to give chase, whooping in anticipation.

Dunn felt no pain, only a seductive weakness that gradually began to steal over him, holding out a promise of peace and rest. Briefly he resisted; then, as memory faded, he allowed himself to succumb and drift slowly into unconsciousness.

It was only Aelfrun's shrill scream that pierced his growing lethargy. He shook his head to clear the mists that shrouded his vision. 'Aelfrun,' he cried, but the word came out as a whisper. 'Where are you,' he called again, struggling with the confusion in his mind.

Dimly, he saw her dragged and thrown to the ground almost at his side. The leader of the band, a man of remarkable height and startling, snow-white hair, was holding Siggi by the ankles, dangling him before her eyes. In graphic and brutal mime he illustrated his intention to smash the small head to the ground, and Aelfrun, with a piteous cry, ceased to struggle against the two men holding her down.

The white-haired man glanced at the limp and unresisting body in his hands and, almost in irritation, tossed the boy aside. Siggi landed on the bank of the river and began to slide into the water.

'Save him,' Aelfrun screamed. The Scots may not have understood her words, but her meaning was more than clear. One of the men rushed to the river bank, and then, looking back at her with a harsh laugh, he gave the almost unconscious child a final push with his booted foot.

Aelfrun stopped screaming. She lay rigid and unmoving, her eyes round, dark pools of horror and disbelief.

Unable to bear the sight of her agony, Dunn fought to overcome his pain and weakness. He struggled to pull the knife from his

156

belt and managed to push it unobserved towards Aelfrun's outflung hand. There was only one thought in his mind; to give his love the means to end her life. By now, her skirts had been pulled up to her waist and she lay exposed to the eager eyes and rough, probing fingers of the raiders as they pulled apart her legs and squeezed her breasts with hard, ungentle hands.

The white-haired man fumbled to undo his leggings while his companions made avid noises of anticipation. No one noticed the knife concealed beneath the hand Dunn stretched out towards her.

The Scot was now moving relentlessly above her, his hips rising and falling with a rhythmic intensity. Aelfrun lay motionless, unresisting beneath him, her face white with shock. With a grunt, the man spent himself, rising at once to allow another to take his place. The other men, waiting their turn, had moved away and were pulling apart the discarded bundles of their victims, scattering and destroying that which was of no use to them, keeping anything of value.

Dunn drew on the last of his strength and touched Aelfrun's fingers with his own, pushing the hilt of the knife almost into her hand. 'Aelfrun,' he pleaded weakly, 'hear me my love, I beg you.' For the first time, her eyes flickered and turned slightly in his direction. 'The knife,' he hissed desperately, 'it's in your hand.'

This time she seemed to hear, and as consciousness left him, he saw her grasp the knife and raise it purposefully above her head.

With all her strength, Aelfrun stabbed the knife into the throat of the man who pounded above her, thrusting himself mercilessly again and again into her bruised and bloodied flesh. He shrieked just once before he died in a fountain of blood, drawing howls of rage from his shocked companions.

Aelfrun closed her eyes and prayed earnestly for death.

Thorkil followed the trail until it was almost dark. He hadn't intended to come searching, he knew it to be hopeless. It was the look on the lady Estrith's face which had persuaded him; a look of such terrible grief and despair that he had been helpless before its power. She had asked nothing of him, but he knew that until every last hope had been exhausted, his conscience would not let him rest.

Estrith had been wrong to doubt the loyalty of her people;

Wulfhere's fair-mindedness and her own unwavering kindness had won their grudging affection long since. Thorkil would not abandon her kin if there was any chance at all of saving them.

He had begun his search from the bridge where the attack had obviously taken place. For some reason the Scots had chosen to turn around and head away from Blackwater at this point. Perhaps, he guessed, they had been discouraged by empty, profit-less fields and villages and had decided to make do with what they had; perhaps it was the smell of snow in the air. Whatever the reason, it was certain that they had gone.

He knelt in the road and fingered a spot of dried blood. A good sign perhaps. It might mean that one of the captives was injured, and, if so, it was also possible that they were all still alive. He had found no bodies; that, at least, might bring some comfort.

He stood up and prodded a pile of horse dung with his foot. It was at least a day old; there was no hope at all of catching up with the raiders. He sighed heavily and began to turn back.

All at once he heard a noise, a strange sound that was not of the night or the forest. He stopped and listened. The sound had come from his right; he cocked his ear in that direction. It came again. He moved cautiously towards the trees, his knife held ready in his hand. It was dark in the forest and his grip on the knife tightened.

Suddenly a flash of fur hurtled past his legs and as he recoiled in shock he caught a glimpse of wild, yellow eyes and lips drawn back from bloodied teeth. The wolf, equally startled, disappeared into the trees and Thorkil stared after it in astonishment. What was a wolf doing so close to the road? What had it been feeding on? He hurried in the direction from which the wolf had come and within moments came upon a sight which brought bile to his throat.

A man, stripped and beaten, hung by his wrists from the branch of a tree, his feet barely scraping the ground. Blood from a head wound had made a bright shawl over his neck and shoul-ders, and the flesh of his belly was torn where the wolf had tried to rip out his entrails.

Thorkil was sure the man must be dead, but then from his lips came the now familiar sound, a low cry of such agony that it drew a cry from Thorkil's own lips as he plunged forward to hack at the man's bonds and lower him gently to the ground.

He examined the man's body with deft fingers and found to his

158

relief that the wolf had been disturbed before it had done much more than break the skin. The wound was nasty, but not fatal. The right arm was broken in several places, the body badly lacerated and almost black with bruises. He had lost a great deal of blood from the head wound, but the bleeding had stopped. He might live, given care.

Thorkil sat back on his heels and pondered while chewing thoughtfully at his lip. He would take the man to Ulla, he decided; she would tend his wounds. She was also a woman who could hold her tongue, and, as an idea began to take shape in his head, Thorkil thought he might need her silence.

What comfort could it be, he asked himself, for the lady Estrith to know that her kin were in the hands of such devils? Should he tell her that he had found them dead? he wondered. No, that wouldn't do, he realized; she would be sure to want to give them a Christian burial.

He frowned and thought again. Inspiration struck! He would make false graves in the churchyard and the priest could say the words over them; no one need see the actual bodies.

Well satisfied with this solution, Thorkil heaved the unconscious Dunn across his powerful shoulders and set off back along the road to Blackwater.

X

January–February 1067

Crouching uncomfortably in the dirt of a filthy back alley, Ceolwynn had one ear tightly pressed to a chink in the rear wall of a cobbler's shop, straining to hear what Cenred and Aldhere were discussing. Their voices were so low that she had difficulty in grasping more than a few words at a time, but she had just begun to make sense of most of it.

The weeks since Aelfrun's departure had seen Cenred regain both his strength and his spirit, and with them the will to carry on the fight against the Norman. Ceolwynn knew that he and Aldhere were involved in something secret and dangerous, but to her intense annoyance he refused to let her know anything at all about their plots and schemes, reminding her often that a wife's role was simply to serve and obey. His attitude infuriated her, and she'd long since made up her mind that she would never marry him, but she was desperately curious to know what he was up to here in Lullingworth.

It was Hild who had had the idea that they should follow the two men the next time they left the village together, and so far her plan had worked.

In their hooded peasant cloaks it had been quite easy to follow the slow-moving wagon. In the crowded streets the men had stopped first at an alehouse, where they sat for about half an hour. Every now and then Hild would wander past the door and glance furtively through it, reporting each time that they were still sitting alone. At last they had come out again, taking care to look about them, before hurrying away towards their meeting here in the shop.

Ceolwynn guessed that they had, in fact, received some

message while in the alehouse, and she began to understand their caution. There were strangers in the streets of Lullingworth; well-armed men with cropped hair and arrogant manners, pushing the English out of their way, leering at the women and helping themselves without payment from the market stalls. They spoke in French and in other tongues that Ceolwynn didn't recognize, but it was all too clear that they regarded themselves as the masters here, and Ceolwynn had suddenly realized that this was no game that Cenred was playing. He was, without doubt, regarded as a traitor by his new king and in very real danger of his life. Small wonder he has been so secretive, she thought.

'What can you hear?' Hild asked again, tugging insistently at Ceolwynn's shoulder. Godmund's will had freed all his personal slaves, including Hild and her mother, Eadburg. Though still a servant, Hild's new status had shifted the balance of their relationship, with the bonds of friendship now outweighing those of mere service.

Ceolwynn got up. 'They're leaving,' she whispered. 'Let's go; I'll tell you all I know once we're on our way. We must get back home before Lord Cenred.'

Once they were safely on the road home, Ceolwynn explained the little she had managed to overhear, but was careful not to say too much. She trusted Hild, but Cenred's caution had begun to affect her too.

'Lord Cenred,' she confided, 'plans to join a man they call Edric the Wild, who's organizing rebellion in the west, but in the north and in Kent and the eastern shires as well, men begin to band together against the Norman. Lord Cenred, by passing information and training men in the use of arms, is to play his part.'

'He will hang if they catch him,' Hild breathed.

'Or worse,' Ceolwynn agreed, and they both shuddered. Ceolwynn looked back over her shoulder and fixed her friend with a fierce look. 'Not a word of this must you speak to anyone, do you understand?'

'Of course,' Hild protested, quite offended.

'Lord Cenred plans to leave for Hereford any day now,' Ceolwynn said, 'and will expect me to go with him. We must think of a way to stop me travelling with him.'

'You're not going?' Hild said, astonished. 'But you are to be married.'

161

'No,' Ceolwynn replied firmly, 'but he mustn't know that until it's too late. What do you suggest? Should I suddenly be taken ill? Could we make that convincing?'

Hild had given up trying to sort out all Ceolwynn's changes of plans and just bent her mind to the immediate problem. 'There are herbs which can give the appearance of illness, but can you be sure that Lord Cenred will just abandon you if you are ill? He is, after all, a man of honour.'

Ceolwynn sighed. 'You are quite right. And if he stays too long he may well be caught, especially now that there are Normans in this area.'

The problem remained unresolved until their arrival back at Cottesham, when they discovered that the whole matter was no longer in their hands at all.

The green in front of the hall was full of soldiers, milling about in undisciplined fashion on their enormous warhorses and shouting orders at a sullen and uncomprehending household.

Realizing that her peasant disguise could be useful, Ceolwynn slid from the horse and signalled Hild to slip back into the woods and wait for her there. There was so much noise and confusion everywhere that no one had seen their arrival, and within seconds Hild and the horse had disappeared from sight. Ceolwynn crept closer to the hall.

'Who is in charge here?' one of the knights kept shouting. Since no one understood him, no one answered, and the knight grew angrier and angrier, raising his voice still more as if that would make things clearer.

'I seek the Lady Aelfrun,' the knight tried again. The name, though ill pronounced, evoked a response of sorts and, heartened by this, the knight singled out one young man for his attentions. 'Where is she?' he asked. 'Where can I find her?'

Unfortunately, he had picked on Bedric, Father Eadric's idiot son, who after seeming to study the question carefully for several moments, began to dribble slowly down his chin.

The knight dealt him such a blow with a mail-fisted hand that the lad fell bleeding to the ground. Father Eadric rushed to his son's aid, anxiously wiping the blood from his face with the hem of his robe. Seeing that he was a priest, the knight began to address him in very poor Latin, but Eadric, beside himself with fury, pretended ignorance.

162

Folca, however, seized the opportunity to ingratiate himself by demonstrating his own knowledge of that language. 'I am Folca, steward of this estate. How may I be of service to you?' he asked with servile courtesy.

'I have a message for the mistress of this manor,' the knight said, 'and must put it into her own hand and no other.'

'Then your journey has been a wasted one,' Folca told him. 'The lady is no longer here and, to the best of my knowledge, has no plans to return.'

The knight looked crestfallen. It was obvious that his orders had not prepared him for this contingency, and he was now uncertain what he should do next. 'Is there anyone in authority here?' he asked, almost plaintively.

Before Folca could speak, the priest, who had just caught sight of Ceolwynn lurking at the edge of the crowd, interrupted him quickly in French. He would have preferred to conceal his knowledge of that tongue, but his concern for Ceolwynn prompted him to try to discover just what this vile intruder wanted of them. 'Our lord is dead, our mistress departed,' he said, 'there is no one else but the steward and myself.'

The knight glowered at him, angry that the priest had pretended not to understand him, but finally decided not to make an issue of it. 'We will stay here tonight,' he said arrogantly, handing his reins to Folca and walking away.

'May I ask your name and whom you serve?' Father Eadric enquired, hurrying after him.

The knight looked as though he was going to refuse to answer, but changed his mind. 'My name is Alain d'Ivry and I serve Roger of Montgomery, lord of Surrey, Sussex and Hampshire,' he said proudly. 'The letter I carry, however, is not from him, but from another.'

'What is the name of this other man?' the priest asked.

Alain shrugged indifferently. 'I was simply told by my lord to deliver the letter on my way. I didn't ask who it was from; all I know is that the man who sent it is to be the new master of these estates.'

'Thank you,' Father Eadric replied civilly, and when Alain left him to make his way to the hall, he sidled over to Ceolwynn and muttered at her from the corner of his mouth. 'I won't ask why you are dressed like that, but I thank God for it. You must find

163

Lord Cenred, intercept him on the road and tell him to flee at once. Goodbye my child, and God go with you both.' He walked quickly away before she could answer him.

He was right, she realized at once, Cenred had to be warned without delay. Swiftly she made her way back to where Hild was waiting, whereupon the girl fell upon her, almost in tears.

'What's happening?' she wailed. 'I thought you were never coming back, and I didn't know what I should do.'

'Stop whimpering and listen,' Ceolwynn said. She spoke sharply to get Hild's attention. 'Go back along the road and find Lord Cenred,' Ceolwynn told her. 'Warn him that the Normans have arrived and that he must flee at once. Tell him that I am in their hands, but that I am safe and being well treated. I don't want him trying to rescue me,' she explained in response to Hild's puzzled expression. 'Give him the horse and come back yourself on the cart with Aldhere. You will be in no danger, the Normans will be gone tomorrow, but be careful not to let Lord Cenred know that. Is that all clear?' Hild nodded and Ceolwynn helped her back up onto the horse. 'Hurry,' she said. 'On no account must Lord Cenred come within sight of Cottesham.' She slapped the horse on the rump, and, with an initial shocked leap, the animal lumbered away at a fast trot, Hild clinging desperately to his mane.

Ceolwynn watched her until she was out of sight, then made her way back to the village. Everyone seemed to have disappeared indoors, obviously trying to avoid any trouble with the soldiers, and Ceolwynn managed to slip into the priest's house without being seen.

At her entrance, Father Eadric almost dropped the spoon he was raising to his lips. 'What are you doing here?' he hissed.

'Don't worry,' she said cheerfully, helping herself to half his loaf, 'Hild will find Cenred. I'm staying here.' She bit into the bread and grinned at his shocked expression.

'But you can't,' he argued helplessly. 'Lord Cenred is supposed to take care of you. It's what your father, and the lady Aelfrun, both wanted.'

'Too late now,' she said. 'I'll stay here tonight until those horrid Normans go, then I'll move back into the hall. Can I have some of that soup?'

'My dear child,' he protested, absently pouring her a bowl,

'don't you realize what you've done? Lord Cenred is your only possible protector. You must have heard what the knight said, our new lord is doubtless on his way here even now. That letter was probably to tell the lady Aelfrun so, and to bid her depart. Where in the world will you go now?'

'Lord Cenred,' she replied, suddenly serious, 'is likely to spend the rest of his life as an outlaw, and will, in all probability, finish it at the end of a rope. I think that I may fare better on my own, don't you?'

Father Eadric looked flustered. He hadn't expected her to be so sure of herself, and he had to admit that she had a point. 'But where *will* you go?' he fretted.

'I don't know yet,' she answered him frankly, 'But I refuse to leave Cottesham one moment sooner than I have to.' She gulped the soup down hungrily. 'If our new *master*,' she said, emphasizing the word bitterly, 'permits me to stay, even as a servant, then stay I shall. As you have been at such great pains to tell me, Father, I have nowhere else to go.'

Father Eadric shook his head and sighed unhappily.

From the doorway of the hall, half hidden in its shadows, Ceolwynn watched the Normans come.

She had put on her finest gown and prepared herself to accept with dignity whatever future the Good Lord chose to thrust upon her, standing stiff-backed and proud in front of her people with her hands clasped tightly together to hide their trembling.

Outside, the winter sun shone with unseasonable brightness, lending to the scene an air of false cheer quite at odds with the fierce hostility in the faces of the waiting men and women. Their resentment and fear created a wall of emotion almost palpable, and Renaud felt the back of his neck prickle as he attempted to lead his men through the silent crowd which blocked his access to the hall and forced him to a halt.

The halt was brief; Renaud paused for only a moment before gently spurring his horse forward again. The crowd parted slowly, reluctantly. Renaud rode up to the hall and dismounted, holding out his reins with such authority that, out of habit, a stable boy took them from him. Renaud grinned inwardly at this small victory and removed his helmet, sweeping the once-familiar scene with his eyes and noticing for the first time the woman in the doorway.

He took a step towards her, wondering who she might be. He knew from Montgomery's messenger that Aelfrun had already left Cottesham and had assumed that Ceolwynn would have gone with her. So, as he stepped forward to make himself known, it never occurred to him that this might be Ceolwynn herself.

A quiet muttering began as some people in the crowd thought they recognized him, but it took Ceolwynn several moments to see in this tall, lean young man with battle-hardened features, the boy who had once been her friend; but recognize him at last she did.

Momentarily faint with the shock of it, she closed her eyes and reached out blindly for the doorframe to stop herself falling, only to find Renaud's strong arm beneath hers, supporting her.

'Come, let me help you inside, lady,' he said. The words were gently solicitous, but his tone was distant, formal.

Ceolwynn, unaware that Renaud had, in fact, no idea who she was, was thankful that at least he was making no attempt to call upon old affections. Wordlessly she accepted his help and allowed herself to be led away from the host of curious eyes that watched them with both a considerably heightened interest and a consequent lessening of tension.

'Are you ill?' Renaud asked, helping her to a seat. 'Is there anything I can get for you?'

Hild was hovering anxiously nearby and when Ceolwynn, still shaken, made no reply, Renaud ordered the maid to bring wine for her mistress.

Ceolwynn sipped the wine and thought desperately how she should respond to this unexpected turn of events. Her first overwhelming sense of relief that this was no fierce stranger come among them had soon been replaced by an awareness that he was, nonetheless, still her enemy. His hands were stained with the blood of her people, and he could have no other purpose here but to steal what was rightfully hers. She remembered her father's bloodied body, wrapped in a sack like a slab of meat, and this strengthened her anger.

Renaud watched her with curiosity, but waited patiently and courteously for her to recover herself. He had barely glimpsed her features, and her hair, braided and covered by her headdress, was concealed from him; yet still he had the distinct impression that this was a singularly lovely young woman.

Eventually, she put down her cup and fixed him with a look from her startlingly blue eyes. 'So, Renaud de Lassay,' she began bitterly, 'you choose a strange way to repay our past friendship and hospitality.'

His reaction was not what she had expected; he looked stunned, and the power of speech seemed to have deserted him.

After a moment, he reached out and took between his fingers an errant tendril of hair escaping from its covering. It seemed to convince him that he was not imagining things and, finding his tongue, he said hesitantly: 'Ceolwynn? Can it really be you?'

'Who else did you expect to find here?' she asked shortly, rather surprised that he had not known her from the start.

'I knew that Aelfrun had gone,' he replied, 'and thought that you must surely have gone with her.'

Fascinated, he studied the face of the young woman whose eyes bored so fiercely into his own, and laughed at his own stupidity. All these years he had imagined Ceolwynn a child still. How could he not have realized that a girl must become a woman just as surely as he himself had become a man? He smiled in wonderment at the transformation, and in sheer delight at seeing her again.

Ceolwynn did not smile back. 'My presence must be a great inconvenience to you,' she sneered. 'No doubt you were hoping to take over my father's lands without ever having to come face to face with those whose friendship you had betrayed. What was it you wrote in your letter to Aelfrun? That we should be gone from here before you arrived? I'm sorry to disappoint you, my lord, but you will not drive me from my home quite as easily as that.'

'That was never my intention,' he protested, but before he could explain she stood up and struck him across the face with the palm of her hand.

Renaud staggered from the force of the unexpected blow and Ceolwynn, her hand stinging painfully, stepped back quickly, half expecting him to retaliate.

He didn't, and the hurt, puzzled expression in his eyes just added fuel to her anger.

'Norman dog,' she spat venomously. 'Coward, traitor, lackey of an ill-begotten bastard,' she shouted.

Renaud just looked at her, rubbing his cheek slowly. He made no effort to restrain her outpourings and his lack of resistance finally defeated her. Sobbing bitterly, she collapsed back onto her stool and pressed her face into her hands.

Renaud was confused; her tears upset him, but her obvious hatred distressed him more. Wisely, he resisted the impulse to put his arm about her, sensing that there was no comfort he might have to offer that she would accept from him now.

He decided that he would have to try to talk to her at another time, when she was calmer and more amenable to reason. Instead, he looked around for the maid, and Hild, always close at hand, quickly came forward at his signal to take Ceolwynn away. The other servants in the hall glared at him, but when he gave instructions for his men to be housed and fed, and for their horses to be stabled, no one resisted his orders.

He began to make Cottesham his own.

Ceolwynn confined herself to her room for five days, half hoping that Renaud would eventually send his men to drag her out forcibly, thereby proving beyond all doubt that he was nothing more than the foul brute that she expected him to be.

The fact that he did no such thing, and that he freely allowed Hild to bring her food, drink and anything else she required, did little to change or improve her opinion of him.

She questioned her maid closely, but Hild's reports of Renaud's irreproachable behaviour caused her even greater annoyance. Each morning, Hild told her, Renaud asked after Ceolwynn's welfare and asked if there was anything she needed. Satisfied that there was nothing he could do for her, Renaud would then not mention her again until the following morning. In the meantime, he busied himself about the manor, earning, if not good will, then at least a grudging respect for his willingness to listen and to learn.

It was increasingly obvious to Ceolwynn that even her maid was being won over, and one day she was infuriated to detect a note of admiration in Hild's voice when she spoke of her new lord.

On the fifth day, Father Eadric came to see her. She greeted him warmly, eager to share her rancour and fury. His first words, however, were disappointing.

'Come, my child,' he said, 'you must stop hiding yourself away like this.'

'I'm not hiding,' she said indignantly, annoyed that her protest might be seen in such a way. 'I'm just waiting to find out what Cottesham's new master intends to do about me.'

'It was Lord Renaud himself who sent me to speak with you today,' Father Eadric started to tell her, but she didn't let him finish.

'Ah ha!' she interrupted gleefully, 'so he could no longer prevent you from seeing me then?'

The priest looked puzzled. 'Not at all; he's never tried to prevent me seeing you,' he said. 'Hild said you would speak to no one, or I would have come sooner.'

Ceolwynn looked momentarily discomfited, but then when she heard the rest of what he had to say she turned on him in astonishment. 'Give thanks?' she cried out, appalled. 'For what, in Heaven's name, should we give thanks?'

'Why, that a man who is so well disposed towards our people should be the one set over us. Truly, God was listening when we prayed that Cottesham should be safe from all harm. I've heard that some Normans are very fiends incarnate, bringing much suffering upon the heads of those they now rule.'

Ceolwynn shook her head in despair. 'Even you, Father,' she murmured accusingly. 'Can't you see? I have lost everything – home, family, even my betrothed.' The priest raised his eyebrows slightly at this last and Ceolwynn was forced to smile at herself just a little. 'Well, all right,' she conceded, 'I chose not to go with Cenred, but you cannot deny the rest. Besides, if the Normans had not come, we would have been married already and I would probably have been quite content. It is only the change in circumstances which has changed my heart.'

'Be that as it may,' Father Eadric agreed, 'things *have* changed and out of several possible outcomes of these tragic events, to have Renaud de Lassay as our new lord is probably the most satisfactory.'

'I am amazed that you can even think that way,' Ceolwynn argued fiercely. 'This man called himself our friend, yet he is perfectly willing that my family should be dispossessed for his own personal gain. How can you defend and support any Norman?'

'Come out and speak to him for yourself, my lady. He asks that you join him at supper this evening so that you can talk about your future. I believe that the young man has a good heart and bears you no ill will. Put yourself in his hands, I pray you, and you will have nothing to fear.'

'I fear nothing now,' she replied, clenching her fists, 'but I will do as you ask. I know I cannot stay in here for ever, and since de Lassay seems to have won over even those I regarded as my friends, I have no choice but to submit to his will.'

Father Eadric tutted irritably. 'There is no question of submission in this, my child,' he said. 'You will only make things worse if you stubbornly persist in rejecting his efforts at reconciliation.'

'I have said I will speak to him,' she answered tersely. 'Go and tell your new lord that I will obey his summons.'

The priest gave an exasperated grunt and left her alone.

Hild, relieved that her mistress was to leave her self-imposed seclusion, dusted off Ceolwynn's best gown, dark green velvet embroidered with gold thread and tiny pearls, and held it up. 'There's no doubt that this one looks very well on you,' she remarked. 'He can't help but notice how pretty you are in this.'

'Hild,' Ceolwynn muttered disagreeably, 'I almost wish my father hadn't freed you after all. It's made you far too free with your opinions.'

Hild just shrugged and went to fetch some water, and later, as Ceolwynn made her way to the hall feeling far more nervous and apprehensive than she would admit, even to herself, she was grateful that Hild had persuaded her to look her best. She was wearing the green gown, and her hair, braided but uncovered, was hanging in one thick plait over her shoulder, crowned with a circlet of gold that had once belonged to Cengifu. She had made a point of hanging the household keys at her girdle, realizing with some surprise as she did so that Renaud had not sent to demand them of her, as he might well have done.

Holding her head high she took her place at the high table without waiting for Renaud to indicate where she should sit, half afraid that he might be planning to humiliate her by placing her below the salt, but Renaud had no such intention. He watched her stately entrance and calm assumption of place with veiled amusement, as aware as she was that her place in this hall, if place she had, was now his alone to decide.

He smiled a welcome as he greeted her and took his place at her side, and she replied to his greeting with formal courtesy, beyond which neither could think of anything to say.

Food was brought and they filled the silence that languished between them with the clatter of spoons and bowls and a pretence of eating. Even the chatter of the lower table was muted, and Ceolwynn noted that the priest and the steward, although both seated at the high table, had been placed far enough away so that any softly spoken words between herself and Renaud might not be overheard. Since neither of them seemed much inclined to conversation, Ceolwynn thought wryly, that seemed a somewhat unnecessary device.

After a while, the continued silence made her feel uncomfortable, but Renaud appeared almost unconcerned by their situation, politely passing dishes and refilling her wine cup so often that she began to feel a little light-headed.

She avoided his eye, keeping hers directed firmly at the table, but occasionally sneaking a glance at his face, curious despite herself to discover what kind of a man he had become. The laughing, mischievous quality she remembered had disappeared from his eyes, but she thought she saw humour in them still, and a gentleness which, in the circumstances, she would have preferred not to acknowledge.

Slowly, the anger she had been nursing so carefully for the past few days began to evaporate. However hard she tried, it was impossible to think of Renaud as some unholy monster when he had offered her no unkindness or discourtesy at all. In fact, if she were honest, he had been exceptionally patient and tolerant. By comparison, she thought with embarrassment, it was possible that her own behaviour might perhaps have seemed just a little childish.

As though he sensed a slight weakening in her armour, Renaud turned and smiled at her, and in that smile she saw again the cheerful, confident boy who had once shared her dreams and brought laughter into her life. The memory warmed her, and she found herself wanting to smile back at him and to find some way to bridge this terrible, yawning chasm between them.

A host of questions flooded into her head, all of them beginning: Do you remember when? – but then she recalled a time long ago when they had laughed together at Cenred and his clumsy, ponderous ways. It was that same brave, loyal Cenred, she remembered, who was now a fugitive in his own land while she dined with his enemies. Flushing with self-reproach, she let any seeds of goodwill towards Renaud wither and die.

Renaud, who had recently come to an important decision relating to Ceolwynn's future, had been quite apprehensive about this encounter, and although he cleared his throat several times as if about to speak, the meal was half over before he ventured to put to Ceolwynn the first of the many questions that had been on his own mind.

'Do you know where Aelfrun has gone?' he asked suddenly.

It came out more abruptly than he had intended and Ceolwynn, startled, hastily swallowed the piece of bread she had been eating and laid down her knife. 'To her sister, Estrith,' she answered stiffly.

'I remember Estrith,' he said with genuine pleasure, but the hard, unblinking stare she turned on him was a clear warning that it would be useless to try to use the past as a means of bringing about some sort of peace between them. 'I take it that she is married,' he tried again. 'Did she marry well?'

'*I* think so. She married Wulfhere.'

Renaud looked surprised, but pleased. 'Godmund allowed that?' he said in amazement. 'I'll wager it was Aelfrun's doing.'

Ceolwynn could hardly believe her ears. How could he sit there, in her father's place, and talk as though nothing had changed? Did he really think that she wanted to sit here with him gossiping about old times, old friendships? She was not going to allow him to divert her so easily. 'Aelfrun left here,' she said bluntly, 'because she feared for the safety of her son at Norman hands. I stayed because this is my home and because here my father lies untimely in his grave, a victim of Norman greed and dishonour.'

'Dishonour?' he protested, stung by the insult. 'There is nothing dishonourable in claiming what is your own. Duke William was promised the crown by King Edward himself.'

'Then did my father promise you Cottesham?' she asked bitterly. 'Is it on a promise unseen and unheard by any other that you base your claim to be master here?'

'Of course not,' he answered impatiently, annoyed with himself for adding more fuel to a fire already raging fiercely enough without his help. Clearly, he thought, this young woman was going to prove every bit as headstrong and stubborn as the child he had known, and it was obvious that if she was to be persuaded to listen to him, he must do all in his power to avoid antagonizing her further. 'Aelfrun has a son, you say?' he said, changing the subject. 'I'm very glad for her.'

'Why?' Ceolwynn asked shortly. 'What has she to give him? At best, another's charity; at worst, poverty and starvation.'

'It was to prevent such a thing that I came here, Ceolwynn,' Renaud said quietly. 'I understand how you must feel about me – I didn't at first, I will admit, and it was stupid of me to think that I might be welcomed here, but, believe me, my intentions were good.'

'What do you mean?' she asked, still angry. 'How can the intention behind theft ever be "good"?'

'I will try to explain,' he said angrily. His raised voice and the thump of his fist on the table caused even the little conversation lower down the table to cease altogether, and Father Eadric glanced towards them anxiously. Ceolwynn retreated into a sulky silence, and Renaud took a deep breath before continuing more calmly: 'Your father's lands were forfeit to William at the very moment King Harold fell. Nothing could or would have changed that fact.

'King William could have given these lands to any man he chose, and anyone else would have had no hesitation in turning out Godmund's family to starve. I asked for these lands, not just for myself, but so that I would be in a position to help those I once cared for. I didn't know Aelfrun would leave; I wanted her to stay here, in safety and honour. That was what was contained in my letter. I would have looked after you both, I swear it, and if Aelfrun ever chooses to return, I will welcome her, and her child.'

Ceolwynn looked up at him then, searching his face for any sign of guile or deceit. There was none. It didn't make things any better, or make her like him more, but at least she felt he could be trusted. 'Aelfrun cannot come back,' she confided hesitantly. 'She left because we heard that someone had sworn an oath to kill her son.'

'You heard that,' Renaud exclaimed. 'How? No one knew of it except Hugo and myself.'

'You know this Hugo?' Ceolwynn asked, just as surprised as he was. 'You knew of this threat to my brother's life?'

'How did you find out about Hugo?' Renaud asked again.

Ceolwynn hesitated. It might not be wise to let a Norman know that Cenred had been here until quite recently. She didn't trust him that much. 'A boy brought my father home for burial,' she told him. 'He hid, waiting until he could take the body, and overheard two men talking.'

Renaud sensed that she was keeping something back, but since she was at least talking to him now he decided not to delve further. Instead, he said: 'I was one of those two men. The other, Hugo, is a friend of mine, and you can rest assured that he is no longer a threat to your brother. He has been persuaded to see reason and now harbours no thoughts at all of revenge towards your kin.'

'You are certain of that?' she cried, and for the first time he saw her smile, her whole face lighting up with joy.

For just one brief moment she was the child Ceolwynn once again and he was simply her friend. He wanted to reach out and take her hands in his, but the moment passed and she turned her face away from him again.

The meal had ended, and Renaud offered her his hand. She took it, and allowed herself to be led to a seat by the fire. Renaud stood warming himself at the flames, stroking the ears of Godmund's greyhounds and talking softly to them in French. They listened with heads cocked attentively to one side, quivering with delight at his attentions.

Everyone seemed to like him, Ceolwynn thought miserably, even the dogs. Cenred was the only one she knew who was not prepared to give up without a struggle, and she had rejected him. Perhaps she had been wrong.

'It grows late,' Renaud said, turning suddenly to face her, 'but there are things, Ceolwynn, that we must discuss. I don't want to have to keep defending myself to you. Can we talk without you attacking me all the time?' Ceolwynn nodded, too depressed for argument. 'First,' he said, 'what happened to your father's steward? I don't remember this man, Folca. Where did he come from? Who appointed him?'

'Dunn went with Aelfrun,' Ceolwynn told him. 'Folca had been steward to Aelfrun's father. Did you know that your people butchered all her family?' she couldn't resist adding.

Renaud winced. 'No, and I'm deeply sorry for it,' he said. He sat down on a stool opposite, his knees almost touching hers, and

174

prodded thoughtfully at the fire with a piece of wood. 'So she left this Folca to take Dunn's place?' he asked eventually.

'Yes,' Ceolwynn replied. 'He seemed the man most suitable, at least until we knew what the future held for us all.'

Renaud grunted and tossed his improvised poker into the flames. 'It is about your future, Ceolwynn, that we must now speak. I have been thinking about you a great deal in these past few days, and I have come to the conclusion that both our interests would be best served if we were to marry.'

Ceolwynn stared at him, dumbfounded. 'Each other?' she got out at last, almost laughing at the absurdity of the idea.

'Of course each other,' he replied quite seriously, 'who else would I mean?'

'That is surely the most ridiculous suggestion I have ever heard,' she answered contemptuously. 'I would have thought I had made it quite clear that I loathe and despise you.'

Renaud shrugged. 'I don't see why that should be an obstacle,' he said with a hint of his old mischief, 'most married people I know both loathe and despise each other. Anyway, if you think about it you'll see that it does make perfect sense. I am here to stay, and marriage to you would make that easier for everyone to accept.'

'It seems to be well enough accepted already,' Ceolwynn remarked sourly, still upset that she alone seemed to view this man as an enemy still.

Renaud ignored her. 'Cottesham,' he went on, 'has always been your home, and had you been willing to leave it you would already have done so. I, myself, am content that you stay, but, if I marry another, you would have to accept her as mistress here. That is a situation which, if I'm not mistaken, you would find intolerable.' Reluctantly she nodded agreement. 'What then are your alternatives?' he asked, and knowing that he was about to tell her, she made no reply. 'Perhaps Aelfrun's sister and her husband would take you in,' he mused. 'You would, of course, then be dependent on the charity of a man who was once your own father's servant. Of course,' he added innocently, 'you could always take the veil.' His lips twitched with suppressed laughter.

'That is a possibility that I have indeed been considering,' Ceolwynn replied with dignity, glaring at him.

'Oh Ceolwynn, Ceolwynn,' he said, openly laughing now, 'do

you really think that you of all people could be happy in a nunnery?'

Ceolwynn stood up and made to leave, more humiliated by his laughter than his words.

'I'm sorry,' he said, reaching out and taking her hand in his to stop her. 'I shouldn't have laughed,' he admitted placatingly, although his grip on her hand was firm and imperative. 'Forgive me, please.'

She snatched her hand free, but she did sit down again. 'Nothing you have yet said convinces me that becoming your wife would bring me any happiness whatever,' she said resolutely, even though part of her yearned to seize the opportunity he was offering her.

Renaud looked surprised. 'I wasn't thinking of happiness, yours or mine,' he said thoughtfully, almost sadly. 'I don't think either of us can expect that, in these circumstances.'

He was quiet for a few moments and Ceolwynn, darting a furtive glance at him, caught him staring bleakly into the flickering fire, apparently lost in thought.

Covertly she studied his face, intrigued by the pain and sadness she saw there. It struck her with sudden appalling clarity that he wanted to marry her no more than she did him. 'Why then do you ask me to marry you?' she asked, breaking the silence.

Renaud slowly turned his head to look at her. 'You have grown very lovely, Ceolwynn,' he said, stroking her hair with great gentleness. 'It would be a crime to hide away such beauty in the cloister.'

Impatiently, she shook off his hand. 'You're not answering my question,' she said.

'Don't you see?' he asked, his eyes meeting hers and holding them for the first time. 'There is a kind of justice in it. If we marry, then, through you, Godmund's own grandson may one day inherit his Saxon birthright. In a sense, you could say that our marriage would restore to your father's line that which has been taken from it.'

Ceolwynn's heart leapt in response to his words. He was right, she thought, she had everything to gain by this marriage; but what then, she asked herself suspiciously, did Renaud have to gain? It was true that such a marriage would assure his peaceful acceptance here, but, on the other hand, there didn't seem to be overmuch hostility towards him anyway.

Hard as she tried, she couldn't think of any good reason for him to make her such an offer, yet she was disturbed rather than reassured by the apparent absence of an ulterior motive. She refused even to consider the possibility that he might have made the offer for her sake alone.

'And that would ease your conscience and wash the blood from your hands, would it not?' she heard herself saying viciously, then felt a pang of regret as he drew away from her, his face suddenly shadowed and unreadable. She had wounded him, she saw, but strangely it gave her no pleasure.

'I will give you three days to think about it,' he said, his tone now curt and dismissive. 'If at the end of that time you choose not to accept my offer ...'

'You'll doubtless turn me out to fend for myself,' she interrupted him fiercely.

'Whatever you may think of me, Ceolwynn,' he answered her, even more coldly than before, 'I would never knowingly allow any harm to befall you. If you choose to leave here, I will provide you with a goodly dower and see you safely escorted to whichever order of holy sisters you cared to join. Never would I leave you alone and unprotected.'

It came into Ceolwynn's head to say all manner of bitter things, but somehow his chilling withdrawal silenced her and the words died unspoken on her lips.

Without another word, Renaud got up and walked away, and his men, seeing that his private conversation had ended, drew closer to the fire, talking and laughing amongst themselves and taking no more notice of Ceolwynn than of the fire-irons in the hearth. They treated her with no particular disrespect, but they were noisy and loud, and their very presence was a harsh reminder to Ceolwynn of the change in her circumstances.

Resentful and inwardly seething she sat there for a further hour, determined not to be driven from her own fireside even though it was impossible to think with such a racket going on all around her.

She had just made up her mind that she could now leave without loss of face when she noticed, half-hidden in the shadows of the flaring torches, the boy, Brand, trying to attract her attention without alerting the soldiers. Intrigued, she rose with unhurried grace and made her way out of the hall, the boy following at a discreet distance. No one seemed to pay any attention to her going, but she felt a thrill of danger and excitement all the same. What, she wondered, could Brand have to tell her that needed to be kept so secret?

Outside, a bright new moon flooded the grass with such brilliance that Ceolwynn was certain that no one could approach near enough to overhear their conversation without being observed. Even so, she moved well away from any possible places of concealment before slowing her pace and allowing the boy to catch up with her.

'What is it?' she asked eagerly, as soon as he fell into step beside her. 'You have a message for me?'

Brand nodded. 'From Lord Cenred,' he said, and Ceolwynn had to stifle an irrational feeling of disappointment. She wasn't sure what she'd been expecting, but word from Cenred was definitely not what she had had in mind. He should have been far away from here by now. Brand was puzzled by her lack of response. 'He wants to see you,' he said tentatively. 'Will you meet him, lady?'

For just a moment, Ceolwynn considered making some excuse to escape this confrontation, but she knew that to do so would be unfair to Cenred who had, after all, a quite reasonable claim on her affections. The least she could do was meet him face to face and explain why she could no longer marry him.

Brand fidgeted impatiently, obviously wondering at her lack of enthusiasm, and Ceolwynn hardly knew what to say to him.

It was a pity, she thought regretfully, that her original ploy hadn't worked as well as she had hoped, but she was forced to admit to herself that it would be cowardly to try to avoid Cenred when he was risking his life to see her. 'Of course I'll see him,' she said at last. 'When and where does he suggest?'

Brand raised himself on tiptoe to whisper in her ear, a needless precaution that made her smile a little.

'I will be waiting,' she agreed, and as the boy slipped away, Ceolwynn was left to spend a sleepless night contemplating all the unpalatable choices that fate seemed to have mapped out for her future.

Brand came for her two hours before dawn, throwing pebbles at her shutters to let her know he was there, and Ceolwynn, already dressed and waiting, hurried out before the noise could rouse Hild.

Brand led her to a charcoal burner's cottage deep in the woods where Cenred waited, unkempt and dirty in his peasant's clothing, already looking very much the rebel and outlaw.

He spoke a few hasty, whispered words with Brand, and in that few moments before the boy left them alone, Ceolwynn studied with renewed curiosity the man she had once agreed to marry. There was something subtly different about him now, she thought wonderingly. He seemed somehow more interesting, exciting even. Hastily dismissing that dangerous thought, she turned her attention back to his situation. 'You're a fool to have come back,' she told him as he came towards her. 'There's nothing for you here but certain death if you are caught.'

'I had to see you,' he answered softly, and the passion and urgency in his voice came as a surprise. He stood very close to her and for the first time she found herself stirred by his nearness. 'I leave for the west tonight,' he said, taking her hands. 'Come with me Ceolwynn, it's not too late. I know that de Lassay has asked you to be his wife – Brand told me,' he added in reply to the startled expression on her face. 'I've come to persuade you not to do it – you made your vows to me, remember? I know I have little to offer you now, and I know that it was your father's wealth that first made me ask for your hand, but believe me, my love, it is you that I want now and I know that you will be better off with me and your own kind than with him, a Norman.' He placed his hands on her shoulders, half holding, half caressing them. 'Help me to strike a blow against these devils,' he urged her. 'One day, I swear, we will drive them back into the sea.'

His closeness, the earthy, animal smell of him, frightened and excited her at the same time. 'I wish you well, Cenred, truly I do,' she answered him nervously. She tried to step back, but his hands restrained her and she found herself being pulled forward into his arms.

He bent his lips to hers and, helpless to resist, she gave herself up to his kiss, melting into an embrace that left her breathless and trembling. Unresisting still, she felt his hand move over her shoulders, her back, pulling her even closer so that she could feel the hardness of him pressing against her, her hips responding almost without her knowing it.

179

With one hand behind her head, holding her lips pressed to his to stifle any protest, Cenred allowed his other hand to move lower, tugging at her skirts, pulling them up until he could brush the silken nakedness of the soft skin beneath.

Ceolwynn caught her breath. Unfamiliar yet compelling sensations flooded over her whole being, so unendurably pleasurable that she had no other will but to give herself up to them. Insistently his fingers stroked and caressed, slipping into the warm dampness between her thighs. She groaned softly, willing despite herself to let him do anything he wanted, but then, suddenly, as he tried to lower her to the ground, she realized with horror that a few moments longer and she would be committed to him for ever.

Frantically, breathlessly, she pulled herself free, pushing him away and struggling to regain control of herself and the situation. Her lips felt bruised, her heart was beating too fast. 'No more,' she pleaded as he tried to pull her to him again, 'please Cenred, we must talk.' She was shaking and her cheeks were hot with confusion.

Cenred stared at her, baffled, uncomprehending. 'Why?' he asked, his eyes full of pain. 'You wanted me. It wouldn't be a sin, if we are to marry anyway. I love you Ceolwynn.'

He took another step towards her and she backed away from him, terrified that if he touched again her she would be lost.

The hurt she saw in him filled her with guilt and self-loathing. 'I'm sorry, Cenred,' she said miserably. 'I came here only to tell you that I cannot leave Cottesham; it's my home and my people need me. I can't go with you.'

'I see,' he replied, suddenly cold. 'You will marry the Norman then?'

'No,' she answered vehemently, and then added, more honestly, 'I don't know.' She hung her head and for a few moments there was silence between them.

'I have to go,' he said at last.

'Don't hate me Cenred,' she said, 'I have to do what I believe is right.'

'I don't hate you,' he said grimly, 'far from it.' They walked outside together and Brand jumped up from where he had been dozing to bring Cenred's horse. 'Tell me,' Cenred asked, 'if things had been different, if Harold had won the day and your father had lived, would you have married me?'

'Of course I would,' she said, quite truthfully, but in her heart she was glad that she would no longer have to keep the promises she had made.

What she had experienced, back there in the charcoal burner's hut, had been powerful, exciting, but it had not been love. She'd found a passion in Cenred that she'd never known existed, and her body had responded to that passion, but it did nothing to change her feelings about marriage to him.

Impulsively, she kissed him, certain that it would be for the last time.

'In better times I will come for you again,' he promised.

'In better times, I shall be glad to see you,' she replied kindly, knowing in her heart that they were never likely to see the better times of which he spoke. 'God go with you Cenred. Take care.'

He swung into the saddle and looked down at her, unsmiling. Somehow, she felt, there should be more to say between them, but she could think of nothing. He turned his horse towards the path and she raised her hand in farewell, but he spurred away without once looking back.

When, on their return, the dark shape of the village church could again be made out in the growing light of morning, Brand turned to Ceolwynn. 'Will you be all right if I leave you here?'

'Where are you going?' she asked.

Brand looked back the way they had come. 'I am going with Lord Cenred,' he answered. 'He is my lord now, and I am going to help him fight for our freedom. Lord Cenred waits for me at the crossroads.' He turned away. 'God be with you, my lady,' he called back over his shoulder.

'And with you, Brand,' she replied, knowing that there was nothing she could say that would stop him. 'Farewell.'

Later that day she agreed to become the wife of Renaud de Lassay.

XI

June 1069

Almost two years had passed when, in high summer, Renaud de
Lassay paid a visit to an old friend. Hugo had been living in
Normandy and had only now returned to inspect those estates in
Hereford which had been his reward for his part in England's
conquest.

It was there that Renaud went to renew a friendship sorely
missed, and it was from there that he now returned home in high
good spirits, for Hugo had given him some news so unexpected
and so very welcome that even the prospect of renewed fighting
left him quite undismayed.

That there would be fighting seemed almost certain. King
Sweyn of Denmark, supported by Malcolm of Scotland, still
hoped to seize the English throne for himself, and the rebel
known as Edric the Wild was still fomenting trouble, this time in
Wales.

Nor was this all. The young Aetheling, Edgar, had been made
very welcome in Scotland by King Malcolm who, as always, was
more than willing to stir up trouble in England. Even the great
northern earls whom William had believed won over to his side,
had melted back into their remote earldoms where they continued
to plot with his enemies against him. But so far William had had
little difficulty in suppressing each uprising as it occurred, though
this new Danish threat had brought him hotfoot back from escort-
ing Matilda, his newly crowned queen, home to Normandy.

It was news of William's return which had so delighted the
young lord of Cottesham, or, to be more accurate, the information
relayed by Hugo that Roger de Virar was travelling with the king,
accompanied for the first time by his wife and child. Nothing

could quench Renaud's joy at the knowledge that soon his beloved Emma would be in England – and with her would be Geoffrey, the son he had never seen.

'Good morning, master,' a voice hailed him cheerfully from the side of the road.

'Good morning, hayward,' Renaud answered, reining to a halt. 'How goes the cutting?' he asked, looking out across the fields with one hand shading his eyes from the sun's glare.

Beyond in the hay meadows, a small army of men, bare-legged and unshod, marched slowly through the long grass, swinging their scythes with rhythmic precision, their wide-brimmed straw hats bobbing jauntily with each movement. Women and children followed behind, raking the grass and tossing it with pitchforks to speed the drying. Snatches of their song and laughter came to him on the wind.

'Well enough, my lord, after a poor start,' the hayward replied, his hat held respectfully in his hands. 'I had begun to fear that we would not see the sun at all this summer.'

Renaud agreed with him and lingered awhile, watching.

'If you are looking for my lady Ceolwynn,' the hayward called out as Renaud began to move off, 'I saw her not half an hour since down by the river, near the mill.'

'Thank you,' Renaud called back, and sending his men on without him he turned his horse away from the direction of the hall to follow the path to the river.

There was a bend in the road, just where it dipped steeply downwards towards the riverbank, and it was here that Renaud paused, hearing the sound of women's voices raised in laughter and light-hearted chatter.

A child's shriek of delight rang out. Smiling at the sound of it, Renaud decided to walk the rest of the way, his footsteps drowned by the noise of the churning millwheel. Before him, sprawled on her stomach in a state of childlike abandon, he saw his wife, dressed in a grass-stained tunic from which poked two small, well-formed feet as bare and dusty as any peasant's.

She was watching the small, tawny-haired boy playing at her side. Renaud, still unobserved, watched the child too, his throat closing almost painfully as a surge of love and paternal pride swept over him. Would he feel this way, he wondered, when he saw Geoffrey for the first time?

The child saw Renaud first and cried out in delight. Ceolwynn looked up, then rose to her feet with a cold, sullen expression. Lightly but firmly she laid a restraining hand on her son's shoulder, preventing him from rushing forward to greet his father. The boy glanced up at her questioningly, but obeyed the unspoken command, and Renaud, forcing himself to smile, made an effort to suppress the irritation he felt at her constant and impenetrable hostility.

'Dismiss your servants, Ceolwynn,' he said, dispensing with any attempt to open the conversation with greetings or pleasantries. 'We'll walk back together, you and I.'

'As you wish, my lord,' Ceolwynn said, and made to hand the child over to his nurse.

'No,' Renaud said firmly, meeting Ceolwynn's eyes with a determination to match her own. 'I will carry Edmund,' he said. 'One of your maids can lead my horse to the stables.'

Ceolwynn knew that there were times when it would unwise to gainsay Renaud. Reluctantly she ordered Hild to see to the horse and released the boy to toddle unsteadily towards his father, who stooped to lift the smiling child into his arms.

'He's grown,' Renaud commented with satisfaction, playfully holding Edmund out at arm's length. 'I've hardly been away a month, but I'd swear that I can see the difference.'

'Perhaps so,' Ceolwynn answered with pretended indifference. She walked quickly away, leaving him to follow.

The three of them made their way slowly back to the hall, Renaud and Ceolwynn saying almost nothing while Edmund played with the lacings at his father's throat and prattled happy nonsense in a seemingly random mixture of Saxon and French.

Suddenly, Renaud stopped and turned on his wife with uncharacteristic anger. 'In God's name, what must I do?' he shouted. Edmund's face puckered in uncertain fear and Renaud quickly gave him a reassuring hug. 'Are you going to hate me for ever?' he asked, lowering his voice.

'To the end of my days,' Ceolwynn replied sweetly and started walking again.

Renaud felt a deep hopelessness. 'I have let you have your own way in many things,' he said, grabbing her arm and swinging her round to look at him, 'but I will not let you do this to me.'

'Do what?' Ceolwynn asked, raising her brows with puzzled, studied innocence.

'You know very well,' he replied. 'Be warned, my lady, if you try to turn my son's heart against me I will take him from you, I swear it.'

Ceolwynn saw that he meant exactly what he said. 'I had no such intention,' she lied, staring down at her feet like a child caught out in some mischief.

Renaud snorted in disbelief but let go of her arm. 'Good,' he said, 'because I have no intention of giving you a second warning.'

Ceolwynn looked down submissively, realizing with sudden shock that her son was a certain hostage for her good behaviour, a weapon Renaud could use against her at any time. She could not hope to best him in this.

She walked beside her husband in thoughtful, subdued silence.

Renaud, too, was thoughtful. How, he asked himself, had he ever imagined that time and gentle forbearance would teach his fierce, proud young wife to resign herself to that which could not be undone? All he wanted was for her to care for him a little, to smile for him and acknowledge that not everything Norman was without exception evil. He didn't expect her love, since he believed he had none to give in return, but it seemed to him now that perhaps he had seriously misjudged her capacity for hatred.

'Doesn't it weary you,' he asked with grim sarcasm, 'to keep ever that scowl upon your face? The occasional smile would be far more becoming on a face so fair.'

Ceolwynn ignored the remark. 'I didn't expect you back for several days yet,' she said. 'Are you intending to stay long?'

It was the kind of blunt, hostile question he had come to expect from her, but today he thought he detected a note of unease in her voice and was a little intrigued by it. 'This is my home,' he reminded her. 'Why so anxious to see me gone?'

'I'm not,' she replied hastily, but her cheeks had coloured hotly and he wondered if perhaps it was the thought that this night he might expect to share her bed which had alarmed her. It seemed unlikely.

Their wedding night had been a disaster, he recalled ruefully, although there could be little doubt that the child now sleeping draped across his shoulder had been conceived on that ill-starred occasion.

His anger faded with that thought and he glanced at Ceolwynn, ready to be the first to try to make peace between them, but her forbidding, closed expression persuaded him that it would be useless to try. He subsided into a morose and unhappy silence.

They had lain together, he remembered, in the wide bed that Godmund and Aelfrun had once shared, a fact which did little to ease the tension between them. The memory was as sharp and clear to him now as though it had been but yesterday.

Silent and unmoving they had lain, their naked bodies separated by a few inches of empty space that seemed to stretch for miles. Renaud had wanted to reach out to reassure her, but felt her trembling each time he stirred. He had wanted to say something to lessen her fears, but knew that there was nothing he could say.

Suddenly, in his mind's eye, he had seen the child Ceolwynn with her hand laid trustingly in his, honey and oat cake smeared on her lips. He'd seen her running from him, laughing, her tunic pulled up over grubby, scabbed knees, and kneeling in the dark of her secret cave, her eyes full of wonder as he wove incredible stories to feed her imagination.

Dear God, he'd thought with something like horror, bedding Ceolwynn was a little like bedding your own sister!

The thought had both amused and appalled him, and he'd found himself trying to smother a laugh born more of nervousness than of humour.

Ceolwynn had felt his suppressed laughter vibrating through the bed and stiffened furiously. 'How dare you laugh?' she'd hissed at him. 'There is nothing to laugh at, you beast. Holy Mary, tell me why did I agree to this marriage?'

'I'm sorry,' he'd gasped, giving in to the laughter and allowing it to explode out of him in great bursts.

Ceolwynn had kicked him, hard, and the pain of the impact on his shin had sobered him remarkably. 'I hate you,' she'd said. Her cheeks had been flushed with temper, but her eyes had gleamed in the lamplight with something that had been neither anger nor fear.

'I know,' he'd replied, kissing her gently, his lips barely brushing hers. Very briefly he'd felt her respond to him, moving closer until he could feel the warmth of her skin and the light touch of hair fragrant with the scent of flowers; but then she had stiffened in his embrace.

Dousing the lamp, he had lain down again beside her, listening to the uneven sound of her breathing and mourning the loss of the friendship they had once known. In the darkness he reached out for her hand and unresisting she let him take it, but left it limp and unresponsive in his clasp. Misery had flooded over him in a relentless, agonizing wave, leaving him filled with bitter despair. Oh Emma, his soul had cried out deep in loneliness, what have I done? In that moment, he had hated his new wife almost as much as she hated him, and in the passion of his hatred he had seized her roughly in his arms, taking her with a ferocity that left her bruised and shaken.

He'd spent the rest of the night in an agony of remorse, hating himself for his brutality, but strangely, and to their mutual surprise, the marriage-bed had become the one place where they met, if not as friends, then at least not as enemies.

Renaud could not know, since Ceolwynn would never tell him, that after the initial pain and shock of his precipitate lovemaking, she had discovered to her own amazement that the agreeable sensations she had once experienced in Cenred's embrace, were as nothing compared to the glorious surge of delight that she knew whenever she lay with Renaud.

Whenever he came to her bed she vowed that she would be cold and indifferent to his advances, but when he kissed her lips and teased her body with sweet and tender explorations, she forgot just how much she loathed him and abandoned herself to the joy and pleasure he gave her.

'Is it true that the Danes are coming?' Ceolwynn asked suddenly.

'You have heard that already?' Renaud answered with surprise. 'You seem to be better informed than the court.'

'Ah yes, but then we have Aldhere,' she replied with a smile, and Renaud laughed. 'You didn't answer my question, my lord. Is it true?'

'It's true that the Danish fleet is preparing to sail, but there is nothing to fear. We will be ready for them.'

'Oh, I have no fear of the *Danes*,' she remarked provokingly, unable to help herself. 'You forget, my lord, that I am myself half Danish.'

'Do not assume that your Danish blood will protect you,' Renaud told her seriously, 'but I am certain it will not come to

187

that. The east coast is well-guarded against their landing. Nonetheless, I will be leaving for Northumbria within the month for there's trouble there.'

'Northumbria,' Ceolwynn sighed wistfully. 'How I wish I could find out if all is well with Aelfrun and Siggi, and with Estrith and Wulfhere. I have heard no word from them in all this time.'

'Have you not sent messengers of your own?' Renaud asked unbelievingly. 'You have only to ask and I will send one of my own men for you.'

'Would that it were so easy, my lord. Only Aelfrun knew exactly where Wulfhere's lands lay, and in the haste of her departure she failed to give me the direction. I would not know where to send my messenger.'

'My dear Ceolwynn, why in the name of all the Saints did you not speak of this sooner? There are records of King Edward's gifts of land. I can easily find out which estates were given to Wulfhere, and if you wish it I will do so before I leave for the north. Will that please you?'

'Very much, my lord,' Ceolwynn answered with genuine pleasure. Not for the first time she wished she could find it in her heart to hate him less. His almost unfailing kindness made something petty and spiteful of her own emotions. She sighed and added hesitantly, 'I am grateful to you.'

'I don't expect gratitude from you, Ceolwynn, but I do hope for your loyalty. Do I at least have that?'

'Of course,' she replied uncomfortably, avoiding his eye, and from the sudden rush of colour of her cheeks Renaud knew for certain that she was keeping something from him.

'Where is Aldhere?' Ceolwynn asked frantically, bursting into the church and startling the priest.

'Is this any way to enter God's house?' he reproved her gently. In Father Eadric's eyes, Ceolwynn was still just a headstrong, wilful child, and he treated her with more affection than deference.

'I'm sorry, Father, but this is urgent. Lord Renaud has come home and I can't find Aldhere. What am I to do?'

'Aldhere has already left, I saw him go,' he told her. 'What is wrong, child? Why so agitated?'

'Lord Cenred is on his way here at this very moment,' she explained breathlessly.

The priest paled. 'Dear Lord, did I not warn you not to become involved in those rebels' schemes? And Aldhere too. If anyone has cause to be loyal, after what Lord Renaud has done for him, Aldhere is that man.'

'Hush,' Ceolwynn cautioned him, glancing round anxiously. 'It's too late to think of that now.'

'Which way will Cenred come, think you?' Father Eadric asked. 'Will he be here before nightfall?'

'If I knew those things, there would be no cause for alarm, would there? I could have sent someone to keep watch for him,' she replied impatiently.

'How deeply are you involved in all this, child?' he asked sternly.

'I thought I could count on you,' Ceolwynn said with dismay.

They had by now reached the privacy of the priest's house and he stood back to let her enter first. 'You can count on me to do all in my power to keep you safe,' he said, closing the door and lowering his voice, 'but I do not believe that any useful purpose will be served by fomenting rebellion and unrest. Lord Renaud is a good man and has proved himself a good master. What more can our people ask for?'

'We want a Saxon king on England's throne; we fight for England and for Edgar,' she protested.

'These are not your own words, I think. Let me ask you, does Sweyn of Denmark seek only to put the crown on the young Aetheling's head? Has he raised an army for no other purpose than to right a wrong?'

'Well no,' she acknowledged. 'But even a Danish king would be preferable to a Norman one. We understand the ways of the Danes, and they understand us.'

'How quickly people forget,' Father Eadric sighed. 'Have you never heard of the Danegeld, money raised from taxes to protect us from the savagery of these same Danes of whom you now speak so fondly?'

'That was long ago,' she argued. 'Today, most Englishmen have some Danish blood in their veins.'

'Very true, but think of it this way: we tried to fight off the Danes, we tried to buy off the Danes, but in the end they came and now no one asks of a man: "Was your grandfather Saxon or Dane?" It will be so for your son. It will not matter whether his lands came to him through his Saxon mother or his Norman father, but, with a Norman father, what guarantee is there that he will keep his lands at all under Danish rule?'

Ceolwynn looked troubled. 'I had not thought,' she said.

'Why is Lord Cenred coming back here after all this time, and what does he want of you?' the priest asked. 'Tell me, I must know.'

'There's little enough to tell,' she said grudgingly. 'When the rebellion in the west failed, Cenred led his men back to continue the fight here. He plans to join King Sweyn's forces as soon as the Danes land, but in the meantime he has been attacking Norman troops for their horses and weapons.'

The priest frowned. 'A dangerous business,' he said, 'but I don't see what part you might have to play in all this.'

'Aldhere passes information to him through a man in Lullingworth. I don't know where Aldhere gets all his information, but sometimes I can tell him useful things – things that Lord Renaud or one of his men has mentioned. That was how he found out about the silver.'

'Silver?'

'Payment for the Bastard's mercenaries, a chest full of silver carried under armed guard from London through Andredsweald. Cenred's men captured it and killed every Norman in the guard. They never even found the bodies. For all they know,' she laughed, 'their own soldiers could have run off with the money themselves! Cenred brought it here, and here it has been hidden ever since, over six months. Now he is returning for it.'

Shocked, the priest sat down heavily. 'Dear Lord,' he said, 'this is worse than I thought. Have you any idea of the danger this could bring down upon us? Who else knows about it?'

'Aldhere, and Afa the smith who helped hide the chest.'

The priest thought for a moment. 'Well, you can't stop Lord Cenred coming. So can you get your husband and his men to be elsewhere when he arrives?'

Ceolwynn looked doubtful. 'He is bathing now, and he seemed tired after his journey.'

'Short of getting them all drunk, I can think of no better idea.'

'That wouldn't work, I'm afraid,' she answered.

'Then go to your lord and ask him to take you hunting. Be kind to him and make him want to please you. I will send someone to find Aldhere. Perhaps it's still not too late to get word to Lord Cenred.'

Ceolwynn nodded and left at once.

In the hall she found Renaud dining alone on stewed eels and fresh baked bread, his hair still wet and his face pink from the heat of the bath house. A servant, newly arrived with a jug of wine, was about to pour a cup when Ceolwynn took the jug from him and poured it herself, handing it to Renaud with a warm and inviting smile.

He took it, looking up at her a little dubiously. 'You haven't poisoned it, have you?' he asked lightly.

'What an unkind thing to say,' she protested.

She moved to stand close to his shoulder and began to break small pieces of bread from the loaf, dipping them in the gravy and feeding them to him, her fingertips softly caressing his lips as she did so.

After a few baffled moments, Renaud seized her wrist and pulled her down so that her face was level with his. 'What's all this about, Ceolwynn?' he asked sternly, although his eyes twinkled with amusement at her transparency. 'What do you want from me that you think I am unlikely to give you?'

'Nothing,' she protested indignantly, 'why do you always have to think the worst of me?' She tried to pull herself free but he held her fast.

'Perhaps because the worst of you is all I ever get to see,' he answered bluntly.

'You wrong me,' she said softly, smothering the urge to sink her teeth into the hand that held her so tightly. 'I've been thinking about the things you said to me, and perhaps I have been at fault. I want us to be friends, my lord.'

'Indeed,' he said thoughtfully, releasing her at last. 'I wouldn't really take Edmund away from you, if that is what you fear.'

'That is not the reason,' she replied, rubbing the red mark on her wrist, 'but I am glad to know it.'

He returned to his food, occasionally glancing at his wife as though expecting her to startle him at any moment with some new, unlooked-for demonstration of affection.

'Perhaps we should try to get to know one another better,' she mused, 'spend more time in each other's company. I would rather like to hunt this afternoon. Would you care to join me, my lord? It would be very pleasant on such a fine day.'

Renaud wiped his lips on a napkin and smiled wickedly. 'So, I'm to be lured to my death in the woods, am I?' he asked, grinning. 'Poison in the wine might have been easier, I never ride abroad without my escort.'

Curiously, Ceolwynn felt genuinely hurt by these teasing accusations. 'I've never wished you harm,' she told him.

'No,' he agreed, rising. 'I don't believe you ever have.' He kissed her lightly on the brow and walked away.

'Will you hunt with me then, my lord?' she called after him anxiously. He stopped for a moment to consider, and she added with what she hoped sounded like real but innocent enthusiasm: 'It would give me much pleasure.'

'Very well, in an hour,' he replied over his shoulder. 'I have business to attend to first.'

In the bustling, prosperous town of Guildford, Folca, the steward of Cottesham, having successfully concluded his business, now turned to the pleasure he had in mind as he bent his steps towards that part of the town where, once the sun had gone down, respectable people feared to tread.

Folca was surprisingly content at Cottesham. He couldn't rob his new master, but he was well paid and comfortable, which meant that he could leave his precious hoard untouched. This suited him well since he enjoyed the possession of wealth more than the spending of it.

Folca was a strange, unhappy man; he wanted what he knew he could never have, and then hated what he longed for because of its very inaccessibility. Now, unwittingly, Ceolwynn had replaced Wilfred's daughters as the focus of his twisted desires. In his fantasies he saw her begging for his aid when the Normans came, but instead she had married the Norman and escaped him. It had been a bitter disappointment.

Folca now made his way with eager tread to the brothel where he knew that his particular and somewhat unusual needs would be catered for without question or comment.

The good lady who ran this accommodating enterprise saw him coming from her vantage place at the window and gave a harsh, mirthless laugh. 'Look out girls,' she warned, 'the Fetterman is on his way.'

As Folca entered, one small dark-haired girl recognized him. It was Nest, Wilfred's former slave girl. She quickly followed the example of the other girls and drifted swiftly into the concealing shadows. She found herself trembling uncontrollably, not quite sure what she feared most about this vile man.

It was the threat to her daughter's safety, rather than her own, that made Nest tremble so. Fear for Rhianwen had haunted Nest's dreams since the very day she had given birth, terrified and alone, in the shelter of an abandoned hovel in a war-ravaged village that no longer had even a name.

Knowing from the start how impossible the existence of a child would make her life, Nest had made up her mind to leave her baby at the door of the very first church on her road, and she'd held firm to this intention all through the long, agonizing night of the child's birthing; but then she'd held the tiny, helpless creature to her breast, and all logic and common sense had been blown to the four winds.

Exhausted and half starved she had reached Guildford two days later, and had immediately set about looking for work, tramping the streets and knocking at every likely door.

Eventually, she had found work as a kitchenmaid in the house of a wealthy mercer, but this had not brought an end to her troubles. Within a few months she had been dismissed without explanation and through no fault of her own. It happened again, twice more, and she realized at last that her child was in fact less of a handicap than her own undeniable beauty, for no matter how hard she worked or how modest her manner and behaviour, when the mistress of the house saw the direction of her husband's admiring glances, Nest would once again be shown the door.

Nest was close to despair when a chance encounter with a plump, pink-cheeked girl at a pie stall on market day had led her to this house and a life of shame, but shame made bearable by warm clothing and a full belly.

'And what is your preference today?' she heard the dame ask her guest, and it seemed as though the whole room held its breath.

Folca's sharp eyes raked the wall searchingly and Nest, wishing she could make herself disappear altogether, drew even deeper into the shadows.

'I want someone fair,' he said, his tongue sliding wetly over his lower lip, 'fair and slender as a willow wand,' he murmured.

His eyes lighted upon a girl not three feet from where Nest stood huddled and his hand shot out at once, pointing at her with trembling eagerness. The dame crooked her finger and the girl came forward, but so slowly and hesitantly that she earned herself an impatient slap from her mistress.

Without further ado and pushing the unfortunate girl in front of him, Folca passed out of sight behind the ragged curtain which divided this room from the pallets beyond, and which was all the privacy the house afforded its guests.

An audible sigh of relief greeted his departure, and soon the girls began to move back into the centre of the room, as careless and unconcerned as a herd of deer once the wolf has chosen his victim and made his kill.

'Why do you call him the Fetterman?' Nest asked Aggie, the plump young woman who had first brought her here.

'It's because he likes his women tied up and helpless,' her friend explained carelessly, helping herself to a sweetmeat from a bowl. 'He can't get it up otherwise,' she added, giggling lewdly. 'He likes to cause pain,' she continued. Nest's eyes widened and Aggie lowered her voice confidentially. 'I heard tell,' she said, 'that one girl died after.'

'Ugh! I do so hate this part of it,' Ceolwynn exclaimed, closing her eyes and turning her head away in disgust.

Renaud laughed at her squeamishness and the head huntsman, already bent over the body of the fallen stag, looked up with a grin before pulling out his knife. With one deft slash he opened up the beast's belly with his long, sharp blade, and the hot, steaming entrails plopped out onto the ground.

The dogs slavered wildly in anticipation, whining and yelping, straining furiously at the leash until the juicy tidbits were at last thrown to them.

'It's done,' Renaud said, and very tentatively Ceolwynn opened her eyes. 'A fine chase,' he remarked cheerfully. 'The dogs performed well.'

'Yes, my father was proud of his hounds, and with good cause,' she replied, but for once Renaud detected nothing hostile in her words. 'Shall we try for new quarry?' she asked.

'No, I think not,' he replied, yawning widely. 'I've spent too many hours today in the saddle.'

'Oh but ...' she began.

'No buts,' he interrupted her, smiling. 'I am glad if my company has given you pleasure, but enough is enough.'

Ceolwynn frowned worriedly. The hounds had started the stag so quickly that it seemed as though the hunt had barely begun before it was all over. Now Renaud signalled impatiently for her to join him, as he turned his horse homewards.

Slowly, she did so, and he waited for her with a slightly quizzical expression. 'Is aught amiss?' he asked, full of consideration. 'Your horse is not lame?'

She shook her head miserably. His kindness disarmed her and to her fear was added a confusing sense of guilt at her deceit and treachery, although treachery was not how she had thought of it at the time.

With Renaud's four men positioned at a polite distance behind them, they set their horses to a canter.

Ceolwynn glanced back once, hating his escort, hating their aloofness, the martial clanking of their gear, their cold eyes in which she read nothing but contempt for her conquered race. They spoke no Saxon, despised everything English and complained frequently and bitterly about the weather. Their very foreignness was a constant reminder that only chance had made her mistress of her own home.

Restored by the exhilaration of the chase, Renaud was whistling softly to himself and thinking how pleasant it would be if only his wife's unusually temperate mood could be counted upon to last. He was vaguely aware that Ceolwynn herself was strangely quiet, but being both weary and full of sweet, secret thoughts of a dark and sultry beauty who might already be here on English soil, it was some time before he noticed that the closer they got to the village, the slower the pace of her horse. Her horse was now walking.

He could only conclude that it was Ceolwynn herself who was holding the animal back, and suddenly this alarmed him, as did the silence which had replaced her earlier bright chatter.

'What mystery is here, Ceolwynn?' he asked with deceptive gentleness. 'What is it that you seek to conceal from me?'

The startled, fearful look she gave him confirmed his worst suspicions. Never before had she shown such fear of him. She had tormented him, fought with him, but she had never really feared him – until now. She was, without doubt, up to some terrible mischief.

'Let's not play games,' he snapped, suddenly furious with himself for having been fooled by her pretence of goodwill, and disappointed, too, that pretence was all it had been. 'All this,' he said, waving an arm about angrily, 'it was all just a ploy to get me away from Cottesham, wasn't it? What's going on there you are so determined I should not see?'

'Nothing, my lord,' she protested urgently, her voice shaking a little. 'What could there be?'

'That's what I intend to find out,' he answered grimly, and signalled for his men to draw near. 'I leave it to you to escort my lady home,' he ordered them. 'I ride on alone.'

'Is that wise, my lord?' one asked.

Renaud made no answer, but spurred away in a cloud of dust and dried leaves.

Renaud's impulse was prompted by fear, not for himself but for his wife. Some part of him had known that his men, fellow Normans and loyal to their king, were too new in his service to aid him in any enterprise which might seem at all disloyal to William. Godmund, he knew, could have commanded such unswerving loyalty from his men, but Renaud had yet to earn it. If any one of the grim-faced soldiers who followed him uncovered any hint of treason, there could be no concealment of Ceolwynn's complicity and nothing could protect her from the king's wrath.

He approached the village with caution, his hand ready on his sword and his eye searching intently for any sign of danger. Would he surprise his own villagers at some traitorous mischief? Would he suddenly find himself face to face with a band of armed rebels? His hand tightened on the hilt of his sword.

Slowly he rode, tense and alert, over the bridge and into the village, his head turning from side to side, watching and listening, but there was nothing unusual to be seen or heard. Workshops rang with the clatter of tools and the sound of apprentices whistling as they worked. A young woman emptied a bucket of dirty slops outside her door and smiled coyly as she disappeared back inside. A man hurried past with a sack of flour on his shoulder, doffing his cap. Small children played outside the cottage doors, and one naked infant, too young to understand the difference between peasant and lord, waved to him with cheerful familiarity and pissed into the dust.

Renaud felt the tension drain from him, almost sure that this normality was no pretence and that there could be no possible intrigue here at all. By the time he reached the church, he had begun to frame in his head the words he would use to apologize to Ceolwynn. He had ruined a fair day with his foolish suspicions.

He had already ridden several yards past the graveyard before it registered in his mind that there, close by the wall and half hidden in the shadow of the yew trees, had been a patch of fresh-turned sod.

He turned and rode back. He had heard of no new deaths in the village.

Suspicion flooded back.

He dismounted and tied his horse away from the poisonous yew before going to take a closer look at the supposed grave, kneeling at the edge and running his fingers contemplatively through damp soil that the sun had not yet dried. This was no grave – it was too short to hold a man, too wide for a child – and from the surrounding mess it was clear that the earth had very recently been shovelled back.

Suddenly he heard a noise behind him and whirled about, rising with his sword already in his hand.

The priest stood there, ashen-faced, guilt written clear in his eyes and in the defeated sag of his shoulders. He carried a pail of dry soil in each hand, evidence of his intent to conceal the mystery.

Renaud lowered his sword, a deep and terrible disappointment in his soul. Of all men here, he had believed the priest most worthy of his trust. 'Well, Father,' he said sourly, 'there is a secret here ripe for the telling, I think.'

Father Eadric stared down at the dark scar in the ground and said nothing. In vain he struggled to find some plausible tale.

'My patience wears thin, priest, and your face tells me that you seek a falsehood to divert me. Be warned; you'll not convince me with untruths. What lies in this hole, or what lay in it perhaps, for I see that is more likely the case?'

'Another hour, half even,' Father Eadric mused, still half in shock, 'and there would have been nothing at all to see. There would have been no harm done at all.'

'Tell me the truth, Father, all of it.' Renaud's face was pale with anger, and with dread of what he might discover. 'My lady is involved, this I do know of a certainty. If you love her, tell me everything, or she may pay for your silence with her life.'

Father Eadric, realizing that he could not protect his mistress, threw down his buckets and fell on his knees before the enraged young man. 'If I had known sooner what she was about, my lord, I would have done all in my power to stop her, I swear.'

Still on his knees, he told Renaud almost everything he knew, babbling the words in a nervous torrent and close to tears as he did so. He omitted, however, the names of those in the village who had also been party to the enterprise.

Renaud, growing paler by the minute as the story unfolded, silently thanked God that Cenred had got away before their return, and then cursed his one-time friend for persuading Ceolwynn to take such risks – endangering herself and all those who aided her.

The priest finished his tale and gripped Renaud's knees imploringly. 'Punish me, if you will,' he pleaded, 'but do not denounce her, the mother of your child. She is young and foolish, I know, but it is in your power to curb her, to make her loyal and obedient.'

'Tell me priest,' Renaud asked, very softly, 'did my wife's affection for her kinsman lead her to any other folly? I know that they were once betrothed,' he added carefully, in case the priest should doubt his meaning.

'Certainly not, never,' he replied, fierce despite his fear. 'You impugn my lady's honour with such a foul suggestion.'

'Her honour?' the young man echoed him with a harsh laugh, but there was a certain relief in his voice. He stared down at the priest's anxious, frightened face for a moment longer. 'Get up,' he said wearily, his decision made. He sighed. 'Finish what you set out to do, Father,' he said, indicating the spilled buckets, 'and make haste. My men will return at any moment and I want no trace of this left.'

'My lady?' the priest asked nervously.

'Do as I bid and she will be safe. As for yourself – you know your own guilt, so set your own penance; I have not the stomach for it.'

Without another word he turned and strode away.

When Ceolwynn returned ten minutes later, Renaud was in the hall and already well into his third cup of wine. He stood up as she entered, and never before had she seen such blind fury, a cold, hard rage that chilled her to the bone.

'My lord,' she began, defiant still, unsure of what he knew but determined to brazen out the storm.

He held up his hand to silence her. 'We will not speak here,' he said, his voice too quiet, too controlled. 'Go to your bedchamber.' She hesitated. 'Now,' he thundered, and she half ran from the hall.

Slowly, he drank another cup of wine, reluctant to do what he knew had to be done; but at last he found the strength to follow her.

Though it was still daylight, the room was dim behind its closed shutters, lit only by a single candle. In its flickering light she waited for him, looking so very young and so very fragile that he trembled as he stripped her of her gown and raised aloft the supple birch wand he carried.

He beat her then, he who had never before raised a hand to any woman, over and over again until her back was striped and bloody from neck to thigh. She cried, she begged him for mercy, she cursed him, but nothing would make him stop; and blinded by her own tears, she could not see that he also wept.

'Do you think you feel pain, madam?' he shouted at her in a voice that rose almost to a scream.

Ceolwynn sobbed and drew herself as far away from him as she could across the bed, curling herself into a ball to protect herself.

'This is not pain,' he said, delivering a last stinging blow across her naked buttocks before throwing aside the blood-flecked switch with a look of disgust and loathing in his pain-filled eyes. 'Let me tell you,' he panted breathlessly, 'the pain you feel now is but a pinprick, a gnatbite, compared to what the king's men could inflict upon you.'

He leaned forward and pulled her round to face him by her hair. His breath stank of wine and there was a madness in his eye which terrified her into silence. 'Do you understand what I'm saying to you, lady?' He shook her roughly, but seemed not to expect an answer – which was as well since she was quite incapable of speech. 'Before God, this is no game. If your doings here came to the king's ears, nothing could save you from the stake.'

He seized one of her hands, squeezing it painfully in his. 'I should hold your hand to that candle flame,' he said, and for one fearful minute she thought he might do just that, 'then you might know what is pain. Think on this when next you are tempted into such folly.'

Abruptly, he released her and walked out of the chamber without a backward glance.

Ceolwynn glared venomously after him, and would have spat if her mouth had not been so dry and her bitten lips so painful.

Hild came to her almost at once, and Ceolwynn knew without asking that Renaud had sent her, a fact which caused her more confusion and, perversely, even more resentment. Hild brought her mistress soothing unguents and clean linen for bandages, and she asked no questions, for which Ceolwynn was grateful.

In the days that followed, Ceolwynn had much time to reflect on her actions and their consequences. She kept to her bed, too sore to move, and at first nursed her anger and hatred with sullen ferocity. Not once did Renaud come near her, but, to her surprise, young Edmund was allowed to visit her quite freely, and soon it became clear that no further punishment was to be forthcoming.

As the days went by and her pain lessened, reluctantly Ceolwynn began to understand what had driven Renaud to treat her so cruelly.

She remembered the terror she had felt when it seemed likely that her treachery had been discovered. Holy Mother of Christ, when she thought of it now, the possible consequences were too terrible to contemplate. Renaud could have denounced her, handed her over to the king's officers, washed his hands of her; but he hadn't. He had punished her, and brutally, but he had undoubtedly shielded her from a terrible death – and in so doing had compromised his own sworn loyalty to his lord.

Renaud left only a few days later, and Ceolwynn rose painfully from her bed to watch him leave, hoping that the gesture might show him that she understood and could forgive. Suddenly it seemed very important that she, too, should be forgiven. Renaud, however, spoke to her hardly at all, chilling her with his cool indifference. Unexpectedly, she found that she missed his smile, his banter, his bright good humour; but he smiled only once, as he kissed his son a fond farewell before taking the reins of his restless stallion and swinging into the saddle.

Father Eadric stood a little aside, his face grey with concern. He seems to have aged ten years, Renaud thought with pity, and beckoned the priest to come close to his saddle. 'Watch her Father,' he said softly. 'Guard her well. It is her very life, priest, that I leave in your keeping.'

Ceolwynn handed him a goblet of wine brought by a servant and Renaud drank slowly, staring out into the distance while his horse tossed its head impatiently and pawed the ground. Surely now he must say something, Ceolwynn thought, but for a long time he said nothing. Someone coughed, and Renaud stirred, looking down at her with an expression she couldn't read.

'Will you pray for me, Ceolwynn,' he asked disconcertingly, 'while I fight the king's enemies in the north country?'

'Oh yes, of a certainty I will pray,' she answered truthfully, and he smiled grimly, wondering what it was exactly that she would pray for.

He leant forward suddenly, cupping her chin in his hand and forcing her to meet his eye. 'Take care, my lady,' was all he said, but she heard the warning there.

'Is there no more than that to be said between us?' she said, her hand seeking his with a kind of desperation.

He jerked his hand away from the intimacy of her touch and shook his head. Suddenly she understood that she had destroyed beyond repair the delicate fabric that had bound them together.

XII

August–December 1069

Summer brought the Danish fleet and rebellion flared across the land – in the north, on the Welsh borders and in the south west; almost everywhere, in fact, but in the southern shires, where Ceolwynn waited, in vain, for word from her husband.

The Danes landed in the Humber in late August, joining forces with the young Aetheling Edgar and the great lords of the north. This vast host then advanced unopposed on the city of York, slaughtering the hated Normans garrisoned there and destroying the castles built for their protection. Suddenly, everything William had achieved since Hastings seemed to be in dire jeopardy.

The king rushed northwards with every man he could muster, and Renaud, who had been sent with urgent messages for William fitzOsbern, found his lord had troubles enough of his own. The south west and the Welsh marcher country were up in arms, Edric the Wild was back, and Shrewsbury had been burned by the Welsh. The king's call for help made fitzOsbern groan, but he gave up over a hundred men for Renaud to lead to York, and it was on this wild ride north that fate took a hand in Renaud's affairs to an extent that he would not discover for some time to come.

Fate, in this instance, took the form of a fever which came stealthily at first, starting with a sudden weakness which Renaud, who was seldom ill, attributed to simple weariness. After all, he reasoned, he'd spent most of these past few days in the saddle with very little sleep – it was hardly surprising that his body ached and his eyes blurred.

'My lord, you are ill,' one of his escort, Broad Thomas, said with some concern as Renaud's horse began to stray out of the road, his grip on the reins weak and useless. 'Shall I call a halt for a while?' he urged. 'You must rest.'

'No, not yet,' Renaud insisted, fighting to force the words past an aching throat and parched lips. 'We ride on.' His body burned and his head screamed in agony, but he took a firmer grip on the reins and brought his horse back into line, assuring himself that all this would soon pass.

An hour later he tumbled from his saddle and knew no more.

It was late autumn and the trees had long since clothed themselves in shades of rich red-gold before Renaud came to himself again, waking early one morning to find himself lying on a pallet in a small, bare cell with only a high, barred window to let in the first thin threads of daylight.

Weakly, he raised his head to study his surroundings, disorientated by the unfamiliarity and a disturbing lack of memory. Walls of rough stone surrounded him, and he felt a moment's alarm, thinking himself a prisoner; but this anxiety was soon dispelled by the atmosphere of simple comfort and care all about him. The bedcovers, though coarse, were clean and warm, and close by there stood a table upon which he saw a jug of water, a wooden cup and a half-burned candle. Next to this was a stool, as though someone had recently been keeping vigil at his bedside.

He fell asleep again and awoke to the sound of distant chanting. He turned his head towards the stool, which some sixth sense told him he would now find occupied, and saw a young man in monkish habit seated there.

Renaud tried to speak; the words came out as a whisper, but it was enough to alert the monk, who gave a broad smile of pleasure.

'God be praised,' he cried, putting his hands together joyfully, 'he lives.' He rushed to pour a cup of water, holding it to Renaud's lips while supporting his head with a strong arm.

Renaud drank gratefully. 'Was it in doubt?' he asked, his voice growing a little stronger.

'Oh yes, most certainly,' the monk assured him contentedly. 'We'd almost despaired of you, but we had faith to strengthen our prayers, and Brother Theodore's potions of course.'

'And your name, brother?' Renaud asked. 'I'm sure I owe you, too, a debt of gratitude,' he said. 'Be assured, I will remember you always in my prayers.'

'I'm Brother Wulfstan,' he answered, 'but truly I have done nothing to deserve your thanks – only my duty, and that I was glad to do.'

'Then tell me, brother, where am I?' Renaud asked, beginning to remember the events preceding his collapse. 'How long have I been here?'

The monk shook his head. 'All in good time,' he said. 'I'll fetch Father Adrian. He'll answer all your questions.'

He bustled out and Renaud, who suddenly found himself ravenously hungry, was greatly pleased when a small boy, barely six years old and dressed like Brother Wulfstan in the drab, unbleached woollen robe of the Benedictine, came in carrying a tray of food which he then placed carefully upon the table.

The meal was simple, broth, fresh bread, a little cheese and apples, but the smell was wonderful and Renaud addressed himself to it with such enthusiasm that it was several moments before he noticed that the child was still there, watching him, his brown eyes round and bright with interest.

'I haven't got a tail, I promise you,' Renaud joked pleasantly, knowing that many simple folk firmly believed that all Normans were demons and possessed a tail as proof of it.

'I know that,' the child answered, indignant. 'I looked while you slept.'

Renaud started to laugh, but the boy looked so affronted that he quickly turned it into a cough. 'Have you been long in this house, brother?' he asked to change the subject.

'I'm not really a brother, not yet,' his young attendant replied, bowing his head so that Renaud could see he was untonsured, 'but I've been here always – as long as I can remember.' He smiled a gap-toothed, radiant smile. 'I'll take my vows as soon as I'm old enough.'

'And does that please you?' Renaud asked wonderingly, his heart and mind recoiling from the thought of a childhood spent solely in study, fasting and prayer.

'Oh yes,' the boy answered. 'I'm very happy here, most of the time.' For just the briefest moment there was a look in his eyes, a sad, forlorn expression, which stirred something deep within Renaud's memory, some vague recollection which fluttered at the back of his mind, then slipped away before he had time to grasp it. 'I'm not always as good as I should be,' the boy admitted regretfully as he gathered up the tray and its empty dishes. 'I do seem to get into a lot of trouble sometimes.'

Renaud smiled, suddenly feeling too tired to talk. The boy left and Renaud had just begun to doze once more when he had another visitor – a man of middle years, tall and dark, with sharp, intelligent eyes and a marked air of authority. This, as Renaud deduced at once, could be none other than Father Adrian.

'Forgive me, my son,' the prior began, in unmistakably Norman French, 'I would have come to you sooner but important matters, you understand ...' He tailed off, shrugging expressively.

'Of course, Father,' Renaud started to say.

Father Adrian sat himself down in one graceful, flowing movement. His manner, both cultured and worldly, struck Renaud as being somewhat at odds with his office, and privately he wondered if this wasn't a man who would be more at home in the court than the cloister. 'You are a very fortunate young man,' the prior was saying, and Renaud quickly dragged his attention back. 'It's very likely that you would have died had your companions not heard our bell ringing for Nones. They would not have found us otherwise – our priory is somewhat remote and set well off your road. God must have been watching over you, my son.'

Renaud nodded, but his mind was racing ahead with more questions. 'So what news, Father?' he asked, tense with anxiety. 'How goes it with the king?'

'Oh, William still has his head and a crown to set upon it, have no fear,' the prior said. 'Did you ever doubt it?' he then queried with a slight, humorous raising of the eyebrows.

Renaud laughed. 'Of course not, but the Danes, what of them?'

'Oh the Danes,' the prior said contemptuously, waving one elegant hand in the air. 'They did what the Danes always do; they plundered what they could then disappeared back to their ships!'

'Then it's all over?'

'Well no, perhaps I exaggerate, just a little. The Danes seem happy enough with their booty and the king seems happy enough to let them keep it as long as they give no more support to the rebels; but they have not gone away, and may yet cause more trouble. The king has deemed it wise to put aside that problem for the time being and turn his attention to the task of crushing the rebellion in Mercia.'

'So it is to Mercia I must ride to join him,' Renaud said thoughtfully.

'Yes, possibly, but not yet. Brother Theodore, our infirmarian, tells me you will need to rest here for many more days.'

'It's true that I still feel very weak, but I must be gone as soon as possible. Father, are any of my men still here?'

'Two only, praise God,' the prior said, raising both hands in mock despair. 'They eat enough in one day to feed one of our brethren for a whole month.'

'I beg your pardon for them, Father. I will of course repay you for your kindness and hospitality.'

'We do only what we have been bidden to do by Our Lord and the holy St Benedict. However,' he added with a wry smile, 'we are a poor house and would receive any suitable donation with much gratitude.' He gave Renaud no time to reply, but rose with a determined air and sketched a brief blessing over him. 'Now, I must go and you must sleep, my son,' he said, and Renaud, obediently, fell asleep almost as soon as the prior had left him.

A few days later Renaud felt strong enough to leave his bed and walk out in the cloistergarth with the amiable Brother Wulfstan ready and willing to offer any necessary assistance. A circuit of the cloisters was a short walk, but the fresh northern air, redolent with the scent of rain-watered earth and damp grass, was sweet and reviving, and Renaud felt the strength begin to flow slowly back into his stiff, bed-weakened limbs.

'Has Father Adrian been prior here long?' he asked Brother Wulfstan curiously.

'No, not all that long – perhaps two years.'

'It cannot have been a welcome appointment,' Renaud said, probing. 'A Norman prior, I mean.'

'No, there was much bitterness at first. It's always been the custom that the brothers should elect their own prior, not have a stranger foisted upon them by the bishop, and Father Adrian seemed, well, out of place up here in these mountains.'

'Yes,' Renaud agreed. 'He looks like a prince who has donned a monk's habit for a prank, and means to throw it off at any moment.'

Brother Wulfstan laughed heartily. 'That's exactly it,' he agreed. 'Indeed,' he added, glancing around cautiously and lowering his voice, 'rumour has it that he's the bastard son of a bishop, at the very least.' In his normal voice, he continued: 'But we were all wrong about him. Make no mistake, Father Adrian is one of the most worthy, most godly men you will ever meet.'

Renaud must have looked surprised because the monk obviously felt that he had to justify his statement. 'St Aidan's has never been a slothful, sinful house, you understand,' he explained. 'We have few tenants and gather few tithes, so we have always had to work hard, just to feed and clothe ourselves; but I think that because our last prior was ill so much of the time, we tended to lose sight of God. Father Adrian brought God back into our hearts and minds, and now, though we work harder than ever, everything we do is done with joy and thanksgiving.'

In his own way, Renaud understood this. Father Adrian was a born leader – a man capable of inspiring men to great achievements in the same way that King William, and even the late King Harold, managed to inspire their armies. Godmund, he remembered, had had that same quality of leadership, and because thinking of Godmund made him think of Ceolwynn, he lapsed into an unhappy silence which Brother Wulfstan took to indicate weariness.

'There, I've overtired you,' he reproached himself, and despite Renaud's denials, insisted that he returned to his bed.

It was a further week before Renaud was finally fit enough to ride, and then word came that William had already routed the Mercian rebels at Stafford and had turned his attention once more to the north, where, it was rumoured, the Danes were planning another campaign in alliance with the Northumbrian rebels. William was now moving back towards York, and Renaud knew he could stay no longer.

Broad Thomas and Little Hugh, the two men who had come with him from Cottesham, were eager to be away once more, bored with the company of monks and the almost unceasing sounds of chanting and bell ringing. They had the horses saddled and ready as soon as they had broken their fast, but Renaud delayed just a little longer to hear Mass, to make his farewells and to hand to the prior a purse of silver in gratitude for his care. All this accomplished, he was making his way towards the stables when he heard a most terrible outcry – somehow shocking in a place of such quiet calm.

Intrigued, he sought out the source of the noise and soon discovered that it came from the scriptorium where a man's voice was raised in anger so loud that it almost drowned the other sound, a child's loud weeping.

He peered tentatively around the door, unwilling to interfere in what was obviously a simple disciplinary matter, but curious to know who and what could have inspired such fury. Somehow he was not at all surprised to see that the culprit was his young friend of the supper tray, looking so small and helpless as blow upon blow rained down upon his frail shoulders that Renaud, moved to pity, felt obliged to intercede on his behalf.

'Good brother,' he said placatingly, moving into the sight of the enraged monk, 'stay your hand I pray you. Whatever the offence, surely the child has been dealt punishment enough?'

'Just look,' the monk said, almost plaintively, pointing in obvious anguish at some small sheets of parchment scattered across one of the writing desks. 'Such a waste,' he wailed. 'God forgive him, it's such a waste. He was set to copy these texts, but just look at what he's done. Scribblings, vain, foolish scribblings on the finest vellum, and to use our most costly inks as well!' He shook his head despairingly.

'Well, if God can forgive him, then surely so can you,' Renaud said sensibly, and picked up the offending scraps of parchment to study them more closely. The little novice had stopped crying and was watching him. Suddenly Renaud was aware that the boy was a true artist. 'The boy has much skill,' he remarked. The drawings – colourful sketches of plants, birds and animals – were accurate and well observed, displaying a talent far beyond his years. 'He does great credit to his teacher,' he added slyly, and was pleased to observe the softening effect of flattery on the angry monk.

'It is true,' the man conceded, much calmer now, 'the lad shows much promise, but he has a tendency towards frivolity and he will allow his mind, and his pen, to wander.'

'Were you never young, brother?' Renaud asked sadly, laying down the sheets of vellum. One fluttered to the ground and he stooped to pick it up, noting with pleasure the delightful picture of a dog cavorting playfully within a border of oak and vine leaves. 'Here,' he said on impulse, offering the monk a small handful of silver coin, 'I will pay for the wasted ink.'

Astonished, the monk hesitated briefly before taking the money. 'Brother Martin,' he said severely, turning to the boy, 'you owe this noble lord your thanks for his generosity.'

'Thank you, noble lord,' the boy repeated obediently, and Renaud laughed.

'Do as you are bid in future, young man,' he said, laying an affectionate hand on the boy's soft, mouse-brown hair. 'You'll find your passage through this life much smoother that way.'

There was no more time to waste. Renaud quickly rejoined his men, now waiting for him at the gatehouse, and they left without further interruption or delay. Broad Thomas, who claimed an amazing ability to memorize directions, had managed to discover a route over the mountains which should lead them safely to York within two days.

Trusting to his skill they followed him along the lonely, tortuous trackways which crossed the high Pennines. It was an uneasy ride, they were few in number and very vulnerable to attack, but Thomas led them unerringly to each promised landmark and by dusk they found that they had made remarkably good progress.

'Were you not told of any village close by, Thomas?' Renaud asked regretfully, dismounting at a sheltered spot they had chosen for their night camp. 'It would be pleasant not to have to spend the night in the open. This ground will make a poor mattress, I'll warrant,' he added, kicking away some of the many small stones littering the ground.

'There is one, so I was told, my lord,' Thomas replied, 'but it's further off our road. There,' he said, pointing down the valley lying to the right of them. 'Can you see the lake?' Renaud strained his eyes to see, and then agreed that he thought he could just make out the faintest sheen of sunlight on water. 'Well, there's a village there somewhere,' Thomas said, 'and I've been told that it's not exactly unfriendly.'

'And what does that mean?' Renaud asked. 'Not exactly unfriendly?'

'I think it means that they might not welcome us with open arms, but nor are they likely to slaughter us in our beds.'

'That's good enough for me,' Renaud said, swinging back into the saddle. 'I've grown soft these past weeks. What's the name of this place?'

'Blackwater,' Thomas replied, and Renaud, stunned by the force of coincidence, stopped dead in his tracks.

There was a chill bite to the wind that whistled down the

Blackwater valley, scarring the surface of the lake with small, sharp-edged wavelets and stirring up small dust storms on the dry road. Shivering a little, Renaud drew his cloak closer around him and held up his arm as a signal for Thomas and Hugh to come to a halt.

'What think you?' he asked them.

The three men studied the village, now only just visible in the gathering dusk, with cautious, watchful eyes. There was little sign of life, but that was not unusual once the day's work was done. A shaggy white dog ambled around the corner of one of the huts, sniffed, then lifted its leg up against a barrel before ambling on about its business.

'It looks safe enough to me,' Hugh said. 'Shall I blow the horn, my lord?'

'Yes, blow your horn, Hugh,' Renaud said, making up his mind. 'If Wulfhere is still master here, he will know then that we come in peace and will respect that.'

He spoke without thinking and seeing the startled expression on the faces of the other men, paused briefly to explain how it was that he thought he might know the thegn of Blackwater. In the telling it seemed to him a matter of some considerable wonder that he should find himself here in this place, at this time, with his promise to Ceolwynn as yet unfulfilled.

Even in his fiercest anger Renaud had not forgotten his promise to Ceolwynn. On his way north, he had been in London for a short time and had made a point of discovering where Wulfhere might be found, intending to seek him out at the first opportunity.

As things had turned out, the events of the past few months had put the whole matter out of his mind, and so it was with some satisfaction that he realized that now, however unexpectedly, at last he had the chance to make good his word.

They moved forward, shadowy figures now in the rapidly descending darkness. Hugh blew his horn and it resounded loud and shrill through the clear, crisp night air. Dogs barked and light suddenly streamed from a dozen places as shutters were thrown wide and doors opened. A small gathering of slightly apprehensive villagers crowded into the single street to see who these unlooked-for visitors might be. At their head stood a man, broader even than Thomas, strong as a young oak, with hair and beard the colour of gold. Renaud recognized him at once.

'Wulfhere,' he cried with genuine pleasure, swinging out of the saddle to grip the young man by the shoulders. 'You cannot know how good it is for me to find you here, alive and well.' There was a strange, uncomfortable silence and Renaud was taken aback to see Wulfhere staring at him in confusion. 'Don't you remember me?' he asked, dropping his hands. 'Renaud de Lassay. I was at Cottesham when you were thegn Godmund's man.'

Wulfhere's face cleared at once as comprehension dawned. 'Well of course I remember,' he replied enthusiastically. 'Renaud, the young Norman lad.' The smile disappeared from his face as suddenly as it had appeared. 'All that was a long time ago,' he said in a voice from which all friendliness had vanished. 'Times have changed and, for us at least, not for the better.'

'Wulfhere,' interrupted a soft, gentle voice that Renaud remembered well. 'Lord Renaud comes to us in peace and friendship. At least let us welcome him in the same spirit.'

Estrith came forward from the back of the crowd leading by the hand two sturdy young boys, like as two peas and as golden fair as angels.

'Our sons,' Estrith told him, 'Godmund and Edgar.'

Renaud returned their grave, hesitant smiles. 'They are fine boys, Estrith,' he said. On an impulse he stepped forward to embrace her heartily and affectionately in the English fashion. 'Right glad I am to see you, dearest Estrith,' he told her, and all at once the tense, almost hostile atmosphere eased.

Before he had time to register the change of mood, the horses were being led away and Wulfhere was striding towards his hall, calling for bread and ale and already deep in reminiscence of happier days.

Wulfhere's hall was very small, hardly more than a large cottage, Renaud observed with some curiosity. Estrith noticed his surprise and told him how their first hall, which had been almost a mile away from Blackwater, had been destroyed by raiders several years before. Wulfhere, she added, had decided to rebuild in the village, a situation they both found more comfortable and familiar.

Once they sat down to eat, Wulfhere talked and talked about the past. He spoke of his pride in his thegnship, and commented bitterly that the honour meant nothing now, in a conquered land. The ale flowed, strong and heady, and Wulfhere drank steadily as he talked, as if to drown all the grief and bitterness in his soul. Renaud, eager to ask his own questions and tell his own news, nonetheless managed to listen attentively and keep a tight curb on his impatience, but all the while his eyes searched the hall, in vain, for other familiar faces.

In a corner, curled together like puppies, slept Wulfhere's twin sons, wrapped in sheepskins and lying in the straw along with the servants. Not for them the ease and comfort their mother had once known. Estrith, older now but no less lovely than he remembered, moved gracefully from man to man, plying each of them with food and drink and making even Renaud's Normans, lost and speechless in this stream of Saxon, feel comfortable and at ease.

Her tunic was shabby, patched, and the soft hands that once had drawn sweet music from the lyre were red and work-roughened. Renaud guessed that there could be little room for music in her present life, and as she leaned over his shoulder to pour his ale he gave her a gentle smile of sympathy. She straightened, meeting his eye with a half amused, half angry glance which told him beyond a shadow of a doubt that although her husband might have become soured by life's cruel twists and turns, she at least was content, happy, and had no need of his pity.

It wasn't until the fourth horn of ale that Wulfhere finally allowed Renaud to put in a word. 'So, Renaud,' he said, 'what brings you to this wild land?'

'I came here looking for the lady Aelfrun and her young son,' he said. 'I need to know that they arrived here safely, and where they are now.' The stricken look on the faces of both Wulfhere and Estrith sent his heart plummeting into his boots. 'They did get here?' he asked softly.

'They're dead,' Wulfhere said and slammed his fist into the table so hard that it set all the dogs barking. 'They died on the road, slaughtered by a band of thieving, murdering Scots, may the bastards rot in hell. They never even reached us,' he added sorrowfully. 'We never saw them alive.'

Renaud found himself speechless. He had not expected to hear anything quite so dreadful, as final, as this.

It was Estrith who at last broke the long silence. 'How did you know about my sister's child?' she asked curiously. 'He was born long after you left us.'

'Of course,' Renaud exclaimed, 'you do not know. I am married now to Godmund's daughter, Ceolwynn. It was she who told me, and it's for her sake that I came to seek you all.'

'Then Ceolwynn is safe,' Estrith cried joyfully. 'Heaven be praised. I have prayed for her so long and so often, and now I know God has seen fit to answer my prayers.'

Renaud wondered if Ceolwynn would view her marriage in quite the same light. 'We too have a child,' he told them proudly. 'A son, Edmund, just two years old, who will one day, God willing, be lord of Cottesham.'

Wulfhere frowned. 'All this time,' he sighed, 'we never thought to send word to her at Cottesham. We were so sure, so certain, she would have gone away with Lord Cenred – he was her betrothed, you know,' he added absently, forgetting that Renaud would have known this. 'Poor little maid. She must have been desperate for news of Aelfrun and the child.' He poured himself another drink and subsided into a morose silence.

Renaud's men took themselves off to sleep at the back of the hall and Estrith, who had finished serving, sat down on the bench, squeezing herself in between Renaud and Wulfhere, who shuffled along to give her room but otherwise seemed to have lost interest in both of them. Renaud suspected that the drink had begun to fuddle his brain.

'Do you have any idea what became of my cousin Cenred?' Estrith asked.

Since this was still a sore subject, Renaud answered somewhat shortly: 'He's still alive, as far as I know.'

'Then I must be thankful that I have not lost all my kin,' she said. 'Dunn told me what happened to my parents and my sisters.'

'Dunn?' Renaud echoed in surprise. 'Dunn was not killed then, along with his mistress?'

'Why no: he was badly hurt, it's true, but the damage to his body healed in time, though sometimes I fear his spirit will never fully recover. I've sent someone to fetch him from the manor farm, knowing he would be glad to see you again.' She laid her hand on his arm and leaned close as if to speak in confidence. 'Whatever has happened between our peoples, Renaud,' she told him, 'we were always fond of you and regarded you as our friend. It doesn't surprise me that you have taken Ceolwynn under your protection, and I for one am glad of it. She always loved you, you know. She cried when you left us.'

'She was a child,' Renaud replied uncomfortably, glad that Estrith could have no knowledge of the last tears he had caused his young wife to shed.

'Yes, she was a child, but I think she knew her own heart.'

She looked up quickly as a sudden draught from an opened door signalled that Dunn himself had arrived. Renaud half expected to find Dunn older but otherwise unchanged, but the man who walked towards him now, he saw, was hardly that same man at all.

Renaud's first astonished thought was that there was nothing at all clerkish now about Godmund's steward. His hair was long, tied back with a throng of plaited leather, and his clothes were rough and work-stained. A long scar, fading now to silver, ran down the left side of his face to disappear into a thick beard more grey than brown. He walked with a limp, and when Renaud gripped his arms in friendship he noticed that one arm was much thinner, far less muscular, than the other.

'I never thought I could find it in my heart to welcome a Norman,' Dunn said, returning Renaud's bear-like grip, 'but I find myself truly glad to see you, Lord Renaud. Seeing you brings back so many happy memories.'

'Renaud has brought us the most wonderful news, Dunn,' Estrith said eagerly before Renaud could make any reply. 'Ceolwynn is safe and well at Cottesham.'

'Can this be true?' Dunn asked, half disbelieving. 'Can you be sure?'

'I am sure,' Renaud laughed. 'She is my wife, and the mother of my son.'

'God be praised,' Dunn breathed, and tears stood in his eyes.

Much later, when all the questions had been asked and answered and all the past memories brought out and shared, Renaud burrowed comfortably into a bed of straw near the fire with his head too full to sleep. He lay restless and wakeful, listening to the snores, the coughs, the muffled gigglings and gruntings in the dark, and started, unexpectedly, to think about Emma, who had hardly been in his thoughts at all since his last encounter with Ceolwynn. Where was she now? he wondered. Would she still be the same? Did she love him still? Sudden panic gripped him: suppose she had already returned to Normandy – the thought made him toss and turn in agitation. How would it would be if Roger de Virar should die? The man was old – it was not impossible. He'd almost forgotten the obstacle of his own marriage.

Drowsy at last, he drifted into sleep, and in his dreams saw Emma riding at his side, her slender hand, clothed in a jewelled glove, resting lightly on his sleeve and her lovely face alight with desire. With them rode a smiling child, dark and handsome, but with features strangely blurred and uncertain. Suddenly the woman on the horse was Ceolwynn, not Emma, and she riding away from him, not fast, but no matter how hard he tried he couldn't keep up with her. She was vanishing from his sight and he called after her as loud as he could, but it was as though he had been struck dumb – no sound came from his mouth. Now the face of the child, too, had changed. It was Edmund's baby face that stared up at him, accusingly, and he was saying – though the voice, mysteriously, was Estrith's – 'but she loves you, but she loves you,' over and over again until Renaud, sweating, woke up with a start to find that it was already morning.

Just before he left, Renaud walked with Dunn in the churchyard. They stopped beside the two graves in which lay, as they both supposed, the last remains of the dearly loved wife and child of Godmund Edgarson.

'Cruel, cruel,' Renaud mourned. 'She didn't deserve this fate.' He knelt at the graveside and laid his hand on the rough-carved stone which marked the place. Dunn had spared no detail in the telling of her last minutes, scourging himself with his memories, and Renaud grieved for her suffering. 'Come back to Cottesham, Dunn,' he said unexpectedly as he got to his feet. The idea had come to him suddenly, but it seemed good to him. 'We have need of you there, and Lady Ceolwynn would welcome you most gladly, I know it.'

Shaking his head slowly, Dunn gazed off into the mountains and made no answer. In his face Renaud saw an expression of such agony and guilt that he understood at once what Estrith had meant when she had spoken of Dunn's unhealed spirit. 'No,' he said at last. 'I am grateful, my lord, but I must stay here, where my lady is.'

'You did all you could to aid them, Dunn,' Renaud told him gently. 'Do you really think she would hold you to blame for what

215

happened? Forgive yourself, man, for no one else could ever believe that there is anything to forgive.'

Dunn shook his head again, and Renaud knew that further argument would be wasted. He left soon afterwards, glad to have renewed old friendships, but heartsick at the news he carried away, knowing it would do nothing to help mend matters between himself and Ceolwynn, even if mending had been what he desired.

Wulfhere had made his farewells just after dawn and was already in the fields, working alongside the women and children in an effort to scratch a living from this inhospitable land. Renaud, seeing how few able young men there were, realized that Blackwater had paid dearly for supporting King Harold.

This thought reminded him of a warning he had in mind to offer Estrith. 'One thing more,' he said to her from the saddle. 'The king is a just man and a good lord, but he can be cruel, merciless even, towards those who would defy him. If you love your husband, lady, keep him from a fight he cannot win.'

Estrith nodded, understanding only too well his meaning.

'Have no fear,' she replied grimly. 'I will keep him safe at home. Gall to us though it may be, William is our anointed king and Wulfhere will commit no treason.'

Renaud rode away, content in the knowledge that Wulfhere's folk at least would be safe from further danger; but as the whole of the north country was soon to discover, guilty or innocent, young or old, none would be spared the consequences of defying the Bastard of Normandy.

'Will you be spending Christmas with the court?' Hugo asked thoughtfully. He had recently arrived in York, with letters to William from fitzOsbern, and had gladly accepted Renaud's invitation to stay with him while he awaited William's reply. The campaign in the north now seemed to be over and Renaud, who had been slightly wounded in a minor skirmish just before the Danes had finally withdrawn from the town, was glad of an excuse to enjoy himself and forget his troubles for a while.

'No, it's time I went home,' Renaud said. 'I've not seen my son since haymaking, and it's time I checked my steward is not robbing me blind.'

Hugo nodded with mock gravity. 'Ah, the trials we landholders have to endure,' he intoned solemnly, and Renaud laughed. 'It's sometimes hard to believe the change in our fortunes, is it not?' Hugo went on, more seriously. 'Less than four years ago we were both landless. Yet look at us now.'

'Yes, but in our different ways we both paid a high price for what we've gained,' his friend replied. 'You lost a father and two brothers, and I lost friendships that meant much to me.'

'You gained a wife,' Hugo said mischievously, having heard something, if not all, of Renaud's unhappy marriage.

'You have a cruel streak, Hugo,' Renaud remarked without rancour. 'How is Emma?'

'She's very well,' Hugo replied, watching Renaud's face over the rim of his cup. 'Actually, it was thinking of my sister that made me ask where you intended to spend Christmas. Emma, and her husband of course, the odious Roger, are to spend the season with me at Mandon.'

'Oh,' Renaud said, expressionless. A maidservant came in with a tray of honeyed fruits and Renaud took one.

'I thought perhaps you might like to join us.'

Renaud hesitated. 'I'm not sure that would be wise,' he said at last.

'Wisdom is for greybeards,' Hugo scoffed. 'Take what you want from life while you are still young enough to enjoy it, my friend.' As if to illustrate his point, he grabbed hold of the maid and kissed her vigorously, forcing her to drop her tray with a shriek, but when he took no further interest in her she flounced out, clearly disappointed.

'Hugo, you baffle me,' Renaud sighed, watching the incident with mingled amusement and disapproval. 'You seem very careless of your sister's honour.'

'Emma is responsible for her own honour, I'm not her keeper; and anyway, I detest Roger de Virar. You can have no idea how much pleasure it gives me to see the man humiliated.'

'But he doesn't even know he's being humiliated,' Renaud argued, 'and God forbid that he ever should.'

'But I do,' Hugo countered happily, 'that's enough for me.'

'Well, I'm not sure,' Renaud said doubtfully, but he was sorely tempted by Hugo's offer. This might well be the only opportunity he would have to see Emma and her child – his child – before they returned to Normandy in the spring.

217

'I've an idea,' Hugo said. 'Why don't you send for this wife of yours to come to Mandon? I'm curious to meet the woman who caused you to sacrifice a possible fortune for her sake, and who repays you with such loathing. She could bring the boy, too, since you seem to be pining for him. Just think how amusing it will be,' he added, grinning impishly, 'you and Emma with your guilty secret, Roger and your wife all unknowing.'

'It's not a jest, Hugo,' Renaud reproved him quietly. 'I really did love Emma, I think perhaps I still do, and I know she loved me once. Do you think she still feels the same?'

'Who knows a woman's mind?' Hugo replied vaguely, with an careless shrug. 'Come, give me your answer.'

'Very well, I will come, and I will do as you suggest – I will send for Ceolwynn and Edmund.'

Resentment and anger had replaced Ceolwynn's early penitence as the months went by without a word from Renaud. She snapped at the servants, and soon everybody was equally miserable and bad tempered.

She was in a particularly ill mood on a day when a band of travelling players stopped to ask for food and shelter for the night. By way of payment, they offered a show for all the company in the hall, and promised news from far and near, gleaned on their travels. Ceolwynn cheered up, just a bit. It would soon be Christmas and they all deserved a little pleasure.

'What news have you?' she asked the lute player, almost shouting above the noise of stamping feet and wild music. Even the two Normans, Alain and Hugh, whom Renaud had left to keep an eye on things, seemed to be enjoying themselves for once. Ceolwynn scowled at them, and one, catching her glance, mockingly raised his cup to her. She turned away, furious and humiliated. How dare Renaud think that she needed to be watched all the time, like a child? 'Has there been much fighting?' she asked her companion, forcing herself to maintain a polite calm. 'We seldom get any news here that isn't already weeks old.'

'Most of the fighting seems to be over now the Danes have gone,' the young man told her, tearing with neat, white teeth at a piece of mutton. 'The king is to celebrate Christmas in York, so I hear.' He belched and wiped his greasy fingers on his leggings, trying not to stare too obviously at the attractive swell of her

218

breasts as she leaned closer to catch his words. 'He's even sent
for his crown to be carried up to him, all the way from
Winchester,' he shouted.

'So his army will be disbanding soon?' she asked, and felt irritated with herself for sounding so pleased.

He shrugged. 'I expect so.' He was bored with this talk of
fighting and armies. He scanned the crowd for a pretty face and a
ripe young body, and saw Hild coming towards them, hips
swaying provocatively.

Music was playing and people were dancing. The young man
jumped up and grabbed Hild by the hand, whirling her off into
the dance with her skirts flying and her face flushed with pleasure
and excitement. Ceolwynn watched them with an ugly knot of
jealousy in her heart, and as soon as Hild caught her eye she
summoned her to her side.

'I'm tired,' she said, brusque and petulant. 'Come, help me
make ready for bed.'

'Then may I come back to the hall, mistress?' Hild asked hopefully, looking over her shoulder at the handsome young bard, who
was already looking round for another partner.

'No,' Ceolwynn answered sharply, 'I want you to stay with me
tonight.'

Hild's face fell and Ceolwynn, who knew she was being petty
and spiteful but couldn't help herself, left the hall in an even
worse mood than before.

'Anyway,' she asked later, as Hild dutifully combed the tangles
from her hair, though rather more roughly than usual, 'aren't you
supposed to be courting – ow! do try to be more careful – the
reeve's boy?'

Hild sniffed with annoyance. 'I heard tell that he is seeing
another maid, on the sly. It may be true – Handel had always a
wandering eye. I planned to make him jealous and bring him up to
the mark at last.'

'Oh, and I spoiled it for you,' Ceolwynn cried, feeling very
guilty. 'Leave this,' she said firmly, taking the comb out of her
maid's hands, 'go back to the hall and fight to win your love.'

Hild beamed. 'Oh, thank you,' she cried, giving Ceolwynn a
quick, grateful hug, followed by a warm-hearted, sympathetic
one. Hild loved her like a sister. She thought she knew what it
was that ailed her now, and, meaning to be kind, she said: 'Have

219

no fear, my lady, my lord Renaud will come back very soon. If any harm had come to him you would surely have heard of it.'

Ceolwynn shook her off angrily. 'Him!' she spat out. 'I hope he's dead.'

After Hild had gone, Ceolwynn drifted restlessly around her bedchamber, picking things up, putting them down, sighing. She really didn't know what she wanted but she knew, and the knowledge was painful, that she missed Renaud dreadfully.

The first time the sound came – a brief rattle, like hailstones striking against the shutters – the noise from the hall was still so loud that Ceolwynn wasn't quite sure what it was she had heard, or even if she had heard anything at all. The second time it was louder, more insistent, and she remembered the night Brand had thrown pebbles at her window. This sound was the same. Brand was waiting for her outside.

She threw on her cloak, but ran out barefoot in case she wasted too much time putting on her shoes and he disappeared back into the woods.

It took some time for Ceolwynn to make out the shadowy, hooded figure of a man in the dark – standing motionless in the shelter of the wall – but in the end it was his frosted breath on the cold night air which gave him away.

'Brand?' she hissed uncertainly. The figure moved slowly towards her, cautious still, until she could see him clearly in the moonlight. It was Cenred. 'What in Heaven's name are you doing here?' she asked, then gasped as she saw that under his cloak his tunic was covered in blood.

He glanced down at his clothes and grinned. 'Not mine,' he said succinctly, and tapped the hilt of the sword at his belt.

'Thank the Lord for that,' she said, then suddenly alarmed she added: 'Whose is it? You know, don't you, that innocent people, our people, will suffer if a Norman dies by violence and no culprit is found? Will this bring danger to Cottesham?'

'You need have no fear. It's old blood, spilt in honest battle. We've come from Stafford, those of us that are left. We're hungry and tired, and we need a safe hiding place.'

'Holy Jesu, not here!' she exclaimed, horrified. 'I cannot hide you. There are two of Lord Renaud's men here, and he himself could return at any time. He knows you were here before and will not trust me now. It's not safe.'

He shook his head. 'It's all right. That's not why I'm here.'

He took hold of her hand and pulled her back into the concealment of the shadows. She was nervous, there was always the
possibility of discovery, but there was also something a little
exciting about meeting Cenred like this, in defiance of her
husband. It seemed, at that moment, as good a way as any to get
her revenge on Renaud for deserting her.

Unfortunately for Ceolwynn, not everyone was either abed or
in the hall. Folca had left the revels to relieve himself, and was
contentedly pissing up against the stable wall when he glimpsed
the two cloaked and hooded figures dart furtively into hiding.

Excitement dried up the flow midstream as instinct warned him
that this was not some commonplace lovers' tryst, but a mystery
that might well be turned to his advantage. His suspicions were
confirmed as he recognized the sound of his mistress's voice, and
hurriedly retying his points he crept closer, with a tread surprisingly light and silent for a man of his build.

Cenred was saying, 'I heard what happened, after we left. It
was my fault, I should never have involved you. It wasn't even
truly necessary.'

'What do you mean, it wasn't necessary?' she asked, puzzled.

'There was no need to bring the silver to Cottesham for safe-
keeping. It could have been hidden almost anywhere.'

'Then why did you?'

'Why do you think, Ceolwynn?' He moved closer and put his
hands on her shoulders. 'I wanted to have an excuse to come here,
to see you, to win you back.'

She gasped slightly and stepped back out of his clasp. 'You
mean you endangered all of us for nothing?' she said, staring at
him in disbelief.

'Not for nothing,' he protested. 'I love you Ceolwynn. I'd do
anything to persuade you to leave Renaud.' He took hold of her
again, grasping her arms so tightly it made her wince with pain.
The wild, intense look in his eye frightened her. 'I know you
don't love him,' he insisted, 'you can't possibly love him after
what he did to you. I would never lay a finger on you, I swear it.
Come away with me now, Ceolwynn. I'll make you happy.'

'No,' she said heatedly, trying to struggle free. 'I can't go with
you, not now, not ever. Let me go Cenred, please.'

'You don't mean that,' he said pulling her close. 'You said I should come back for you. You promised you would come away with me when I did.'

'No, no I didn't,' she protested fiercely. 'I promised you nothing, Cenred, nothing.'

But it was obvious that Cenred wasn't listening. She could feel his heart pounding and smell the rank odour of sweat and blood on his clothes. 'Don't be frightened, little one,' he said soothingly, and there was something oddly menacing in his tenderness. 'I'll make you change your mind,' he whispered, and suddenly his hand was inside her clothes, stroking, squeezing, but there was nothing pleasurable or exciting in his touch now.

Ceolwynn struggled, beating at him uselessly with her fists, still protesting in a fierce whisper that made no impression on him whatsoever. 'Please, Cenred, please don't,' she begged, her mind struggling frantically to find some way of escape that would not bring Renaud's men-at-arms down upon him. She was frightened, but if she screamed then Cenred would most surely die, and his death would be on her conscience for ever.

She tried to jerk herself backwards, out of his grasp, but now he had her pinned against the wall, his hand suddenly beneath her skirts, his fingers brushing with shaming intimacy the springy curls of her bush. He groaned and began forcing his hand between her thighs, the sound of his breathing harsh and loud in her ear. Ceolwynn knew that if she didn't scream now it would be too late; but then he was kissing her, silencing her, and the coppery taste of blood filled her mouth as his teeth bit painfully into the soft flesh of her unyielding lips. Frantically, she wrenched her head sideways and opened her mouth to scream.

At that very moment, Folca, creeping closer in his efforts to see and hear better, kicked over a wooden bucket which rolled away with a quick succession of loud, heavy thuds. Cenred leapt away from Ceolwynn, his hand reaching for his sword.

Folca held his breath, as alarmed as they at the thought of discovery. He stayed very still. It was very, very dark, and darkness was all that lay between him and the unknown man with the sword.

As the seconds passed, Ceolwynn, suspecting that it was perhaps a cat which had caused the disturbance, realized that if she didn't seize her opportunity now, she would be no better off than before. She turned on Cenred, pushing him away, towards the woods. 'Run,' she hissed urgently, 'it's Renaud's Normans. They always patrol the village at this time. You stand almost no chance at all against the two of them.' Cenred still hesitated, obviously prepared to argue with that assertion. 'Go!' she ordered with all the authority she could muster, 'go now.'

She pushed him again, and at last he went, disappearing from her sight within seconds. Heart beating much too fast, Ceolwynn hurried to bar herself in her room, trembling with relief and promising that never, ever, would she allow herself to be trapped like that again.

Folca, equally relieved, walked back to the hall deep in thought. So, he thought gleefully, the lady Ceolwynn, that proud, haughty piece, was no better than a common fornicating slut, keeping secret assignations with her lover while her husband was from home.

How best could he use this new knowledge, he wondered? He could expose her as an adulteress – she wouldn't look anything like as proud or as pretty with her nostrils slit, the fate of many an adulterous wife – but there would be small satisfaction for him in that. Who, he asked himself, had been the man with her? Hadn't there in fact been something vaguely familiar about him, his voice? He pondered deeply, then slammed his fist to his forehead in sudden realization. Of course, it was that young oaf she'd been betrothed to before the Normans came. What was his name? Cynwulf? No, Cenred, that was it, Wilfred's nephew – outlawed now and leader of a notorious band of rebels.

Folca stopped short, quivering with excitement. This wasn't just a matter of adultery now. Lady Ceolwynn was consorting with rebels and that made her a traitor.

Just what price, he wondered gleefully, would that arrogant young miss be prepared to pay to save herself from the axe or the stake?

XIII

December 1069–January 1070

Ceolwynn ripped the seal from Renaud's letter with eager fingers, her eyes lighting up with relief at his request that she and Edmund spend Christmas with him at Mandon. It was only when she read the few brief words a second time that she realized just how very cold and impersonal they really were, with no hint at all of forgiveness or affection. Hiding her distress she thanked Broad Thomas, the man sent both as messenger and escort, and began to prepare for her journey.

Thomas, unhappy at having been assigned to what he called 'nursemaid duties', was inclined to be disagreeable and unhelpful, setting what Ceolwynn thought were unreasonable limits on the size of their party. Unwillingly, she agreed to take only one servant, Hild, but stood her ground over a second mule, refusing to leave behind her best clothes and jewels. In the end, Thomas had been obliged to back down – but had got his revenge by forcing a gruelling pace which had left both women saddle-sore and exhausted, all excitement and interest in their week-long journey utterly quenched by the pain of aching limbs and the discomfort of perpetually damp clothing. Only Edmund seemed to find any pleasure in the journey.

They arrived at their destination late in the afternoon of Christmas Eve, cold, travel-stained, bone-weary and very, very hungry – but all these things Ceolwynn forgot as Hugo's great new castle finally appeared on the horizon, its forbidding grey walls stained blood red by the setting sun.

Started in King Edward's reign, Mandon Castle was still only part built and would take many more years to complete. There was a ragged, unfinished look to its walls, but Ceolwynn hardly noticed. She saw only the massive stone towers which, high on a hill, dominated the landscape with awesome and imposing grandeur. She shivered, and had to force herself to spur her horse forward into the shadow of those grim, menacing walls.

They clattered over the drawbridge, through the gatehouse arch and into the bailey. Thomas called a greeting to one of the men on the gate, who gave him a casual wave in return and stared with mild interest at the two women and the child.

No one else took much notice of their arrival. It was Christmas Eve and servants were rushing in all directions, and everyone seemed to be shouting orders at everyone else. Only the two half-naked spit boys remained stationary, as they turned a huge ox over an enormous open fire outside the kitchen.

The delicious smell of roasting meat, coupled with that of fresh-baked bread from some nearby oven, made Ceolwynn's mouth water. 'Where are we supposed to go, Thomas?' she asked, more than ready to leave the saddle at last.

'I don't know,' he admitted, glancing round hopefully for a sight of the steward. 'Wait here, my lady. I'll try to find out.'

He trotted off, leaving them alone in the bailey. The mules started to graze, and Ceolwynn let her eyes wander curiously around the castle grounds. In many ways, life here was no different from life in any other busy village. There were huts where the soldiers and the servants lived, and workshops for making tools and barrels and harness. There were granaries, and bakehouses, stables and cattle-sheds, and even the familiar foul-smelling midden. Slowly, she began to feel a little less overwhelmed and apprehensive.

'Can I help you?' a voice asked unexpectedly, and Ceolwynn started, causing her palfrey to step sharply sideways.

There was a soft laugh, and suddenly a slender hand appeared on the reins, restraining, quite unnecessarily, the startled horse. Ceolwynn felt foolish and glowered at her self-appointed rescuer, finding herself looking down at a very lovely young woman dressed in a fur-trimmed gown of crimson velvet under a matching cloak, the hood of which had been thrown back to reveal a mass of raven-black hair.

Her dark eyes, slightly slanted and cat-like, travelled slowly over Ceolwynn's shabby, travel-stained clothes and her full, sensuous lips curved into a smile. 'You look lost,' she said kindly, but with veiled mockery beneath the concern. 'Are you looking for your mistress?' she asked sympathetically.

Ceolwynn seethed, convinced that the young woman knew exactly who she was. 'I'm looking for my husband,' she replied, through gritted teeth, 'Renaud de Lassay.'

'Oh, Renaud,' the woman laughed, using his name with easy familiarity. 'He's out hunting with my husband and my brother, Hugo. So, you're Ceolwynn, his little Saxon. I'd like to say that I've heard so much about you, but in truth Renaud hardly ever mentions your name. Never mind, we have all the time in the world to get to know one another, and I'm sure that we'll come to love one another like sisters. I am Emma.'

The name meant nothing to Ceolwynn and though tempted she declined to say so. Emma, she suspected, was already far better at verbal swordplay than she would ever be. She adopted a tone of cool and dignified civility. 'I'm glad to make your acquaintance, Lady Emma,' she said.

'Just call me Emma, and do get down from that malodorous beast,' she added, screwing up her nose with distaste. 'You won't want to greet your husband reeking like a stable boy.'

Ceolwynn dismounted, flushing with annoyance. No one could be expected to arrive spotlessly clean and sweet-smelling after such a long journey, but Emma's remarks made her feel as though she ought to have done just that. Once she was on the ground, she felt even worse, for the lady was unusually tall and exceedingly beautiful, possessed of a cool elegance which made Ceolwynn feel graceless. To cover her discomfort, she went to take Edmund from Hild so that the maid, too, might dismount.

'Is this your son?' Emma cried, almost snatching the boy from her arms. 'Isn't he sweet?' she gushed, smothering him with kisses. Edmund, who hated a fuss, struggled to escape. 'He's quite adorable, my dear,' Emma said, handing him back with a slight grimace, 'but also a little damp.'

Ceolwynn hid a smile. 'He's very young still,' she said, 'and it has been a long journey. Do you have any idea where we will find our quarters?' she asked, as politely as possible. She was beginning to dislike Emma quite heartily.

'Oh yes, I chose the rooms for you myself. Renaud is always too busy to deal with little details like that, isn't he? Come, follow me, I'll take you there at once.'

'What about the horses?' Ceolwynn asked. 'We can't just leave them here.'

'No, of course not,' Emma answered with a pretty tinkling laugh. She raised one arm, snapped her fingers, and suddenly two servants materialized, almost from nowhere. 'Take these horses to the stables,' she ordered. 'Unload them and bring everything to the top of the west tower – at once.' Grinning like idiots the two men almost fell over themselves in their eagerness to obey. 'Fools,' Emma muttered contemptuously as she strode briskly away with Ceolwynn and Hild, still stiff from the saddle, struggling to keep up.

By now Ceolwynn was feeling exceedingly grateful that she would have the opportunity to wash and change her clothes before Renaud set eyes on her again, but this was not to be the case. Before they had gone more than a dozen steps they heard men's voices, loud and merry, and the sound of hoofbeats thudding rapidly over the drawbridge. Emma quickly turned back with a pleased, well-satisfied smile on her face, and Ceolwynn had no choice but to stand waiting next to her, horribly aware of the sharp contrast in their appearance.

Her first sight of Renaud made her heart leap unexpectedly with happiness, and with pride. Dressed in an elegant black tunic decorated with pearls, and with a smart red velvet cap perched jauntily on his head, he looked so very handsome and courtly that Ceolwynn hardly recognized him for the soldierly young man she had married.

Next to him rode a young man who was so much like Emma that he could not possibly be mistaken for anyone other than her brother, and slightly behind them, busy passing the hawk on his wrist to one of the servants, rode a man, very much older, whose clothes fairly sparkled with precious gems.

With some surprise, Ceolwynn realized that this must be Emma's husband, and not only was he very old, but also, she thought, exceedingly ugly. There was something cold, almost cruel, about his eyes, and his face, skull-like in its fleshlessness, was dominated by an enormous, pock-marked nose. The whole effect was intimidating, and for just a moment she found herself feeling sorry for Emma, but then that young woman was dragging her forward by one arm, almost causing her to drop the baby and managing to make her look both clumsy and foolishly reluctant.

'Look who has arrived,' Emma enthused, now half pushing Ceolwynn forward. 'Aren't you happy to see your wife, Renaud?'

Renaud looked down and his face lit up in a smile. He swung quickly down from the saddle and strode towards her eagerly, arms outstretched. Full of relief and happiness, Ceolwynn stepped forward to meet him, but then, hardly glancing at her, he took Edmund into his arms and lifted him high into the air with a shout of pleasure.

Ceolwynn felt a flood of humiliation sweep over her.

'Why Renaud,' Emma protested, rubbing salt into the wound, 'shame on you. Poor Ceolwynn has ridden all this way and you, it seems, have not one kiss to spare her.'

There was a burst of laughter from the other men, and Ceolwynn noticed Renaud and Emma exchange a quick look that she could not interpret.

'My apologies,' Renaud said, smiling to make light of the omission. He put Edmund down carefully and signalled for Hild to take him out of reach of the horses' hooves before he stepped back towards Ceolwynn and gave her a brief kiss on the brow. 'I trust you made the journey without mishap?' he said.

Ceolwynn nodded, numb with disappointment and pain. There was so much she wanted to say to him, but at this moment he seemed like a stranger to her.

Hugo, who by now had also dismounted, was studying Ceolwynn with undisguised interest. 'Is that the best you can do, Renaud?' he asked with mock surprise. 'Allow me. I'm sure I can do such beauty greater justice.'

Before Ceolwynn knew what was happening, Hugo was kissing her full on the lips and, at first, she was merely startled by the unexpectedness of it, then suddenly she felt his tongue in her mouth, deep and probing. Shocked, she stepped back quickly, her cheeks flaming, but Hugo's laughing eyes met hers boldly, daring her to protest. Helplessly, she looked away.

Hugo grinned, amused by her embarrassment. 'Ralf, look to the horses,' he ordered, holding out his reins to one of the servants. 'Ralf,' he said again, more sharply.

Ralf, his squire, an attractive, red-headed man in his mid-twenties, who until that moment had been gazing at Hild with a rather stupid look on his face, hurried to obey.

Ceolwynn noticed that Hild did not seem too displeased by his obvious admiration, and wondered if young Handel of the roving eye might not have a rival here. For some reason the thought cheered her a little, and when Emma introduced her to Roger de Virar, she even managed to smile and make some polite small talk as they walked side by side towards the west tower.

'I hope you won't be too weary to join us for tonight's festivities,' he was saying. 'You must be very tired from your journey.'

'Not at all, my lord,' she said untruthfully, turning her head away slightly to avoid the stench of his breath, made foul by rotted teeth. 'It would take more than a little weariness to keep me from a Christmas feast.'

'Good, good,' he said, a little sourly, and she noticed that he was watching his wife walking with Renaud some way ahead of them.

Renaud was speaking, and Emma, her head close to his, was laughing softly at his words, her hand resting in a proprietary fashion on his sleeve. Ceolwynn began to suspect that perhaps it was simple jealousy which lay behind Emma's thinly veiled nastiness, but there was small comfort for her in the thought since Renaud obviously preferred Emma's company to her own.

Roger de Virar politely excused himself and moved to separate his wife from her companion, and Ceolwynn, hoping that Renaud might now join her, tried to catch his eye, but he ignored her and began chatting with Hugo. By the time they reached the tower, Ceolwynn was feeling quite miserable and depressed.

It was a long climb up to the rooms that Emma had had prepared for them, but somewhat to her surprise Ceolwynn found them to be warm and comfortable. The walls were hung with huge tapestries to lessen the chill, and a fire burned cheerfully in the hearth. The bed, generously covered with soft furs, half filled the room, and at its foot was a chest for her clothes and a pallet for her maid. A smaller bed, suitable for a child, had been provided in an alcove, and off to one side there was a smaller room pierced with several small windows. A fire burned here too, and refreshments had been laid out on a table.

'I'll leave you now to rest awhile,' Emma said. The rest of the party, Renaud included, had turned off for the great hall two floors below. 'Have I forgotten anything?' she asked.

Ceolwynn looked around, determined not to seem too impressed. Her travelling chest had been brought up and, at her nod, Hild laid the very sleepy Edmund down on his bed and started to unpack. 'Just some water to wash with, if you please,' she said at last.

'It's already being heated for you and should be here in just a few minutes. Would you like someone to help you bathe and dress? My own maid, Alys,' Emma remarked, with an amused glance at Ceolwynn's tangled locks, 'is particularly good with hair.'

'No thank you,' Ceolwynn replied. 'Hild serves me very well.'

'Really?' Emma replied, raising her eyebrows almost imperceptibly. 'Well, you know best, of course.' She drifted towards the door. 'I'll look forward to seeing you later,' she said. 'I'm sure we'll find we have a great deal in common.'

'I'm sure we will, madam,' Ceolwynn growled to herself as the door closed. Hild looked up, a questioning look on her face. 'It doesn't matter,' Ceolwynn said, reverting to English.

'She seems kind, the lady,' Hild remarked, 'and very lovely.'

'The foxglove and the nightshade, too, are beautiful, Hild,' Ceolwynn answered her thoughtfully, 'but they are also deadly. You would be wise not to be deceived by appearances.'

Hild looked fierce. 'Are you in any danger here, mistress?' she asked, glaring round as if at some unseen enemy.

Ceolwynn laughed and kissed her, touched by her defensive glower. 'There's no danger of that sort,' she promised, suddenly understanding something that she had half known all along. Emma really was jealous of her. 'If there is to be a battle between myself and the lady Emma,' she said grimly, 'then it is one I must fight alone, dearest Hild, using no other weapon than my wits. Pray God they serve me well,' she sighed, 'for in beauty and grace the lady surely has the advantage.'

Later that same evening, Ceolwynn found herself seated, at Hugo's insistence, between himself, to her left, and an unusually quiet and withdrawn Renaud on her right. She was enjoying herself immensely. A wash and a short rest had restored both body and spirits, and she had come down into the great hall determined not to let Emma or anyone else make her feel stupid or uncouth. She wore a gown of pale, river-green silk, every graceful curve of her body highlighted by the soft, clinging folds of its drapery. Well aware that she could never match Emma's dark beauty, she had forgone bright jewels in favour of pearls – a net of them in her hair and a single string at her throat – and had entered the hall with her head held high, as ethereal and shimmering as a sea-nymph.

Admiring glances had followed her progress through the long hall to her seat between Hugo and Renaud, and Emma's furious expression had amply repaid all her efforts. Only Renaud had seemed unimpressed, hardly looking at her at all, but she refused to allow herself to be upset by his apparent lack of interest and turned her attention to Hugo who, devouring her hungrily with his eyes, seemed quite prepared to devote almost all his conversation to her alone.

The hall was loud with music and chatter as the usual motley crowd of tumblers, jugglers and musicians vied for attention. Servants, heavy-laden with dish after delicious dish, formed a seemingly endless stream between the hall and the distant kitchens far below. To be sure, the food often was a little cold by the time it reached the table, but for all that Ceolwynn was impressed. It did surprise her to see that there were no beggars waiting patiently in the warm hall for scraps from the lord's table, and she would have been shocked to know that any leftover food would be thrown outside for the poor to quarrel over like brute beasts; but not knowing this, there was nothing to dampen her pleasure and in a general spirit of goodwill she firmly resolved to heal the breach between herself and Renaud. Unfortunately, Renaud himself remained sullen and uncommunicative. After exchanging a few stilted and formal pleasantries with him, she gave up in irritation and turned her attention to Hugo, gratified that he at least seemed more than glad of her company.

Renaud poured himself yet another drink and wondered at his own stupidity. Why was he behaving so unkindly? He loved Ceolwynn. The dreadful anger that had been born of his terror for her safety had taught him that. Why then had he come here to Mandon at all? The answer, of course, was obvious – Emma. He'd loved her for so very long that the sudden knowledge of his love for Ceolwynn had left him confused and bewildered, and the lure was, as always, irresistible. He was like a fly, caught up in Emma's web of enchantment, helpless to break free. Could he, did he, love them both?

He had no answer to that, but he hated himself for the way he'd treated Ceolwynn earlier. He'd seen the expression of naked hurt in her eyes when he had lifted Edmund so joyfully from her arms. He'd known at once that he'd been needlessly cruel, and if Hugo had not stepped in so quickly with his embrace, and if Emma had not been there to lure him away with silken words, perhaps he could have made amends, welcomed her properly, but now it was too late. She would never forgive him.

He glanced at her out of the corner of his eye, watching her throw back her head in laughter. Her throat was beautiful, he thought with a kind of wonder, so white and slender: he remembered suddenly how sweet it had been to run his lips over that delicate neck, to kiss the warm hollow at its base and feel the heat and passion of her eager, willing response. It seemed a lifetime since they had shared such passion.

He sighed and glanced at her again, unexpectedly jealous of Hugo and irrationally angry with Ceolwynn for seeming to take pleasure from his attentions.

Bright, witty and charming, Hugo had soon made Ceolwynn feel at ease, sharing with her his cup and trencher, and lessening the pain of Renaud's brooding silence with a stream of amiable, flirtatious chatter, to which she responded heartily, hoping to annoy Renaud, and, had she but known it, succeeding very well.

'I should be angry with Renaud for keeping such a jewel hidden from me for so long,' Hugo remarked lightly, handing her a cup of wine.

'Had he known the distress it would cause you,' Ceolwynn laughed, 'he would surely have taken pains to remedy the situation sooner.'

'Not if he were wise,' Hugo replied, holding her eyes with his own as she sipped the sweet, red wine. She handed back the cup, and pointedly he turned it so that he drank from the side that her lips had touched. 'What think you of my sister's husband?' he asked suddenly, his lips close to her ear, although the noise from the music makers and the loud buzz of conversation round the long table made such discretion almost unnecessary. 'They make a good pair, don't you think?'

Ceolwynn leaned forward slightly and glanced at the sour-faced old man seated next to his wife, and wondered what reply she was expected to make. 'He seems a little old for her,' she offered cautiously.

'True,' Hugo agreed, leaning closer and keeping his voice low, 'but he is very, very rich, and in my sister's eyes that makes up for any lack of charm or vigour. Which is as well, because Roger de Virar is singularly lacking in both.'

'They have a child, though, do they not?' Ceolwynn remarked, thinking that Roger could not be quite so lacking in vigour as his wife's brother seemed to believe. Hild had obtained that piece of information from Alys, although how, when neither woman spoke the other's language, was a mystery to her.

'Ah yes, my young nephew, Geoffrey,' Hugo agreed. He laughed unexpectedly, as if at some secret jest.

For just a moment Ceolwynn thought he was about to say something more, but he hesitated, his lip hovering on a word, before apparently thinking better of it.

'Is he here at Mandon?' Ceolwynn asked. 'Perhaps Edmund could share his company: I believe they are quite close in years.'

'No. Emma did bring Geoffrey to England, but he was taken ill soon after they landed and Emma thought it best to leave him behind rather than subject him to such a long journey. Roger has property in Guildford and she left him there.'

'I see,' Ceolwynn said, wondering how any mother could leave a sick child alone like that in a strange land.

'Has Renaud told you that we will be returning to Northumbria as soon as the Christmas festivities have ended?' he asked.

'I have hardly spoken to him since I arrived. It seems that he has other, more pressing, business.' She glared at Emma, who was now deep in conversation with Renaud and obviously had his wholehearted attention.

Hugo noted with an inward smile the bitterness in her voice, but made no comment. The angrier she was with Renaud, he thought cheerfully, the easier it would be to coax her into his own bed, which had been his intention from the moment he'd set eyes on her. Amoral as a tomcat, the knowledge that to seduce Ceolwynn would be to cuckold his oldest friend presented him with no real problems of conscience, and any rift between her and Renaud had to be to his advantage.

'Well, it's true,' he continued, shaking his head sadly. 'I shall have the pleasure of your delightful company for only a week or two longer.' He leant closer, his warm breath teasing her ear and his knee pressing hard against hers under cover of the table. 'I

233

hope we can use what little time we have to get to know one another very, very well.'

Even Ceolwynn, whose experience was undoubtedly limited, could hardly mistake his meaning. Startled, she took a large gulp of wine to cover her confusion, but then embarrassed herself even further by swallowing the wrong way, provoking a coughing fit which drew all eyes in her direction.

Emma looked amused, she noted between coughs, and that made her so angry that she failed to notice the concern in Renaud's voice as he asked if she was all right. She nodded, her coughs subsiding, and kept her eyes fixed firmly on the table until the hum of conversation around her returned to normal.

'I'm sorry,' she heard Hugo say. 'I think that was my fault, was it not? I did not intend to alarm you so.'

'I wasn't alarmed,' she protested, 'I was just surprised, that's all. It was unexpected.'

'What was?' he asked innocently.

For a moment she wondered if she had made a mistake and felt herself becoming hot and flustered again, but then she saw the mischief in his eye and knew that she had not misunderstood him. 'You know very well what I'm talking about,' she said reproach-fully. 'You should be ashamed of yourself.'

Hugo grinned. 'Why should I feel shame for desiring the love of such a beautiful woman?' he asked softly.

'You would betray your friend?' she asked severely, but in truth she had begun to feel flattered and unexpectedly excited by his attentions.

'Look at him,' Hugo said, nodding towards Renaud. 'Do you really think he notices anything else when he is in my sister's company? He's been lovesick for her since they were little more than children.'

'She's very lovely,' Ceolwynn sighed, 'but Renaud is an honourable man, and a man of honour,' she added pointedly, 'would never attempt to seduce another man's wife, however much he admired her.'

Hugo gave a sharp bark of laughter. 'Do you really believe that?' he asked, shaking his head at her wonderingly.

'Of course I do,' she answered, but he could hear the uncer-tainty in her voice and scenting an opportunity to weaken her defences he pressed home his advantage, forgetting his own private resolution that there were certain things, dangerous things, best left unsaid.

'Perhaps you would think differently if young Geoffrey was here,' he said. 'Perhaps you would be surprised to see how much he resembled your own boy, just as an older brother might.'

Ceolwynn turned pale with shock as his meaning became clear. She felt winded, as though someone had struck her a sharp blow to the stomach. Unconsciously, she clasped her hands tightly together and forced herself to speak calmly. 'I don't believe you,' she insisted fiercely. 'You're making it up just to provoke me, but it's a cruel and unkind thing to say.'

'It's probably a cruel thing to discover, I agree,' Hugo replied carelessly, 'but none the less true for all that. Renaud is the father of Emma's child, and to the best of my knowledge they are lovers still – Roger's absence permitting, of course,' he added with a small chuckle. 'My point is,' he went on, returning to his attack on Ceolwynn's virtue, 'you owe no particular loyalty to Renaud, since his marriage to you is purely one of convenience, and one that he will undoubtedly regret just as soon as Roger de Virar has the good taste to relieve the world of his unsavoury presence; an occasion, I might add, which all who have the misfortune to know him, await with some eagerness.'

Ceolwynn shook her head in protest: she wasn't a child, she knew that it was common enough for a man to take a mistress, especially when, like Renaud, he was away from home for months at a time, but she hadn't realized how much it would hurt her to know that Renaud could really love someone else.

'Are you all right?' Hugo asked, his voice gentle and comforting.

'Yes, of course,' Ceolwynn replied, swallowing the lump in her throat and trying desperately to blink back the threatened tears. Hugo looked as though he was about to say something more when, to her relief, his attention was distracted by the sudden quiet that fell as the musicians unexpectedly ceased to play.

In the hush that followed, a small boy, dressed in a long, white robe and with his fair curls decorated with a crown of ivy and holly leaves, began to sing, in a sweet, childish treble, a haunting Saxon cradle song. 'Oh, listen,' Ceolwynn breathed, glad of the opportunity to change the subject, 'isn't that beautiful?'

Hugo nodded and listened appreciatively. 'Once, I have heard tell,' he remarked thoughtfully as the last notes died away and the child was showered with gifts of food and coin, 'that long ago, in a far-off land, there was a bishop, Gregory, I think he was named, who saw some English children in a slave market. He is said to have declared that they were more like angels than Angles. It's easy to see what he meant.'

Ceolwynn smiled uncertainly, warming to him despite herself, Hugo confused her. She felt herself attracted to him, but she wasn't really sure whether or not she actually liked him. He charmed her, she was flattered by his obvious admiration, but at the same time she found his readiness to betray his friend, both in word and deed, quite detestable.

On the other hand, part of her argued, shouldn't she be grateful to him for being honest with her, even when that honesty had brought her such pain?

She could find no easy answer to her own question and spent the remainder of the evening in a very subdued humour, picking unhappily at her food and hardly noticing what was going on around her.

Hugo, well-satisfied with his progress so far, had decided that his purpose would be best served by leaving Ceolwynn to brood on what he had told her, and was now performing to the full his duties as host to his other guests.

Even Hild, later that night, sensed that her usual chatter would be unwelcome and undressed her mistress in virtual silence. Humming softly to herself she brushed Ceolwynn's silken hair, putting all the comfort and affection she could into each brush stroke. She was still brushing when they were both startled by a sudden loud knocking at the door, which then burst open before Ceolwynn had a chance to recover from her surprise and invite their unexpected visitor to enter.

It was Renaud. He stood in the doorway looking furiously angry, swaying slightly as though somewhat the worse for drink. After a moment's hesitation, he signalled Hild to leave with a sharp jerk of his chin over his shoulder.

'No,' Ceolwynn countered nervously. 'You've no right to order my servant away.' Hild, who knew better, gave her mistress a small, encouraging pat and scurried out, squeezing past Renaud who was still blocking the doorway.

'Don't speak to me of rights,' he said furiously, moving into the room at last. He looked as though he was about to slam the door shut behind him, but his eye fell upon the sleeping child and instead he shut it very quietly. 'It seems to me that you would do better to remember your duties before you insist on your rights,' he continued heatedly. He was waving his arms wildly and trying to shout at her, but since he was anxious not to disturb Edmund, the shouting was in fact little louder than a whisper and Ceolwynn, finding the whole effect faintly ridiculous, giggled nervously, which incensed him still further. 'You put me to shame,' he railed, 'behaving like that, in front of everyone.'

'Like what?' Ceolwynn protested indignantly, jumping to her feet, any fear of his anger forgotten in her own.

'Like a ... like a whore,' he hissed, his jealousy finally brought to the boil. 'If Hugo had but crooked his finger at you, you would have been in his bed by now. By God, I thought you were about ready to eat out of his hand down there.'

'How dare you?' she cried, stamping her foot. 'How dare you call me a whore, while you deliberately flaunt your wanton here under my very nose. I did nothing of which I need be ashamed. I may hate you, Renaud de Lassay, but I at least have never dishonoured my marriage vows.'

Taken aback by this sudden accusation, Renaud stopped his furious pacing and stared at her. 'Nor have I,' he said defensively, but he had been put off balance and his protest sounded weak and unconvincing. The amount of drink he had consumed during the evening had made him strong on bombast but weak on reasoned argument. 'Whatever you've heard, it's not true.'

'Not true,' Ceolwynn replied with a small, mocking laugh. 'Don't you think I have eyes in my head? Deny, if you can, that Emma is your mistress.'

'I do so deny it.'

It was Ceolwynn's turn to be taken aback. She had not expected a flat denial, and knew that Renaud was generally too honest a man to lie. 'You are saying you have never had knowledge of that woman?' she asked, a certain hope dawning in her breast.

Renaud hesitated, and the hope was dashed. 'I didn't exactly say that,' he hedged. Ceolwynn glowered at him, saying nothing, and Renaud, horribly aware that he had lost all the advantages in this encounter, had no choice but to explain himself. 'Once, long ago, we were lovers,' he said, slumping down into Ceolwynn's vacated chair, 'but not now, I swear it. Certainly not since our marriage.' He looked very tired suddenly, and remarkably sober. He reached out to take her hand in his and despite herself she let him take it. 'Do you really hate me, Ceolwynn?' he asked unexpectedly.

'How can I not?' she answered, not with anger now but with weary resignation. She believed him, but the pain was still there. 'You will always be my enemy, that will never alter.'

'You should learn to love your enemy,' he said, drawing her close and taking her onto his lap. 'Did Father Eadric not teach you that?'

She gave a soft laugh and let her head rest on his shoulder while his hand caressed her gently through the thin stuff of her shift. She wanted to ask him if it was true about Emma's child, but the moment was sweet, an oasis of calm in a turbulent marriage, and part of her didn't want to know the truth.

'I've missed you,' he said, his words slightly muffled in her hair as he kissed her head.

'Truly?' she asked, genuinely interested and very grateful that his past anger seemed forgotten. 'Do you really think of me when you are away from home?'

'Truly,' he affirmed. 'In fact,' he said, suddenly remembering what anger had driven quite out of his mind, 'I did for you exactly what I promised to do.'

'What?' she asked, raising her head and looking at him with eager curiosity.

'I found Wulfhere and Estrith.'

Ceolwynn gave a shriek of joy and leapt off his lap. 'Where?' she cried. 'Are they well?' She flung herself down so that she was kneeling between his knees, looking up at him with a child's delight illuminating her face. 'Tell me everything,' she insisted, pounding impatiently at him with her fists.

Renaud sighed, cursing himself for not having waited until morning. He began to relate the whole story, good-humouredly putting up with all her exclamations and questions, even though his head was thumping and there was nothing more he wanted now than to fall into bed and sleep.

It was only when he got to the part about the tragic deaths of Aelfrun and Siggi that he realized how bad a mistake he had made in bringing up the subject at this moment, just when a reconcilia-

238

tion between them had seemed almost certain. Now, the light had gone out of Ceolwynn's eyes, to be replaced by a look of horror and dismay. She had drawn away from him in disgust, blaming him once again for all the terrible things that had happened to her family since William of Normandy had decided to take the English crown for his own.

'It's not my fault,' he said lamely, knowing full well that she wouldn't listen. 'If they had stayed at Cottesham I would have protected them, treated them with all honour; you know that, don't you?'

'They were forced to go. How could they have stayed with the man who slew my father howling for Siggi's blood?'

'Hugo would never have harmed your brother,' Renaud argued, though fully aware of the futility of his words when it was too late for anything to be put right, 'not once he had calmed down. He spoke only in the heat of the moment.'

'Hugo?' she said, her eyes widening in horror. 'Hugo is the man who killed my father?' It had never occurred to her to make a connection between this Hugo and the unknown, vengeful Hugo that Cenred had spoken of in years past.

Renaud looked surprised. 'I thought you knew,' he said.

Ceolwynn stumbled to her feet, still half numb with shock. 'How could I know?' she asked bitterly. 'How could you bring me here, knowing this thing?' She shuddered with self-loathing as she remembered how she had actually been attracted to the man who had slain her own father.

'I had hoped all this was forgiven by now,' Renaud said, trying to win her over with reason. 'No one should be held to blame for an honourable death on the field of battle. Hugo doesn't hold you to blame for the fact that it was your father who killed his kin.'

'My father was defending his own land; his cause was just.'

Renaud sighed wearily. 'Whoever was right or wrong, William is now King of England and likely to remain so. It's time to put all past enmities to rest.'

'Never,' Ceolwynn said defiantly.

'Then I'll leave you to your hatred,' he replied, rising. 'I think you'll find it a cold bedfellow.'

Ceolwynn turned her back on him as he walked to the door. With his hand on the catch he paused and turned back. 'Do you remember the days when we were such friends?' he asked sadly.

She kept her back to him and said nothing, but he knew she was crying. 'I still have the cup you gave me then. Do you still have the little bear?'

'No,' she answered curtly. 'It was a child's toy. I threw it away years ago, along with any belief I had in your promises.'

Renaud looked puzzled. 'What promises have I ever made to you that I have broken?' he asked.

She turned to look at him. The tears had dried but her eyes were heavy with pain. 'You gave me a promise in exchange for that cup,' she replied. 'You promised that I had but to call upon you for whatever favour I desired.'

'I remember,' he said, recalling the two of them kneeling in the flickering light of an oil lamp in a dark hollow, musty with the smell of earth and leaf-mould. He laughed softly. 'I was to be your guardian giant, waiting to be roused from sleep by your summons.'

'I summon you now,' she said. 'Fulfil your promise to me.'

'What do you want of me?'

'Bring back to me all those I loved,' she commanded with quiet venom.

'Before God, I would, were it only within my power,' he said regretfully. Then, knowing that to stay would only make things worse, he left her.

After he'd gone Ceolwynn went to her coffer and pulled out a roll of cloth. She unwound it slowly to reveal a small, carved wooden bear, well-worn from much handling. She took it over to the fire and stood undecided for several minutes with the toy in her hand before carefully rewrapping it and placing it back in the chest.

Roger de Virar observed with a certain detached amusement the breakdown in the relationships all around him. Renaud was hardly speaking to Hugo, and his wife was barely speaking to either of them. Renaud was obviously avoiding Emma, and she, in her turn, was waspish and ill-humoured with everyone. Roger thought he knew exactly why.

It suited Roger that they should all think that he believed the friendship between Emma and Renaud was born only of child-hood affection. No one suspected what he really knew. Even Emma had quickly forgotten about the young page who had disappeared so soon after she'd told Roger of her pregnancy. Only Roger and a trusted servant knew what agonies young Richard had suffered, his body torn and broken by hours of torture, and only Roger knew the name he'd spoken before he died.

Roger had nursed his hatred well. One day, he knew, he would destroy Renaud de Lassay – but not yet. It was not enough to kill him; Roger wanted him to suffer first. He was astute enough at reading the emotions of others. It was plain to him that Renaud loved his wife, Ceolwynn, very dearly, and it was also very clear that the same knowledge had seriously enraged Emma, however hard she tried to disguise it.

Roger smiled to himself. He would bide his time, and when his opportunity came, he would be ready.

'I hear your wife is to leave us, Renaud,' Emma said, oozing a regret that Renaud knew quite well to be thoroughly false.

He was really in no mood to discuss Ceolwynn, least of all with Emma, but finding himself trapped on a turn of the narrow tower stairs with no way of escape without causing offence, he had little choice but to stop and allow her to engage him in unwilling conversation.

'It was time,' he replied carelessly, making no mention of the fact that Ceolwynn's barely concealed loathing had made the past few days so uncomfortable that eventually he'd been forced to agree that she should return to Cottesham.

'Oh! but it's a great shame, is it not?' Emma continued blithely. 'I was so sure we would become such friends.'

Renaud laughed shortly. 'You and Ceolwynn, friends?' he replied. 'Snow in August would be more likely by far.' Impatient to be gone, he tried to squeeze between Emma and the wall, but she blocked his descent with her arm, leaning against him provocatively. 'Come, let me pass, I pray you,' he said irritably. 'I have things to do.'

Emma pouted. 'Why so angry with me, Renaud? I have done nothing to offend you, surely?'

Renaud sighed inwardly. 'I'm not angry with you Emma, but I really do have things to do which will not wait.'

'Oh, and when will you have time for me, the mother of your child?' she asked petulantly.

Renaud started and glanced apprehensively behind him.

'Hush,' he said fiercely, 'before you bring us both to ruin.'

'Well, answer me then,' she replied, equally fierce. 'I won't be ignored just because that stupid little Saxon you married has a tantrum and puts you in a temper. If I didn't know better, I would think that it was her you loved, not me.'

The statement was half a question, and for just a moment Renaud hesitated, tempted to deny that anything had changed between them, but lies had never sprung easily to his lips. 'I think that what you say is true, Emma,' he said quietly, and winced at her sudden sharp intake of breath. 'God knows,' he hurried on, convinced that he had wounded her deeply, 'there was a time I would have died for you, Emma, believe me, but ...' he tailed off, helpless to explain how Ceolwynn's presence here had finally broken the spell of his long infatuation.

He noted her startled expression with sad regret. He'd loved her once with a passion hot as fire, but that had been long ago, before the boy became a man and discovered that love and desire were not the same thing at all.

'You choose her?' Emma gasped incredulously. To his relief there were no tears, she was far too indignant for that. 'All these years I have prayed each day for my husband to die, just so we could be together at last, and now you abandon me. You seduce me, then toss me aside like a worn-out glove, shattering the heart which ever has loved none but you.'

Renaud almost smiled with relief. He knew Emma too well to be taken in by this histrionic tirade. Her anger stemmed from defeat, not from sorrow. Her heart, he mused, if indeed she had one at all, was most certainly not in the least shattered. 'I seduced you?' he queried reproachfully. 'That's not quite as I remember it.'

'You're a swine, Renaud,' she hissed, stamping her small, slippered foot ineffectually, noiselessly on the stone steps.

She was incredibly beautiful, he thought, studying her fury with an indifference that amazed him; but there was a hardness in her beauty, a cold self-interest in her eyes which suddenly repelled him. 'Then you should be glad to be rid of me,' he told her.

'Perhaps I am,' she retorted furiously; then, too enraged to think of anything more to say, she gathered up her skirts, pushed her way past him and stalked proudly up the stairs without a backward glance.

Unbidden, Renaud's feet made to follow her, moved by an

unexpected and painful sense of loss; but the impulse was brief, overwhelmed by an enormous sense of release.

He was finally and completely free of her enchantment.

Feeling as though a great burden had been lifted from his shoulders, Renaud hurried down the stairs and made his way to the stables where Thomas, in a foul mood because he had to escort Ceolwynn back to Cottesham, was waiting for the horses to be saddled and the mules reloaded.

Hugo was there too, and in no happier frame of mind than Thomas. Baffled by Ceolwynn's sudden hostility towards him, and disappointed of a quarry he'd been convinced was almost his, he'd been complaining bitterly at being deprived of her company ever since he'd heard that she was leaving.

'It's sheer folly to send them away in weather like this,' he protested. He glanced up at the leaden skies and shook his head. 'There's snow on the way, I feel sure.'

'She wants to go,' Renaud replied, shrugging. 'Thomas will make sure they come to no harm, won't you Thomas?'

Thomas growled something incomprehensible, and a few moments later Ceolwynn herself appeared, holding Edmund firmly by the hand, having learnt from experience that her son could vanish in the blink of an eye when the mood to explore came upon him. Anxious to be gone, she didn't want to risk delaying her departure searching for him.

Behind her, following with dragging steps, came Hild, accompanied by Hugo's manservant, Ralf, who was carrying a large bundle of furs to wrap around the child once they were mounted. It was obvious from their glum faces that both servants were every bit as miserable as everyone else.

Renaud knelt to kiss his son farewell before passing him over to Thomas. Howling with anger, Edmund struggled in Thomas's arms, reaching for his father. Renaud took him back and hugged him hard. 'Go with Thomas now, little one,' he said. 'I have a gift for you, but only if you are good.' Only slightly mollified, Edmund reluctantly allowed himself to be carried away.

Ceolwynn watched them both with irritation. It never failed to annoy her to see how much Edmund loved the father he hardly ever saw, and when Renaud came to bid her farewell she submitted coolly to his embrace, turning her face so that his lips merely brushed her cheek.

243

'Are you sure you really want to go?' Renaud asked her quietly, but not quietly enough.

'Tell her she must stay, you have the right,' Hugo insisted over his shoulder.

'My wife is free to come or go as she pleases,' Renaud answered him sharply. Annoyed, Hugo turned away and left them alone. 'I don't want you to go,' Renaud said, taking both her hands in his, trying to make her look at him. 'You know that, don't you?'

'I cannot stay,' she replied, refusing to meet his eyes.

'Just think of poor Hild,' he said, attempting humour. 'You're breaking her heart, forcing her to part from her beloved like this.'

Ceolwynn gave a contemptuous snort to show just what she thought of love, but it saddened her that Hild, who really did seem to have fallen in very much in love with her roguish Norman admirer, was to have her chance of happiness snatched away. This time she was truly smitten.

Accepting at last that there was nothing more he could do or say to make her change her mind, Renaud released his hold on Ceolwynn's hands and helped her to mount.

He hated to part from Ceolwynn like this, in anger once more, but perhaps it was really better for her to go. He had seen too many women succumb to Hugo's charms to be absolutely certain that, however unlikely it might seem in the circumstances, even Ceolwynn would not, in the end, yield to his persistence.

Nonetheless, he watched her ride away with a heavy heart, and it was only after she had gone that he remembered, with wonderful clarity, exactly where it was that he had first seen the dancing dog drawn with such skill by the little oblate of St Aidan's.

XIV

February 1070

Renaud stirred, roused by the early-morning clatter of the waking camp. For a few moments he lay, listening to the familiar sounds outside the tent: the rattle and clink of harness and armour, the shouted orders and muttered responses, the stamping and snorting of impatient, hungry horses.

At last, shivering, he dragged himself from the warmth of his makeshift bed and struggled to pull on his boots. The only other occupant of the tent snored on, a huddled heap under his coverings, as he stepped quietly past and, grabbing his cloak, went outside. There he stood for a few moments, flapping his arms and shifting from foot to foot in a vain attempt to keep warm.

The frost-white grass crunched loudly underfoot and his breath made clouds in the chill air. He sniffed the air like a hunting dog, pulling a face at the lingering stench of burnt flesh and hide, so pungent and greasy that it made his empty stomach churn. It was a smell, he reflected uneasily, that would become terrifyingly familiar throughout Mercia and Northumbria in the coming weeks, a smell that for hundreds of helpless men, women and children would soon come to mean freezing misery, starvation and almost certain death – and he, God help him, was part of the cause: hating it, he still had no choice but to be part of it.

Would Ceolwynn accept that as an excuse? he wondered wryly. Would she listen if he tried to explain that it was his duty to persecute her people? Would she see that they had brought it upon themselves, these rebellious northerners, and that the king, driven beyond patience, had no choice but to destroy them? Would she understand why every habitation from the meanest cot to the richest monastery had to be burned to the ground; why every scrap of food, every store of grain or seed must be destroyed; why every fowl, every beast from the great plough oxen to the smallest unweaned pup was to be slaughtered without mercy? He thought not.

He yawned, wearily, and relieved himself against a nearby tree as he reflected on a restless and troubled night plagued by dilemmas of duty and conscience for which the slow coming of dawn had brought no answers. He was the king's man, a soldier and a loyal Norman. Pity had never yet prevented him from carrying out his orders, however cruel, but it was impossible for him to think of Wulfhere and his family, or even the monks of St Aidan's, as the enemy. Yet they, too, must surely soon fall victim to William's merciless policies – unless, of course, there was something he could do to save them.

There was something he could do. The question was, should he do it? Last night he had almost made up his mind that to give his friends some warning of the impending danger would be only a very minor breach of his duty, but in the cold light of day, and remembering the king's almost incandescent fury over this latest rebellion, he was certain that William himself was unlikely to view the matter in quite the same light. Nor was that the only problem. Just how could he get far enough ahead of the advancing wave of destruction, of which he was very much a part, in order to give his warning?

From the tent behind him came the voice of the chief obstacle to his half-formed plans. 'Why didn't you wake me?' Roger de Virar growled. 'God's teeth, the day's half gone,' he snarled. 'You know full well we move today. Where's my page?'

'I'll find him for you,' Renaud offered, while imagining what it would be like to run his sword through Roger's ugly, scrawny neck. Without realizing it, he allowed his hatred to push him into making his final decision.

He found Roger's page still dozing by the dying embers of one of the camp fires, oblivious to the soldiers around him breakfasting noisily on bread and ale. Stirring the lad awake with his foot, Renaud warned him cheerfully that his master had woken in a foul temper and that he'd better look sharp.

Left alone and quietly munching a lump of dry bread, Renaud allowed his thoughts to drift back to his problem. What could he do, he pondered, to get word to his friends? If de Virar, ever alert to the possibility of finding fault in others, had any hint of Renaud's intention, he would surely have a messenger on his way to the king within the hour.

The unexpected arrival of Hugo, two days later, brought him not only a solution to his problem, but also a great deal of personal distress.

Hugo found Renaud by a mill just outside a small port which after this day would cease to exist. The mill itself was still standing, although the wheel and the great millstone itself had already been smashed into a thousand pieces, leaving just a rubble-filled shell. The miller and his family stood nearby with a few pathetic bundles of possessions, watching dazed and uncomprehending as Renaud's men prepared to fire the building.

Renaud himself, mounted and ready to follow Roger into the town, reached automatically for his sword as the loud and rapid tattoo of horses' hooves caught his attention. 'Hugo, by all the Saints,' he called out, relaxing as he recognized the distinctive red stallion Hugo rode. He wheeled his own horse back to greet his friend. 'What brings you here in such haste?' he asked, smiling broadly.

Hugo hesitated and wouldn't meet his eye. 'I must speak with Roger,' he said, unusually grave. 'The matter is most urgent. Where will I find him?'

'No, my friend, you rest right here,' Renaud ordered in a manner that precluded any discussion or argument. 'I'll find him for you.' He glanced around, looking for one of the boys who, along with the cook and a few guards, had been left here with the baggage. He spotted Roger's page, the side of his face bruised from a recent blow, watching the newcomers with obvious curiosity. 'Gilbert here will tend your horses,' he said, summoning the boy forward, 'and will bring you whatever you need.'

Hugo nodded and dismounted, his escort swift to follow his example. 'My thanks,' he said, gratefully surrendering the reins and pulling off his helmet.

'Have you come from York?' Renaud asked.

'No,' Hugo answered. Then added, almost reluctantly, 'From Guildford.'

Renaud frowned, worry beginning to replace his pleasure at Hugo's arrival. Emma, he remembered, had planned to go to Guildford. Hugo's unusual reticence began to disturb him. 'What is it you don't want to tell me, Hugo?' he asked. 'Is it Emma?'

Hugo hesitated. 'No, he said, 'it's not Emma. I'm sorry, Renaud, but Geoffrey is very ill. He may be dying.'

Renaud paled. Hugo was waiting for him to speak, but his throat had closed and the words wouldn't come. His horse fidgeted restlessly under him and he soothed it with a gentle slap on the neck. I ought to feel more pain, he thought. My son is dying and I don't know what I feel. I never even knew him.

'Why didn't you tell me at once?' he asked.

'Geoffrey is de Virar's son, Renaud. Had you forgotten? It is his right to be the first to hear such news.'

'You know that's not true,' Renaud said bitterly.

Hugo shrugged and Renaud shook his head in bafflement. The way Hugo's mind worked had long been a mystery to him. He lived by his own strangely distorted rules. 'Rest then,' he said heavily. 'I'll find him for you.'

Roger de Virar was watching with brutal satisfaction the countless fires spreading rapidly through streets teeming with terrified townsfolk fleeing with what few possessions they could carry. On the river, too, every ship was ablaze, the flames leaping playfully amongst the flapping sails.

'Hugo is here, my lord,' Renaud called out above the roaring of flames on the wind, 'but I fear he is the bearer of bad tidings. He waits for you at the mill.'

'Just tell me,' de Virar snapped impatiently. 'I've no particular wish to speak to that creature.' Roger had never made any secret of his dislike of Hugo.

'It is your son, my lord,' Renaud told him with genuine sorrow. 'He is very sick, and thought to be close to death.'

Roger's reaction took him by complete surprise. He lost what little colour he possessed and his hands began to quiver uncontrollably. 'Geoffrey?' he said, tears standing in his eyes. Renaud said nothing, amazed to find himself feeling pity for the man. Regaining control of himself, de Virar spoke with decision. 'I will go to him at once,' he said. 'You will take over my command here until I return.'

Renaud nodded, wondering at the love de Virar must surely have for the boy he believed to be his son. Emma, he thought, must have been very convincing.

Watching Roger ride away, he let out a deep sigh of relief, not just at the unexpected answer to the problem that had been taxing him for several days, but in the certain knowledge that the fears he had nursed for Geoffrey, the unsuspected hostage in de Virar's hands, had been completely groundless.

'Just what are we doing here, my lord?' Hugh asked under his breath.

Renaud smiled at his two gruff companions, Little Hugh and Broad Thomas, both of whom had been with him here and at Blackwater last autumn. He couldn't ride alone, that would be a great folly, but he was beginning to believe that he could trust in the loyalty of these two. 'What any traveller would do at a monastery gate,' he replied lightly, 'begging a night's shelter and a hot meal.'

They had ridden hard and fast to get here before the army moved any closer. Hugo had been happy to deputize for him in his absence, and had asked no questions, for which Renaud was grateful. Hugo could be capricious, he knew, but he could also be a good friend when he chose.

He rapped a second time at the heavy oaken door until at last the grille slid open and the familiar face of Brother Oswald, the gatekeeper, peered out at him curiously.

'Why, I know you, don't I?' the old man said in pleased surprise. He unbolted the gate and flung it wide. 'Come in, and welcome, brother,' he said heartily. 'I'll find someone to tend your horses and then I'll tell Father Adrian you're here.'

'Thank you, Brother Oswald,' Renaud answered. 'It is Father Adrian I am here to see, and my business is urgent.'

'Then I'll waste no more time in idle chatter,' the old monk replied agreeably. 'Just leave your horses here, then get you into the guest house and warm yourselves at the fire. You'll remember the way, I'm sure.'

The three of them were soon settled round a roaring fire, each of them with a foaming cup of ale in his hand. Renaud was fidgety, watching the door with growing impatience; but it was time for Nones and the prior, he knew, would not miss a service, no matter how important or urgent the business.

Father Adrian arrived ten minutes later with a cordial welcome on his lips.

'There are important matters I must discuss with you, and at once,' Renaud said, once greetings were over, and glanced towards his men. 'Is there anywhere private where we can talk?'

The prior looked surprised, but nodded. 'Come with me,' he said, and led Renaud out and through the cloisters to his own sparsely furnished cell, a lodging no more comfortable than the dormitory in which the other monks slept.

Father Adrian pointed at a stool and Renaud sat down, shivering a little now that he was away from the warmth of the guest house. There was no fire here, he noticed, nor even the comfort of rushes to blunt the chill of the cold stone floor.

'I can see from your eyes that you have nothing good to tell me,' the prior said calmly as Renaud hesitated, unsure how to break his terrible news. 'Just say what you have to say, my son, bad news is no better for pretty words.'

'You're right,' Renaud agreed heavily. 'There really is no way to soften what I have to say.' They spoke in French, which Renaud guessed few of the monks would speak. Still cautious, however, he glanced at the door, which the prior had left open.

'We shall be able to hear anyone approach,' Father Adrian reassured him with a faint smile, and Renaud, who had been about to ask that the door be closed, flushed slightly at the realization that it had been left open to prevent any suspicion of improper behaviour between them.

'Father, if you want to save the lives of the brothers and your villagers,' he began hurriedly, to hide his embarrassment, 'you must do exactly as I tell you. You must drive your livestock to a safe hiding place in the mountains. You must conceal as much food and grain as you can, buried in the ground or sunk in weighted casks in the river, but leave enough to convince an enemy that you are unprepared.'

'Wait, wait,' the prior cried, raising his hand, 'you go too fast. What enemy, what are you talking about?'

Renaud explained, feeling a growing shame at his part in William's brutal crushing of the north.

'But this is a monastery,' Father Adrian protested. 'King William has always been a godly man: he would never order the destruction of a house dedicated to the Lord.'

'No doubt he will insist on doing penance for it,' Renaud replied a little cynically. 'Believe me, Father, everything I have told you is true. Not even Jarrow has been spared.'

He waited for this news to register. Prior Adrian's eyes widened in horror. The ancient monastery of Jarrow, with its famous holy relics and wonderful library, gone?

'How much time have we got?' the prior asked, accepting the truth at last. His face was suddenly pale with anxiety, and Renaud knew it was not for himself, but for those in his care.

'It would be safest to assume only a few days. It may be longer.'

'The soldiers will not lay violent hands on the brothers?'

'I cannot promise there will be no violence done,' Renaud admitted, well aware of just how many innocent, helpless folk had died recently at the end of Norman swords. 'Their orders are to destroy livestock, stores, crops and buildings. If no man resists them, it is to be hoped you will be left unharmed.'

The prior was silent for a few moments. 'Tell me,' he said at last, 'would the fact that I, too, am Norman make any difference? If I, a fellow countryman, were to plead for mercy for this house, would they listen?'

Renaud's reply was blunt and unequivocal. 'No,' he said, and the prior sighed.

'To bring us this warning, you have put your life at risk,' he said quietly, understanding, as only a Norman could, just how enraged William would be if he knew of it.

'I have gone to rather a lot of trouble not to be found out. I'm relying on you not to tell anyone else,' Renaud said.

'God bless you, my son,' Father Adrian said, 'you are a good man.'

Renaud made as if to go, then hesitated. 'There is one other matter, Father,' he said. 'I want to ask you about the young oblate, Brother Martin.'

Father Adrian looked at him in startled surprise. He had not expected this. 'Brother Martin?' he queried. 'What is it you wish to know?'

'What is his parentage? How did he come here, and when?'

'It is strange you should ask these things,' the prior remarked, 'for indeed the child's origins are something of a mystery to us here. It was before my time, but I have heard the story many times from Brother Wulfstan.'

'Tell me, I pray you,' Renaud asked eagerly, his hopes raised still further now he knew for certain that the boy's parentage was unknown.

251

'What is your interest in the child, my son?' the prior asked curiously.

'Tell me what you know first, Father, then I will tell you everything.'

The prior considered this, then nodded his agreement. 'It was before my time, perhaps two years before I arrived. A traveller came to the gate with the boy, then little more than a babe, and asked the late prior, Father Edwin, if he would take him in. He said that he had found the child caught up in reeds and tree roots at the edge of a river, a good day's ride to the west of here. The child had been wet through and half dead of cold, apparently, but he had been wrapped in a sheepskin which had billowed up around him like an inflated pig's bladder, thus saving him from drowning.'

Renaud leant forward, listening intently. Everything the prior had told him so far had helped to fuel his belief that little Brother Martin might indeed, by some miracle, be Ceolwynn's lost younger brother. 'Did he try to find the child's mother?' he asked.

'Of course; he looked everywhere, he said. He searched for many days, making enquiries in every village he passed, but no one knew the child or his family. The child himself could tell him nothing.'

'Why was that?' Renaud interrupted him. 'He must have been, what, three years old? Old enough to speak, surely?'

'I believe the boy must have been through some terrifying ordeal. It took him many, many weeks to find his tongue again, and by then he could hardly remember anything, not even his name. Fright can do that, I have heard.'

'So Martin is not even his rightful name?' Renaud asked, finding it hard to contain his excitement.

'No, that's quite right. St Martin is the patron of charity, so it seemed appropriate to Prior Edwin – after all, the boy was just another mouth to feed. Anyway, I can tell you no more, so what is it that you know, or suspect, about him?'

'My story,' Renaud answered, 'is somewhat longer than yours.'

'I have time to listen, my son.'

'Not much,' Renaud reminded him, and the prior smiled wryly.

So Renaud told him how a young visitor to a strange land had been befriended by a good man and his daughter, a sweet and lovely child who had shared with him her secrets and shown him a hidden cave and the picture of a dancing dog. He told of how the man had become his enemy and had died a bloody death, and of how the child had become his unwilling bride and hated him. He told him of a babe, brother to his wife, who had been brought here to Northumbria where he had met a cruel fate, and finally, he told of the day he had seen Brother Martin's drawings, and how one of them had been of a dancing dog, a picture that the child could have seen only if he had been admitted to that hidden cave far away in the south.

'There can be only one explanation,' he concluded. 'The boy has to be my wife's brother, Siggi, saved by God's mercy and brought here so that one day I might find him and restore him to his family.'

'That would surely be a wonder,' the prior agreed slowly, 'but what if you're wrong? What if the boy is not who you think he is? You saw the boy's drawing only once, perhaps you have let your imagination see more in it than was really there.'

'No, I have no doubts at all, Father,' Renaud replied firmly. 'The boy's face was familiar to me, also, but it took time for me to realize that it was his mother I saw in him.'

'I say again, what if you are wrong?' the prior persisted, and Renaud saw suddenly what was being asked of him.

'Then I will continue to take care of him,' he promised. 'He has taken no vows, he could take service in my own household.'

Father Adrian shook his head doubtfully. 'He knows no other home but this house,' he argued. 'He knows no other life.'

'If he wishes to return to the church, I will not deny him his wish, but this house will no longer exist, Father, make no mistake about that. Coming with me can do the child no harm, whoever he might be.'

The prior nodded thoughtfully, but Renaud understood that he was accepting the promise, not giving his consent. 'Give me a little time to think and pray,' he said. 'I'll give you my answer in the morning.'

'I must leave in the morning,' Renaud reminded him, rising, a little stiffly, from the stool.

'I will not delay you,' the prior replied, 'but I cannot give you my answer any sooner.'

'Can I at least see the boy?' Renaud asked hopefully.

The prior hesitated, but only briefly. 'Have I your word that you will say nothing to him yet of this matter?'

'Of course.'

'Then go back to the guest house now and I will send him to you.'

'Thank you, Father,' Renaud said gratefully as he left, but the prior, already on his knees before the tall wooden cross, was no longer hearing him.

True to his word, Father Adrian sent the boy with food for them all. With him was Brother Wulfstan, as full of noisy exuberance as ever. Renaud was pleased to see him and while the young monk chattered on, hardly noticing that his listener did little more than nod and smile in response, Renaud studied the child Martin as he moved round the table, carefully laying out the cups and bowls and cutting the bread into untidy chunks.

It took Renaud only a few minutes to be certain that he was not mistaken. The boy had grown a lot in the five months or so since he had last seen him; his face had lost its infant plumpness and Renaud could see more clearly than ever the likeness to Aelfrun, his mother. Strangely, he could see her also in the boy's movements and expression as he went about his business with a thoughtful frown, moving things around the table until he was satisfied they were in the right position.

'Don't you remember me?' Renaud asked him when Brother Wulfstan paused for breath.

The boy didn't answer, but he smiled a smile which tore at Renaud's heart and made him want to ignore his promise to the prior and tell the child everything.

'I'm sorry,' Brother Wulfstan said. 'I don't know why, but he's not allowed to speak to you. Father Adrian's orders.'

'I see,' Renaud replied, annoyed that the prior had not trusted his word.

'He told me to tell you not to be offended,' the young monk continued apologetically. 'He said I was to tell you that some promises are harder to keep than others.'

Renaud laughed, remembering how close he had come to breaking his word only moments ago.

The food was now ready. A pottage of salt pork, leeks and barley had joined the bread, along with a dish of beans and, amazingly, a flask of clear red wine from Bordeaux – a generous gift which quite dissipated any residual annoyance Renaud might have felt towards the prior. Hugh and Thomas were hovering by the table, willing him to join them so they could eat.

'Tell Father Adrian from me that he is right,' Renaud said to Brother Wulfstan, 'but tell him also that I know for certain now that I, too, am right. He will understand what I mean.'

Brother Wulfstan nodded seriously. He didn't understand what was going on, but being involved made him feel quite important. He left, taking Martin with him, and to the great relief of his men, Renaud at last sat down to eat.

Blackwater village looked just as still and undisturbed, Renaud thought, as it had last year when the three of them had come across it so unexpectedly on their journey to York.

It had been Thomas, the walking map, who had led him here then, and without Thomas now, he realized, he would have found it difficult indeed to find his way back – something he hadn't considered when he'd first set out. Appreciating his good fortune, he made a mental note to offer formal thanks to God as soon as a suitable opportunity presented, and to offer both Thomas and Hugh something a little more tangible to reward their patient, unquestioning service.

'I suppose we're only here to beg a night's lodging,' Hugh muttered to Thomas with heavy sarcasm.

Thomas grinned. 'Is that right, my lord?' he asked.

'Perhaps,' Renaud answered, glancing down at the child Martin dozing in the saddle in front of him, warmly wrapped in and virtually hidden by Renaud's large, enveloping cloak.

Brother Wulfstan had insisted that they take with them the clothes that the infant Martin had worn on the day he had first arrived at St Aidan's, and although Renaud could see little point in keeping them, still he found himself reluctant to throw the bundle away once they were on the road.

Martin had accepted his departure from the monastery with surprising calm. He had asked questions, but had accepted Renaud's careful half-answers with thoughtful gravity and had seemed content. Renaud wished he could tell him the whole story, but Prior Adrian had convinced him that to do so before all doubt was removed would be cruel.

Now, Renaud hoped, the truth was about to be revealed, and he

255

felt excited, almost elated. He was bringing dreadful, devastating news to Blackwater village, but somehow he felt sure that the presence of this child in his arms would bring such joy that, as far as Estrith at least was concerned, he would be forgiven all else.

As before, everyone turned out to watch the visitors arrive. He could see Estrith there, shading her eyes against the glare of winter sun on the bright snow, but there was no sign of Wulfhere or Dunn. At this time of day, he guessed, they were probably attending to their livestock.

Estrith stepped forward to greet them with a fragile smile of welcome on her lips and a frightened look in her eye. She had recognized him, Renaud had no doubt of that, but he understood that she could never be absolutely certain that he had come as a friend. The knowledge of her fear saddened him and stole away the fond words of greeting he had planned.

It was Estrith who eventually had to break the silence between them. 'If you come in peace, then you are welcome here, my lord Renaud,' she greeted him stiffly.

'How else would I come here?' he asked, almost reproachfully. 'You forget, we two are almost kin, and I have never willingly been anything other than your friend.'

'Of course,' she replied, allowing a smile to smother the worry in her eyes, but casting an anxious look towards the sheep-folds.

Renaud, following her glance, saw Wulfhere charging towards them at a run with his hand on his sword hilt. He waved reasuringly, and Wulfhere's advance faltered briefly, resuming at a more dignified pace as he realized that there was no immediate danger.

'Come, enter,' Estrith said, signalling for someone to take care of the horses. 'I long to hear news of Ceolwynn, and of your son. They are well, I hope?' she asked anxiously.

'They are both very well,' he assured her, relieved to hear the growing warmth in her voice. He hoped he was telling her the truth, but as he'd had no word from Ceolwynn since she'd left Mandon in such a rage, he couldn't be sure.

Thomas and Hugh had already dismounted and were moving away. Estrith waited expectantly for him to follow them, and he knew that this was the moment he had been waiting for. Without warning, he flung aside his cloak, revealing the child concealed beneath. Woken by the sudden movement, Martin opened his eyes and stared sleepily around him.

Estrith's reaction was all that Renaud could have hoped for: her hands flew to her mouth as expressions of shock, wonder and hope swiftly followed one another across her startled face.

'Whom do you see, Estrith?' Renaud asked fiercely, determined to get an answer before she could convince herself that she could not have seen what she thought she saw. 'Tell me now, whom do you see?'

'My sister, my sister Aelfrun,' she gasped. 'But that's not possible.' She moved closer, studying the child intently. 'It cannot be, yet those eyes, the shape of his mouth, even the colour of his hair.' She shook her head in disbelief. 'In God's mercy, Renaud, who is he?'

Before he could answer, Wulfhere reached Estrith's side, and he too stared in astonishment at the boy, who was now fully awake and staring back with almost equal interest.

'Who are they, my lord?' Martin whispered back at Renaud over his shoulder. He spoke in French, pleased to practise the tongue that Prior Adrian had taught him.

'Hush,' Renaud replied tenderly, stroking his hair.

'If I didn't know that he was already dead,' Wulfhere said bluntly, 'I'd swear that to be Aelfrun's child, for all I never once saw him.'

Estrith burst into tears.

Wulfhere comforted her with a kiss while she clung to him, sobbing. Renaud dismounted, then lifted Martin out of the saddle and led him to his aunt.

'Estrith Wilfredsdottar,' he said, speaking formally as befitted such a solemn occasion, 'it is my joy to bring to you Siggi Godmundson, your sister's son. Will you welcome him to your house?'

Wiping her eyes, Estrith let go of Wulfhere and knelt to hug the child to her breast. 'Siggi, dearest Siggi,' she crooned, rocking him in her arms, 'welcome, welcome to our home.'

Martin looked up at Renaud with a small, puzzled frown. 'My name's not Siggi,' he protested quietly, but made no effort to shake off Estrith's warm embrace.

'Here, your name is Siggi,' Renaud told him with a smile.

Content with this, Martin allowed himself to be led by the hand into the hall where young Edgar and Godmund descended upon him at once, chattering like magpies. Smiling, Renaud turned to untie Martin's bundle before the horse was led away.

'What miracle have you managed to work here?' Wulfhere asked. 'It really is Aelfrun's child, is it?'

'Can you doubt it?' Renaud said, falling into step beside him.

'My eyes tell me one thing,' Wulfhere replied, sounding dubious, 'but we had good cause to believe the child was dead. Where did you find him? How did you know who he was?'

'By great good fortune,' Renaud said, 'or by the will of God,' he amended as they walked together into the hall. 'Is Dunn here?' he asked as they shed their cloaks and sat themselves close to the fire. 'I'd like him to be here before I tell you the whole story.'

'He'll be back soon,' Wulfhere replied, 'he's been gone for most of the day, hunting a wolf that raided the sheep-folds in the night,' he added.

Estrith joined them, bringing a jug of mead which Renaud found rather sticky and sweet, but which quickly warmed and revived him.

'Was bringing the child here your only purpose?' Wulfhere asked unexpectedly. 'Something tells me you have other matters on your mind.'

Renaud hesitated, staring into his cup and swirling the thick liquid around and around. 'Is it so very obvious?' he asked, still stalling for time.

'You seem ill at ease.'

'I would prefer to wait until Dunn gets back.'

'Then you need wait no longer,' said a voice behind him, and Renaud turned to find Dunn himself already at his shoulder, the bloody hide of a dead wolf draped over one shoulder.

'Dunn,' he cried, rising quickly to grasp the other man firmly by the upper arms.

'Oh, Dunn, Dunn, you will not believe it,' Estrith cried. 'Only look over there, with Edgar and Godmund.'

Obediently, he looked where she pointed. His reaction was startling and unexpected; he staggered, his face drained of all colour. 'It cannot be,' he whispered hoarsely, crossing himself, 'it just cannot be.'

Renaud cursed himself for a fool. How could he have forgotten that of them all, Dunn alone had actually known Siggi? Small wonder the man looked so shocked. With that thought came the sudden realization that Dunn was the one man who could probably identify the boy beyond all doubt. 'Dunn,' he said, grabbing the bundle of tattered clothing and offering up a fervent prayer of thanks for Brother Wulfstan, 'look at these, do you recognize them?'

Dunn fingered the tiny tunic, the ragged sheepskin. 'She cut this with my knife,' he said almost dreamily. 'It was still too big, but it would have kept him warm.'

'It did keep him warm, Dunn,' Renaud said, guiding him to a seat. 'It saved his life.'

'God be praised!' Dunn answered him. 'Aelfrun, was she saved too?' he asked, grabbing Renaud's arm.

'No, Dunn, no man could save her,' Renaud said gently, 'but you tried. You almost lost your life trying.'

'I lost my life when I failed,' Dunn replied, coming slowly to himself again.

Estrith brought a drink and pressed it into Dunn's hand. He took it and drank gratefully, hardly noticing the tears that streamed down her face.

'Well,' said Wulfhere, sounding more cheerful than he had sounded for some years, 'if only we had the makings of a feast, a feast is just what this occasion deserves.'

Estrith laughed, drying her face on her sleeve. 'I'll find something, never fear,' she answered him. 'It may be a small feast, but a feast we shall have all the same.'

'No, wait!' Renaud interrupted, hating to mar their happiness, but knowing that to wait would only make matters worse.

Alerted by the sudden tension in his voice, the others turned to look at him, Dunn and Estrith puzzled, Wulfhere watchful.

'I didn't come here because of Siggi alone,' Renaud began, in answer to their questioning stares.

Remembering what Father Adrian had said about breaking bad news, he plunged straight in and told them bluntly all that he'd told the prior, including his advice on what they could do to protect themselves. To his amazement, no one said a word after he had finished speaking; there was no outcry, no anger, just quiet resignation.

'I'm very sorry,' he said, to break the silence.

'It's not your fault,' someone answered, and he realized with some surprise that it was Wulfhere who had spoken, the very one he would have expected to be most bitter, most unforgiving.

259

'I was expecting your anger, your hatred even,' Renaud said.

'Attacks on our village are nothing new,' Dunn told him. 'We have our hiding places in the mountains, and this time we will, at least, be well prepared for a long stay.'

'We have cause to be grateful to you yet again, Renaud,' Estrith said softly. 'Your warning will save many lives.'

Dunn stood up. 'I'm going to speak to Siggi now,' he said, putting all thought of impending danger aside for the moment. 'I wonder if he'll remember me at all.' He sounded wistful.

'He doesn't remember any ...' Renaud started to say, but Dunn was already walking away.

'Tomorrow,' Estrith said firmly, 'I will tell Siggi exactly who he is, and I will tell him about his mother and his father. Then I will show him his mother's grave and let him light a candle for her, and for his father, Godmund, too.'

Renaud, who had been watching Dunn as he crouched to talk face to face with the children, turned his head sharply towards her. 'His mother's grave,' he repeated slowly.

'Why yes, we showed you, last year.'

'You showed me two graves,' he reminded her, 'one of them Siggi's.'

'But Siggi is alive,' Wulfhere breathed wonderingly, catching the drift of Renaud's thoughts.

'Indeed,' Renaud agreed, 'and if that be the case, who, then, lies buried in your churchyard?'

Summoned into the hall and faced with the living evidence of his well-intentioned lies, Thorkil the smith confessed at once to everything he had done the day he had gone out to search for Aelfrun and her son.

'I meant no harm, I swear,' he finished, his eyes pleading with Estrith for understanding and forgiveness. 'I was so sure they had to be dead, or worse, I thought it would bring you peace to think they were buried here, amongst kin.'

Dunn, more enraged than anyone there had ever seen before, lunged forward with his fist ready to strike the man. Wulfhere caught his arm before the blow reached its target. Dunn shook him off furiously. 'Don't you understand what he's done?' he shouted, turning on Wulfhere. 'Everyone thought she was dead and stopped looking for her. She might have been alive, injured in the forest as I was. She might have died there, all alone, while it was still possible to have saved her.' The force of his imaginings made him more distraught than ever. 'If only you'd kept looking,' he cried, turning again, wild-eyed, towards Thorkil, 'she might have been found, she might have been here with us now.'

Pale but calm, Estrith addressed the smith. 'Is that possible?' she asked.

He shook his head. 'I read the tracks,' he said.

'What did the tracks tell you?' Renaud asked.

Thorkil hesitated. It was this above all which, in the kindness of his heart, he hadn't wanted his mistress to know.

'Speak, man,' Renaud snapped, 'it's too late now for silence.'

Thorkil hung his head. 'They carried her off,' he said, 'the Scots. I think she was hurt, bleeding, but she was alive.'

'Dear God!' Wulfhere exclaimed. 'If only you had told of this at the time, men could have been sent after them. What stupidity, what cowardice made you hide the truth?'

'Do you think I would have done what I did if I had believed there was any hope of saving her,' Thorkil protested, stung into defending himself. 'The trail was already a day old and snow was falling. It would have been impossible even to follow their tracks, let alone catch up with them before they crossed the border.' He turned to Estrith, his look imploring her understanding. 'Lady, if I was wrong, forgive me.'

Estrith was still confused. 'I truly believe you meant no harm, Thorkil,' she said, placing her small hand on his huge, bear-like arm. 'I trusted you then, and I want to trust you now, but I cannot understand why you lied to us. Make me understand, Thorkil, then perhaps I can begin to forgive you.'

Thorkil sighed hopelessly. 'You were not Northumbrians, my lady,' he answered her. 'We came to honour my lord Wulfhere,' he continued, 'and to love you for your gentleness, lady; but you were not Northumbrians. You came here, the two of you, innocent as babes. Border raids are no new thing here; generation upon generation it's been going on. We frighten our children with tales of the terrible things those Scots devils do to their captives.

'Suddenly, I find my lady's sister has fallen into their hands. What can I tell her? Her husband is wounded, perhaps close to death. She is alone, with two babes still at the breast and danger all about. How should I burden her with the sufferings of a sister

261

she can do nothing to help?' He swung his head towards each man in turn, as if demanding an answer.

'You pitied us?' Wulfhere asked incredulously.

'If you like,' Thorkil acknowledged, shrugging.

Renaud laid a restraining hand on Wulfhere's arm. 'I think,' he said quickly, 'that we can all accept that Thorkil, however misguidedly, acted from the best of motives. Surely, what we must now consider is whether or not there is anything we can do to find out what really happened to the lady Aelfrun, and whether she is still alive. That, I believe, is what we all want to know.'

There was a general murmur of agreement.

'Very well,' he continued, taking charge. 'Then, the hour being late, I suggest we sleep now and talk again tomorrow, when we are all a little calmer.' He glanced towards Hugh and Thomas, already bedded down in the straw. Tomorrow, he decided, he would have to tell them the truth and let them choose for themselves whether to stay or go. For him, it seemed that there was no longer a choice.

XV

January–February 1070

Ceolwynn had returned from Mandon tired, dispirited and very confused. She hated Renaud, she knew she did: she hated him for being Norman, for being Emma's lover, for being everything she should despise. Why then, she asked herself miserably, did the thought that she had lost his love for ever leave her feeling so very heartsick and so unutterably lonely?

Father Eadric, a little concerned by her unexpectedly sudden return, hurried to meet her. 'My lord Renaud is well, I hope?' he asked, probing, after the civilities had been exchanged.

'Better than he deserves to be,' Ceolwynn replied shortly.

The priest laughed uncertainly, disappointed to find that there had been no improvement in her relationship with her husband.

Edmund, who had been hovering excitedly nearby, waiting to speak, finally managed to get the priest's attention. 'Look,' he commanded, waving a pair of wooden soldiers, Norman soldiers, under Father Eadric's nose. 'They fight, watch.' He made them wave their swords and stamp up and down. 'My father gave them to me,' he announced proudly.

Ceolwynn, taking one of the toys and holding Edmund's free hand in hers, started to walk towards the hall. 'I have to admit,' she said, 'the child ran wild at Mandon. He found the castle very exciting.'

'Ah, yes, the castle!' Father Eadric said eagerly, falling into step beside her. 'Tell me, what was it like?' He'd never seen a castle and was intrigued by the thought of life lived high above the ground with staircases and passages and no need to go outdoors to get from one place to another.

Ceolwynn thought for a moment. 'Impressive,' she admitted,

squeezing the word out reluctantly. 'But very cold,' she added quickly, 'and not at all welcoming, not like our own hall.' She was about to say something more, but at that moment she saw Folca striding towards them, and she forgot the words as a sudden overwhelming feeling of revulsion swept over her.

'My lady,' Folca cried effusively, halting her progress by stopping directly in front of her, 'welcome home, welcome home indeed. Your presence has been most sorely missed.'

'Thank you, Folca,' she said, starting to edge around him. Folca, standing close enough to make her feel uneasy, sidestepped with her, blocking her escape.

'Not at all, not at all,' he replied, smiling a smile so ingratiating and familiar that even Father Eadric, usually slow to anger, scowled in annoyance.

'Step aside, man,' he said irritably, 'can't you see your mistress wants nothing more than her own hearth at this moment. Hold your noise for a better time.'

Folca hid his venom beneath a conciliatory bow as he stood aside. Things would soon be very different, he thought viciously. It would be the priest who would then have to hold his tongue, if he wanted the lady to keep hers.

Ceolwynn moved away, her hand, shaking slightly, placed gratefully on Father Eadric's arm, comforted by his reassuring presence. She was furious with herself for allowing Folca, a mere servant, to intimidate her the way he did. She, not the priest, should have been the one to order him aside. 'He has to go,' she hissed, glancing over her shoulder to make sure he wasn't following them.

'That's a decision your husband must make,' Father Eadric reminded her. 'You'll need his permission to dismiss the man.'

Ceolwynn didn't answer and they entered the warmth of the hall in silence. Once inside, Ceolwynn left him to greet others in the hall and Edmund, released from her grasp, ran off to show the village children his new toy. Ceolwynn, about to call him back for the one still in her hand, stopped herself and took the opportunity to seek out Aldhere, the crippled woodcarver.

'I hope I find you well, Aldhere?' she asked politely, finding him surrounded by woodshavings and small heaps of new-made bowls and spoons. Talking to Aldhere always made Ceolwynn feel nervous and wary. He was a man full of dangerous secrets. Part of

264

her sensed that he saw her as only temporarily strayed from the Saxon cause: sooner or later, his sharp, accusing eyes seemed to say, you will be one with us again.

'I'm well enough, thank you, my lady,' Aldhere answered, grinning his ugly, goblin grin and making her smile despite herself. 'As are others whose names you might not care to have me mention.'

Her smile vanished. 'Then don't mention them,' she answered curtly.

'As you wish,' he replied unperturbed, holding a piece of his work out for her inspection.

'It's very fine,' she commented, examining closely the intricate design of acanthus leaves around the rim of the proffered bowl. 'You take a lot of trouble over something of little worth.'

'It gives me pleasure,' he said, taking it back.

'Tell me,' Ceolwynn asked, handing him Edmund's wooden soldier, 'have you ever seen one of these before?'

Aldhere pulled experimentally at the toy, his face lighting up with pleasure as the knight waved his sword and stamped his feet. 'No,' he said, 'I've never seen a toy quite like it. It's very clever.'

'Can you make one the same?'

'Oh yes, it's very simple really. You see,' he began, full of enthusiasm, 'if you pull this rod here ...'

'I don't need to know how it works,' Ceolwynn interrupted him, 'I just want you to copy it. Can you do that for me?'

'Of course. Do you want it exactly like this one?'

She frowned thoughtfully. 'No,' she said, 'I want it to look like us, like a Saxon. I want my son to know he is as much Saxon as Norman. More so, since he was born on English soil.'

Aldhere nodded gravely. 'Yes,' he said, catching her glance and holding it, 'we should never forget who we are and where our loyalties must lie, is that not so, my lady?'

Ceolwynn felt the accusation in his words, and because she was tired and miserable, and because she half believed it to be just, she quailed before it. 'Please don't judge me, Aldhere,' she pleaded wretchedly, 'I am torn in two.'

Quick to seize upon her moment of weakness, Aldhere leant forward. 'Let me bring Cenred to you,' he whispered, 'Talk to him, let his certainty heal your doubts.'

'No, I cannot,' Ceolwynn protested.

'Have you forgotten how your father died?' Aldhere persisted. 'Can you look at your son and not remember that your brother was no older when he was driven from his home, his rightful inheritance? Their cause is your cause, my lady.'

Ceolwynn shook her head helplessly. She knew that Aldhere despised her cowardice, but how could she explain that it was Cenred himself whom she feared. Cenred, she realized with an unexpected flash of insight, had little need of any help she could give; what he really wanted was to steal her back from Renaud, to revenge himself in the only way he could on the one-time friend turned foe.

'Your father was a brave and noble lord,' Aldhere went on in gentler tones. 'He'd expect his daughter to be worthy of him.'

This was too much for Ceolwynn. 'Are you saying that I am not?' she demanded angrily. 'What right have you to censure me, you who owe everything to this house?'

'It's because I owe so much that I must say what I believe, my lady. Your father's house will always have my undying gratitude and loyalty.'

'It is a curious kind of gratitude that expresses itself in plots and deceits against the very one who has shown you such kindness.'

Aldhere looked puzzled. 'I don't understand your meaning,' he said.

'My father rescued you from beggary and gave you a position of dignity,' she said. 'But he did it idly, without overmuch thought, simply because he was in a good humour and willing to please. It was Lord Renaud who begged him to help you. He was the one whose heart was moved to help a fellow man in distress. It is to him you owe your debt.'

Aldhere sat back looking disconcerted and uncomfortable.

'Don't you think,' Ceolwynn continued, astonished to find herself in the position of Renaud's advocate, 'that for his kindness alone he deserves our loyalty. He has been a good lord to our people, has he not?'

Aldhere nodded reluctantly, but she hardly noticed as she argued less with him than with herself. 'Was it not generously done,' she continued, 'to offer me marriage so that Godmund's line might continue here at Cottesham? Doubtless,' she added unhappily, the image of the lovely Emma indelibly sharp and clear in her mind's eye, 'he could have made a far better match elsewhere.'

'The words you speak are true,' Aldhere agreed, having made up his mind that what she said changed nothing, 'but your heart speaks a different truth, does it not?' He waved Edmund's soldier triumphantly under her nose. 'It rejects the usurper, however kind, however generous.' He leant forward once more, his eyes bright, his voice intense and compelling. 'You will never find peace until you accept what you are, your father's daughter, and do his will.'

'His will?' Ceolwynn repeated, puzzled. She was aware that she had once again allowed Aldhere to take control of the conversation.

'He bound you to Lord Cenred. You were betrothed,' he said, 'in the sight of God.'

Ceolwynn felt a cold finger of superstitious dread run the length of her spine. Could Aldhere be right; was God angered? Was this the reason why her marriage to Renaud lurched from one confrontation to another, condemning them both to perpetual misery? 'Our betrothal was annulled,' she protested weakly. 'My lord Renaud attended to the matter. He showed me papers.'

Aldhere made a contemptuous, dismissive gesture. 'While Lord Cenred lives,' he said, 'before God you may have no other husband.'

Shocked, Ceolwynn gave a small gasp, but before she could say anything further she caught the warning look in Aldhere's eye and looking up saw that Folca, silent as a cat, had joined them. Aldhere returned wordlessly to his work.

'My lady, I must speak with you,' Folca began. 'The matter is urgent,' he added, seeing from her face that she was about to send him away unheard.

Ceolwynn indicated that they should walk to a relatively unoccupied space in the crowded hall, but Folca shook his head.

'I would speak to you *privately*,' he insisted.

'I can think of no matter between us which may not be discussed here in the hall,' she said, her flesh creeping at the thought of being alone with this man.

Folca smiled. 'Not even adultery?' he asked softly. 'Or treason?'

'Adultery?' she repeated weakly. Coming so hard upon what

267

Aldhere had just said about her marriage, the word filled her with alarm. As for treason, her conscience wasn't so clear that she could afford to ignore the implied accusation. What, in God's name, did the man know?

Folca's smile widened as the colour drained from her face. He gestured for her to walk ahead of him out of the hall and numbly she obeyed. Aldhere watched them leave with a worried frown. After a few moments' thought he called for his apprentice and sent the boy away with an urgent message.

Once outside Folca began to walk briskly through the village towards his cottage, glancing back at her occasionally and grinning with insolent confidence to see her still behind him.

Ceolwynn followed, unpleasantly aware of just how isolated his cottage was from the rest of the village. She hesitated a moment, then hurried on, dismissing her fears as ridiculous. At his door she found him holding it open, waiting for her to enter.

It had been a long time since she'd last been inside this cottage – Dunn's old home – and she paused for a moment to remember fondly the place where once, in happier days, she had pestered that ever-patient young man with ceaseless questions and played at counting games that she hadn't realized until much later were not really games at all.

Folca fidgeted impatiently. She sighed and stepped over the threshold, staring in dismay at the dirt and neglect which had overwhelmed the neatness and order she remembered so well. Old bones and unswept embers littered the floor, unwashed cups and bowls covered the trestle, and even the bed, which most people would roll up each morning and put away, was still exactly as Folca had left it on rising. There was nothing in this gloomy room to remind her of the man who had once been like a second father to her, and she hadn't known until now just how very much she missed him.

Folca closed the door behind them, shutting out the daylight. In the darkness Ceolwynn could hear his rapid, over-excited breathing as he paused to light a candle. 'You wouldn't need to waste a light if you opened the shutters,' she commented nervously, moving to open one.

'Leave them,' he ordered sharply, 'our business is best kept from prying eyes and ears.'

'What business, Folca?' she demanded, still apprehensive but angered by his manner towards her. 'Say what you have to say and have done.'

'Very well,' he said, 'I won't waste words. With my own eyes I saw you fornicating with a known outlaw and enemy of the king – an act of both adultery and treason.'

Shocked beyond words, Ceolwynn grabbed at the edge of the trestle for support. The food-soiled table felt slimy beneath her fingers and acid bile rose in her throat. Desperately she fought to recover her wits, but Folca didn't wait to hear what she might say.

'I'm sure I don't need to tell you,' he continued, 'that your very life depends on my willingness to keep silence.' He moved closer and seized her arm when she tried to move away. 'That willingness goes without saying – just as long as you are willing to show me your appreciation.' To make sure she knew exactly what he meant he pulled her to him and squeezing her breast painfully with his free hand he tried wetly to press his lips to hers.

Furious despite her fear, Ceolwynn fought free of his grasp and thrust him away. 'I'll have you flogged for this,' she spat at him. 'Touch me again and I swear you'll hang for it.'

Folca laughed and made a lunge towards her. She darted behind the trestle and groped frantically for something with which to defend herself, not daring to take her eyes off him for a single second. Her fingers closed on an iron ladle, a poor weapon but better than none.

'It's you that will hang, lady,' Folca assured her with soft menace, 'if I choose to tell what I know.'

Ceolwynn thought fast: it must have been Folca who had disturbed Cenred on the night he'd tried to force her to go away with him. But without proof it was his word against hers. 'I don't know what you're talking about,' she protested furiously. 'Let me out of here this minute if you value your life.'

'I saw you,' he said, 'you and that stubborn fool who thinks the world will change because he wills it. I saw you, rubbing up against him like a bitch on heat. What do you think your husband will think of that, eh?' He grinned and moved closer, always keeping his body between her and the door, her only escape. 'I wonder what he'd do if he found out his wife was a traitor's whore? What do you think he'd do? I don't think just a beating would serve, oh no!' Unconsciously his tongue flicked with anticipatory glee over lips already glistening with saliva, and for the first time Ceolwynn understood that she was in very real danger. Folca was indeed mad, and probably beyond all reason.

She forced herself to stay calm. 'You're mistaken,' she replied firmly. 'You saw two lovers in the dark and mistook another for me. Let me go now and I'll forget all that has passed here between us.'

Folca made no sign that he had heard and the strange, absent look in his eyes made her wonder if she might risk a move towards the door. Tightening her grip on the ladle she began to edge slowly and carefully around the trestle, and for several seconds Folca seemed genuinely unaware of her movements. Then, suddenly, his head jerked towards her and with a howl of rage he grabbed the edge of the trestle, hurling it effortlessly out of the way. There was now nothing between them but a scattered debris of broken pots and half-eaten food.

Ceolwynn raised the ladle and backed away from him, only to find her retreat blocked all too soon by the rear wall. Folca dived towards her and she swung the ladle at his head, but he was ready for her and before she knew it his hand was around her wrist, squeezing it in an iron clasp that made her drop her only weapon with a gasp of pain. At once he had her pinned against the wall, one sweaty hand pressed over her mouth.

With almost practised ease he grabbed her hair, twisting it round his hand and forcing her head back so that her every movement sent agonizing waves of pain through her head. He laughed softly as her frantic struggles quickly subsided.

'That's better,' he said, removing his hand from her mouth. 'I wouldn't try to scream, if I were you,' he warned her, almost gently, 'no one will hear you, but it might make me angry. You wouldn't want to make me angry, would you?' he asked, jerking violently at her hair when she didn't answer.

'No,' Ceolwynn gasped, her eyes watering. Helplessly she felt his lips and teeth on her exposed neck, half kissing, half biting, and for one terrifying moment imagined him tearing out her throat. 'Please, no, I beg of you,' she sobbed, despising herself but helpless to stop the words.

'Not so proud now, eh, my lady?' Folca gloated, his breath hot and foul in her face. 'Soon, I think, you might even begin to like the arrangement I have in mind for us, don't you?' he asked, giving her hair another little tug.

'Yes,' Ceolwynn agreed desperately, thankful to have his teeth away from her throat: but her relief was short-lived. With calm deliberation he set about unlacing the neck of her woollen gown, then with equal calm ripped away the fine linen of her undertunic, exposing her breasts and drawing from her a whimper of shame and revulsion as his tongue flicked over her nipples and his teeth nipped painfully at the tender flesh. She began to struggle again, pounding at him with her fists, oblivious to the searing agony of his relentless grip on her hair.

'Let me go,' she shrieked, still punching and trying to kick, but to her dismay she discovered that her resistance only excited him more. For the first time, she realized, she could feel the hardness of him pressing against her stomach, and the certain knowledge that he was about to rape her hit her like a blow.

Clutching at straws, she went limp, hoping desperately that if her struggles aroused him, then perhaps her passivity would have the opposite effect, but it was too late. His free hand began to explore her body, reaching beneath her skirts to follow the soft curve of her thigh while his lips sucked greedily, obscenely, at her nipples. She bit her lips as he raised her skirt up above her hips and began to fumble with the lacings of his own clothes, but she sobbed aloud at the touch of his hot, throbbing organ on her naked belly.

Forcing her legs apart with his knee, he began to lower her to the floor.

Suddenly the door burst open, ripped from its hinges by one enormous blow. Ceolwynn sagged with relief as Afa the smith hurtled into the room, closely followed by the reeve, Walter, and Aldhere's lad.

With a snarl of rage Folca thrust her away from him and turned on the intruders, ready to do or say anything to save himself. With a silent prayer of thanks Ceolwynn noted that there were no Normans amongst her rescuers. There was no one here, she knew, who would listen to Folca's accusations. Folca, it seemed, had come to the same conclusion.

'She was willing,' he shrieked as they seized him. 'She wanted it, the bitch,' he spat at them. 'Why else would ...' A vicious blow across the face reduced his protests to a high-pitched squeal of pain. Blood poured from his shattered nose.

'How did you know?' Ceolwynn gasped, her face flushed with

271

humiliation as she struggled to cover her breasts with the remains of her torn clothing. Afa, shielding her from other eyes with his huge body, discreetly turned his head away.

'Aldhere sent us,' he replied, 'he was worried about you.'

'Just you three?' she asked carefully. 'No one else?'

'Just us,' he confirmed. 'Aldhere knows each one of us may be trusted to hold his tongue.'

Ceolwynn nodded, relieved but surprised to find Walter the reeve to be one of Aldhere's confederates. How many more of her people, she wondered, were involved in Aldhere's dangerous games without her knowledge?

'What do we do with him?' the boy asked. They all looked at Ceolwynn.

'I don't know,' she said uncertainly. She couldn't let Folca stand trial; he'd be sure to tell all he knew or suspected and who knew what might be believed.

'Why don't you just leave it to us,' Walter suggested quietly. 'He'll just be gone, that's all.'

Folca, hearing this, struggled frantically until Afa punched him again.

Ceolwynn winced at the blow but considered the suggestion carefully. The thought of Folca silenced for ever was very tempting, and for just a moment, remembering all too vividly the terror and humiliation he had inflicted upon her, she revelled in the knowledge that his very life lay in her hands.

She stared at him, a trembling, pathetic creature with his leggings pooled around his ankles and his penis hanging limp and unthreatening below the edge of his tunic. His battered, terrified face stared beseechingly back at her, and she felt ashamed of her thoughts.

'Lock him up,' she ordered at last, 'I have to think about what to do. We can't just kill him out of hand.'

Walter looked as if he was about to argue but Ceolwynn raised a silencing hand. 'We will talk about this, but later,' she said firmly, forestalling him.

Afa, seeing his mistress was still struggling to keep herself modestly covered, quickly threw his cloak around her. Ceolwynn gave him a weak smile of thanks and walked to the door, drawing the cloak tighter as she edged past their prisoner.

She was shaking by the time she got back to her own chamber, and thankful to find it empty. Feeling weak and sick she was in no mood to explain to Hild about the state of her clothes, or the bruises and bite marks on her neck and breasts – she had far more important things to worry about.

What, for instance, was she going to do about Folca?

Folca, certain he was about to die, had at first succumbed to a terror which left him passive and unresisting as his captors locked him away in the abandoned charcoal burner's hut that Cenred used as a meeting place. No one went near it any more, and it was far enough from the village for any cries for help to go unheard. As the days went by, however, and still nothing dreadful happened, hope resurfaced and Folca began to think about escape.

There was no guard, and although the door could be locked from the outside, the walls themselves were so flimsy that with very little effort he might well have been able to smash his way out had Afa not chained him by the ankle to a huge log. The chain, firmly stapled to the log, was so short he could barely stand, let alone walk.

His eye lighted on a broken chisel amongst the discarded debris on the floor. It was a long way out of his reach, but Folca pulled off his tunic and used it to try to flick the chisel across the muddy floor towards his hand. Sometimes he caught it just right and it moved nearer by an inch or two, but then his next flick always seemed to send it scudding away in quite the wrong direction. After several hours of concentrated but futile effort he sank back exhausted, almost ready to give up.

It was just then that he heard a familiar tuneless whistling drawing steadily closer and closer.

Struggling up onto his knees Folca cupped his hands around his mouth and shouted as loud as he could. 'Bedric, Bedric, come here.' The whistling stopped for a moment, then started again, tentative and uncertain. 'Bedric,' Folca almost screamed, 'I'm in the hut, come here now.'

In the silence that followed Folca held his breath, willing the priest's idiot son to do his bidding. Bedric was unpredictable: he was just as likely to run off home to tell what he'd heard as to obey the command.

'Master Folca, is that you?'

Folca started, his heart hammering with relief. He hadn't heard

Bedric moving towards the hut and the unexpected, puzzled query from so close at hand had made him jump.

'Yes Bedric, and I need your help,' he replied carefully. He had not been kind to the boy in the past and knew he must take care not to frighten him away.

'What are you doing in there?' Bedric asked curiously.

'I locked myself in, accidentally. I need you to get me out.'

There was a long pause while Bedric digested this. 'I can't,' he said at last, 'the door's locked.'

'Yes, I know it's locked,' Folca agreed, forcing himself not to snap, 'but you can break it down can't you? You're a big, strong lad.'

'I'm not allowed to break things,' Bedric answered, shocked.

Folca began to feel a growing sense of panic. Bedric was his last and only hope of escape, but there was barely an hour until dusk, the time when his food was brought to him. If he couldn't get the boy to co-operate soon it would be too late.

'Bedric, listen,' he said as patiently as he could, 'you have my permission, just this once, to kick a hole in the wall. Nobody will mind, I promise you, and I'll give you a penny if you do it very quickly.'

'A whole penny?' Bedric asked, awed by the thought.

'Yes, yes, but only if you do it right now.'

To his delight, Bedric hesitated no longer but began kicking vigorously at the wall. Within moments his round, beaming face appeared in the hole he'd made.

'Good lad,' Folca said. 'Come inside now and pass me that chisel over there.'

Bedric, who was beginning to enjoy this game, obeyed willingly, even helping Folca prise the staple free without once enquiring how the steward came to be chained to a log.

Folca scrambled to his feet, stamping and striding about to get his circulation going again, wincing at the pain which shot through his calf muscles. He bent over and rubbed them energetically.

'Can I have my penny now?' Bedric asked.

'Yes,' Folca said, straightening. 'Hand me your knife.'

Unquestioningly, Bedric did so, removing it from his belt and handing it carefully to Folca by the handle, as he'd been taught. It was a small knife, useful only for cutting meat and whittling

sticks, but Folca found to his satisfaction that applied with sufficient force, it was quite long enough to reach the heart of a
skinny, half-grown boy.

It was Walter the reeve who found the body and carried it home.

'In God's name, what happened? Was it Folca?' Ceolwynn
cried, drawing the man aside.

Walter nodded and described briefly what he'd found at the
charcoal burner's hut. It wasn't difficult to work out just what had
happened.

'But why kill the boy?' Ceolwynn protested helplessly. 'He'd
done him no harm – quite the opposite.'

'Spite,' Walter replied, 'revenge, who knows? It doesn't really
matter why, does it? It's what he does next that concerns us, and
if the sheriff's men catch him, God alone knows what he'll tell
them.'

'They wouldn't believe him,' Ceolwynn argued. 'A man facing
the gallows might well say anything to try to save his neck.'

'Who knows what they'll believe or not believe? As long as that
man lives you are in grave danger, my lady.'

Ceolwynn nodded, aware that only luck had so far prevented
disaster. What if the Normans had been here still? Renaud's men-
at-arms had returned to Mandon only the previous day. 'You're
probably right,' she agreed worriedly, 'but there's nothing we can
do about it now though, is there?'

'No, there isn't,' he agreed, 'except to make sure the sheriff
doesn't get word any sooner than he has to.'

'So if I am to be saved, Folca must escape unpunished,'
Ceolwynn said bitterly.

'There seems to be no alternative, my lady,' Walter replied.
'You should have let me deal with Folca in my own way,' he added
reproachfully.

'Perhaps,' she sighed, 'but God will judge him.'

'Man's justice is swifter,' Walter muttered under his breath as
he left her.

Ceolwynn wanted to talk to Father Eadric, comfort him, but
faced with the depths of his sorrow she hardly knew what to say,
knowing that if only she'd allowed Walter and Afa to have their
way, his son would still be alive. But she saw that the priest
preferred to be alone and instead went to find Aldhere, wondering

worriedly how much Folca really knew about what had been going on at Cottesham? If he'd seen her together with Cenred, just what else had he seen? Folca, alive and at liberty, was a menace to them all. Perhaps she'd been wrong to spare him.

Aldhere's advice was unequivocal. 'You must leave,' he said. 'Go with Lord Cenred. It's the only way you will be safe.'

'Safe,' she almost laughed, 'living with outlaws?'

'Speak to him,' Aldhere persisted. 'While Folca lives your life is in peril, my lady. Lord Cenred is the only protector you have. Your husband,' he said, putting a sneering emphasis on the word, 'should this come to his ears, is hardly likely to dismiss Folca's accusations lightly, is he?'

Ceolwynn shook her head despairingly. Aldhere was right. Renaud would never forgive her if he heard what Folca had to say. He wouldn't believe she was innocent of any wrongdoing. He probably wouldn't even try to defend her. 'I will speak to Cenred,' she agreed miserably. 'I don't know what I'm going to do yet,' she said, 'but I will speak to him.'

Cenred had learned that to try to force Ceolwynn would only drive her away from him; but he was certain that if he could only persuade her to leave Cottesham, and Renaud, all else would surely follow. She would come to him in time; he just had to be patient.

He'd arranged to meet her at the charcoal burner's hut, just before dawn, waiting patiently for her there with Brand, the two of them half-dozing in the doorway. Once, Cenred thought he heard her footsteps and jumped to his feet, alert as a cat, but there was no sign of her and he relaxed again, sending Brand to water the horses at a nearby stream.

When Ceolwynn arrived a few minutes later, looking very frightened and unhappy, he embraced and kissed her, taking care to keep the greeting no more than friendly, cousinly. 'My poor, dear Ceolwynn,' he said, full of concern, 'Aldhere has told me everything. It doesn't look as though you are left with many choices, does it?'

She shook her head and gently disengaged herself from his arms. 'If we could only find Folca before the sheriff does,' she said anxiously. 'Can you help, Cenred?'

'I already have men looking,' he promised her. 'He'll not get a second chance if my people find him. I swear.'

This time, Ceolwynn was not prepared to argue on Folca's behalf. The man deserved to die. 'And if you don't find him?' she asked.

'Ceolwynn,' he said seriously, 'I don't think you should wait to find out what may or may not happen to Folca. You're in danger and I want to help and protect you. Come with me – to Denmark. We can start a new life there.'

'Denmark?' she said, startled by the unexpectedness of it.

Cenred sighed. 'The fight is over, Ceolwynn, even I know it. We can't win against the Bastard; we are too few and he is too strong.' He took her hand. It felt very cold and he warmed it tenderly between his. She'd never known him so kind and thoughtful. 'I cannot live under the Norman's rule,' he went on, 'so Denmark it has to be. Will you come with me?'

Ceolwynn didn't know what to say. 'When do you leave?' she asked, avoiding his question.

'Very soon,' he told her, 'but there's just one last blow to strike before we go.' Unconsciously, he glanced around and lowered his voice a little. 'Have you ever wondered why William has a garrison stationed at Lullingworth?' he asked, then laughed at her confused expression. 'No, of course not.' He laughed again. 'I only discovered why quite recently. You remember the consignment of silver we seized last year?'

Ceolwynn nodded. 'How could I forget?' she said. The scars on her back were only just fading. She smiled at Brand who had returned with the horses and was waiting patiently nearby.

'Well,' Cenred was saying, 'it seems that William has a vast store of treasure in Lullingworth, the silver was only a small part of it. Now he plans to move it all to London, very secretly, in just a few weeks. I intend to make sure it never reaches its destination.'

'If it's all so secret, how do you know about it?' she asked, alarmed but interested just the same.

'William is not the only one to have spies. Soldiers like to drink and in drink become careless of speech. A word here, a word there, it all adds up. When they move, we'll be ready.' He kissed the hand he held. 'Will you be ready, my dear one?'

Ceolwynn looked sad. 'It seems strange to think of leaving Cottesham,' she sighed, 'but you're right, I've little choice. Poor

Edmund,' she said, 'he must learn to be a Dane now.'

'Edmund!' Cenred exclaimed without thinking. 'I'll not raise the Norman's brat,' he said. 'You must leave him behind.'

'No,' Ceolwynn said, pulling her hand sharply from his grasp. 'That I will not do. If I can't have Edmund then I'll take my chances here.' She began to walk away, angry with herself for believing that Cenred really cared what she felt. How could he expect her to desert her child?

'And let him see you burn at the stake?' he called after her.

She slowed, alarmed by the possibility that he could be right. On reflection, perhaps Edmund *would* be better off with his father. Thinking of Renaud brought a lump to her throat.

Cenred caught up with her and grabbed her arm. 'Have you forgotten,' he asked, quite harshly, 'how once you swore vengeance on these Normans?'

Ceolwynn shook her head. 'I haven't forgotten,' she said.

'Then take your revenge,' he urged passionately. 'Let's seize their silver, kill their soldiers and humiliate that two-faced, treacherous Renaud de Lassay into the bargain.'

She found herself wanting to defend Renaud from this attack, but then she remembered Mandon and the way he'd deceived and humiliated her. Anger surged through her yet again, but still she hesitated to commit herself.

'You don't have to decide now,' Cenred told her, sensing that her mood had changed. 'I'll come back for you in sixteen days. That's when the treasure is to be moved. If anything happens before then and you have to hide, go to the cobbler in Lullingworth. He'll shelter you.'

Ceolwynn nodded, softening towards him. There was no point in being angry with Cenred; he had his own point of view and if she was honest with herself she could understand it.

Cenred let go of her arm and she hurried away, anxious to be back in her bed before Hild woke. A few moments later both Cenred and Brand left in the opposite direction.

When all was still, Folca emerged carefully from his hiding place in the undergrowth. Under cover of darkness he'd come to recover his stolen silver, his path by chance taking him past the place of his recent imprisonment. He'd been frightened half out of his wits to find himself within a few feet of Cenred and Brand, ducking out of sight just in time as Cenred heard his footfall, but he could hardly believe his luck at all he'd seen and heard next.

He looked up at the reddening sky. It was getting too light to think of fetching his silver now. Too many people would be up and about their business.

The silver could wait, he decided contentedly, turning back towards Guildford, but the time for his revenge had come.

XVI

January 1070

Dunn's description of the tall, white-haired Scotsman drew a sharp intake of breath from Thorkil.

'You know of whom he speaks?' Renaud asked quietly.

'God help me, I do,' Thorkil said, hanging his head. 'Dunmail Whitehair of Kilbar it has to be, my lord. We've not seen him in these parts for several years, but there was a time when his name alone struck terror into the bravest heart – the man was merciless beyond belief.'

Dunn paled, but Renaud refused to be disheartened. 'Tell me Thorkil,' he asked, 'can this man be found?'

Thorkil nodded slowly. 'Dunmail's lair lies perhaps four days ride north of here. If he kept the lady as his own, that's where she'll be. If he sold her, of course, she could be anywhere.'

'Can you show me the road to Kilbar, Thorkil?' Renaud asked coldly, wondering how different things might have been if all this had been known years since.

Thorkil swallowed nervously. 'No,' he said, then hurried to add, 'but border raids are not all one way – there are men here who know their way into Scotland. I'll find you one to be your guide.'

Renaud nodded. 'Good, then I will leave before dawn.'

'We will leave,' Dunn corrected him. 'It would not be wise for you to ride into Dunmail's village alone. You forget that the Scots have no great love for Normans.'

Renaud nodded. 'You're quite right,' he agreed, 'a direct approach might be a mistake, but I can see no other way.'

'We must go as Saxons, both of us,' Dunn said.

'I could never pass as a Saxon,' Renaud protested.

'You could if you travelled as my servant,' Dunn said excitedly, 'I could do all the talking, and if you have to speak, well, they barely understand the southern tongue up here anyway.'

Thorkil and Renaud exchanged glances. 'It could work,' Thorkil said.

Renaud would have liked to discuss matters with Wulfhere, but both he and Estrith were fully occupied preparing for the move into the mountains. Thomas and Hugh, a little bemused, were actually helping with the loading. Their reaction to his plan was unexpectedly matter-of-fact.

'We have chosen to serve you, my lord,' Thomas said seriously, 'and whatever you choose to do is right with us, isn't that so, Hugh?' Hugh nodded. 'I daresay there's those as might see it differently,' Thomas added, 'but friends are friends and it's no sin to be loyal to a friend in need. We've got no wish to see these folk suffer; they were kind enough to us, last year, all things considered.'

Renaud smiled with relief and gratitude. 'Well then, Hugh,' he said, 'I want you to take a letter to my lord fitzOsbern. He, at least, has a right to know what I'm about, and Thomas, I want you to rejoin the king's forces at Hexham, taking the boy Martin with you. I entrust him to your care. Guard him well.'

'Is it true,' Thomas asked, 'that young Martin is the lady Ceolwynn's brother?'

'Yes, that is so, and he is, therefore, precious to me.'

'Then I will guard him with my life, my lord,' he promised.

Renaud knew without a doubt that Thomas meant what he said. For the first time he felt that he was truly their lord, not merely their paymaster. It was a good feeling.

The letter to fitzOsbern proved to be as much of a challenge as Renaud had expected. It was not easy to explain to his lord why he was off chasing about Scotland when he should have been with the army, but he excused himself as best he could, saying nothing, however, about Blackwater or St Aidan's. At least he was leaving four fully armed men to serve in his name, and this, he hoped, coupled with fitzOsbern's goodwill, would be enough to soften the king's anger at his temporary desertion.

Finally satisfied with his efforts, he took up the sealing wax, then stopped and quickly added a footnote before writing a few words on another piece of parchment and rolling the two pieces up together. Finally he affixed his seal and handed the package to Hugh, who was waiting to leave. 'On your way to the stables, Hugh, find young Martin and send him to me,' he said, wondering how the boy would take the news that he was leaving his new-found family so soon.

Martin appeared almost at once and Renaud got up to greet him. Someone immediately took the chest he had been sitting on, so Renaud suggested they walk outside and Martin obediently fell into step beside him. The boy was very quiet, and Renaud realized that he hadn't yet had a chance to ask Estrith how the child had taken the news of his origins.

'Your aunt has told you who you are?' he began.

'Yes,' Martin replied, staring at his feet.

'Do you understand who I am?' Renaud tried next.

'Yes, I think so. My sister's husband.'

'Yes, that's right,' Renaud said, pleased that the child had understood that much. 'That makes us brothers, of a sort.'

'Like Brother Wulfstan and Brother Oswald and Brother Theodore?' Martin asked, suddenly more interested.

'No,' Renaud replied with a sigh, 'that's a different kind of brother. Listen, Martin,' he said, still finding it hard to think of the boy as Siggi. 'Your aunt and her family have to go away for a while, but I want you to go with my man, Thomas, who is to look after you until I can take you to your sister. Do you understand that?'

Martin nodded. 'Then will you take me home?' he asked.

Renaud sighed again and swung round to face the boy, kneeling so that their faces were on a level and putting his hands on his shoulders. 'Martin,' he said gently but firmly, 'I tried to tell you on the way here, St Aidan's is no more. The brothers are gone and there is no home for you there. Your home is with us now, with your sister and with me.' Martin's eyes filled with tears. 'You'll be happy, I promise you,' Renaud said, stroking his hair. 'Be brave now and things will seem better before too long. Aren't you glad to have found your family?'

Martin nodded, not very convincingly.

Sigurd, the man Thorkil had found to be their guide, proved to be well worth the whole shilling Renaud had agreed to pay him, leading them through country so remote and isolated that they saw not another living soul until they were almost at their destination. They had approached Kilbar from the south, following hidden paths and tracks that only their guide could see, and were now less than two miles west of the village.

At this point Sigurd said he would go no closer, but would wait in hiding for them there. He warned them to mark the place well or they would never find him again, and he would wait, he said, only until the second sunrise. This left them some forty hours to complete their search.

Dunn, looking every inch the thegn in Renaud's borrowed mail, led the way mounted on one of Wulfhere's better horses, with Renaud, dressed in peasant clothing and with a cap pulled firmly down over his too dark hair, following apprehensively.

As they approached Dunmail's village, three heavily armed men rode out to meet them, mounted on small, shaggy ponies. Renaud watched them uneasily, preparing himself for any sudden attack, but Dunn, showing no sign of fear or hesitation, trotted boldly towards them, his empty hand raised to show he came in peace. He greeted them in the Northumbrian tongue, which they seemed to understand well enough, explaining that he was a Saxon fugitive needing shelter for the night on his way to seek refuge at King Malcolm's court. His manner was so very much that of a nobleman and warrior that Renaud couldn't help but be both surprised and impressed by the performance. The Scots, too, were convinced, and soon they found themselves being escorted quite amicably towards the place where, if God was willing, they hoped to find the lady Aelfrun.

If Renaud had any doubts at all that Dunmail Whitehair was the man they sought, they were dispelled as soon as he saw Dunn's reaction to the tall Scot who emerged from his hut to greet them as they entered his village. Setting eyes on him, Dunn's face turned to stone and his knuckles whitened as they clenched the hilt of his sword. Fearful that Dunn might actually attack the man and ruin everything, Renaud allowed his horse to jostle Dunn's quite hard.

The frozen look faded from Dunn's eyes and he quickly recovered himself. 'Greetings,' he called blithely, all goodwill. 'My name is Cenred Oswaldson of Bosham, loyal follower of Edgar Aetheling and enemy of William of Normandy. I seek a night's shelter on my way to King Malcolm's court.'

Renaud threw him a glance of surprise, quickly suppressed.

283

He'd never even given a thought to false names and was amazed that Dunn had had the forethought to use that of a man whose reputation as an outlaw and rebel might be known even here.

'Who is the other man?' Dunmail asked. He spoke Northumbrian of a sort, and although Renaud couldn't understand all the words, his meaning was clear enough.

'My servant, Dunn,' Dunn answered without hesitation, and Renaud had to bite his lip to smother a startled laugh.

Dunmail studied them both with careful, cold, pale eyes. 'You are welcome, Cenred of Bosham,' he said at last, accepting their story. 'Enter and warm yourselves. Soon we shall eat.'

Both men dismounted and, as their horses were led away, Dunmail took them into his hut through a crowd of dirty, ragged women and children who stared at them with undisguised curiosity. Renaud's eyes scanned the crowd carefully as he walked, but he saw no one who looked even remotely like Aelfrun.

Disappointed, he followed Dunn inside, through the low, narrow doorway, noting with some surprise that Dunmail the chieftain lived no better than the rest of his clan. His ramshackle hut was small and dirty, shared with the beasts penned at one end and lacking even the most basic of homely touches.

He was a little puzzled by Dunmail's unexpectedly friendly welcome, but it soon became clear that the man was hungry for news, asking question after question about matters south of the border, especially about King William's movements. Dunn, Renaud was surprised to find, had an answer for almost every question, and lied with amazing conviction. Renaud, ignored by Dunmail, watched everyone who came and went, hunting desperately, but in vain, for a familiar face.

As evening drew on, the trestles were brought out and food appeared. Women came and went carrying bowls and dishes and jugs of ale. They spoke little and smiled less, serving and moving away without meeting Renaud's eyes, ignoring his efforts to get their attention. Several of them, he noted, were Saxon slaves, but there was still no sign of Aelfrun. Reluctantly, he began to accept that their quest was hopeless.

Dunn, wearied by Dunmail's relentless questions, was trying to turn the conversation to his own advantage. 'Do you believe King Malcolm really intends to aid young Edgar to oust the Bastard?' he asked.

'I've heard that he plans to marry the lad's sister, Margaret,' Dunmail replied through a mouthful of mutton. 'That sounds to me as if he's on your Aetheling's side.'

'It's not quite the same thing as putting an army in the field, though, is it?' Dunn asked. 'And it doesn't necessarily mean peace on the border, does it? The raids continue.'

Dunmail laughed, spitting food on the table. 'Peace on the border,' he chortled, 'that's a different matter altogether.' He belched and wiped his mouth on his sleeve. 'Life on the border doesn't depend on the mood of princes,' he said, 'it goes on the way it always has and always will. You're my guest tonight, Saxon, and safe under my roof, but another day I might kill you without a second thought.' He grinned wolfishly.

Renaud could hear the menace in Dunmail's voice and looked up from his food, instantly alert and watchful.

'Then I must be grateful that I chose a good day to pass your way,' Dunn replied easily, smiling in his turn.

Dunmail laughed again, and Renaud, who had never suspected Dunn's talent for play-acting, was astonished at his sangfroid.

'Enough now,' Dunmail announced abruptly. 'The hour is late.' He got up, calling for the servants to clear away the dishes and trestle. He took one man aside and spoke a few words to him quietly. The man left, grinning.

Dunn and Renaud exchanged a look, each warning the other to be wary.

Other servants came in carrying armfuls of fresh bracken and heaped them up close to the fire as beds for the guests, and soon the lights were being doused, leaving Dunn and Renaud with no option but to retire to bed. Dunmail had already thrown himself under a bearskin on the other side of the fire.

Renaud and Dunn exchanged another look, this time of despair. They had learned nothing and must leave in the morning with their hopes in tatters.

The last light went out, and Dunn, lying in the bracken, heard it crackle as someone crept to his side. He tensed, reaching for the sword only inches away. Suddenly, he felt his visitor lie down by his side, and knew it was not a man.

Dunmail chuckled. 'I thought I would offer you a gift,' he called out laughingly, 'a woman of your own kind to pleasure you.' His 'gift' was an insult, and meant to be.

Dunn could feel the woman tremble as she pressed herself against him, her heart beating far too fast. Clumsily, her hand moved to touch him, but he caught it gently in his, moved to pity for the degradation she endured. He put his mouth close to her ear. 'Have no fear,' he whispered, 'I won't touch you, I swear, but it might be as well to pretend.'

He pulled himself over her, noisily scuffling in the bracken and drawing a harsh laugh from where Dunmail lay, obviously listening with amused interest in the dark. Grateful that the fire had burned low enough to make such a pretence possible, Dunn grunted a couple of times and threw himself down again.

Slowly the woman started to relax, trusting him, and Dunn was suddenly aware that at last he had the opportunity to ask some important questions. He waited until he could hear Dunmail snoring before he whispered, 'What's your name?', more to soothe her fears than satisfy his interest.

'Aelfrun,' she said.

Dunn was dreadfully afraid that he must have misheard. 'Aelfrun?' he repeated. 'Aelfrun of Cottesham?' He felt the shock of his question in the sudden stiffening of her body.

'Who are you?' she asked, and this time he knew her voice.

'It's Dunn,' he said, almost frantic with joy. He wanted to hug her and shout the news to Renaud, but Dunmail and his men lay all about them. He had to force himself to stay calm and keep his voice to a whisper. 'I came to find you,' he said softly, 'and God in His mercy has answered my prayers.'

'Oh, can it really be you?' she said, her voice catching with emotion. He reached out to touch her, tenderly tracing the line of her cheek with his rough, workworn hand. Her face was wet with tears and it seemed the most natural thing in the world to want to kiss them away. He kissed her eyes, her cheeks, and then before he knew what he was doing, his lips were on hers and she was kissing him back, almost desperately, her hands holding his head fiercely to hers while his own hands found their way under her skirt to stroke the curve of her buttocks, the sharp ridge of her hips, unexpectedly thin under his hand.

Breathless with desire, he forgot all about Dunmail and Renaud and the danger surrounding them. All he knew was that his beloved Aelfrun was alive and here in his arms.

His lips moved from hers to cover her face, her neck, the swell of her breasts. She sat up suddenly and pulled her gown over her head before sliding down naked into his embrace. With only touch to guide him, he explored every inch of her, kissing and stroking until it became almost too much for them to bear.

She took his hand, guiding it between her thighs, gasping at his touch. Soon she was pulling him towards her, urgent and demanding. Dunn struggled out of his leggings, fumbling clumsily with the laces, hardly daring to believe what was happening. Then he was inside her, moving slowly at first, then thrusting faster, deeper and harder until she cried out softly, clinging to him, and he came in a spasm of sheer inexpressible joy.

For a long time afterwards they lay unspeaking in each other's arms, with Aelfrun's head laid trustingly on his chest, her arm wrapped around his waist. Dunn sighed contentedly, hardly daring to speak. They would have to talk soon, but this moment was good beyond words and he hesitated to spoil it.

It was Aelfrun, however, who broke the silence. 'Have I dreamt this?' she whispered. 'I thought you dead, just when I had learned to love you.'

'It's no dream, dearest Aelfrun,' he murmured gently, kissing her again and rejoicing at her wonderful, astonishing declaration of love. 'We came to find you, and now we'll get you away from here, I promise. Can you get away to meet us just a little way along the road after we leave?'

'No,' she replied without hesitation. The dull certainty in her voice made him frown with concern.

'Why not?' he asked.

She didn't answer for a moment. 'I'm kept in chains,' she said at last, her voice full of shame and bitterness, 'and I'm never alone. Sometimes, though,' she added with a glimmer of hope, 'I fetch water from the spring, which is close by but out of sight of the village, just through the trees and up the hill. In daylight you will see clearly the path trodden to it.'

'Can you find an excuse to go there tomorrow, no sooner than two hours after we leave?'

'I think so. I will find a way, but remember, I won't be alone.' She sat up. 'I have to go now,' she said.

'Take care, my love,' he whispered as she kissed him and rose to leave. 'Tomorrow all this will be over, I swear.'

287

Renaud was quiet the following morning, and Dunn thought he sensed a certain disapproval in his aloofness. He wasn't sure whether to be offended or amused by Renaud's obvious assumption that he had taken advantage of Dunmail's offer, but until they were alone he was in no position to explain.

Dunmail, breaking his fast with them, was in a good mood, and his conversation full of lewd remarks and gestures that made Dunn want to strangle him with his bare hands; but it was obvious that he was by now quite happy to be rid of them, and as soon as they had eaten, their horses were brought and directions given as to their road. Dunn pretended to listen, nodding and smiling, but his eyes searched restlessly for a glimpse of Aelfrun, and more particularly for the path to the spring. There was no sign of Aelfrun, but, as she had told him the night before, the path was clear and well trodden. Carefully, he made note of the direction they must take to approach it from behind without being seen.

It was a blessed relief to be able to break the news to Renaud, which he did just as soon as they were out of sight and earshot of the men who had guided them a little way along their road. 'I have found her,' he burst out excitedly, whirling his horse round in front of his stony-faced companion.

'Aelfrun?' Renaud exclaimed, his expression changing to one of such happiness as understanding dawned. 'The woman of last night,' he said, 'that was Aelfrun?'

Dunn nodded. There was no time for detailed explanations. 'We must go back,' he said. He pointed towards the hill where Aelfrun had told him they would find the spring. 'We must get up there,' he said, 'that's where she will try to be within the next few hours. We must be there, waiting, when she comes.'

Renaud was already turning, following his pointing finger. Soon they had both left the road to pick their way carefully across the half mile of rock-strewn, pitted land that lay between them and the end of their quest.

As he made his way along the road to Guildford in the early dawn light, Folca's excitement began to give way to a growing sense of annoyance and frustration. He knew he would have to take his information to some important Norman, but he spoke no French and it would certainly not be easy to find a Norman who spoke Saxon. Besides, he couldn't take the chance of being dismissed as soon as his information had been given; he wanted to be there when Cenred and Ceolwynn were caught; he wanted to see them brought down and punished; he wanted her to see him and know that he had won. Her accusations would count for nothing then, he gloated, and there would no longer be any need for him to run and hide like some wild, hunted beast.

It would be a mistake, he decided regretfully, to act precipitately. In the meantime he must find somewhere safe to hide while the sheriff's men were hunting him. He felt the purse at his belt, comfortingly heavy. His captors had taken his knife, but the fools had not even thought to rob him of his money. It came to him suddenly that, as long as he had money, he knew exactly where he could go.

Surprised and not at all pleased at being woken at such an early hour, Elfrida the brothel-keeper was happy enough to see the silver Folca waved under her nose. She welcomed him in, quickly agreeing to shelter him in return for a generous payment negotiated shrewdly to her own satisfaction, and Folca, weary from his night's adventures, tumbled gratefully into the bed she offered him, not emerging until late in the afternoon.

So it was that Nest, returning from a visit to young Rhianwen, walked in to find him sitting on Elfrida's favourite stool, warming himself at the fire and enjoying a mug of ale.

He glanced up as she came through the door and Nest found herself tensing with fear as their eyes met. Folca eyed her briefly, then turned away with no sign at all of interest or recognition. Slowly she released the breath she'd been holding and moved cautiously into the room.

Folca hadn't been here for so long she had almost forgotten about him, but now he was back, and looking very much at home – actually living under their roof, she discovered from Aggie. Was it possible, she asked herself, that in time he would come to remember her? Even hearing her name might be enough to jog his memory? She bit her lip and sat hardly daring to move or speak for fear of drawing his attention, but before long trade became brisk and he retired out of sight into Elfrida's private quarters where, to Nest's immense relief, he stayed most of the time from then on.

After a few days Nest's fear of Folca began to be replaced by curiosity. Why was he here, and so obviously in hiding? She took to sitting close to the door of Elfrida's room, listening intently to the muffled snatches of conversation within, but learning little beyond the fact that he was hoping that one of the many Norman soldiers who came here would speak Saxon. Why, she wondered, was he so anxious to speak to a Norman?

Then, a week after his arrival, she overheard him say that he was going out into the town that day, and, on impulse, she decided to follow him. Elfrida grudgingly allowed her a few hours off and she slipped outside to wait for Folca to leave.

Almost furtively, with his hood pulled up to hide his face, Folca walked into that part of town where the Norman soldiers, in their off-duty hours, spent much of their time drinking and dicing. Following him now became very difficult. Several of the soldiers recognized her and called out, inviting her to join them with loud laughter and lewd gestures. Horrified, she expected Folca to turn and see her at any moment, but he was too busy trying to find a Norman who could speak his tongue.

At last he discovered such a man, not a soldier but a red-headed squire called Ralf, a man who served Hugo de Caen and who waited now for his master's return from the north in the house of Roger de Virar.

'Will you be going back to Northumbria now that Geoffrey is out of danger?' Emma asked her husband, disguising very well, she thought, her eagerness that he should do so.

She wished now that she hadn't been so quick to send Hugo to him with the news of Geoffrey's illness, but if the boy had died without Roger even knowing how ill he was, he would have been sure to make her life a living hell. Not that it wasn't already, she thought to herself with an inward sigh.

Roger smiled, not at all deceived by her casual manner. 'I thought I would stay a few days more,' he replied, 'just to be sure, and to enjoy your charming company just a little longer, my dear.' It amused him to know just how much she hated him. It added spice to their marital encounters, he always thought.

Guessing at his thoughts Emma got up and wandered to the window. Unconsciously she wrapped her arms protectively around herself, shuddering at the memory of his revolting demands. 'It's raining again,' she remarked heavily. 'Mother of God, how I wish I were at home once more.'

'You were eager enough to come,' Roger said. 'Has the place suddenly lost its attraction?' He smiled to himself, thinking of the obvious rift between Emma and her erstwhile lover.

Emma turned to see him watching her with undisguised amusement. Something in his manner alarmed her. 'No,' she replied defensively, 'I just want to go home now, to Normandy. I hate this outlandish place, with its horrible, incomprehensible language and dreadful people.'

'Oh, it's not that bad,' he protested, laughing at her. 'In fact, since I intend to stay a while, I've made a point of learning a little of their language myself – especially useful if the servants don't know you can understand them.'

'Do you refuse your consent for me to return home then, my lord?' she asked, thoroughly dismayed by the news that he intended to stay here. Since Renaud's humiliating rejection of her at Christmas she wanted nothing more than to get away from this cold, dreary place for ever.

Roger hesitated. He would have liked to make her stay, if only because it would annoy her so very much, but unfortunately this climate did not agree with Geoffrey at all, and since the boy was, it had to be admitted, a sickly child, it was for the best that he should return home as soon as he was well enough to travel. 'No,' he said at last, 'you may take Geoffrey home as soon as it seems wise to do so. I would rather he was in your care than in that of servants.'

Emma nodded gratefully. Her maternal feelings were far from strong, but she did have an affection for the child, and while he lived her husband did at least honour her as the mother of his heir. It amazed her, just as much as it did others, how devoted a father Roger had become.

At that moment there was a knock at the door and Ralf, her brother's squire, appeared, followed by a small, dark man with strange, yellow-coloured eyes. 'My lord,' Ralf said, 'this man has something to tell you which, he declares, is of much import. Will you hear him?'

Roger looked contemptuously at Folca, staring him up and down as his rain-sodden clothes dripped water all over the floor. 'Leave us,' he said suddenly to his wife, and Emma quickly left the room, glad that her husband had found something other than provoking her to amuse him.

Roger was, at first, only mildly interested in Folca's story. The details were hard to grasp, for his knowledge of Saxon was imperfect, but Cenred's name was clear enough and Roger quickly realized that he was being offered the chance to capture a notorious rebel, something that would do much to earn him the goodwill of the king. He began to listen very much more carefully to the details that Folca began to reveal.

It was only when he heard the name of Cottesham, however, and remembered exactly who it was who ruled there, that Roger knew that at last the opportunity to revenge himself on Renaud de Lassay lay within his grasp.

Nest really didn't know what to do next. Part of her wanted to forget the whole business, but another, less timorous part really needed to know what it was that Folca was plotting. Fear of the man was only one reason for her interest; she remembered the stolen bag of silver and suspected that he still had it secreted away somewhere. That silver could change her life for ever. She could even take Rhianwen home to Wales, a dream that she had held in her heart since the day of the child's birth.

So she found a doorway to shelter in and waited and watched outside Roger's house all afternoon until she heard the vesper-bell and knew that if she didn't return soon she would be in serious trouble with Elfrida. Then, just as she was about to leave, Ralf emerged from the gate and began to make his way, whistling, down the road.

Quickly she chased after him, smiling and inviting, and Ralf, ever susceptible to a pretty face, allowed himself to be led away towards Elfrida's house, where Nest hoped to humour her mistress with a new customer while at the same time finding out as much as she could from Ralf about Folca's activities.

Ralf, a man of naturally friendly and talkative disposition, was happy enough to sit and drink with Nest for a while before they went behind the curtain, and Elfrida was content to let them do so since she made a nice profit on the watered ale she sold. Nest knew she had to be very careful what she asked, but the fact that Folca actually lived in Elfrida's house made it easy enough for her to bring him into the conversation.

'I saw you with my mistress's friend this afternoon,' she mentioned innocently, refilling his cup for the third time, and not with the watered stuff, 'Folca is his name.'

'Folca?' he replied, surprised that she knew the man.

'He lives here,' she said. 'I wondered how it was that you knew him.'

'He wanted to speak to my lord Roger de Virar, that's all. I don't really know him. Truth to tell, I found him most unpleasant and certainly wouldn't choose his company.'

Nest struggled to make sense of all that; Ralf's grasp of Saxon was quite good, given the short time he had spent in England, but it still left a lot to be desired, and his accent was quite appalling.

'How strange,' she said at last, 'what could he possibly have to say that would interest such an important man?' She was sitting on his lap by this time and running her fingers playfully through his bright shock of hair.

Disappointingly, Ralf refused to be drawn any more on the subject, turning his attention to squeezing her breasts and trying to get his hand up under her skirt. With a resigned sigh she got up and led him behind the curtain, letting him get on with the business in hand while her mind busily explored all the questions she might ask to get the information she wanted.

After he'd finished, Nest persuaded him to stay for another drink or two. Business was slack and she knew Elfrida wouldn't mind as long as the man kept spending his money.

'I wonder where he came from, before he came here,' she mused as she sat in the straw, her head resting against his leg.

'Who?' Ralf asked, having forgotten their earlier conversation.

'That Folca,' she replied thoughtfully, 'he's not a Guildford man, and I just wondered where he was from.'

'Some place called Cottesham,' Ralf replied, belching a little. He'd already been warned to keep a tight rein on his tongue for fear of alerting the rebels to what they knew, but now he was very relaxed, more than a little drunk, and badly off his guard. 'No loyalty though,' he said with disgust. 'Ready to throw his mistress to the wolves.'

'What do you mean?'

He leant forward, whispering confidentially in her ear. 'His mistress consorts with rebels,' he said, nodding to himself in drunken confirmation of his own words. 'She dismisses this Folca, probably with good cause,' he added, 'so then he comes here to make sure she pays for it. Not a pleasant man, not a pleasant man at all.' He whispered a little more, saying things that would have cost him his life had Roger learned of it. As he spoke his head drooped lower and lower until it was almost resting on hers. He was nearly asleep.

Nest pushed him upright and left him leaning up against the wall while she went to get her supper. Ralf hadn't told her much, but the little he'd said had raised some intriguing questions. Wasn't it to Cottesham that the lady Aelfrun had gone on her marriage? Was Aelfrun the lady Folca planned to destroy? Was Folca's silver still hidden at Cottesham? If he'd been dismissed in disgrace, perhaps he'd not had time to recover it. Folca's future movements would undoubtedly be worth watching, but she knew that it would be almost impossible for her to follow him any more. She was hardly ever allowed to leave the house.

Then it suddenly occurred to her that there might actually be another way to escape this dreadful life. She had no cause to love Wilfred's family, but the lady Aelfrun had always been kind and generous. Ralf's information had now placed her in a position to do Aelfrun a great service, a service that in all honour Aelfrun would be bound to reward most handsomely.

Within moments Nest had made up her mind what she would do. Tomorrow she would leave this house for ever, and taking Rhianwen with her she would find her way to Cottesham to warn the lady Aelfrun of the terrible danger that lay in wait for her.

Dunn was worried, and he knew without asking that Renaud was worried too. All day they had lain hidden in the rocks above the spring, but Aelfrun had not come. The sun was sinking fast and the likelihood of her coming at all before nightfall grew more and more remote. They could wait here tomorrow and the next day if they had to, but Sigurd would be gone by sunrise, greatly reducing their chances of a successful escape.

Renaud stretched his cramped muscles and glanced up at the sun. Dunn knew he was about to voice his own fears and prepared himself to argue for a longer wait. At that moment, however, they heard voices on the path and held their breath, praying that this time they would not be disappointed. So many women had climbed this path during the day with their buckets and jars, but not one of them had been the one they sought.

Almost before they saw them, Dunn knew that his prayers had

been answered, for he heard the clink of chains, the cruel reminder of Aelfrun's servitude.

There were two women with her, one carried a leather bucket while the other held a stick which she used sharply every now and then to hurry the stumbling Aelfrun up the hill. Aelfrun carried two buckets and struggled with a length of chain which, running from ankle to ankle, would have tripped her if she hadn't held it up with one hand. Her wrists, also, were chained, and around her neck she wore an iron collar.

Renaud heard Dunn catch his breath with fury and quickly placed a restraining hand on his arm. It was too soon to move. 'I'll get the one with the stick,' he whispered, 'you take the other. Silence her swiftly,' he added.

Dunn nodded, then at Renaud's signal they burst out of their hiding place, falling upon the women before they could recover from their shock. With no hesitation at all, Renaud ran his sword straight through his target's throat and she died without a sound; but Dunn faltered, suddenly horrified to find himself about to kill an unarmed woman. His hesitation was momentary, but it was enough. With loud shrieks of alarm she took off down the hill and Renaud, cursing furiously, threw Aelfrun over his shoulder and made for the horses as fast as his feet could carry him.

It took him only a moment to see that, encumbered by her chains, Aelfrun could not hope to ride astride, so he tossed her without ceremony over his saddle and leapt up behind, glancing round to make sure Dunn was still with him. He was, and they made off into the gathering dusk, just as the sound of loud and angry shouts reached them from the village below.

They headed west, back towards the place where Sigurd waited for them, but Renaud was dismayed by the upset to his plans. He'd hoped for a head start to see them well clear of the village before Dunmail discovered what had happened. Then, all being well, they could have made for the road and headed back at a gallop. Now, however, they had to make their way slowly over treacherous, unknown terrain, in the dark and unable to use the road until they were certain it was clear. With their knowledge of the land, Dunmail's men had a distinct advantage, either on foot or on their stocky hill ponies.

He made a sudden decision and reined abruptly to a halt. He dismounted and helped Aelfrun back onto her feet, noticing, just as Dunn had, how very thin she was. 'Aelfrun,' he said, feeling the weight of her chains, 'do you think you can walk three miles like that?'

'Three hundred if I have to,' she responded resolutely, wondering who this man was who had come with Dunn to rescue her. There was something familiar about him, but she just couldn't place him.

Renaud looked at Dunn. 'I want you both to cross those fields above the village on foot,' he said, 'and to keep heading towards that ridge there.' He pointed to a line of trees on a distant hilltop, clearly outlined by the light of a bright, rising moon. 'The road lies below it, and if you can remember the markers you should be able to find Sigurd before sunrise.'

'What are *you* going to do?' Dunn asked, but, having no intention of questioning Renaud's instructions, he had already dismounted.

'Exactly what I hope they'll expect us all to do. Head for the road and make eastwards. That way I should be able to draw them away from you.'

'They'll kill you,' Aelfrun protested.

'They'll have to catch me first,' Renaud replied with a grin, and suddenly she knew him.

'Renaud!' she exclaimed, but before she could say any more he was in the saddle and leading Dunn's horse away.

'Good luck,' he called softly, 'and if I'm not with you by sunrise, I'll meet you in Hexham for sure. Seek the protection of one Hugo de Caen and wait for me there.'

Then he was gone.

With no time to waste, Dunn and Aelfrun set off across the fields, their progress greatly hampered by her chains and by the unevenness of ground deeply ridged by winter ploughing. The muddied skirts of her tunic clung cold and wet around her legs, leaving them chafed and sore, but still she struggled on, her hand in his, exhausted but uncomplaining.

Renaud, meanwhile, had made his way back to the spring, moving cautiously forward until he could hear voices and see the light from a dozen or more torches flaring in the night. They were still trying to pick up the trail, but he would have to act fast if he were to distract them before they found it.

Still hidden by the rocks he made his way carefully downhill towards a point in the road close enough for them to hear the hoofbeats, but far enough away for them not to see that one of the horses was riderless. If he could only get them to give chase and give up the search above the spring, he was sure that Dunn and Aelfrun would be safe.

Making as much clatter as he could, he spurred his horse out from behind his cover and dived out onto the road, dragging Dunn's horse close alongside and galloping as fast as he could towards a bend that would quickly hide him from view. There was no time to look back, but he grinned triumphantly as he heard the sudden clamour of angry, excited voices behind him.

Within moments he heard the sound of several horses on his trail, but he just laughed and gave his horse its head, confident that Wulfhere's horses could outrun anything in Dunmail's stables. Once he'd shaken them off, he decided, he'd leave the road and find somewhere to hide until daylight, then head south across country for the border. It would probably take a few days, very hungry days at that, but as long as he kept heading south, he thought rather optimistically, he was bound to find himself in England sooner or later.

The following hoofbeats grew fainter and fainter until at last Renaud felt safe enough to allow the horses to slow to a walk for a few minutes. The second horse was a great hindrance to him and he wondered whether he should take a chance and turn it loose. It seemed safe enough; the sound of pursuit had died out altogether and he began to think that the Scotsmen had given up the chase as hopeless. He started to dismount, meaning to strip the animal of its gear.

Suddenly, from a hidden gully to his left three men burst out in front of him, their ponies mud-besplattered and lathered with sweat.

'Did you really think you could outfox Dunmail Whitehair on his own ground?' Dunmail called out, sneering, but there was a baffled, disconcerted look in his eyes as he took in the riderless horse and the fact that Renaud was alone.

Renaud caught his breath and grabbed for his sword, charging straight at Dunmail without waiting for the man to prepare for the attack. One of the other men quickly dived between them, a huge, long-handled axe raised high above his head. Before he could bring it down Renaud had plunged his sword into the man's exposed armpit, wrenching the sword free with a deft twist before whirling his horse away to prepare for the next assault.

Too late, he saw that the second man had dismounted and was already hanging onto the reins, plunging a knife deep into his horse's neck. Blood spurted everywhere, and as the horse screamed and staggered, Renaud threw himself clear, quickly rolling away as the animal collapsed to the ground. He leapt to his feet, his sword miraculously still in his hand, and turned to face the attack once more. He was breathless and bruised, but his blood was up and his eyes sparked with excitement. This is what he had been trained for all his life.

The second man, not quick enough to avoid being knocked over by the horse he'd killed, had only now got to his feet, dazed and bloody, and with one arm apparently hanging useless by his side. For the moment, at least, the man was out of the fight, while Dunmail, shocked by this swift and unexpected defeat of his men, had only just drawn his own sword to enter the fray.

Renaud, unhorsed and without mail, a situation that left him feeling more than vulnerable, used the delay to grab the second horse.

Dunmail, realizing at last that he was dealing with a warrior, not a peasant, withdrew himself a little way and called out, 'You have me at a disadvantage, fellow. Meet me on foot, these ponies are not trained for battle.'

'This is no tourney,' Renaud shouted, 'why should I concede any advantage?'

'For honour's sake.'

Renaud laughed contemptuously, but Dunmail had struck a nerve. 'Unmounted, then,' he agreed reluctantly, cursing himself for his own stupidity even as he spoke. Dunmail was taller, heavier and hadn't just taken a nasty, bruising fall.

He let go of the reins as Dunmail cautiously dismounted and walked forward. The two men faced each other in the bright moonlight, circling warily, each taking the measure of the other, their hands clasped over their sword hilts, testing the weight, perfecting their grip.

Dunmail struck first, lunging forward with a mighty down-wards swing of the sword. Renaud countered it swiftly, the jarring as their blades met sending bolts of pain up both arms. They both retreated a little, still assessing one another.

Renaud struck then, but with little more success. Dunmail was good, his reflexes fast. This showed signs of being a long fight, a steady wearing down of each other's defences. Suddenly, Dunmail bared his teeth in a disconcertingly confident grin, but just at that moment Renaud caught a movement at the corner of his eye and turned his head just slightly towards it. The injured man had recovered enough to try to join in the fight, and with his knife in his good hand he was attempting to sneak up unobserved in order to stab Renaud in the back.

Without hesitation, Renaud spun on the spot, his sword outstretched, almost cutting the man in half. Disappointed, but quick to seize his opportunity, Dunmail darted forward with his sword aimed at Renaud's head. Renaud ducked just in time, but the edge of the blade had laid open his cheek and blood poured down his face and neck. Dunmail, having missed his target, was momentarily off balance and Renaud struck with all his might at his enemy's sword arm, severing the hand.

Dunmail stood staring with astonished disbelief at the gushing stump of his arm, but not for long. With a final gasping effort, Renaud plunged his sword into the man's heart, his own rejoicing in this final revenge for Aelfrun's sufferings.

Out of long habit he carefully cleaned the blood from his sword with a handful of grass, and then looked around for the horse. It had disappeared, taking itself off into the night, but at the side of the road two of the hill ponies were cropping placidly at the grass. With a resigned sigh, Renaud caught the reins of one of them and swung himself onto its bare back. He didn't feel very dignified, but he had to admit that this was the better mount to see him safe across the hills.

Well pleased with himself, Renaud headed south.

XVII

February 1070

Just twelve days left, Ceolwynn thought to herself with growing misery. Just twelve days to choose whether or not she would abandon everything in her life that she held most dear – her son, Cottesham, even Renaud. If only he would come home, she sometimes thought, but in her heart she knew that his return would solve nothing. He had protected her once, but if Folca's accusations ever came to his ears it would be a different matter. He would never forgive her if he believed, however unjustly, that she had given herself to Cenred.

Reluctantly she began to accept that her situation was quite hopeless. Her future, like it or not, lay with Cenred in Denmark, and this is what she told Brand, two days later, when he came to get her answer.

The decision made, she started to spend as much time as possible with Edmund. They were playing together with the soldier puppets Aldhere had made, when a strange man in rich and handsome livery rode into the village, setting all astir with the news that William fitzOsbern, the king's most trusted friend and adviser, was about to descend upon them.

Ceolwynn was appalled. In just ten days she would be in the company of wanted outlaws, deeply involved in a plot to steal King William's treasure, and here was the king's own Seneschal about to pay them a visit!

Hastily she prepared herself to greet him, trying hard to remember everything that Renaud had told her about the man. Renaud had always spoken of his lord with great admiration and respect, even affection, but the man himself still surprised her. Of middle years, tall and well built, with a bluff, genial manner that didn't quite conceal the astuteness in his eyes, he was certainly not as Ceolwynn had envisaged. She had expected him to show her the same barely concealed disdain that she had come to expect from most Normans, but in fact he proved to be both charming and courteous, disarming her with his obviously genuine pleasure at meeting her at last.

'Why,' he said at once, 'Renaud is indeed a fortunate man to have for his wife one so fair to look upon; and is this your son?' he asked, beaming down at Edmund who was staring at him with unabashed curiosity. 'A fine, sturdy boy,' he said agreeably, 'and much like his father.' Unexpectedly, he summoned forward one of his men and, with a dramatic flourish, produced a large, wriggling mastiff puppy from a sack the man carried. Edmund's eyes opened very wide as fitzOsbern told him that the dog was for him.

'You are indeed most kind,' Ceolwynn said, a little uncertainly as fitzOsbern, laughing at Edmund's obvious delight, turned back to her. 'Will you come in and take some food and wine, my lord?' she asked.

'Thank you, no,' he replied. 'I'm on my way back to York, but as I was passing close by I thought I'd stop to give you word of your husband. He wrote to me from Northumbria, and asked me to give you this if I could.' He handed her a small, rather crumpled roll of parchment, not noticing at all the happiness, and then the despair in her eyes. She took the letter and held it tight, not wanting to read it until she was alone. 'He's in good health, it appears, although as usual he seems to be up to some mischief of his own; which means, I suppose,' he added with a rather dramatic sigh, 'that it will be up to me to soothe some ruffled royal feathers.'

'I am most grateful, my lord,' Ceolwynn told him weakly, stuffing the letter in the scrip at her girdle.

'I've wanted to meet you for a long time,' he remarked suddenly. 'I've always wondered why it was that a man with such rich rewards in his grasp should throw it all away for an estate as insignificant as this Cottesham.' Ceolwynn bristled visibly. 'Forgive me,' he said hastily, laughing a little. 'I didn't mean to insult you. I was about to say that he chose well after all. His wife is undoubtedly worth an earldom.'

Ceolwynn blushed furiously, both with embarrassment and at

the compliment. 'Could he really have had an earldom?' she found herself asking curiously.

'Perhaps not an earldom,' fitzOsbern admitted, 'but if he hadn't annoyed the king by demanding Cottesham and almost coming to blows with Hugo de Caen over the matter, he certainly would have been given far richer estates.'

This was news to Ceolwynn, and she began to see Renaud's desire to possess Cottesham in a new light. In this, as in many other things, she realized that she'd misjudged him.

'In more settled times I hope to see you at court, Lady Ceolwynn,' fitzOsbern said, kissing her cheek with the friendly familiarity of a fond uncle. 'The king never stays angry with Renaud for long. He'll doubtless expect to see him at his Easter court in Winchester, and your presence there will be sure to put our Norman ladies on their mettle.'

Ceolwynn smiled wanly. 'You are too kind, my lord,' she returned politely, wondering where next Easter would find her.

He stood for a moment pulling on his gloves and casting a professional soldier's eye over the lay of the land and such meagre fortifications as the village boasted. 'You're in a poor position here for your own defence,' he commented absently, more to himself than her, 'but there's plenty that could be done to improve matters, if at no little cost.'

Ceolwynn, mentally shrugging, made no reply.

As soon as he'd gone she rushed to her bedroom, shooing out Hild, who was busy shaking the mattress, and closing the door firmly behind her. Then, pulling out the letter and unrolling it with fingers that trembled slightly, she began to read.

My dearest wife,
I greet you well and send you God's blessing and mine. My most dear wish is that I could be with you now to make all well between us, for nothing is so like to distress me than to know that I have caused you pain. Forgive me if you can for aught I have ever done to deserve your hatred and despite, and know that no other has such a claim on my heart as you. May Jesus in his great mercy watch over and protect you.
Your loving husband,
Renaud.

302

With tears running down her face, Ceolwynn read this letter over and over again. If only, she thought, he had written something cruel and unkind to make leaving him easier, and how like Renaud it was to make her feel even more confused, guilty and miserable than ever, when all he'd obviously wanted to do was to make amends.

Renaud arrived in Hexham very much the worse for wear, starving hungry after four days without food, and covered with dried blood. He smelt, as Hugo was later to remark, like a slaughterhouse in summer, and an ugly black scab had formed itself unattractively over the wound on his cheek.

William's army had been halted here in Hexham for some days, preparing to turn back south towards York. The king, however, had no intention of bringing his harrying of the north to an end just yet. The whole of Cheshire was now to be laid waste, its people dying while their lords fled to safety abroad.

The camp was large, but it didn't take Renaud long to find Hugo, who raised his eyebrows in amusement at the sight of his friend mounted on the scruffy little mountain pony. 'God's bones!' he exclaimed, 'you never were a pretty fellow, Renaud, but you'll certainly scare the maids away now.'

Renaud tried to laugh, but it hurt his face too much.

Hugo, who was more concerned for his friend than he cared to show, hurried to help him from his pony and led him into his tent, where Martin was sitting at a board game he'd been playing with Hugo before Renaud had arrived.

'Run and get the surgeon, Martin,' Hugo ordered, 'and your lady mother.' Martin dashed off at once.

'Aelfrun is here then,' Renaud said, sighing with relief. He lowered himself carefully onto Hugo's cot.

'She is,' Hugo replied, 'and,' he continued, a shade reproachfully, 'she has told me who the boy is, Renaud.'

Renaud shook his head wearily. 'I swear that three years ago, Hugo, I honestly didn't know that Godmund Edgarson had a son. I wouldn't have lied to you.'

'All the same, didn't you think it was taking a bit of a risk to send his family to me, of all people, for protection?'

Renaud smiled, then winced. 'I had no choice,' he said, 'but really I had no fear for them in your hands. You're not quite so bad, Hugo, as I think you would like me to believe.'

Once he had rested and eaten, Renaud, still lying on the cot, asked Aelfrun to stay and talk with him for a while. Hugo, with unusual tact, made himself scarce, taking Martin with him, and Aelfrun sat down on a low stool, her hands busy with a salve she was mixing in a small bowl.

He watched her fondly for a few moments, but if his gaze made her uncomfortable, she didn't show it. She was looking very much better now than she had a few days ago, he observed with pleasure. He could see the scars on her wrists where the chains had chafed her, but in a new, clean gown she had lost the pathetic, bedraggled look of her enslavement. 'You found Sigurd then?' he asked her, knowing it to be a foolish question but at a loss to know how to begin.

She carried on stirring the contents of the bowl in her hands, ignoring the question. After a few moments, though, she turned her head to look at him, her eyes full of warmth and affection. 'I have no words to thank you for all you've done for me, Renaud de Lassay,' she said. 'For an enemy, you have been a very, very good friend.'

He saw she was close to tears and reached out his hand to her. Putting down her bowl she placed both her hands around his and then, to his great embarrassment, raised it to her lips in gratitude. 'I could do no less,' he said, withdrawing his hand gently and striving to lighten the moment, 'you and I are kin now, of a sort.'

'So I hear,' she said, recovering herself and smiling. She tipped her head thoughtfully to one side. 'I always thought you and Ceolwynn the perfect match. Are you content together?'

'It has not always been easy,' he admitted, 'but I do love her, and our son is, of course, quite perfect.'

She laughed, something she hadn't done for a very long time, and he rejoiced to see her so happy after all she'd endured. 'And your own son,' he said, 'he is a fine young man also.'

'Yes, he is,' she agreed, sighing, 'and to find him alive is wonderful beyond all things, but he's not really Siggi any more. We are strangers to one another. He prefers Lord Hugo's company to mine.'

Renaud was at a loss, knowing there was little he could say to comfort a mother who still mourned for the child she had nursed at her breast. 'He may be called Martin now,' he ventured, hoping to say the right thing, 'but he will always be Godmund's son, and his father would have been proud of him.'

'Yes, you're right,' she said with a brave smile, 'he would.'

'And remember,' Renaud added, 'he has lived half his life in a world of men, and of course a boy of his age doesn't want to be seen always at his mother's skirts. Hugo is pleasant and entertaining company for a child, but that doesn't mean that the boy isn't happy to know that you're his mother.'

'You comfort me,' she said, 'and since I have so much to be grateful for, it is very wrong of me to complain that all is not exactly as I would wish it.' She stood up, suddenly brisk and businesslike. 'Lord Hugo said you complained of a headache. Where is the pain?'

He pointed to the side of his head and with a large goose feather she began to apply the sticky, rather slimy salve to the opposite temple. 'What, in the name of Heaven, is that?' he protested, trying to pull his head away.

'Green rue and mustard seed in egg white,' she replied, smiling a little. 'The best remedy I know for the headache.'

'I think I would rather suffer,' he grumbled, but submitted anyway as she plastered away in silence. 'Dunmail is dead,' he said suddenly, which was what he had been preparing himself to say all along.

Her hand faltered only briefly. 'Good,' she said, with unexpected and uncharacteristic venom, but she asked no questions.

The next day, Renaud was ready to escort Aelfrun, Dunn and Martin back home to Cottesham. Thomas and Little Hugh were to go with them, for protection against the bands of starving, homeless peasants turned outlaw, now roaming the north.

Hearing that William fitzOsbern was in York, Renaud decided that it might not be a bad idea to show his face and find out just how unpopular he was with the king, who, by great good fortune, had not yet arrived in Hexham with the other half of his army. Renaud was anxious to be gone before he did.

It was not a happy journey. They passed through a wilderness of slaughter and destruction, sights which shocked even Renaud, who had known only too well what to expect. Every town and village, every barn, sheep fold, coop and mill, had been burned to the ground. The bloated, stinking carcasses of slaughtered livestock and massacred peasants, men, women and children, all lay rotting where they had fallen.

'God in Heaven,' Dunn muttered bitterly the first time they came upon such a sight, 'was there no one left to bury them?'

'The ground is frozen,' Renaud replied, knowing that every tool that might have been used to dig the graves would have been broken and burned beyond repair.

Aelfrun and Dunn, horrified by all that they saw, said little after this, even to each other. They forced themselves to look away from the eyeless corpses and the ugly, glutted crows, but Martin, riding with Renaud, became especially quiet and subdued, praying often under his breath and hardly touching his food when they stopped to eat – not that any of them had much appetite by then.

At last they reached York, and this nightmare part of the journey was finally over. While the others rested, Renaud sought out fitzOsbern, who was here to restore some order and government to a town almost destroyed by a devastating fire the previous year.

Charged with the task, among many others, of rebuilding the castle, William fitzOsbern was a very busy man, never in one place for two minutes together. Renaud finally tracked him down to the proposed site of the new castle, and found him surrounded by a bevy of clerks, carpenters and other tradesmen, all talking at once.

'Renaud,' he called out with pleasure, seeing the young man approach. He pushed past the crowd, which fell back respectfully out of his way. 'I wondered when you'd decide to put in an appearance,' he said. 'What happened to your face?'

'The Scots didn't like me,' Renaud replied cheerfully, and with some relief. He could see that fitzOsbern was in a good temper and obviously not about to berate him for his shortcomings. Which could only mean that he'd managed to placate the king as well.

'So you were successful, then, in what you set out to do?' fitzOsbern asked, suddenly serious. 'You found the woman?'

'Yes, I did. She is safe,' he said, and then recounted briefly the events of the past week.

'Well, I'm glad of it,' fitzOsbern commented when he'd finished. 'Your wife will be most happy, I thought she seemed concerned for you when I took her your letter.'

'You've seen her?' Renaud asked with surprise, but rather gratified that his lord should have taken the trouble to deliver the letter in person.

'Yes. A charming young woman. She seems very fond of you.'

'Really?' said Renaud unguardedly, taken aback by the thought of Ceolwynn actually showing herself to care for him.

FitzOsbern laughed at his expression. 'Actually, I'm very glad to see you Renaud. I've been thinking about your manor, Cottesham, and I've had a word with the king about the place.'

'Oh?' Renaud said, a little dubiously.

'Have no fear, all I have in mind is that you should think about building a castle there. Where the village is now, of course, is hardly suitable, but the general position of the place, between London and the coast, could prove useful.'

'I'd agree with you, my lord,' Renaud said, quickly recovering from his initial surprise, 'but Cottesham could not support the cost of building a castle. It's prosperous enough, but not that prosperous.'

'Oh, I know that,' fitzOsbern replied impatiently. 'The king has promised to hand over to you all of Godmund Edgarson's confiscated lands, and I intend to give you five pounds so that you can start the work without having to wait for your next rents to come in.'

Renaud was staggered. William fitzOsbern was a man noted for the generosity of his gifts to his followers, but this was generous indeed, and hardly deserved. Five pounds would pay for nearly two years' work! Before he could collect himself enough to speak his thanks, fitzOsbern was off again.

'So that's settled then,' he said, obviously anxious now to get back to work. 'What are you planning to do next?'

'With your leave, my lord, I would like to escort my wife's mother back to her home.'

'You have my leave,' the earl replied, 'and now Godspeed, I must return to my labours.'

Renaud wasted no more time and soon had his party back on the road home, with every intention of going straight there without further delay. He had no idea what made him change his mind, but when they reached the fork in the road which, taken in one direction would lead them to Lullingworth and thence to

Cottesham, instead of going that way he found himself taking the other road, leading them all towards Guildford.

Was it his concern for Geoffrey, he wondered, which had changed his mind, or was it knowing that Emma, too, was in Guildford? He'd been so sure he was over his infatuation for her, but still he felt a strange excitement at the thought of seeing her again. At least, he thought ruefully, being in love with Emma had not meant fighting one battle after another.

'Why are we heading for Guildford?' Dunn asked curiously, voicing the question for all of them.

'I have a little business there,' Renaud replied guiltily. 'It won't take long, and you can take the opportunity to rest and buy some new clothes. It's going to be enough of a shock for Ceolwynn without her seeing us all like this.'

This was quite a good spur-of-the-moment argument and fore-stalled any further questions. Dunn then suggested that they seek shelter at the house of a wool merchant called Wulfric, with whom he'd had dealings in his days as Godmund's steward.

Wulfric was glad to welcome them, and leaving his companions to the kindly ministrations of Eadhild, the merchant's wife, Renaud wasted no time in making his way to de Virar's house, hoping that Roger wouldn't find anything too strange in his visit. After all, he persuaded himself, as a long-time friend of both Hugo and Emma he might be expected to have some small inter-est in Geoffrey's welfare. As it happened, he needn't have worried; Roger was not at home. Renaud was a lot more relieved by this than he would have been had he known what it was that had taken Roger to Lullingworth, and what he was discussing there with the captain of the guard.

Emma was glad to see him, always ready to believe that he found it impossible to stay away from her, but she was a little disappointed by the coolness of his greeting kiss.

Beautiful as ever, her presence stirred him as it always did, and he withdrew as quickly as he could from her embrace. 'I just came to ask after Geoffrey,' he said hastily. 'Does the child live?' he asked with growing hope, watching her face and seeing no sign of grief in it. 'I have prayed for him.'

'Then the prayers of us all have been answered,' she replied frostily, annoyed by her obvious failure to recapture his interest. 'My son has made a good recovery.'

'Can I see him, Emma?' he asked. 'I've waited three years.'

She hesitated. 'He's still very weak and frail,' she hedged. 'It might not be wise to excite him with visitors just yet.'

Just at that moment, the sound of loud, childish shouts and laughter rang out from some nearby room. Renaud stiffened angrily and looked at her as if demanding that she explain how a child as sickly as she claimed could sound so very lively.

'I'm sorry,' she said, refusing to meet his eye, 'but I think you should go now. My husband may return soon and since I think he has little love for you, I would not have him angered by your presence here.'

Aware that there was nothing he could do to force her to let him see his son, Renaud turned to go.

'I'm taking Geoffrey back to Normandy in a few days,' she said suddenly. 'Perhaps you would like to come and see us both there, when you tire of that silly child you married.'

Renaud turned back with a look of shocked astonishment. 'Are you saying that to see Geoffrey I must leave my wife?' he asked.

Emma, who hadn't quite meant it to sound that way, had the grace to look a little ashamed. 'Of course not,' she said, flushing with embarrassment. Recovering herself, she moved closer until he could smell the jasmine and musk that perfumed her clothes. 'I just want you to know,' she said, smiling seductively, 'that, for me, nothing has changed.'

'Unfortunately,' Renaud answered her coldly, 'for me, everything has changed.' Then he turned on his heel and left her.

Ralf, happening to be in the courtyard where Renaud waited impatiently for someone to bring his horse, wondered idly what his master's friend was doing there. He wasn't really all that interested, but he had his eye on Alys, Emma's maid, and was looking for an excuse to engage her in conversation. 'What's Renaud de Lassay doing here?' he asked her, arm outstretched to help her with a heavy basket of freshly washed linen.

She handed him the basket, but she knew well enough the price Ralf tended to ask for his favours, and he'd be getting none of that from her, not if he was to carry a hundred baskets. 'Why shouldn't he call?' she replied tartly. 'He's an old friend, and his home lies almost no distance from here.'

'Oh!' he said, pricking up his ears. 'Where exactly?' He'd suddenly lost all interest in pursuing Alys. If Lord Renaud lived close by, then that meant that Hild, the one woman he knew he really loved, was close enough for him to find again. The thought set his heart pounding.

'Some place called Cottesham, I think,' she said, having heard Emma mention it. 'A few miles from Lullingworth.'

To his utter horror, Ralf realized just what harm he'd done in bringing the Saxon, Folca, to talk with Roger de Virar. After he'd left the two of them together, he'd been quite happy to put the whole matter out of his head, believing it to be none of his business: but now it was very much his business. Anything that endangered Cottesham endangered Hild.

He threw down the basket and raced across the courtyard, leaving Alys, hands on hips, staring with fury at the pile of muddied linen. 'Well!' she exclaimed indignantly.

Renaud had just mounted and was about to spur away when he suddenly found the squire hanging onto his stirrup.

'Hello, Ralf,' he said, recognizing the man. 'What are you doing here?'

'I must speak with you,' Ralf panted, breathless from his sprint. 'It's very, very important.'

The day had finally come and Ceolwynn knew that there could be no turning back. Brand had arrived and was waiting for her in the hall while she went to fetch the carefully hidden bag containing the few personal things she'd be likely to need, including a lock of Edmund's hair, the carved bear that Renaud had given her, and the letter that fitzOsbern had brought.

She took one last, sad look around her room before bracing herself to say goodbye to Edmund. She'd sent Hild on an errand just to keep her out of the way until she'd gone, but it hurt her bitterly to leave without a word.

'We have to go, my lady,' Brand warned her quietly as she tried to tear herself away from Edmund. Still hardly more than a boy himself, Brand had grown tall for his thirteen years, and carried himself like a man. He came and went almost without comment in Cottesham, but living as an outlaw had made him cautious and wary.

'I'm ready,' she said, and followed him outside, hiding her bag beneath her cloak, hiding her pain and sorrow behind a grim resolve.

An hour's ride saw them into that part of Andredsweald where Cenred's outlaw band had made camp. There must be close on half a hundred men here, she thought with surprise, but it was obvious, even to her, that few of them were trained soldiers.

Cenred was more relieved to see her than he cared to admit, half convinced that at the last minute she'd change her mind. For three years his main aim in life had been to win Ceolwynn back from Renaud, and finally he had succeeded. 'At last,' he said warmly, smiling and helping her from the saddle.

She accepted his kiss, but quickly pulled herself away. 'What happens now?' she asked. 'Am I to wait for you here?'

'No indeed,' he answered her. 'You, Ceolwynn, are very much a part of my plan. William's men will be riding fast and stopping for no man while they have his silver in their care; but they might slow just a little for a damsel in distress, and that's all my men will need to come upon them unawares.'

Ceolwynn, who saw at once that this plan could leave her in the thick of an armed battle, didn't think very much of it at all. 'Is there no other way?' she asked doubtfully. 'I'm not sure I care to be your bait.'

'Don't worry,' he said, impatiently brushing aside her objections, 'I'll make sure you come to no harm. All you have to do is stand in the road with a dead horse, looking beautiful and helpless, and no man could resist stopping to help, not if he had all the silver in the world in his train.'

Ceolwynn wasn't so sure, but she let herself be persuaded since she really didn't seem to have much choice. Cenred had produced a very elaborate gown for her to wear instead of her drab work-a-day clothes, which, she had to agree, were hardly likely to set any man's pulses racing, and in almost no time at all she found herself standing on a forest road holding the reins of a doomed horse and dressed, as she told herself with a nervous laugh, like a court whore.

In the undergrowth and in the trees, Cenred and his men waited patiently. Ambush was much easier these days, Cenred had told her on the way. Since the Normans came no one troubled themselves any more about the old laws that had kept the highways safe. Now, no one kept the sides of the road clear, and in just three years there was almost enough undergrowth to hide an army.

A large man with a heavy club stood next to Ceolwynn, and at

311

Cenred's signal he hit the horse between the ears and vanished into the trees. The horse collapsed, and Ceolwynn, shocked, even though she was expecting it, presented just the right picture of distress and dismay. No one, Cenred thought with satisfaction, watching from no more than ten feet away, could possibly resist helping her.

The Normans came into view, at least twenty well armed and armoured men with twelve packhorses led by mounted grooms. The captain, raising his arm at the sight of Ceolwynn standing there, slowed his men to a halt. Cenred, seeing his plan work even better than he'd expected or hoped, gave his signal and with a wild cry led his men out of the undergrowth with their weapons already in their hands.

They swooped on the Normans, outnumbering the soldiers more than two to one and confident of a swift victory. Suddenly the grooms dropped their lead reins and threw aside their cloaks. One glance at their swords and mail and Cenred knew that he was caught in his own trap. It came as no surprise to hear the sound of rapid hoofbeats approaching as the Norman reinforcements arrived. All that was left for them to do was to try to fight their way clear and run for it. Caught up in the fighting he had no time to do more than pray that Ceolwynn would see that all was lost and make her escape into the forest.

Ceolwynn, however, had no clear idea at all as to what was going on. Before she could grasp that for Cenred this fight was over, the second troop of Normans had arrived, and several of them headed straight for her, surrounding her. She whirled round with alarm, looking for a place to run, but it was too late. Defiantly, she looked up into the faces of her captors, paling as she saw the ugly but familiar face of Roger de Virar leering down at her; but then, to her absolute horror, she saw Folca behind him and knew that nothing short of a miracle could save her now.

After hearing what Ralf had to tell him, Renaud headed straight for Cottesham without even going back to Wulfric's house to tell the others. His first and only thought was to get home before Ceolwynn did something so stupid and reckless that it would cost her her life. Fear for her drove him, a blind panic that wouldn't even allow him to blame her or feel any anger at what she planned to do. There would be time enough for anger if only she was safe.

He rode into Cottesham like a whirlwind, throwing himself out of the saddle and rushing into the hall calling her name at the top of his voice.

Hild stared at him with startled surprise. 'My lady went riding, my lord,' she said.

'When?'

'About noon, I think. I can't be exactly sure because I wasn't here.'

'That's over three hours ago,' he said with a sinking heart. 'She never rides out for so long.' Hild frowned, suddenly worried. 'I'm going to look for her,' Renaud said, and rushed out again, hardly knowing what to do next.

Hurriedly going over in his head all that Ralf had told him, he decided to follow the London road from Lullingworth through the forest. Ralf hadn't been sure when the ambush was due to take place, but Ceolwynn's disappearance made it likely that he was already too late to prevent her involvement. Dreading what he would find, he drove his horse relentlessly onwards.

It was already growing late when Renaud reached the place where Roger had sprung his own trap, but even in the dusk it was clear that a fight had recently taken place here. The trampled undergrowth and churned mud were all the evidence he needed.

With desperation in his eyes he rode back and forth, round and round, trying to make sense of the tracks. Most of them, he saw, led back the way they'd come, towards Lullingworth. As well as hoofprints he could just make out the tracks of boots and shoes, a sign that some at least of the foiled attackers had been taken alive.

Knowing how little mercy was likely to be shown to Roger's captives, Renaud didn't know whether or not to pray that Ceolwynn was one of them.

'The place is a nest of traitors,' Roger said, plying the captain with more drink, 'trust my word for it. If the lady of the manor is a traitor, can her people be anything else?'

'What you say makes sense,' the captain agreed hesitantly, 'but her husband is one of us, you say?' He drank deeply. 'I'm confused.'

'Oh, I don't claim that he is involved,' Roger said, 'far from it. The man is something of a favourite with the king. What I'm trying to say is that he would probably be grateful if we cleaned out the whole nest for him and saved him the trouble and embarrassment of doing it for himself.'

'Cleaned out the whole nest?' the captain repeated hazily, waving his mug in a wide, expansive circle.

'That's right; and remember, you will share the credit for capturing Cenred of Bosham.'

The captain nodded, quite liking this idea. 'Tomorrow?' he said.

'Tomorrow,' Roger confirmed with a triumphant smile. Renaud had not just lost his wife, he was about to lose his whole village as well, with any blame falling squarely on the head of an overzealous captain and a handful of overexcited mercenaries. He almost laughed aloud at his own cleverness.

Leaving the captain to his ale, Roger took himself off to gloat over his fair captive. Cenred and the other prisoners had already been sent under armed guard to Guildford for interrogation, trial and, of course, execution, but Roger had quite different plans in mind for Ceolwynn.

Folca was waiting for him outside her cell, almost frantic with excitement and anticipation. Roger de Virar had agreed to the one thing he'd requested as a reward for his information – and now he could hardly wait to lay claim to his prize.

Roger hunted for the right key on the large iron ring, deliberately taking his time just to annoy the man. Eventually he found it and went inside, with Folca almost treading on his heels in his eagerness.

Ceolwynn, alerted by the jangling of the keys, was already on her feet and facing them with a frightened, hunted look. Folca's presence terrified her even more, but suddenly remembering what was to be expected of her father's daughter, she drew herself up and tried to look far braver than she felt.

Roger slowly circled around her, unnerving her with his silence and his cold, assessing eyes. It didn't take her long to guess what these two intended, but she was wrong about Roger, who wasn't much attracted by her at all. He preferred boys; young boys, frightened boys, boys like Richard who never lived to tell the world of the hideous things he did to them. Even so, the thought of watching the repugnant Folca defile the loveliness of this creature amused and excited him. Only one thing spoilt his pleasure: Renaud was not here to see it.

Folca could contain himself no longer. 'Now?' he said, grabbing hold of Roger's arm.

Roger threw him off with distaste. 'Perhaps not quite yet,' he said thoughtfully.

Folca groaned, his groin throbbing with suppressed desire. 'Why not now?' he hissed.

'I have my reasons,' Roger replied, finally deciding that there could be no pleasure in this unless Renaud de Lassay was here to watch her scream and struggle, helpless to act while Folca forced himself into that slim, white body. Only then could he be sure that Renaud truly suffered. 'I wonder,' he said, one elegant finger scratching the side of his menacing hawk's-beak nose, 'does your husband love you enough to risk his life for you?'

'Yes, he does,' she shouted at him, full of defiance, 'he'll kill you when he hears of this,' she said less certainly, knowing in her heart that her own actions had made it impossible for Renaud to do anything to help her. Roger was acting within the law to imprison her, and rape was a common enough fate for women in gaol.

Roger stared at her contemplatively. 'Then perhaps we should wait for him to return and give him that opportunity,' he said at last. He walked briskly towards the door, pushing the reluctant, infuriated Folca in front of him and leaving her alone with her anguished thoughts.

Aelfrun looked out of the window for what Dunn guessed must be the hundredth time. 'He'll probably be back soon,' he said. 'He didn't actually say he would be staying here last night.'

'I know,' she sighed, 'but I'm worried all the same. I just have this strange feeling that something is wrong.'

'What can possibly be wrong?' he said. He got up and stood behind her, letting his hands rest on her shoulders. She half turned her head and smiled at him. 'Stop worrying,' he said, kissing her ear, 'I command it.'

She opened her eyes wide at that and laughed. He let his arms slip around her waist. 'Did you really kill one of Dunmail's men?' he asked unexpectedly. He felt her stiffen and try to draw away from him, but he just held her tighter. 'I want you to tell me everything, Aelfrun,' he said gently. 'Won't you trust me enough to tell me?'

315

'You will hate me,' she said.

'Of course I won't. How could I ever hate you?'

'You say that, but do you know how many men have used me in these last few years?' she asked bitterly. 'Do you really want to know that?'

'It hurts me to think that you would believe I would value you any the less for that,' he said, wounded.

Aelfrun turned and wrapped her arms around him, her cheek resting on his chest, wondering at the steadfastness of his love for her. Falteringly then, she told him how she'd used his knife, and how Dunmail, at first furious, had suddenly laughed, admiring her spirit and sparing her life. Her punishment, though, had been the chains she had worn almost constantly for the three years of her captivity, and Dunn was not the first man whose bed she had been forced to share.

She was crying softly by the time she'd finished, and Dunn stroked her hair and held her, comforting her with whispered words of love and tenderness. Eventually her tears dried, but they stayed locked contentedly in each other's arms until the sound of Martin returning from Mass made them jump apart, both blushing like maids.

'Isn't Lord Renaud back yet?' the boy asked, looking around with disappointment. 'He told me we'd be going home today.'

'And so we shall, I expect,' Aelfrun said. 'Let's take a walk through the streets and look at all the shops and stalls. Perhaps we'll see him riding through the town.'

'All right,' he agreed, bored with being cooped up indoors.

Dunn decided he'd stay behind in case Renaud came back while they were gone, so Aelfrun and Martin set off on their own up the steep hill to the market square. It was a new experience for Martin, all the crowds and bustle, and he didn't much care for all the noise and the awful smells from the tanneries and open sewers. Aelfrun had almost forgotten what it was like to walk through a town like this, and her overwhelming joy at the freedom to do so far outweighed any minor unpleasantness.

So engrossed was she in examining all the wonderful goods on display, that she didn't even notice the dark young woman staring at her across the square.

Nest could hardly believe her eyes. She'd just stepped out to buy some goat's milk for Rhianwen, who was only just recovering from the sudden fever which had completely upset all Nest's plans to find Aelfrun, when whom should she see but the lady Aelfrun herself. She hadn't been quite sure at first, but a second look confirmed that she'd made no mistake. The lady was thinner, and very pale, but it was definitely she.

She hurried across the street, leaving a trail of spilt milk in her wake. 'Lady Aelfrun,' she called out urgently, and Aelfrun looked up in surprise. 'Lady Aelfrun,' Nest repeated, coming up to her, 'don't you remember me?'

Aelfrun frowned in puzzlement, then suddenly her brow cleared. 'Nest!' she exclaimed. 'The little Welsh girl.'

Nest nodded. 'That's right,' she said, wondering how best to go about breaking her news. 'Do I remember aright,' she asked, 'aren't you the mistress of a place called Cottesham?'

'Why, yes,' Aelfrun began, then stopped. 'Actually, no,' she corrected herself. 'I used to be, but not any longer.'

Nest's face fell.

'Why?' Aelfrun asked curiously. 'Was it important?'

Nest hardly knew what to say. All her hopes seemed to have been dashed in one go, although she did, of course, have one other chance to persuade Aelfrun to help her. 'Will you come with me, my lady? It isn't far, I promise you, and there is someone there you might want to meet.'

Aelfrun glanced doubtfully in the direction of Wulfric's house, wondering if Renaud was there waiting for them.

'Please,' Nest pleaded.

Intrigued, Aelfrun gave in and agreed to come, sending Martin back to tell Dunn that she wouldn't be long. She followed Nest through a few back alleys to a squalid little house so close to the tanneries that one of the many stinking heaps of waste fat from that trade was almost on the doorstep.

They ducked under the low doorway and Nest, with a few hurried words of explanation to Rhianwen's foster-mother, led Aelfrun to her child's bedside.

Rhianwen, now almost well again, was sitting up in bed with her hair freshly washed and combed, the soft curls framing a delicate heart-shaped face from which wide, dark eyes studied Aelfrun with bright, intelligent interest.

'This is my daughter, Rhianwen,' Nest said proudly. 'It means "pretty child" in my own tongue.'

'It suits her well,' Aelfrun said kindly, wondering what she was doing here. She was anxious to be gone and started to move back towards the door.

'Wait,' Nest insisted, 'I haven't told you yet. Rhianwen is your own half-sister, your father's child.'

Aelfrun turned back to stare at the child with amazement. She could see no resemblance – the child's handsome looks had all come from Nest – but she didn't doubt for a moment that Nest spoke the truth. It was a shock, but not an unpleasant one for a woman who had lost almost her entire family in the most brutal of circumstances.

Seeing the expression on Aelfrun's face and guessing that her gamble had paid off, Nest quickly explained that they were all but destitute and in desperate need of her help.

'Oh, Nest,' Aelfrun said sadly, 'of course I'd help you if I could, but I have nothing at all to give you. All I can do is ask my daughter's husband if he will extend his charity towards you both. I can promise nothing, but he is a good man and I'm almost sure he will not refuse me if I ask it of him.'

Nest was dreadfully disappointed, but at least Aelfrun was willing to do what she could for them.

'Come with me now,' Aelfrun said suddenly. 'Leave this awful place and come with me now. Renaud will understand if I tell him I need a maid. You can both come with us back to Cottesham.'

'But you said you weren't mistress of Cottesham,' Nest said, confused.

'No more I am,' Aelfrun replied, 'but my daughter Ceolwynn is.'

'Oh, no!' Nest wailed, seeing yet another hope for safe sanctuary disappear, and in no time at all a very alarmed Aelfrun had heard the whole story and was racing back to Wulfric's house with both Nest and Rhianwen at her heels.

Exhausted by a day in the saddle and then his desperate dashes between Guildford, Cottesham and Andredsweald, Renaud had had no choice but to tie his horse to a tree and snatch a few hours' sleep at the roadside. Before dawn he was on the road once more, and as soon as he arrived he began to question the soldiers of the garrison, who answered him freely enough, having nothing to hide.

318

Yes, they told him, they had captured Cenred of Bosham. Yes, there had been a woman among the prisoners. No, the prisoners were no longer here but in Guildford, although the woman had not gone with them. Someone suggested that she might be being held at the small town gaol, and Renaud hurried there to be told that Roger de Virar himself had taken the prisoner into his own custody just that morning. The guard had no idea where he'd taken her, but he had brought a horse for her so it was likely he was taking her out of the town.

Renaud stood outside in the road, frantically asking himself, which way, which way? Towards London, Guildford, where? Suddenly he saw a blind beggarman on the corner of the street and hurried over to drop a few coins in his bowl.

'Thank you, my lord,' the beggarman cried, catching the healthy sound of Renaud's generosity.

'How are your ears, man?' Renaud asked. 'Some say the blind can see with their ears.'

'They're not wrong,' the man agreed. 'I know you put two whole pennies and one half in my bowl.'

'Then can you tell me if you heard a woman being taken from this place this morning?'

'Yes, I did, my lord. The woman was struggling and I think a man was kicked, quite hard if his cry told a true story.'

'Then think well, and it will be worth another two pennies to you,' Renaud told him urgently, 'how many were there in the party, when did they leave and which way did they go?'

'That's easy enough. There were two men, the bell had not long sounded for Prime, and they left that way,' he added, pointing down the Guildford road.

'My thanks,' Renaud said gratefully, and quickly handing over the promised payment he threw himself back into the saddle and tore off in pursuit of his wife who was now no more than half an hour away from him.

With her hands tightly tied to the saddle, Ceolwynn shared a horse with Folca, enduring the touch of his hands exploring her body while he whispered in her ear all the things he planned to do with her once Roger let him have his way.

Frantic to get away from him, if only for a few moments, Ceolwynn called out to Roger, begging him to let her relieve herself. Roger thought about it and then agreed, telling Folca to untie her and lead her to the side of the road.

'Won't you make him turn his back,' she protested as Folca waited for her to squat in the grass.

'Why?' he asked indifferently.

'Have you no honour, no decency?' she shouted angrily, hoping to shame him. 'You may hate my husband, but you have no cause to use me so ill. What harm have I ever done to you?'

Roger scowled, but the attack on his honour stung. 'Turn your back then, Folca,' he said impatiently, 'but keep hold of that rope.'

Folca grudgingly did as he was told, and Ceolwynn, who already had her eye on a broken branch in the grass only a few feet away, waited just long enough for Roger to move on down the road before she grabbed it and whacked Folca over the head with all her might. With a loud scream Folca grasped his wounded head, dropping the rope that held her, and before the startled Roger could whirl around she was already more than half way to the trees. White with rage he set off after her, leaning from the saddle and grabbing her by the hair just seconds before she made it into the dark, sheltering woods.

Roger was almost insane with rage. Through letting himself be persuaded to show a little kindness he'd almost lost her, but he'd never make that mistake again. Still holding her by the hair he dismounted and slapped her backhanded across the face. His gloved hand, studded with gems, left long, red weals across her cheek. She cried out with pain and he raised his hand to hit her again, but the blow never landed for suddenly Renaud was there, bearing down upon them on his foam-flecked destrier, his sword in his hand and a look in his eye to strike terror into the stoutest heart. Folca, whose heart was cowardly to the core, ran for his horse and disappeared down the road in a cloud of dust.

'Let her go, de Virar,' Renaud commanded, reining to a halt so abrupt that his horse was thrown back on its haunches.

'You have no right to command me,' Roger snarled, drawing his sword. 'This woman, your wife, is an outlaw and under arrest. There's nothing you can do about it.'

'Except kill you,' Renaud replied with quiet menace.

Roger licked his lips nervously. This was not at all how he had hoped to confront Renaud de Lassay. He was not a coward, but he knew that Renaud was a match for the best of men, let alone one more than twice his years. He tightened his grip on Ceolwynn and backed carefully towards his horse, his sword pressing against her neck. 'Move one step,' he threatened, 'and I'll cut her throat, I swear.'

'And then what?' Renaud called, pointing his sword straight at Roger as if about to charge. He found it hard to speak calmly for the rage and hate he felt for the man who had laid such violent hands upon his wife.

Roger faltered. Had he made a mistake? Did Renaud not even care if his wife died?

He'd made it to the horse and now stood irresolute, hardly knowing what to do next. Ceolwynn, almost faint with pain and fear, felt his uncertainty and began to hope. She tensed, ready to move at the first opportunity, and when Roger let go of her hair to make a grab for the reins, she threw her head back with all the force she could muster, hearing his nose crack and feeling the blood gush down the back of her neck.

Roger squealed like a stuck pig and almost dropped his sword, giving Ceolwynn the chance to duck under his arm and dart out of reach.

Renaud, recovering swiftly from his surprise, lunged forward and, with vicious satisfaction, sliced the man's head from his shoulders.

XVIII

February–March 1070

Hearing what Nest had to say, Dunn knew they had no choice but to confide in Thomas and Hugh, trusting in the faith he knew that Renaud had in them. To his great relief, their reaction was all that he could have hoped for, their concern solely to protect their lord's interests.

Within minutes they had the horses saddled and a couple of Wulfric's apprentices out scouring the town for any sign of Renaud himself. Privately, Thomas suspected that Renaud had already heard something of the matter and was out there trying to do something about it, so the only sensible thing they could do at this stage was to go to Cottesham and hope to nip the whole thing in the bud – at least as far as the lady Ceolwynn was concerned. If they were too late of course, then the matter would be out of their hands.

Aelfrun had now taken Nest and Rhianwen firmly under her wing and insisted that they should come too; and despite her fears for Ceolwynn, she could hardly contain her excitement as they drew closer and closer to Cottesham. It seemed impossible that anything bad could happen now, not after all they'd been through. Ceolwynn would still be there, overjoyed to see them and they would all be happy together once more.

The first intimation they had that all was not to be as they'd hoped, came within a mile or two of Cottesham itself. Staggering along the road, weak from shock and loss of blood, was young Brand, one of the few to escape the trap in the forest. Aelfrun recognized him at once: how could she ever forget the boy who had brought her husband's body home to her?

'Brand!' she cried, leaping from her saddle and rushing to help

him. 'Quick, Dunn,' she said urgently, 'give him some wa
before he faints away.'

Brand drank the water gratefully, and after a few minute
recovered sufficiently to tell her what had happened. Aelfrun and
Dunn stared at each other in horror. They were too late.
Ceolwynn was lost to them for ever.

'Don't give up hope,' Thomas said gruffly, upset to see
Aelfrun's eyes filling with tears. 'We still don't know what Lord
Renaud's doing, do we? He won't let any harm come to her if he
can prevent it.'

'But what if he doesn't know?' Aelfrun sobbed.

Thomas had no answer for this, but he saw no point in them
staying here in the middle of the road. 'Let's go on,' he said. 'We
might find out more when we get to Cottesham.' He helped Brand
up behind him in the saddle and set off down the road, leaving the
others with no reason not to follow.

The second shock came with a change in the direction of the
wind. Suddenly they could smell smoke, and then they saw great
clouds of it rising above the place where Cottesham lay.

Without a word Thomas and Hugh broke into a gallop. Dunn,
shouting over his shoulder for the rest of them to stay back,
wasted no time in following them. Aelfrun waited for a few
minutes in a state of great agitation, but then quickly chased after
them, leaving Nest to look after the children.

It was really all over by the time they got there. Roger, had he
lived to know of it, would have been well pleased by what his
soldiers had accomplished. The entire village was ablaze, the
frantic cries of the villagers mingling with the dreadful screaming
of animals trapped in the flames.

Thomas took one look at what was happening and galloped into
the heart of the village to see if they could save the hall. He
shouted for men to bring water, but the people just ran away in
terror at the sight of yet more mailed knights in their midst, not
recognizing them as Renaud's own men. It was Hild, smoke-
blackened and scorched, who first realized who they were and
rushed at them, screaming for help, tears streaming down her
face. Edmund was still in the hall – she'd brought him out, but
he'd run back in for his puppy and now she couldn't reach him
for the flames.

All of them raced for the great doors, but there was no way in.

323

Dunn and Thomas tried to run through the wall of flame but the heat and smoke drove them back time and again. It was Brand who thought to soak himself with water and pull a wet cloak over his head before plunging into the inferno.

It seemed an eternity before he reappeared, his hair in flames, with the wet cloak wrapped around the bundle in his arms. Already weak, he could hardly make it back to the door, but with a last desperate surge of strength he threw his prize through the doorway into Dunn's outstretched arms, then, as the roof fell in with a deafening roar, he fell, screaming, back into the flames.

For a moment they all stood rooted to the ground, shocked and helpless, until a weak cough reminded them why Brand had sacrificed his life. Dunn hastily unwrapped the wet cloak, and Edmund, pale and frightened, stared around him dazedly, then started to cry, his sobs punctuated by an ugly retching as he vomited the smoke out of his system. Hild, still crying, hugged and kissed him with relief. Only then did she recognize Dunn and Aelfrun, her mouth falling open in astonishment as she stared at them, too stunned for speech.

'Was there anyone else in the hall?' Hugh asked her, not that there was any hope for anyone in there now.

Hild snapped out of her trance. 'I think everyone got out in time,' she replied, but then she remembered one who wouldn't have been able to run for safety. 'Except for Aldhere,' she amended sadly.

Thomas looked around for other casualties. Bodies there were, here and there, but not many; only a few men had tried to fight back. Walter the reeve was among the dead, and Afa was wounded, though not seriously. Thomas scratched his head, wondering what to do now, then turned to Dunn. 'It would be best if you took the lady Aelfrun and young Lord Edmund back to Guildford. Hugh will see you safe there, then he can come back and help me sort out some of this mess. We can't leave it like this for Lord Renaud and his lady to find, can we?' he added with an optimism he was far from feeling.

'He found her then?' Hild asked innocently.

Four heads turned in her direction. 'Who?' Dunn asked.

'Lord Renaud, of course,' she said, puzzled by their obtuseness. 'He was here yesterday, looking for my mistress.'

'There, I told you,' Thomas said with satisfaction. 'I'll wager

he's looking for us in Guildford at this very moment. You shoul.
do as I've already suggested.'

Dunn now agreed that this was probably the best plan, but
added that Hild would have to go with them since she was the
only person whom Edmund knew. Hild was content enough with
this; she had a million questions to ask and a long ride would give
her plenty of opportunity to ask them.

They headed quickly back towards the place where they'd left
Nest with the children. Martin was there, clearly very relieved to
see them, and Rhianwen was asleep on the grass wrapped in his
cloak, but of Nest there was no sign at all.

Martin quickly explained that they'd not been waiting long when
Nest, alarmed by the sound of hoofbeats coming up from behind
them, had made them hide in the trees. A man had passed by and
Nest had suddenly become very excited. Telling Martin to look
after Rhianwen she'd set off to follow the unknown rider down the
road towards Cottesham.

Aelfrun was puzzled. They had seen no one between here and
Cottesham, and there was nowhere else to go, except into the
woods. 'We should try to find her,' she said. 'We can't go back
and leave her behind.'

Hugh looked very unhappy. 'All right,' he said, 'but if we don't
find her before the sun passes the top of that tree, we'll have to
move on.'

Aelfrun glanced at the sky. He was giving them about twenty
minutes. 'She can't have gone far,' she said thoughtfully. 'Let's all
look for tracks leaving the road.'

They rode slowly back towards Cottesham and, sure enough,
within a quarter of a mile they found what they were looking for,
two sets of tracks heading into the woods. They followed them to
a point where both horses had been abandoned, the riders forced
to go on foot.

'The rest of you stay here,' Hugh ordered. 'Dunn and I will go
on alone.'

'No, I'm coming too,' Aelfrun insisted, and Hugh thought it
hardly worth the trouble to argue.

They crept through the trees, following without difficulty the
clear path of trampled undergrowth and broken twigs left by
their quarry. Suddenly, they were on the edge of a wide glade

dominated by the ruin of what had once been a mighty oak, but which now lay with its rotted trunk tilted sharply to one side and its roots ripped savagely from the earth on the other.

Hugh, halting them swiftly and silently with a raised hand, cast his eyes carefully around. Slowly he lowered his hand. 'She's here,' he said heavily, 'and so, by the look of it, is the man she was after.'

He walked boldly out into the glade, and Aelfrun, following, soon saw why he'd abandoned his earlier caution. The man was there, certainly, but he was dead. Spinning slowly back and forth his body dangled from the branches of the fallen oak, the straps of the leather bag he carried twisted tightly around his neck, his feet barely inches from the safety of the ground.

'God alone knows what he was doing up in that tree,' Hugh muttered, 'but it looks as though he came down with it when the tree collapsed.' He paused, thoughtfully weighing up the situation. 'He must have hung the bag around his neck to leave his hands free,' he went on, drawing his knife as he spoke, 'but then, when the strap snagged on that branch as he fell, it was all over for him.' He reached up and cut the man down, turning the body over, none too gently, with his foot.

'Folca!' Aelfrun gasped, half in shock, half in relief. It *was* Folca, she was certain of it. Even the swollen, empurpled face and bulging eyes failed to disguise that man's loathsome features.

Hugh nodded. He, too, had recognized Cottesham's unpleasant steward and thought his death no great loss. He did wonder, however, what it was that had brought the man here, what it was that had led Nest to follow him and, perhaps even more curiously, just what it was that had brought down such a mighty tree on what was, after all, an almost windless day.

Ceolwynn, had she been there, might well have been able to answer that question, for it was in the oak that sheltered her secret place that Folca had chosen to hide his stolen silver. The ancient ruins that had supported an oak for centuries had finally crumbled away, leaving nothing but a gaping hole beneath a tree already teetering on brittle, dry and long-dead roots. Folca's weight had been all it took to bring it finally crashing down.

Much later, when Ceolwynn learned of all that had befallen in this place, she would wonder if it was chance alone which had led to the downfall of the vile and murderous Folca. She would never speak to anyone of these thoughts, not even Renaud, but she would always believe that the ghostly guardians of her childhood dreams had played their part.

Dunn picked up the bag, the straps of which had proved so effective a noose, and opened it curiously. His eyes widened slightly at the quantity of silver inside. 'Did Nest go after him for this?' he asked, hardly believing it.

'Oh yes, I should think so,' Hugh replied, 'but she paid a heavy price for her folly.' He pointed to the far side of the oak where, almost hidden by the tangle of roots, Nest lay huddled in a wide pool of blood.

Aelfrun, stricken to realize that she had forgotten all about Nest in the shock of discovering Folca's body, now rushed to the girl's side. 'She's alive,' she cried as Nest's eyes flickered open.

Hugh said nothing. He'd already seen the gaping sword wound in her belly, and now Aelfrun saw it too. 'Nest,' she cried, kneeling beside her, as close as she could get for the tree roots. 'Nest, can you hear me?'

Nest opened her mouth and blood poured out of it. 'I wanted your father's silver,' she managed to get out, the words bubbling on her tongue. 'He stole it, that Folca, but I knew: oh yes, I always knew.' She tried to laugh, then cried out in agony, clutching at the wound as if trying to push her tortured guts back inside.

'Dunn,' Aelfrun cried out in anguish, 'can't you do something? Please do something, anything.'

'Take her away,' Hugh said quietly to Dunn. 'I'll deal with this now.'

Dunn nodded and took Aelfrun by the arm, half pulling her to her feet. Both of them knew what Hugh intended, but there was nothing else that anyone could do.

There was hardly anything left at all of Godmund's hall, nothing but smouldering ashes and the stink of ruin. Ceolwynn, dry-eyed, stared around her at the devastation, her grief and shock too deep for tears. Everything had gone: homes, byres, storerooms, stables, kitchens; even the church.

Renaud dismounted, spoke a while with Thomas, then followed her at a distance, hardly trusting himself to speak. Relief at her safety had so far kept his anger at bay, but now, faced with such appalling destruction, he found it hard not to speak his mind.

After all, he fumed inwardly, all this was almost entirely of her own making. If she hadn't been so stupid, so reckless, none of this would have happened. He scowled, mentally calculating the cost of rebuilding and restocking.

Suddenly, burying her face in her hands, Ceolwynn gave a small, sobbing cry and Renaud, touched to the heart and unable to help himself, rushed to console her, all thought of reproach and recrimination utterly forgotten.

'Don't weep, Ceolwynn, please don't weep,' he urged gently, laying a comforting arm across her shoulder. 'Praise God that at least Edmund is safe. All of this,' he said, waving his free arm to emcompass the whole village, 'is just timber and thatch. What man has once built, he can build again.'

'What would you know of it?' she sobbed bitterly, shrugging off the comfort he offered. 'It was never your home,' she said, fighting back the tears, 'just one of your possessions, like me.' Moving away from him she picked up a charred stick and began to prod angrily at the ashes. Already the thankfulness she'd felt at being saved from Roger had evaporated in the face of this new horror, again at Norman hands.

'Wherever you are is my home,' he replied, his voice so low she almost didn't hear him. Startled, she turned, wiping away her tears with her sleeve and leaving her cheeks streaked and smeared with ash. She looked just like a grubby child, Renaud thought, almost smiling. 'I love you, Ceolwynn,' he said.

'No,' she half-whispered vehemently, her head shaking in denial. 'I know you lie.' She didn't want him to love her, she didn't deserve his love.

He moved closer. 'If only you could stop hating me so much, perhaps you would find that you love me too.'

'Never!' she protested, refusing to meet his eye. 'Rurik said you would bring disaster,' she blurted suddenly, dredging up a new reason for hating him. 'Blood and fire, remember?'

It was Renaud's turn to turn away and when she looked up he was already at the horses, already mounting. Irrationally disappointed, she hurried to his side, unconsciously laying a restraining hand on his leg. 'Where are you going?' she asked, almost frightened. Would he really leave her? It was a thought too awful to contemplate. She might want to hate him, but she couldn't bear the thought of losing him again. Suddenly, incredibly, losing Cottesham seemed the lesser of two evils.

'*I'm* not going anywhere,' he answered, '*we* are going to Guildford.'

'Guildford?' she echoed. 'Why? Is Edmund there?'

'Don't ask questions, for once in your life just do as I say.'

Too weary to argue further, Ceolwynn placed her foot in the cupped hands Broad Thomas offered and obediently mounted her horse.

Aelfrun was glad to be back in Guildford, back in Wulfric's noisy, bustling and friendly household. When Hugh unexpectedly returned again from Cottesham with the news that both Renaud and Ceolwynn were safe and well, it seemed as though she lacked nothing for perfect happiness. She waited impatiently for their arrival, pacing up and down, too excited to sit for more than a few minutes at a time, and at the sound of horses outside she leapt up and looked excitedly at Dunn. He smiled and got to his feet as well.

From inside the shop Eadhild had already seen the newcomers clatter into the courtyard, and now stuck her head round the door to confirm the news. 'Your friend has returned,' she announced cheerfully. 'He has a young lady with him.' Aelfrun and Dunn exchanged quick, pleased glances. 'I'll fetch them in then,' she said and bobbed out of sight again.

Outside, Renaud was helping Ceolwynn dismount. She accepted his hand, still too puzzled by his strange insistence on this journey to pretend to despise his assistance. He'd hardly said a word to her the whole way, and had certainly made no effort to answer her questions. 'Are you ever going to tell me what are we doing here?' she asked, piqued, apprehensive and curious all at once.

'I want to ask you something first,' he said very seriously.

'What?'

'Do you always keep your word?'

She frowned, even more confused. 'I think so,' she said, a little doubtfully. 'I try to, anyway. Why?'

Renaud smiled. 'Go inside now,' he said, 'the goodwife is waiting to see you in.' She didn't move. 'Go,' he said, giving her a small push. 'I promise you'll not regret obeying me this one time.'

Following Eadhild's broad back Ceolwynn passed through the

shop and into the house. Renaud followed them to the door but didn't cross the threshold, knowing that he had no part in what was to come. This moment was for Ceolwynn alone. It was his gift to her, the long-delayed payment of a debt.

It was gloomy indoors after the brightness of the morning and at first Ceolwynn hardly noticed the small group of people staring at her so intently. When she did, she thought it odd, no one else in the house had more than glanced in her direction, but these people were just standing and staring.

All at once the woman stepped forward. 'Ceolwynn,' she said, struggling not to weep for joy. Her voice was shaking.

Ceolwynn felt the world spin. She knew that voice. She shook her head in disbelief. Aelfrun was dead – this could not be Aelfrun, it was impossible. She didn't even look like Aelfrun – Aelfrun had been round and plump and nut-brown with health, never like this, skeletal and pale as milk: and yet!

'Oh, Ceolwynn, don't you know me?' Aelfrun cried, unable to hold back the tears any longer. 'See, here is Siggi, your brother, and Dunn. You must know Dunn. My dear, dear Ceolwynn, won't you speak to us?'

Ceolwynn swallowed hard. 'Aelfrun,' she finally managed to say. She looked from one to the other of them, hardly daring to believe what she saw. 'Are you real?' she asked almost fearfully. 'You're not ghosts?'

Aelfrun laughed through the tears rolling down her face. 'Come kiss me, dearest Ceolwynn,' she said, 'and you'll see just how real I am.' She held out her arms and Ceolwynn, finally convinced of the wonderful truth, threw herself into them, laughing, talking and crying all at once.

Renaud returned in time to share their evening meal, and later, after yet more talk, more explanations, more exclamations of surprise and horror, he managed to persuade Ceolwynn to step outside with him for a few moments. The moon was full and the air cool, but its coolness was balm after the heat and smoke inside. Ceolwynn closed her eyes and breathed in deeply, delighting in the freshness of the night.

'Will you keep your promise now?' Renaud asked taking hold of her arms to prevent her slipping away from him.

Ceolwynn smiled. 'What promise?' she returned innocently.

Unable to help himself he kissed the tip of her nose. 'You know

330

right well,' he said, gently chiding, 'you promised me your love if only I fulfilled my vow. Surely I have done all that could be expected of me?'

She looked at him then, carefully studying his bruised and battered face, the sword cut on his face. He would have a scar, she thought, running her fingers gently down the length of the wound. He caught her fingers and kissed them.

'Yes,' she said at last, 'you have done all I could expect of you.'

'Then will you confess that you love me?'

Ceolwynn blushed and looked down, 'I confess it,' she said.

Renaud's face lit in triumph. He pulled her close, kissing her hard. She threw her arms around him, returning the kiss and almost crying with happiness, the burden of having to keep hating him lifted for ever.

Suddenly, she pulled away, not rejecting him but remembering something she knew she should not have forgotten. 'What about Cenred?' she asked anxiously. 'What will happen to him?'

'Cenred will hang,' Renaud replied gravely. 'I'm sorry, Ceolwynn, but there is nothing I can do to prevent it.' He shook his head with genuine sorrow. 'It was only possible for me to save you because Roger de Virar kept you in his own hands. He turned Cenred over to the king's men.'

Ceolwynn was puzzled. 'I don't understand,' she said. 'Why did he do that? Why didn't he just hand me over with Cenred?'

'He wasn't interested in Cenred; it was me he wanted. He held on to you in order to punish me. He wanted me to suffer, and knew full well that he could make that happen by harming you.'

'Would you have suffered, Renaud?'

Renaud put his arms around her again. 'Of course I would, my dear one. I love you, and Roger knew it. He knew that I would have to try to rescue you, and he planned that I should die in the attempt.'

Ceolwynn sighed and allowed herself to lean trustingly against his chest. 'Poor Cenred,' she said sadly. 'It seems wicked to feel so happy when he faces such a shameful, ignoble death. It would have been better had he died with my father.'

Renaud said nothing, but silently he agreed with her. If Brand had not brought Cenred to Cottesham, so much suffering might have been avoided. Aelfrun would never have fled from Hugo into far greater danger; Dunn would soon have sent the vile Folca packing and the boy Bedric would still be alive (not to mention Nest and poor, courageous Brand himself); de Virar would not have had an excuse to use Ceolwynn as the means of his revenge, and Cottesham would still be standing.

Dear God, he thought with dismay, what disaster a child's courage and loyalty have wrought!

Ceolwynn stirred in his arms and he remembered that there was still something more he had to tell her, something he'd been avoiding. 'Ceolwynn,' he said, holding her away from him a little so that she had to look at him, 'there is still some unfinished business I have to attend to.'

'It won't take you away from me, will it?' she asked, only half playfully.

'For a very little while,' he answered seriously. Her face fell. 'You will hate me for this, I know,' he went on, 'but I have to see Geoffrey before Emma takes him back to Normandy.'

He waited for the explosion he was sure would come, but Ceolwynn merely nodded. 'I don't hate you,' she said calmly, 'I have promised myself that I will never hate you again.' She reached up to kiss his lips softly, as if to prove she meant it. Her arms crept around his neck. 'Do you still love Emma?' she asked, unable to stop her voice trembling a little.

'No,' he answered firmly. 'No, I don't.' He brushed her hair with his cheek. 'I'm not even sure now that I ever loved her,' he said thoughtfully. 'She captivated me once, that I'll admit, but what I felt for her is as nothing compared to what I feel for you. She has no power over me at all now, but I have to see Geoffrey, at least once. He is my son after all, even if he never knows it.'

'I understand,' Ceolwynn said, quite truthfully. She smiled and let him go. 'What do you want me to do while I wait for you, my lord?'

'Praise be!' he laughed, 'it seems I have at last a dutiful and respectful wife.'

'Perhaps you have earned one,' a voice put in. Aelfrun stood in the doorway, a smile of real happiness on her face.

'Oh, Aelfrun!' Ceolwynn cried, hugging her. 'I'm so very happy. I can hardly believe all this is true. Renaud was right, Cottesham can be rebuilt. How can I grieve for its loss when I have been given so very much in return?'

'I was about to tell Ceolwynn,' Renaud interrupted, 'that I want you all to go back to Cottesham. I expect you and Siggi to make your home with us, Aelfrun.' Ceolwynn shot him a quick look of gratitude and would have spoken, but he held up a restraining hand and continued. 'Thomas has his orders and will have had something built to shelter you all until I return. Dunn, of course, may resume his duties as Cottesham's steward as soon as you get there. There's much for him to do.'

'No, Renaud,' Aelfrun replied firmly, drawing a look of startled surprise from both of them. 'I thank you for your generosity and kindness, but I cannot live as a dependant in my own husband's hall – even a rebuilt hall,' she added wryly.

Ceolwynn was about to argue but Renaud nodded his understanding. 'I'm sorry, Aelfrun,' he said. 'I have been thoughtless, but I had no intention of demeaning you.'

'Demeaning me?' Aelfrun laughed humourlessly. 'Do you think after what I have endured it is possible for me to feel demeaned by acts of love and goodwill? No, Renaud, do not regret offering me charity from a loving heart. It's not pride that keeps me from accepting your offer, merely sorrow for that which once was mine.'

'But what will you do, where will you live?' Ceolwynn protested.

'I am going to marry Dunn.'

'What!' they both cried in unison.

'Why so shocked?' Aelfrun asked, sounding unusually self-assured. 'Surely a better husband would be hard to find. I don't need to list his qualities to either of you.'

'But you were my father's wife,' Ceolwynn argued, full of indignation. 'How can you possibly think of marrying his servant?'

'I will marry Dunn because he is good and kind and because he loves me. What does our rank matter now? I'm not a thegn's wife any more, Ceolwynn. I'm really no more than a freed slave. If you accept that,' she said, smiling a little, 'you will see that a steward becomes a very good match indeed.'

'Renaud,' Ceolwynn said protestingly, turning to him for support.

'You know, Aelfrun is right,' he said, recalling just how long the faithful Dunn had secretly loved his mistress, 'Dunn will make her an excellent husband.'

'Renaud!' Ceolwynn said again, shocked at his defection.

'Thank you, Renaud,' Aelfrun said, kissing his cheek. 'At least I will have your blessing.'

'Oh, you will have a great deal more than that,' he promised.

Aelfrun looked puzzled. 'I don't understand,' she said.

'You have forgotten Folca's silver, I think,' he told her. 'According to Nest it was stolen from Wilfred, your father. To my mind, that makes it your dowry, Aelfrun. You will not go to Dunn empty handed.'

Overcome, Aelfrun was lost for words. Tears sprang into her eyes and she threw her arms around his neck in gratitude.

Ceolwynn, almost in tears herself, threw up her hands in defeat. 'Since it's all settled anyway, you may as well have my blessing as well,' she conceded, sniffing a little.

Releasing Renaud, Aelfrun hugged her, laughing delightedly.

'But where will you live?' Ceolwynn asked suddenly. 'You will still come back to Cottesham, won't you? And what about Siggi?'

A cloud passed over Aelfrun's face. 'Ah,' she said sadly, 'that is your one failure, Renaud. You have returned my son to me, but I have lost him all the same.'

Renaud nodded regretfully. 'I rather thought that was going to be the case,' he said.

'What do you mean?' Ceolwynn demanded, looking from one to the other of them anxiously.

'Siggi has chosen to return to the church,' Aelfrun answered, trying to sound more resigned to it than she felt. 'It's all the life he can remember and what he's seen of the outside world has not encouraged him to stay. He's very young, but I think he knows he will be ready to take his vows when the time comes.'

Seeing Ceolwynn's stricken look she added quickly, 'But we mustn't feel sad. At least we'll know he is alive and content, and we'll surely be able to visit him once in a while. He won't take his vows for at least five more years.'

'It's not the outcome I would have wished,' Renaud commented, 'if only for your sake, Aelfrun, but it is probably for the best. Who knows what resentments might have festered in his breast in later years, knowing what he has lost.'

'I thought that too,' she agreed seriously. 'I should hate for him to become your enemy, after all you've done for us. I won't be totally childless, though,' she added with a sudden laugh. 'I will have Nest's child, to raise, won't I? She is, after all, my own half sister.'

'Speaking as a daughter who loves you very dearly,' Ceolwynn said affectionately, 'the child could hardly be more fortunate in her new mother.'

'Well then,' said Renaud contentedly, slipping his arm round the waist of each of them, 'let us go and offer the groom our heartiest congratulations. I think there may be just time enough for me to toast your future happiness before I leave.'

Knowing that Emma planned to sail from Dover within the next few days, Renaud had very little time to act on a decision he had made soon after his last conversation alone with Ceolwynn. It was not an easy decision; he would find it hard to reconcile what he was about to do with his conscience, but he knew that, if only for his wife's sake, he could not let Cenred hang without making some effort to save him.

His first intent, soon dismissed, had been to go to the king and simply plead for mercy. It took only a few seconds' thought to realize the futility of such an act. Not only was William in a mood very far from merciful at this time, but he might well begin to ask uncomfortable questions about Renaud's interest in a known outlaw and rebel – questions that might easily lead to Ceolwynn and the death of Roger de Virar, which had already been attributed to a revenge attack by outlaws. So, after hours of painful heartsearching, Renaud was forced to accept that to save his erstwhile friend he must yet again betray the trust of his king.

Cenred was being held at Guildford gaol and Renaud, once his mind was made up, made his way there without delay, a small purse of silver at his belt, a knife hidden carefully beneath his tunic and absolutely no idea what he was going to do.

He found the guards, Breton mercenaries for the most part, friendly and co-operative. They saw no reason to query the right of a Norman knight to interrogate a Saxon prisoner and willingly shared a drink with him, bought at his own expense, accepting without question the false name he gave them. Renaud, at his most charming, chatted and joked with them, elucidating detailed answers to questions they were hardly aware they had been asked.

Before he left to see Cenred, Renaud knew exactly who would be on guard that night, when their Norman officers were likely to

335

be off duty, and just how susceptible they were likely to be to a combination of good wine and hard cash. That last part, he saw, was going to present much less of a problem than he'd anticipated. Mercenaries were always remarkably susceptible to bribery. His plans, fragmentary and incomplete as they might be, were laid.

To Renaud's great relief Cenred shared his cell with no other prisoners and, what was even more important, he wasn't chained. Chains, as Renaud now realized, would have made his hastily formed escape plan totally unworkable, but he hadn't even considered the possibility until he'd been halfway down the dark prison stairs. He was shocked at his own stupidity.

Cenred's cell was dark and foul, the walls running with putrid, green slime. Cenred himself, hunched miserably on stinking straw under what little light the high, barred window allowed, was already filthy and verminous. Listless and dispirited he made no effort to look up when the door was opened and Renaud, nodding for the guard to leave them, stepped cautiously inside.

'It's been a long time, my friend,' he said.

'Friend? What Norman calls me friend?' Cenred hissed venomously, still without looking up.

'I do, Renaud de Lassay.'

'Renaud de Lassay,' Cenred repeated slowly. He looked up at last and even in the dim light Renaud could see the unconcealed hatred in his eyes. 'You are no friend of mine, Renaud Wifestealer, Renaud the Thief. Had I a sword in my hand at this moment I would not hesitate to run you through.'

'All the same, I come as a friend,' Renaud said.

'You have come to see me hang, you mean; to gloat over my downfall.' Suddenly he placed his head in his hands and groaned. 'Ceolwynn,' he said, 'what has become of her?'

'Ceolwynn is safe, no thanks to you Cenred. It's very hard for me to forgive you for leading her into such danger, but for her sake I do.'

'Thank God,' Cenred whispered, visibly relieved. 'She has been on my conscience,' he said earnestly. 'I really did mean no harm to come to her.'

'I never doubted it,' Renaud replied, feeling more pity than he expected for one who had nearly cost him so dear.

Cenred smiled briefly. 'Have you heard when I am to die?' he asked. He sounded resigned, almost apathetic.

'No,' Renaud replied coming nearer, 'but, if you have the will for it, perhaps I can help you live.' He lowered his voice. 'Listen well,' he said. 'I cannot promise, but if all goes well then tonight a man may be careless with his keys. Another man, swift to act and determined of purpose, might find a horse waiting for him just two minutes from here, where the corn merchant's shop lies just north of the bridge.'

To Renaud's astonishment, Cenred began to laugh, a wild, bitter sound with little humour in it. 'Oh, Renaud, Renaud,' he said, shaking his head from side to side, 'you haven't changed at all. You always did believe you could put all to rights, didn't you?' The laugh subsided and he beckoned Renaud closer. Warily, Renaud knelt on one knee beside him and Cenred, wincing, pulled himself a little more upright. 'Take a look at this, my friend,' he said, jerking aside the rags that covered him. 'Here is something even you cannot mend.'

Unable to help himself, Renaud recoiled in horror. 'Dear God!' he breathed and struggled not to retch. What remained of Cenred's legs was crushed and mangled beyond all recognition, the broken bones gleaming whitely through torn, seeping flesh. Disturbed by the light, a rat scurried out of the blood-soaked straw and disappeared into the dark. Renaud's stomach lurched violently and he turned away with his hand to his mouth.

'I don't think I'll be needing that horse, do you Renaud?' Cenred asked, mocking.

'I'm sorry, I didn't know,' Renaud said weakly. 'I didn't know they had done this.' He clenched his fists, helplessly.

'Do you really want to help me?' Cenred asked quietly.

'Of course,' Renaud replied, 'if I only could.'

'You could kill me,' Cenred said with great calm.

Renaud stared at him appalled. 'I couldn't do that,' he said, 'just kill you in cold blood.'

Cenred raised his eyes heavenwards. 'Don't be a fool, Renaud,' he snapped impatiently. 'In the name of God, you must have killed other men in your life. Have you never hastened the end of a wounded comrade on the battlefield?'

Renaud still hesitated, even though he could see the sense of Cenred's argument.

'Just leave me a knife then,' Cenred urged, 'I'll do it myself.'

Shocked, Renaud stared at him in disbelief. 'Would you imperil your immortal soul?' he asked.

'I would hand it to the devil himself to put an end to this,' Cenred replied grimly. 'And who knows what names I might be forced to speak,' he added cunningly, 'if your gentle comrades choose to continue with their questions.'

It was a convincing argument – as long as Cenred was alive, Ceolwynn would always be in danger. Renaud hesitated no longer, but it was with great sadness that he drew the hidden knife from his tunic and handed it over. Cenred took it eagerly and, without another word, deftly opened the veins first on his left arm, then, with rather more difficulty, his right. He watched with curious detachment for a moment as his life's blood soaked into the straw, then, letting the knife drop from his hand, he looked up and smiled at Renaud with relief and gratitude.

White-faced, Renaud made the sign of the cross. 'I will have prayers said daily for your soul, Cenred, I swear it,' he promised. Cenred nodded. There seemed nothing more to be said and Renaud started to move away.

'Renaud, don't go,' Cenred begged suddenly. 'Don't leave me to die all alone.' Renaud hesitated, knowing he should be gone. 'I won't delay you long, I promise you,' Cenred said, his voice pleading and already little more than a whisper.

Renaud returned to his side and held him gently in his arms. Nothing more was said between them and soon, with his head resting like a sleeping child's on Renaud's breast, Cenred slipped swiftly into unconsciousness and death.

Renaud, accompanied by Thomas and Hugh, left Guildford at once, arriving in Dover two days later to find that Emma's ship was due to sail that same day. Emma herself was still not aboard and it took him another hour to find her lodgings, only to discover that she had gone walking with her son along the beach while the last of her baggage was carried to the ship.

Leaving his men to rest and eat, he hurried off on foot in the direction he was sent, finding her almost at once where she had stopped to rest, her cloak spread out comfortably on a large rock. She was gazing rather absently out to sea while further down the beach a servant – he thought it must be Alys – watched the boy throw pebbles at the seagulls.

Unobserved, Renaud paused for a moment, watching as the wind from the sea whipped dark tendrils of hair across a face of quite breathtaking loveliness. He smiled, admiring her beauty but more than content that it no longer had any power over him. 'Greetings, Emma,' he said at last, startling her out of her thoughts.

'Renaud!' she exclaimed delightedly. For a moment he thought he saw an almost triumphant gleam in her eye. 'What are you doing here? How did you know where to find me?' She jumped up and seized his arm, unashamedly offering her lips for his kiss.

He kissed her cheek lightly, for old times' sake, and studied with curious detachment the face that had once meant all the world to him. 'Hugo, of course,' he answered, smiling a little.

'Ah! Of course. Hugo was always our friend, wasn't he?' she said with a meaningful glance. 'I'm a widow now,' she added slyly. 'Did you know it?'

'Yes,' he replied, 'but I am not.'

She looked at him curiously. 'Renaud, you are very serious. Is something amiss?'

'No, not at all. I just wanted to say farewell to you, and to Geoffrey,' he added pointedly. He let his eyes stray down the beach to where the boy, curious to see who it was talking to his mother, had started to make his way back in their direction.

'Oh! I see,' she said, letting go of his arm. 'So, you haven't changed your mind. It's still the little Saxon you want, is it?' Her disappointment was obvious and she lapsed into silence. 'Do you know,' she said after a while, her lips curling in a sardonic smile, 'I really never expected to lose you to that one, Renaud. She is such a child.'

'Perhaps, but I love her,' he said simply.

'You said you loved me once,' she sighed. 'But still, I've no intention of pining away for your sake, Renaud. A rich widow never lacks for suitors.'

Renaud laughed. 'You and Hugo are really quite the most inconstant people I have ever known. I don't think either of you need fear dying of a broken heart – neither of you has one.'

'You are cruel,' she accused, tapping his chest with a reproachful finger. Over his shoulder she saw the small, plump figure of her child draw near. 'You wanted to meet my son, Geoffrey,' she said, her eyes crinkling with suppressed laughter. 'Well, here he is.'

There was mockery in her voice, but Renaud hardly noticed it as he turned, with almost bated breath, to greet the son he had waited so long to meet.

Renaud arrived back at Cottesham within the week, and with him came Ralf, his new squire. After what the man had done for him, Renaud could hardly refuse his request to leave Hugo's service for his own, and Hugo made no fuss about it. Renaud knew full well that it was not for his sake that Ralf wanted to join his household, but he saw no reason to deny Hild the happiness her loyalty deserved. He rather hoped, watching the man rush off to find her, that Ralf's wild oats had finally been well and truly sown.

Ceolwynn, seeing him arrive, rushed joyfully to meet him with Edmund trotting excitedly in her wake; and trotting just behind him came the mastiff puppy that, escaping the blazing hall unseen, had so nearly cost the child his life.

Leaping from the saddle Renaud kissed his wife heartily, then scooped Edmund into his arms and tossed him high.

'More, more,' Edmund shouted delightedly, but Renaud shook his head.

'Not now, later. Run along to your nurse and let me speak to your mother,' he said, smiling as Edmund scurried off, tripping over the hem of his petticoats as he went. 'It will soon be time for the boy to shed his baby clothes,' Renaud remarked, smiling after the tottering figure.

'Oh, Renaud,' Ceolwynn complained good-naturedly, 'is that all you have to say to me after so long an absence?'

'It has been only six days,' he replied, offering her his hands.

'An eternity,' she laughed, taking them. Suddenly she was serious. 'Did you see him?'

'Yes, I did.'

'And Emma. . . ?' she started to ask, but they were interrupted by the arrival of Dunn, dust-covered and dishevelled.

'I heard you were back, my lord, and came as soon as I could,' he panted.

'More's the pity,' Ceolwynn grumbled quietly. Renaud squeezed her hand reprovingly and gave Dunn an encouraging smile.

'You wouldn't believe how well things are going,' Dunn carried on, full of enthusiasm. 'I brought in more labourers, and the masons will be here in just a few days. Everyone has been working like demons to get the village rebuilt before the shearing starts, and the ditch is well under way.'

'Yes, Renaud,' Ceolwynn interrupted sharply, remembering a grievance, 'I wanted to ask you about that. Why have you ordered the village to be rebuilt over there?'

She pointed to where half a hundred men, women and children, every one of them turned builder, scurried like ants over the site where Renaud had chosen to rebuild Cottesham. The air was filled with the noise of chopping, sawing and hammering, while above it all could be heard the clang of hammer on anvil as Afa the smith went about his work, fashioning nails and bolts and all manner of vital hardware. Carts full of lumber and straw trundled ceaselessly up and down a stretch of raw, newly built road, and cross-legged on the ground the wattle-makers sat weaving new wall panels, their deft fingers flying like shuttles over the springy hazel wands.

The sight was pleasing and Renaud smiled, but Ceolwynn still wanted to know why Cottesham was now to be half a mile from its original site. Nor was that her only question. 'And why,' she asked, 'are they digging that ditch over by the river? Dunn refused to tell me,' she complained, looking accusingly at the steward. 'He said you would explain.'

'And so I shall,' Renaud promised placatingly, 'if only you will let me get a word in.'

'The first loads of stone are arriving,' Dunn said suddenly. 'I'll go and see to them.'

'Stone?' Ceolwynn queried ominously as Dunn hurried to meet the convoy of wagons now to be seen toiling slowly and laboriously towards the new village.

Renaud took the reins of his horse in one hand and offered Ceolwynn the other. She took it and they began to follow in Dunn's footsteps. Renaud looked serious now and Ceolwynn, having learned at last how far she could provoke him, waited patiently for him to speak. 'We are starting a new life, Ceolwynn,' he began slowly. 'You and I, Aelfrun and Dunn, all our people. Our people, Ceolwynn,' he emphasized, 'not yours, not mine – ours.'

'I understand that,' she said, nodding.

'Well then,' he continued, 'old wounds, I decided, would surely mend fastest where everything was started anew. We had to have a new village anyway, so why not move it closer to where the castle is to be?'

'Castle?' she cried out in astonishment, letting go of his hand and swinging round to face him. 'What castle, for sweet Mary's sake?'

'Cottesham Castle,' he replied, quite unruffled. 'Didn't I tell you?' he asked, pretending surprise.

'No you didn't, as you know full well.'

She wanted to be angry with him, but somehow it was impossible. What he said about a new start made sense, and the idea of a castle did seem very grand. Edmund would be its lord one day, she reflected – Renaud's son, to be sure, but also the grandson of Godmund Edgarson. She smiled to herself.

'You are pleased?' Renaud asked, a little taken aback. Ceolwynn could be so very unpredictable.

'Yes,' she answered thoughtfully, taking his arm again. 'Yes, I rather think I am. Is that what the stone is for, the castle?'

'No, the stone is for the new church. It will be a fine church, I promise you, but I'm afraid your castle will be just timber for several years yet. There won't be much money for luxuries once all this is paid for.'

Ceolwynn was only a little disappointed. Father Eadric deserved his church, he had suffered much, but now, God be thanked, all the pain and suffering was finally over. Aelfrun and Dunn would be married and stay here for ever, Siggi was already happily settled at St Albans, and Renaud had promised that Estrith and Wulfhere would be safe, even if poor, wretched Northumbria did lie torn and bleeding all about them.

As for herself and Renaud? She sneaked a look up at his face as he walked beside her deep in thought. What was he thinking about? she wondered. The rebuilding? Money? Or might it be that he still thought about Emma? Could he really forget her so easily, the mother of his first-born son? Surely the tie between them would always be there. She realized sadly that doubt still lingered.

'Renaud,' she said, tentatively.

'Umm?' he replied.

'You say you saw Geoffrey?'

'Yes, I did.'

'And was he very like Edmund?'

'No, not at all.'

342

'Hugo said he was.'

'You can't always believe everything that Hugo says,' he assured her, eyes twinkling suddenly.

Ceolwynn stopped short. He was laughing at her.

'You're hiding something from me,' she cried. 'Tell me,' she insisted, pounding his chest in mock anger.

He laughed again and took her in his arms. 'Emma has had the last laugh after all,' he said. 'All these years she has used my guilt about Geoffrey to keep me tied to her, and I let her do it. What a fool I've been.'

Ceolwynn caught her breath. 'What are you saying?' she asked, hope rising as his meaning started to become clear.

'Edmund, dear heart, is my first-born and my only son,' he told her gently, cupping her face in his hands. 'There can be no doubt at all that Geoffrey is Roger de Virar's true son, not mine.'

'Oh, Renaud!' she gasped, almost too happy for words. 'Are you really sure?'

'Oh yes,' he said, kissing her lips and laughing again for sheer happiness. 'The evidence is as plain as the nose on his face.'

Catch The Moment
Euanie MacDonald

A compelling Scottish saga

Annie Ramsay is fourteen when she travels to Ayrshire to work as a milkmaid on Clachan's farm. Annie's spirited nature immediately makes an impression on the farmer's only son, Ian – a match considered above her station.

Then she rescues Alexandra Cameron, the daughter of the Laird of Craigdrummond, and is swept away by her new friend to the Paris of the Belle Epoque. There, Alexandra's loyalty proves to be fickle and Annie is left to fend for herself in the exciting but depraved Café Society of Montmartre. As the new century approaches, Annie experiences great happiness and deep sorrow.

But, for all her willingness to catch the moment and use it well, fate is not done with Annie Ramsay yet...

The Weeping Tree
Audrey Reimann

From the author of *Wise Child*

When Flora MacDonald leaps from the balcony of an Edinburgh reform school she falls, literally, into the safe arms of Andrew Stewart. A sailor on leave in the days before the outbreak of WWII, he might be expected to have the worst of intentions, but he is touched by her bid for freedom and helps her escape.

With such a beginning how could they not fall in love? But the tides of war conspire to part them.

Surrounded by danger on all sides, the one thing Flora and Andrew can cling to is their love for one another. But someone is conspiring to keep them apart, for their own secret, selfish, even murderous reasons... It may be a long time before the lovers' vows made under a willow tree can be fulfilled...

The very best of Piatkus fiction is now available in paperback as well as hardcover. Piatkus paperbacks, where *every* book is special.

☐ 0 7499 3082 9	The Gift and the Promise	Sarah Pernell	£5.99
☐ 0 7499 3123 X	The Weeping Tree	Audrey Reimann	£5.99
☐ 0 7499 3110 8	Catch the Moment	Euanie MacDonald	£5.99
☐ 0 7499 3069 1	The Seaweed Gatherers	Jessica Blair	£5.99
☐ 0 7499 3061 6	The Jewel Streets	Una Horne	£5.99
☐ 0 7499 3107 8	For All The Bright Promise	Elizabeth Lord	£5.99
☐ 0 7499 3100 0	Like A Diamond	Malcom Ross	£5.99

The prices shown above were correct at the time of going to press. However, Piatkus Books reserve the right to show new retail prices on covers which may differ from those previously advertised in the text or elsewhere.

Piatkus Books will be available from your bookshop or newsagent, or can be ordered from the following address:
Piatkus Paperbacks, PO Box 11, Falmouth, TR10 9EN
Alternatively you can fax your order to this address on 01326 374 888 or e-mail us at books@barni.avel.co.uk

Payments can be made as follows: Sterling cheque, Eurocheque, postal order (payable to Piatkus Books) or by credit card, Visa/Mastercard. Do not send cash or currency. UK and B.F.P.O. customers should allow £1.00 postage and packing for the first book, 50p for the second and 30p for each additional book ordered to a maximum of £3.00 (7 books plus).

Overseas customers, including Eire, allow £2.00 for postage and packing for the first book, plus £1.00 for the second and 50p for each subsequent title ordered.

NAME (block letters) _____

ADDRESS _____

_____

I enclose my remittance for £ _____

I wish to pay by Visa/Mastercard   Expiry Date:_____
